An Uncommon Collection
fifteen tales from the Colorado Springs Fiction Writer's Group

Edited by Michael Reid and Melissa R. Kary

Colorado Springs Fiction Writers Group
6045 Wildfire Ct.
Colorado Springs, CO 80908
http://www.csfwg.org/

An Uncommon Collection
Copyright © 2012 by The Colorado Springs Fiction Writers Group.

ISBN 13: 978-0615716022
ISBN 10: 0615716024

Interior and cover design by Michael Reid
Cover photograph by Kimberly Evans

Edited by Michael Reid and Melissa R. Kary

Colorado Springs Fiction Writers Group
6045 Wildfire Ct.
Colorado Springs, CO 80908
http://www.csfwg.org/
president@csfwg.org

The Colorado Springs Fiction Writers Group is a 501c3 nonprofit that welcomes writers of all levels to improve their skills through peer critique groups, lectures, seminars and retreats in a supportive setting. More information about our organization can be found at http://www.csfwg.org/

 # Table of contents

Human nature never ceases to amaze. Never happy with their lot, always looking for something more. Something different. Keeps me in business, I suppose. But the young woman today? I don't see that very often. ET

If Wishes Were Horses ...

By Hollie Snider

Oh, hello. Where did you come from? I thought I was alone here, the only one hanging out in a dingy, musty, filthy bus station at two in the morning. Just got off the bus from Chicago, huh? I thought I heard one pull in.

So what's your story? Not much of a talker, huh? You want to hear mine? Well, all right, but you asked for it.

You know the old saying, "Be careful what you wish for, you just might get it?" Well, I never really paid much attention until recently. I mean, how often do wishes really come true in the real world anyway? Fairy tales, sure. But real life? I can't count how many coins I've thrown in fountains, birthday candles I've blown out, first stars I've seen, and no wishes have ever come true. Until now. Well, last week actually.

I am also quite familiar with the phrase, "You can't go home again." Only in my case it's true. I can never go home again. I know, I know, you're asking why. Just be patient. I'll get there.

I guess it all started about a week ago. See, I really like vampire stories, the good ones, like the old Hammer films. Christopher Lee, Bela Lugosi, those guys. They were vampires, scary bloodsuckers that only come out at night. Not like the modern ones, not like George Hamilton in "Love at First Bite." Dracula with a tan? Come on.

Anyway, I was reading this really bad book and just getting annoyed with it. Another one of these vampires walking in daylight, picking up crucifixes, crossing running water type deals. I ended up throwing it across the room. Now normally, I am not one to abuse books that way, I won't even dog-ear a page, but this one deserved it. The name of it? I really don't remember. I wish I did, then I could tell you to stay away from it.

Reading that book, that's the only time I can remember ever being thankful for an interruption. Our housekeeper yelled at me. Something about being late for school. I see that look in your eye. The one that says, "Spoiled little rich girl." I know what you're thinking, "She has it all, designer clothes, manicured fingernails, yadda, yadda, yadda. Why is she sitting in a bus station at two in the morning?" I already told you, I'd get there.

I decided to skip school that day, and find another, better written vampire novel. I had no desire to go school anyway. Teachers and other kids alike give me nothing but grief about my condition. You didn't notice? You're sweet. A liar, but sweet. No one fails to notice albinism. But that's not the point.

Somehow I ended up in front of a bookstore I'd never seen before. Odd, considering how often I go book hunting. It looked abandoned, and probably should've been condemned, but the screen door was open so I went in. Looking back, it wasn't the wisest decision of my life.

The shopkeep stared at me, like he'd never seen an albino. Come to think of it, he probably hadn't. But he was no looker either. Ever seen the "Wizard of Oz?" Remember Scarecrow? This man could've been his double. In costume, I mean. Thin and raggedy, long teeth yellow from age and tobacco. A real sight.

When I went in, I caught my finger on a nail. See, you can still see the scar. Anyway, I've never been one for blood, but for some reason I couldn't stop staring at it as it welled this time. It just fascinated me. I remember it dripping from my finger and falling to the floor, like it was in slow motion. I even remember it hitting the wood with a plopping sound. I don't know why I remember it so clearly. I stuck my finger in my mouth, something I never do, and the taste of blood actually made me hungry. It makes me hungry now, just thinking about it. You're looking at me like I am insane, but I swear it's truth. The shopkeep looked at me that way too.

But he asked if he could help me find anything, and I told him my whole story about wanting a good, old-fashioned, sleep-with-the-lights-on vampire story. "Real or fiction?" he'd asked me. I know, I said the same thing. Vampires aren't real.

He assured me they were and pointed me back to the Occult section. He keeps the vampire, werewolf, any sort of monster fiction stories in his Occult section. "Why not? Who's to say what's fiction and what isn't?" he'd said. I probably should have run out of the store right then, but I'm a dumb teenager and didn't.

Anyway, I found a book, paid an enormous sum for it because "it's an antique," and left. I have the book with me. Do you want to see it? No, I didn't think so. No one does. People hear about my experience in that odd little shop and don't even want to see the book. They just skooch away from me, like you're doing, or get up and leave. That's okay, though, you probably shouldn't read this one anyway. I don't think I should have, but too late now. I've read it cover to cover several times. The odd thing is, every time I read it, the stories keep changing and I get dizzy. Bullshit, you're thinking. Books don't change their contents. Well, this one does. It's the reason I can't go home again.

So here I was, sitting in this bus station, wondering where my next meal was coming from and contemplating reading this book again, when you show up.

I guess you just have to really wish for something meaningful before it comes true. Nothing frivolous like a million dollars, but rather the means to change your life, or even something as simple as food, when you're hungry.

What? No, I don't need money. I've been really lucky the last few days. Things have just come when I need them. Like I said, I never believed wishes could come true before last week. Now, I do.

I wished for a way to change my life, and, poof, I find this book. I was feeling hungry, and, poof, you come along.

Some people just need a little push in the right direction. A little encouragement to see what's right in front of them. And some people need a bit more than a little. EF

Pinwheel

by Melissa R. Kary

Pinwheel, pinwheel, breezy and bright.
Spin me good morning, spin me good night.
~ Janet Gardner

Chelsea forced the outside door to shut faster, causing the bells to bang loudly against the glass. The bitter cold rushed into her naked fingers as she fought with the jammed lock and her overfull key ring.

Fuck, it's cold.

She jiggled the key back and forth, hoping to finally catch the illusive pins against the teeth. *I need a new key. No, I need a new job. New life. Some place warmer. Fuck, it's cold.*

The little hairs in her nose pricked as they coated in ice. Clouds of moisture billowed from her nose a brilliant white, illuminated against the January night sky by the street lamp a few yards away.

The key slipped into place, and Chelsea gave it a full clockwise turn. She grabbed the handle of the locked door and shook it to check that the lock held. Satisfied, she pulled the keys out of the lock and jammed them into her messy purse.

Chelsea stuffed her right hand into the pocket of her parka and grabbed a pair of knit gloves, putting them on as she walked past the storefronts. Stuffing her left hand into her parka's pocket, she pulled out a set of fluffy pink mittens and shoved them on over her gloves. As she rounded the corner of the final building, the brilliant full moon came into view. *Great, moondogs. I thought it was more than just cold. The seventh circle of Dante's Hell is here on Earth. The vast universe, in its infinite freezing cold, presses down on this little spot of Hell.*

The sapphire-blue VW beetle was the only car in the small employee parking lot. Out of habit, she looked past the street lamps into each dark shadow, checking for any suspicious people. She laughed to herself. *As if there would be any bad guys around tonight. It's too fucking cold. That's one reason to live in North Dakota … it keeps the riffraff out.*

The cloudless night was too cold for snow, but the beetle's windshield was white nonetheless. Chelsea hated the routine of hopping in the car, starting it and spending the next fifteen minutes scraping off the frost while the engine warmed up. The car door creaked in protest as Chelsea opened it and plopped into the driver's seat. She dug her keys out of her stuffed purse, vowing to clean it out later tonight. Chelsea slid the key into the ignition and turned it.

Click click click.

"Not tonight! Oh, come on Jezebel, start for me, please?" Chelsea turned off the radio, heater and every other auxiliary accessory she could find, closed the car door and turned the key in the ignition again.

Click click click.

"Stupid car! Start!"

Click click click click click.

"Damn it!"

Chelsea pounded the steering wheel, sighed, and pulled her keys from the ignition. She grabbed her purse and dug for her cell phone among the mess. Her hand finally settled on the thin plastic phone, which she pulled out in triumph. She stared at the blank screen for half a minute before letting her head drop back and rolling her eyes. The battery was dead.

"Oh, can't just one thing go right?"

Chelsea sat for a moment and weighed her options. She couldn't stay with the car. She would freeze to death. Her apartment was a little over five miles away. It was something she would bike in the summer, or walk if she had nothing better to do. In this weather, walking was not a good option. *That would be too much like "To Build a Fire." I know better than to try that kind of trek in this weather. I also wouldn't be stupid enough to build the fire under a tree, but that's moot 'cause who builds a fire in the middle of a city?*

She mentally ran through her friends and where they lived. No one lived within walking distance. That left going back to Red River Roasters, unlocking it, disarming the security system and using the landline to call for help. Unfortunately, if she disarmed the system now that it had been armed, the security company would automatically call the owner. The last time Chelsea had gone back in, Rob got the call and accused her of trying to steal the cash. *As if the grand in the safe is worth losing my job and my freedom.*

Gritting her teeth against the future argument, Chelsea sighed, opened the car door, got out, hit the lock button and slammed the door shut. The crisp bang echoed off the nearby brick building. *Given my luck, I shouldn't slam it so hard. I'm likely to break the door to boot.*

As she silently cursed Jezebel, North Dakota, her job and her life, Chelsea stormed out of the parking lot and around the corner. Even though it was nearly one in the morning, Chelsea scanned both sides of the street for an open business. Her eyes fell upon a well-lit frosted glass door across the street. In the dim light, it was hard to make out the words on the large wooden sign above the facade. As she crossed the street, she pushed her glasses up her nose, squinted and leaned in. The white Gothic lettering made the sign even harder to read in the dim night. Halfway across the street, the words clicked into place in Chelsea's mind, "Librorum Taberna."

When did this place open? I must have been in a bubble to miss it when it's right across the street. How strange.

The glass door was encased in wood and had a simple leaded design of rectangular beveled panels. Chelsea grabbed the wrought iron door handle and entered. Her glasses fogged up in the warmth of the store, rendering Chelsea blind. She remained by the doorway and removed her mittens and gloves, while enjoying the familiar smell of old musty books. *I'll have to come back here and check it out when it's not so late. I bet there are gems on every shelf.*

"May I help you?"

Slightly startled by the deep soft voice, Chelsea replied "Um, yes. My car won't start. May I use your phone to call for a jump?" She thought about adding that she had cables in her trunk if he had a vehicle and the time to help, but she held her tongue.

"Certainly. Do you need a phone book as well, or is this a common enough occurrence that you have the number memorized?"

The man's accent was intriguing. Chelsea couldn't quite place it, but it was certainly different from the somewhat Scandinavian accents she commonly heard around Grand Forks.

"Uh, I'll be needing the book. I only have problems when it's super cold out. I forgot to go run my car on my lunch break ... well, really, there was no time. We got slammed and I almost didn't get a break at all ... and, well, you know how it goes." *Too much information. Stop talking. Smile.*

"Right this way, miss."

The fog on her glasses dissipated enough that she could look around the store and at the man she was following. Both were fascinating, but the books won Chelsea's attention first. The store was huge. It was easily larger than the campus bookstore, which, until now, was the largest bookstore in town. The unfinished, vaulted ceilings showed off the red iron beams and retrofitted heating ducts. Library-style bookshelves haphazardly filled the main floor, creating a maze. The walls had specially built shelving units that ran from floor to ceiling. A brass pole near the ceiling held several rolling library ladders, allowing access to the tops of the nearly twenty-foot high shelves. The books on the shelves were treasures; the vast majority were leather-bound and looked to be in excellent condition. *I will never take a paycheck home again. I might as well tell Rob to direct-deposit my checks here.*

"Here we are," the man walked behind a counter. "One telephone, one local phone book. Is there anything else you desire?"

Chelsea nearly jumped as she looked into his face. His eyes were solid white, but he still managed to gaze piercingly into Chelsea's eyes, almost like he could see her, both inside and out. Shaking the eerie feeling away, she stammered, "Uh, I … wha … oh, yes. This is good. Thank you."

The man gave a little nod and disappeared into the stacks of books.

The phone looked like it had been rescued from a second-hand office supply store. The fat, squatty body was a drab tan and had an old-fashioned rotary dial. The phone book, on the other hand, was current and in perfect condition. She flipped to the yellow pages and searched under "T." After a quick conversation with Tow & Go, Chelsea hung up the phone and looked around the store once more. *Half an hour to kill. I'll have to keep an eye on the time, or else I'll be in trouble.*

"Uh, excuse me, sir?"

"Yes?" The voice carried over the stacks.

"The truck won't be here for another half hour. Do you mind if I just hang out here? I mean, when do you close?"

"Librorum Taberna will remain open for a while. Feel free to browse while your wait."

"Oh, thank you. I- I'm studying lit up at UND. Could you point me in the direction of the classics?"

"I could."

She waited a moment before realizing her wording mistake and adding, "Um … Where are the classics?"

"The classics line the walls. They are organized by time period and then by author's last name."

"Thanks."

Chelsea weaved through the maze of books while contemplating which authors were most absent in her collection. As she walked through one of the aisles, a cover caught her eye. Unlike most of the tomes, this one was turned out so the front was showing rather than the spine. The coffee-table book was simple yet striking. The dust jacket was solid white with the word "Tattoos" in black across the top. Below the simple lettering was an elaborate tribal-inspired pinwheel. Frozen in mid step, Chelsea adjusted her footing and picked up the book. As she flipped from page to page, each black and white photo drew her in deeper. Near the center of the book, she glimpsed a small movement in one of the tattoos. Blinking her eyes, Chelsea stared at the tattoo. It remained still. *I must be more tired than I thought.*

Chelsea turned another page. This time the tattoos did not stop moving. *How the Hell ....*

Chelsea tried to drop the possessed book, but found it glued to her hands. On one page, a butterfly flapped its wings lazily, while on the opposing page the vine of a flower flowed out into curly cues. The tendril did not stop when it reached the edge of the page. Chelsea's fingers burned as the ink flowed into her fingertips, then up her arms. The excruciating pain felt like millions of ants walking over her body and biting as they stepped. The ink vine moved along her body, under her skin, spreading tribal-style lines and curves over every inch of her skin. Unable to drop the book, Chelsea stood motionless as a silent scream left her lips.

Beep beep beep.

The sound of the alarm clock pulled Chelsea from her dream. She hit the snooze button without bothering to open her eyes. *What a strange variation.*

Images of what actually happened on that cold winter night seven months ago flashed through Chelsea's mind. The coffee shop ... calling the tow truck in the dark ... the police knocking on the glass door ... Rob showing up ... throwing the store's key at Rob after both quitting and getting fired ... the long wait in the back of the police car ... the tow truck finally arriving ... crying in the cold car while it warmed up. *I liked this dream better ... well, up until the tattoos attacked me. I wonder what Seph would say about that dream.*

Beep beep.

Faster this time, Chelsea hit the snooze then turned off the alarm. As she reached for her glasses, Chelsea noticed a strange tickling and a black smudge on the inside of her right arm. Brushing the apparent bug off her arm didn't work, so she plopped the glasses on her face and took a closer look.

What the fuck!

Centered halfway between her wrist and the crook of her elbow was the tattoo from the cover of the book. And it moved. The blades of the pinwheel slowly turned counterclockwise, as if a gentle breeze set it in motion. Touching the tattoo with her left hand, as if to verify its presence, Chelsea felt the minute ridges as the ink shifted under her skin. She let her left hand fall and raised her right arm up to eye level. As she stared, a tingle pulsed under her skin as the ink flowed. The movement was not painful and felt a lot like a stray hair brushing against her arm.

This is really fucked up. God, I hope I'm still dreaming.

Chelsea grabbed an inch of skin on her left arm and pinched. Nothing happened. She pinched again, harder.

"Ouch!"

Okay, maybe I can't just wake myself up. Right. Now what?

Chelsea's heart raced as she stared at the spinning pinwheel. Her head felt heavy and her vision narrowed to a pinpoint as her heartbeat pounded in her ears. The world turned black as Chelsea fainted.

Keeping her eyes closed, Chelsea thought, *Just a dream, just a dream. I'm going to open up my eyes, look at my arm and see nothing there. It's just a dream.*

Very slowly, Chelsea opened one eye, and looked at her arm.

Fuck.

She snapped her eye shut again and considered her options. Chelsea could not concentrate with the tattoo's constant tickling motion. She opened her eyes again and watched it spin faster and faster as she lost hope that she was dreaming. She searched her mind for a reasonable explanation, but nothing added up.

Chelsea threw back her sheets and went to the bathroom. She tried scrubbing off the pinwheel with soap, then toothpaste and finally bleach. Her skin turned pink, but the tattoo remained.

This is crazy. Only in a sci-fi movie ... hmm, what would the character in the movie do? Well, if this tattoo is real, maybe the bookstore is real too. Maybe that old creepy guy knows what's going on here.

Chelsea grabbed a pair of jean shorts, a t-shirt and a bra off the floor and dressed. She ran a comb through her long brown hair, snatched her purse and keys, slid her feet into a pair of flip-flops and walked out to her car.

As she drove, Chelsea went over the dream in her head. Some of the details were vanishing as she concentrated on putting the dream into her memory. *Remembering a dream is like trying to catch smoke. Hmm ... that would make a good poem. I should write that down.*

Typical of a Thursday morning, cars filled the downtown street. While driving, Chelsea scanned the brick building for the "Librorum Taberna" sign and the leaded glass door. Not seeing either, she decided to park and get a closer look. *I bet I just missed it in all the traffic.*

The street parking was full, so Chelsea pulled into the familiar employee parking lot. She followed the same path from her car to the bookstore as she took in her dream. Even before crossing the street, she knew it was for nothing. Once on the sidewalk, she stopped and gazed at the solid brick wall. There was no door, no sign. There wasn't even enough room in the building to contain the bookstore. It looked abandoned. The flood of '97 caused a lot of destruction, and the downtown revitalization project obviously had not touched this building yet. She stared for at least five minutes, mind racing, but unable to come to any conclusions. She looked once again to the pinwheel on her arm and watched it spin to an unending gentle breeze.

I can't just stay here all day. The door isn't going to magically appear. I wonder if Seph will have any ideas?

Chelsea pulled out her phone and checked the time. *I could call her, but this isn't the type of thing I can tell her on the phone. She'll think I'm nuts. If I go up to class now, maybe I can catch her before Literary Myths and Legends starts.*

Chelsea was thankful for the relaxed summer class feel on campus. She found a spot in her favorite parking lot, only a few buildings away from the English department. She walked to class, hastened by fear and missing her normal load of books and binders.

She jaunted up the steps to Merrifield Hall, flung open the door and ran right into TJ.

"Oops, sorry, man."

"Hey Chelsea, nice running into you."

Chelsea fought the urge to be rude and matched TJ's pace as he wandered in the general direction of the classroom door. "Yeah, sorry. Say, have you seen Seph today?"

"Are you okay? You look a bit out of sorts."

"Uh, I just have this ... problem. I'm sorry, I just ... I need to talk to Seph."

"Hey, that's cool ... she's in class already, cramming."

Chelsea gave TJ a painful look.

"Don't tell me, you forgot about the quiz on Hercules?"

"Yeah."

"I've heard it's going to be essay. Something about comparing Hercules to the archetype of a hero."

"Okay, that's not too bad ... I think I can do that."

"Without a paper or pencil? Where are your books?"

"I had ... an interesting morning," Chelsea shrugged and weakly gestured with her right hand.

"Holy cow! When did you get a tattoo? Let me see it!" TJ grabbed Chelsea's wrist, and gawked at her forearm. Chelsea watched the pinwheel spin and waited for TJ to flip out.

"That's a cool design. I never pegged you for the tribal flower type. I figured you would be more the butterfly tramp stamp type. Where'd you get it? I've never seen a design quite like that."

"Uh, it's a pinwheel."

"Oh yeah, I guess so. That's better. So many girls go for the flowers and frilly crap. I don't think I've seen a pinwheel before. Wow, they must have really killed you when they did this ... I can feel the ink lines. You didn't say, where'd you get it?"

"Uh, just downtown. I guess it hurt."

"Downtown? But there aren't any parlors downtown. What, were you drunk and forgot where you went?"

"Yeah. I was out with my friends last week, and this is the result."

"You suck at lying. That tat is at least a month old. Given how deep they did it, maybe even longer. And what 'friends?' Seph and I are the only people you hang out with. Why all the deception?"

"Look. You wouldn't believe me, so just ... can we be done?" Chelsea pulled her arm away.

"Okay, fine, whatever."

TJ flung the classroom door open and entered without holding it or even glancing back. Chelsea followed, weaving through the mess of tables and chairs to her typical spot next to Persephone.

"Hey, Seph, how's it going?"

"Can't talk. Studying."

"If you don't know it now, I doubt anything you read in the next minute will help."

"Keep your negative energy to yourself. Positive energy for a positive test."

"Okay, sorry. Good luck."

Chelsea barely finished talking when Dr. Hardy walked in and announced, "Books away, pencils and paper out. I want at least five good paragraphs, not including the introduction and conclusion." As he talked, he wrote on the white board.

The three hour long class dragged on. Chelsea doodled on the paper she borrowed from Seph, while mostly watching the tattoo spin. The pinwheel was actually a rather pretty thing. If it hadn't appeared so magically, it may have been a welcome break in the pale alabaster of her arm. The tribal style design combined graceful curves with sharp points. The stem pointed to the crook in her elbow, making the pinwheel right side up from Chelsea's point of view. Each of the six blades of the pinwheel featured a fishhook design at the tip. If it had been still, the pinwheel would have resembled a columbine, but the constant counterclockwise movement made it hard for Chelsea to imagine it as anything else. The spinning was not always even. It was generally slow enough to make out most of the details of each of the blades, but at times it blurred to a faster pace. Though she tried, Chelsea could not find a reason why it spun faster or slower, or why she could see it spinning and TJ obviously couldn't.

The sounds of chairs scraping, books closing and binders clacking open and shut brought Chelsea's attention back to the room.

Persephone turned to Chelsea and said, "So, what did you think of that essay? I think I did all right. I hate writing by hand. I wish he'd let us use a laptop or something. My hand always cramps after the first couple paragraphs, and I can't write as fast as I can type."

"I was distracted. I don't know how I did," Chelsea paused, contemplating how to ask her friend about her dream and the tattoo without sounding crazy.

"I know you're distracted." Persephone placed a hand on Chelsea's arm and looked her in the eyes. "I just thought you were in a funk again. Is there something more this time?"

Chelsea sighed.

"Okay, I may be empathic, but I can't exactly read every thought on your mind. What's wrong? Maybe I can help?"

"Look, it's a little strange, and I want to talk to you about it, but I also don't want you to think that I'm making assumptions about your religion. I mean, I only know a little about Wicca, but I think this problem might … I don't know. Maybe you know what it's about?"

"Wow, that's a bit esoteric." Persephone laughed. "Now you have my curiosity. Spill it."

"Hey you two," TJ interjected as he plopped down on the table. "Am I interrupting some girly secret society conversation or can I join in?"

Persephone gave Chelsea a smile and a shrug indicating it was up to her. Chelsea sighed and closed her eyes for a moment.

"Okay," opening her eyes, Chelsea looked first at TJ and then at Persephone. "This is going to sound really crazy. I'm actually still kinda hoping that this is a dream, and I will be waking up any minute now."

"Wow, cool. Simultaneous dreams ... do you dream of me often?" asked TJ.

Persephone swatted him and then gave him the "this isn't joke time" look.

"So ...," Chelsea continued, "I had this dream last night. It started like so many of them do with the night I was fired from Red River Roasters. But this time I went into this bookstore. The dude who ran it was really creepy. Anyway, I was looking at books, and this one on tattoos attacked me." At the bewildered expressions of her friends, she amended, "Well, the book itself didn't attack me, but the tattoos did. I mean, like the ink ran into my fingers and under my skin and all over my body."

"So, you want a dream analysis? You don't have to make a big production about it. I've analyzed your dreams before."

"No, Seph. Well, maybe, but there's more. After I woke up ... this is so crazy." Chelsea stopped and both her friends waited. She glanced around the room, but found that everyone else was gone. "So, when I woke up this morning," Chelsea turned her arm tattoo side up, "I had this tattoo on my arm."

"No way. You're pulling my leg." Persephone grabbed Chelsea's arm and held it up to her face. "This is magic marker, right? Nice joke. Was the dream fake too?"

"I'm not making it up. Go ahead, try to wash it off."

"Don't bother. It's real enough. No way that's a marker," said TJ.

"So, it's real then, but you just got it last night," Persephone let go of Chelsea's forearm. "That's why you didn't want to study at my place. You were busy getting inked."

"Again, no way," said TJ. "That tattoo is fully healed. It has to be at least a month old, unless Chelsea has a genetic mutation that allows her to heal super fast, but last I checked, this isn't a movie."

Near tears, Chelsea stammered, "This is *real*. *Everything* I told you. I don't know why or how, but I'm scared. Won't you listen to me? Won't you *help* me? Some friends I have."

Chelsea stood up and took a step for the door. TJ grabbed her arm, preventing her from leaving. In a calm voice, he said, "Ya know, I was thinking about the tattoo during class. You've been wearing short sleeves since May." He paused and looked at Persephone then back into Chelsea's watery brown eyes. "I was trying to figure out how you went for a month or more hiding that tattoo. It's mostly black … makeup would do a poor job of covering it." The bright crimson that filled his cheeks nearly obscured the little brown freckles on his pale face. "Not that I would know about wearing makeup or anything," he finished sheepishly.

Persephone closed her eyes and rested her forehead on her hand. "So, you're saying this isn't a joke? The dream, the tattoo, the bookstore, it's all real?" She looked up and gestured with her hand, "How?"

"I don't know," Chelsea said. "That's why I was asking you. You're the one who knows about magic and other weird stuff; I thought you would know or at least have an idea."

Persephone looked deep in thought for a moment before responding. "There is absolutely nothing I know of in paganism that would leave a real tattoo after a dream of one. Sorry. Maybe there is a clue in the dream." Persephone pulled out a clean sheet of paper while she talked. "Tell me the whole dream, as much as you can remember."

Chelsea recited every detail she committed to memory while Persephone jotted down key words. TJ simply nodded.

"Okay, so the key points were books, pinwheels, tattoos, butterflies, flowers, and vines. Do you remember what kind of flower it was with the vine that attacked you? Most flowers have a meaning."

"It was … I don't know. Just a flower, I suppose. I was kind of more focused on the vine. The flower was white, like it had white ink, not skin tone."

"Okay, well, some of this I know off the top of my head, but I want to double check before I say anything. Don't worry, hun. There must be a good explanation. I'll try to do some research. Maybe my high priestess will know something more. I'll see if I can contact her."

"Thanks. You were the only person I could think of that would have any ideas."

"I'm sorry I didn't take you seriously sooner. We'll help you get through this." Persephone sucked in a breath and bit her bottom lip before adding, "I do sense that you're holding something back. Is there anything else?"

"You always freak me out when you say crap like that, Seph," TJ inserted.

"I know," she said with a smile.

TJ rolled his eyes.

Sighing, Chelsea said, "Okay. Yes. So, I know it looks like a normal tattoo to you, but every time I look at it, the pinwheel is spinning."

"Really? Does it hurt?" asked TJ.

"No, actually it feels like a hair tickling me."

"Crazy. I so want a tattoo that does that … it would be sick. I'd get a dragon that breathed fire and flapped his wings. I've heard that maybe in the future they'll be able to do that, with like computer chips and micro LCD's."

"Wait, is there any way that this tattoo is something like that?" Chelsea asked.

"Nope. Technology isn't there yet, and even if it was, how'd they do it without your knowing about it? And even that would leave you all swollen and red, not fully healed."

Chelsea threw back her head and stared at the ceiling. "This is just impossible. How could it happen? Am I going crazy—"

"Okay, let's assume you are not crazy," Persephone interrupted, "Otherwise we're all crazy, 'cause I know you didn't have that tattoo yesterday. Here's the plan: let's split up, do some research and then meet at Chelsea's place at seven. We'll order pizza and brainstorm. I'll look at dream analysis and paganism, TJ can look into the tribal aspect. Maybe there is some aboriginal thing that can explain this, and Chelsea, try to get creative and explore everything else, no matter how wild. Sound good?"

"Sure."

"Yup."

Nada. Zilch. Nothing.

Chelsea turned over again in bed as she thought about all the research. The meeting of minds resulted in more questions than answers. The dream analysis was interesting, but it gave no real answers. It played like a broken record through her thoughts. *Books — knowledge, intellect, or wisdom. Pinwheel — childhood, carefree and succeeding on your own power. Tattoos — sense of individuality, longer lasting effect than expected. Butterfly — need to settle down, creativity, joy, romance, spirituality and experiencing a transformation. White flower— sadness. Vines — hopes, ambitious thoughts or ideas, feeling trapped and searching for a break through. It mostly makes sense as a dream, but why would the tattoo actually appear on my arm?*

She sighed. The analysis told her what she knew. She was sad. Depressed. Trapped in her life. Things had been going so well until the night she repeatedly dreamed about, the cold winter night when she was fired. Then one thing led to another and like dominoes, her life fell to shambles. She desperately wanted to fix it but felt powerless.

Pinwheel — succeeding on your own power.

The answer was literally tattooed on her arm, but it seemed so unlikely. *Why this? Why me?*

As thoughts tumbled through her head, she felt her body become heavy. The veil of sleep seeped into her mind as the thoughts of the dream slowly turned into the dream.

Snow crunched and squeaked under her feet as she went through the motions of locking the door and attempting to start her car. She floated through seeing the bookstore and calling the tow truck. Again, she asked for the classics and again she plunged into the maze of books. As Chelsea made her way to the back of the store, she passed rows and rows of books. The store was never ending. The back wall was always just a few rows away.

Then she saw a book she felt compelled to examine. Her arms moved almost without her, reaching for the glossy white cover. The picture was simple. Just a rounded silver ring. The title in a plain black font was one word: Piercings.

Pages turned without effort as she was drawn in, staring at the black and white photos of assorted body parts with various metal and plastic piercings. As she neared the center of the book, a picture of a woman's naked back enthralled her. The metal rings ran in two parallel lines down her back, and a black ribbon was woven between them, making her skin into a corset.

Chelsea reached a tentative finger to touch the picture.

Her finger slid through the picture, and she felt the hot naked flesh and the warm metal of one of the rings. At the moment of contact, the rings and ribbon came alive. The ribbon quickly unlaced as the freed rings flew off the woman's back and bit into Chelsea's flesh, first piercing her exposed skin, then sliding beneath the thick layers of her coat and finding the naked skin under her clothing. The pain was intense as each silver ring clamped down.

Unable to drop the book, Chelsea screamed.

The scream brought her back into her bed where she was tangled in the sweaty sheets. Breathing hard, she almost knocked over her lamp as she felt for the switch. She grabbed her glasses, but already knew what she would see. The cold metal rings burned on her back, as if they just pierced her skin and had not yet warmed up. She yanked the back of her shirt with one hand and felt the rows of piercings connected by grosgrain ribbon with her other hand.

This can't be happening. Not again.

She fingered the metal rings, feeling for the clasps to remove them. Unable to feel a break in the metal on any of them, Chelsea threw the sheets back and went to the bathroom to study the rings in the brighter light and the mirror.

Pulling her nightshirt off, then grabbing a hand mirror, Chelsea examined her back. She used the full-length mirror and hand mirror for a better view. The skin seemed fully healed. The two sets of rings started at the small of her back and formed a line that ended right below her shoulder blades. Sixteen rings. The thick black grosgrain ribbon crisscrossed through each piercing, but there was no bow or knot. The ribbon looked like an Escher drawing, no beginning or end, as if it were woven on her back.

She twisted the lowest ring on her right side through her skin, hoping that the clasp had slid inside. After turning for several moments, she was sure that there was no way to remove it. Chelsea tried the next ring up and the next, both without any hint of an opening.

What now?

Scissors.

Chelsea left the bathroom, grabbed a pair of scissors off of her desk and then returned to the double mirrors. She carefully placed the scissors over the ribbon then clamped down as hard as she could. Seeing little results, Chelsea tried pumping the handle. She felt the scissors slip slightly, and opened them to look. The ribbon was not even frayed. She looked at the scissors and gaped at the flat dent in each blade and the bent rivet that only loosely held the scissors together.

Holy crap.

Lost for a moment, Chelsea felt her arm drop and a veil of fear and sadness flow from her heart to every part of her body. *What now? Can I never sleep again? What if I end up in that awful bookstore again?*

Chelsea went for her cell phone and looked at the time. It was nearly three in the morning. After three rings, Persephone answered.

"It happened again," Chelsea whispered, the thought of speaking the words out loud and making it real, too scary for her to grasp.

Groggily, Persephone asked, "Another tattoo?"

"No, piercings this time." The line went dead. "Seph? Are you still there?"

"Yeah ... I'll call TJ. Can you come over?"

"Already out the door."

The scent of lemon poppy seed muffins greeted Chelsea as she knocked on Persephone's apartment door. TJ answered, still in his pajamas and rubbing the sleep from his eyes. He lived a floor above Persephone, but treated her apartment as an extension of his own.

"Hey, Chelsea. Seph's making muffins. Come on in."

Persephone called from the hidden kitchen, "Don't get too excited, it's just a mix."

"I've got tattoos and piercings attacking me, and you're making muffins?"

"Well, I was hungry, and I think better when I'm full," TJ said. "Don't worry, we'll figure this out, but it's not gonna kill you to eat something while we talk. Besides, we had to wait for you to get here from across town."

"Fine, okay. I suppose the muffins aren't insensitive."

They made their way to the kitchen table where the hot muffins cooled, and Persephone poured milk into three glasses.

"Morning, Chelsea. Sorry to hear your night was so bad," said Persephone.

Chelsea sat and snatched a muffin from the pan. She peeled the paper off and took a large bite of the fluffy hot treat. TJ and Persephone joined her and each grabbed a muffin. They munched in silence for a moment, lost in their own thoughts.

"So, this time you dreamed about piercings," Persephone began. "Did you wake up pierced?"

"Yeah. Sixteen rings on my back and a black ribbon running between them."

TJ asked, "Have you tried taking them out, or taking the ribbon off?"

Chelsea smashed the muffin crumbs with her finger as she spoke. "Didn't work. There aren't any clasps, and the ribbon doesn't have any knots or bows. When I tried cutting it, the scissors pretty much just broke."

"I have a pair of wire cutters upstairs. Mind if I try?" TJ got up and started for the door before Chelsea could answer.

"Sure, guess it can't hurt," she said to his back.

Persephone set down her glass and asked, "Was there anything else in the dream that was new?"

"Everything was the same except the book. The picture that attacked me was a woman's back with piercings that made a corset." Felling a little ill from the memory, Chelsea picked at her muffin, breaking it into small pieces.

"I googled piercing dreams before I made the muffins but got nothing. The site I found just said that dreams about piercings can mean a person is feeling anxious about getting a piercing. If it had been your tongue …,"

Persephone paused while TJ bounded through the front door, brandishing a pair of black wire cutters. "If it had been your tongue, it would mean you regret something you said, but I can't think of a logical meaning in getting your back pierced."

"But what about the corset? That has to have a meaning," said TJ. He pointed to Chelsea's muffin and added, "You gonna finish that or pick it to death?"

"I'm done." Chelsea shoved the demolished muffin away.

"Cool." TJ picked it up and used the paper to guide the muffin fragments into his mouth.

Seph took a bite of her muffin before saying, "Well, the meaning of a corset is pretty obvious. It means restriction, feeling limited."

"I suppose that fits with everything else I've been dreaming about, but why this? Why now? Am I supposed to live off of caffeine forever and never sleep again? I'm so frustrated and so tired." Chelsea felt her heart skip a beat as an answer to the 'why now' popped into her mind. *It can't be that. That was just a coincidence.* She tried to push the thought from her mind when she suddenly felt the ribbon pull tighter.

Chelsea screamed.

"What is it? What happened?" Persephone jumped from her chair and grabbed Chelsea into a hug.

"Shh, shh, it'll be okay, you can stop screaming," TJ cooed while stroking her hair.

"I ... ," the tears welled in Chelsea's eyes, and she silently opened and closed her mouth a few times, unable to find the words.

"It's okay, take your time, tell us when you're ready," TJ smiled and continued to run his hand through Chelsea's brown locks.

"The ribbon ... it pulled tighter. It hurts," Chelsea whispered, choking on her tears.

"May I look?" asked Persephone.

Chelsea nodded.

TJ stepped back and Persephone carefully pulled Chelsea's t-shirt up in the back. The only sound was the clock ticking as the pair of friends stared at her back.

"Is it bad?" asked Chelsea after a moment.

Persephone took in a large breath. "Well, the ribbon is pulling on the rings, but only a little. It must hurt, but honestly, it doesn't look all that bad."

"Can I try the cutters?" TJ asked.

"Go for it. I want it all gone."

Persephone held Chelsea's shirt as TJ's warm soft fingers slid along her back, under the ribbon and carefully grasped the lowest ring on the right. Chelsea felt a slight shiver at his touch, but quickly ignored the feeling.

"I think I'm going to have to pull on it a little or else I might pinch your skin in the cutters. Is that okay?"

Chelsea nodded.

The pain was minor. She felt tugging and TJ's hand wiggling against her back as he attempted to cut the ring. Minutes passed. TJ grunted often, but said nothing. Then he stopped and pulled both hands away.

"This isn't working. The ring isn't even scratched, but my cutter is all bent to hell." TJ held the wire cutter up for Chelsea to see. The blades looked like a set of jagged teeth, knocked at uneven intervals with semi-circles.

"What now?" Persephone asked. She let go of Chelsea's shirt, and it fell gently back over her skin corset.

The three friends sat quietly, each deep in thought while the kitchen clock mercilessly ticked on.

"So, I saw this movie a few months ago—" TJ started to say.

"Muffins, movies, what kind of friends are you? I need *help*." Chelsea's voice broke on the last word and tears overwhelmed her, preventing her from saying more.

TJ grabbed Chelsea's hand and looked sincere as he said, "I *am* trying to help. The movie gave me an idea."

"I'm sorry, TJ, I just ... I'm so sorry."

"Calm down, it's okay. So, in the movie they invaded people dreams and stole thoughts. Obviously that's fiction, but it got me thinking about how we could control your dreams in real life. I think maybe we should see a hypnotist."

"What does that have to do with dreaming?" asked Chelsea.

"Actually, that's not a bad idea," said Persephone. "Both deal with the subconscious, so they are related. Maybe a hypnotist could walk you through the dream and get your subconscious to tell us what to do about it."

"Really? You think it could work?" asked TJ.

"I do. That's a really good idea."

TJ beamed. "So, where do we find a hypnotist at four a.m. on a Friday morning?"

"Google, I suppose." Persephone rose.

TJ shook Chelsea for the third time in the last half an hour. No one was surprised when the closest hypnotist with an open appointment was in Minneapolis, and the miles of empty prairie caused Chelsea to nod off. TJ sat in the back of Persephone's Sonata with Chelsea, trying to keep her awake and shaking her when he failed.

"Sorry. I just can't seem to keep my eyes open."

"Yeah, I know. It's actually kind of funny to watch. Here I am, telling you about the exciting sword fights I was in at the last SCA festival, and your jaw starts hanging down and you bang your head on the window."

"Well, we're almost there," said Persephone.

With only five minutes to spare, Persephone pulled her car into a small parking lot next to the prefabricated building that held the hypnotist's office. A painted plywood sign with "Jason Larsson, Hypnotherapist" assured them they had arrived at the correct building.

Once inside, the secretary had Chelsea fill out new patient paperwork and pre-pay for the session. She barely sat on the faded southwestern print chair, when a tall thin man with salt and pepper hair called her name.

When her friends rose to join her, the man said, "It would be better if you came alone. It's harder to relax when you have an audience."

"Oh, okay," Chelsea said and gave her friends a smile. "I'll tell you all about it after, okay?"

"Sure, Chelsea. We'll be waiting," said Persephone as she and TJ sat back down.

The man led her back to his office. The room obviously served two purposes. Half was dedicated to a large wooden desk and surrounded by filing cabinets and bookcases filled mostly with textbooks. The other half resembled a cozy living room. There were two different couches in an L shape that both indirectly faced a large picture window. Outside the heavily draped window was a little garden with a birdbath and wind chimes. The gentle scent of lavender filled the space, mingled with wood and parchment.

"Please, have a seat. Pick a spot that looks comfortable to you."

Chelsea sat on the plushy green sofa, further from the door.

The man offered his hand and said, "Hi, I'm Jason Larsson, feel free to call me Jason."

Chelsea shook his hand. "Hi, Jason."

"So, I gather from our conversation this morning, you've been having a reoccurring dream?"

"Yeah. I've been dreaming about the night I got fired back in January for months now, but the last two nights it got really weird, and I was hoping that maybe I could talk to the old guy who wasn't in the dream before, so I can find out why I am dreaming about him."

Jason sat on the other couch and took a legal pad from the end table. "So, tell me more about how the dream changed. How was it 'weird?'"

"Well, the last two nights, I don't get fired. Instead I go into this bookstore and meet this old, creepy guy."

"That sounds like an improvement. Getting fired over and over again in your dreams can't be a pleasant experience."

"Well, at first the dream was better, but then the books in the bookstore attacked me …," *How can I finish without sounding crazy. . . ?* "And it really freaks me out. I can't sleep because I am afraid of the books. I just think if I talk to the owner of the store, maybe he'll tell me why the books are attacking me."

"Alright. Let's see what we can do. It isn't unreasonable to attempt to talk with this man, because he is simply part of your subconscious, and it seems like he is trying to tell you something."

Jason explained that he would put Chelsea under and then wake her up a few times, so she would get used to the process. While he did that, he would also plant a wakeup signal that would trigger if she touched a book in her dream. Once she was comfortable with the process and he could get her into a deep "sleep," they would then try to contact the old man from the dream.

Already sleepy, Jason's relaxing description of rocking back and forth, back and forth on a hammock in a garden immediately put Chelsea to sleep. It did not take her long to get used to the process of both going into trance and coming out of it.

"Are you ready to talk with the bookstore owner?" Jason asked.

"I think so. I think it'll be okay."

Once again, Chelsea's body grew heavy as she rocked in the hammock. Her arm shot up in the air when Jason mentally attached the huge helium balloon, then fell to her side when he clipped the ribbon. Then his voice took over the narration of her dream.

The cold air bit into her naked fingers as she locked the coffee shop door. The dream was the same, but different. The elements were all there, but everything was fuzzy and dull. She floated in her dream from coffee shop to car to bookstore, without really feeling present in the dream. Once inside the bookstore, the dream became a little clearer but still kept its otherworldly quality. She felt more present, but still detached. The old man did not meet her at the front door. She floated to the desk where the old man kept his phone. She noticed a sign she didn't remember, printed on yellowed parchment, "Ezra Finfrock, Proprietor."

"Mr. Finfrock?" she called out in a hushed whisper.

The skeletal old man stepped out from behind a bookcase. "Chelsea Schmidtkunz?" He pulled a silver pocket watch from a pocket in his black wool vest and checked the time. "I wasn't expecting to see you for several more hours. You look a bit fuzzy. How did you arrive here?"

Still unable to talk louder than a whisper, Chelsea said, "I'm being hypnotized."

"Well, that explains why you're blurry. You aren't fully here. Go back now. I'll talk with you tonight as scheduled."

"No, please! I need to talk to you. I need to ask you something."

The dream started to dissipate, and Chelsea could feel the office and the couch she laid on taking over the feeling of being in the bookstore.

"Please, Ezra, please!"

The bookstore became clearer once again, as the feeling of lying on the couch left.

"Fine. Ask your question. I'm not saying I will answer, but I will consider it."

"Oh thank you, thank you."

Ezra checked his watch again. "Get on with it. I don't have all day. I have an appointment with Spirit, and you need to be gone by then."

"I need to know ... why am I having these dreams? How do I stop them?"

"That's more than one question." His thick, bushy eyebrows formed a line across his forehead as he scowled.

"Please."

"Fine. If you go as soon as I finish talking."

"I will, I promise."

"You've been wishing for a change in your life. Well, you got your wish. Be glad you didn't pick up the book on vampirism."

"But, I didn't wish for this. I wasn't looking for tattoos and piercings. I just wanted things to go better for once. I wanted life to stop sucking."

The bookstore began to fade once again, and this time, Chelsea was sure it would not refocus. "Please, how do I stop it?"

The store was gone. In the distance Chelsea heard Ezra's faint voice, "I can't tell you that. Perhaps there is a book on the subject."

"So that's all he said? 'Perhaps there is a book on the subject'? That's *so* not helpful." Persephone rolled down the car windows to let in some fresh air while they chatted in the heat.

"But he knew who I was, and he said he was expecting me tonight. I don't know what to do. What if I wake up with vampire fangs or something tomorrow?"

"Or what if you pick up a Lovecraft novel and end up with tentacles all over?" asked TJ.

"Ack, don't even say that!" Chelsea screeched.

"Well, hold on, maybe he was giving you a hint. Maybe he was trying to help," Persephone said in a calm voice. "Maybe there is a book you need to find."

"I am *so* not touching any books in that store anymore."

"I don't mean in the store, I meant in real life. Maybe there is a book on … well, I really don't know what the subject would be," Persephone finished weakly.

"Well, according to my phone, we're close to the Ridgedale Library. It looks like the biggest one here. Shall we try that?" asked TJ.

Persephone started her car. "Tell me how to get there. It's at least a step in the right direction. I can't stand just doing nothing."

The glass and brick structure reminded Chelsea a little of the Sydney Opera house, with its arched roof, though she had only ever seen photos of the famous building. The three friends scoured every subject they could think of that was related to dreams, tattoos, piercings, wishes and making changes. The number of books and the variety of subjects made it nearly impossible to look at every book individually. They researched until the announcement that the library would be closing at five came on over the speakers.

"This is hopeless. There just isn't enough time. Why do they close so early on a Friday?" Persephone said.

"Because everyone in his right mind is partying on a Friday night, not hanging out at a library." TJ said as he snapped a book shut. "Yeah, this is hopeless."

"Well, I don't know what to do," said Chelsea, flipping her right hand out into an "I don't know" gesture.

"Aaah!" Persephone squealed. "It's moving! I can see it! Holy crap!"

"Me too, what the fuck?" asked TJ.

"Language, young man," and a dirty look from an older lady with a stack of books reminded them to keep their voices down.

"You can see it spinning? What changed?" asked Chelsea, in a hushed voice.

The three thought a moment then Persephone smiled. "Let me see your arm." She stared intently at the tattoo. Chelsea watched Persephone as several different emotions filled her cherub-like face.

"I have a theory," said Persephone after a minute. "Chelsea, look at it and see what happens when you think about the worst day ever in your life."

Chelsea looked curiously at her friend.

"Just try it, okay?"

Chelsea focused on the tattoo, and thought about the day her mother died in a car accident. The pinwheel spun so fast, she could only see a circular blur.

"Now, think of something hopeful … like what you would do if you won a hundred million dollars and never had to work again."

"Okay …." Chelsea thought about the little used book store she would open on the beach that specialized in fun summer novels that tourists could read and return while visiting the shore. The pinwheel slowed, and finally stopped as she felt the calm happiness the fantasy always made her feel.

"So, did it change speeds?" asked Persephone.

"Yes, how did you know?"

"TJ and I both said we were feeling hopeless, then we both saw it spin for the first time. I think it is like a hope meter. You've been feeling hopeless for so long, maybe that's why you see it spinning all the time."

"Really? Let me try." TJ grabbed Chelsea's arm and stared for a moment. "Woah, cool. It works. It's like having a magic eight ball on your skin. I wonder if the bookstore does requests."

Chelsea pulled her arm away. "I don't know. It's not like it's telling me the future. It's just making it obvious when I'm feeling bad."

"I think we're on the right track though. I think we just need to look at some more books. Perhaps there is one with a title about succeeding on your own power, thus the reason for a pinwheel."

"But the library is closing," said Chelsea.

"TJ, will you look and see if you can find a large bookstore on your phone? I'm thinking one with new and used books, not a chain."

The female voice on the speakers interrupted the trio. "Please bring your final selections to the checkout counter. The library is officially closed. We will reopen tomorrow morning at ten. Thank you for visiting the Ridgedale Library."

Chelsea and Persephone lead the way through the deserted library, while TJ trailed behind, googling bookstores on his phone as he walked. As they left the glass entryway, TJ stopped and said, "I think I found one that looks good. Called Magers and Quinn. This says they're open 'til eleven tonight."

"Okay, let's go," said Persephone.

The three-story bookstore had a great selection of books. Where the library had an exceptionally good selection of reference and non-fiction books, Magers & Quinn was especially well stocked in fiction.

"So, if the pinwheel means self-powered," Chelsea said as the three friends entered the store, "maybe I need to look by myself for a bit. How about we split up? I know you both want to look around and deserve a break after all the help you've given me. I'll go look in the self-help section, and you can meet me there after you browse. If I haven't found anything in like an hour, I'll find you guys."

"Are you sure? We can help," asked Persephone.

"No, really. I think you're right. I think the book I need, if it exists, will say something about pinwheels or self-powered something or another."

"Succeeding on your own power."

"Right, that."

"Are you sure?" TJ hesitantly asked.

"Positive. Have fun."

Chelsea asked an employee for the self-help section of the store. She carefully looked at every cover and title on the pale maple shelves. Some of the book's titles came close, and she set them aside to study further. Once she was sure that she looked at every book in the section, Chelsea went back to the small stack she pulled from the shelf. Reading the table of contents and flipping through each book, Chelsea found a few books she wanted to buy, but none of them seemed to be the magical solution.

Chelsea went to the help desk to see if anyone in the store had heard of a pinwheel book. An elderly lady with snow-white fluffy hair sorted books behind the counter. As Chelsea approached, the woman greeted her with kind green eyes.

"May I help you?" The store name badge identified her as "Eliza."

"I'm trying to find a book, but I'm not sure it exists. I know it's a gamble, but maybe you know of it?"

"Well, I will certainly attempt to help you, dear. I spend a great deal of time looking through all the books that come and go here." Eliza pushed a stack of books aside and picked up a pen and slip of paper.

"Okay, well, I am looking for a book that might be in the self-help section that has a pinwheel on the cover and something about succeeding on your own power."

Eliza's vivid green eyes turned from kind to piercing as she looked up from the paper. "Is your name 'Chelsea' by chance?"

Chelsea's voice caught in her throat. For the first time since the trip to Minneapolis, Chelsea felt the icy stab of fear.

Kinder, Eliza said, "I'm sorry, love. I didn't mean to frighten you. I've been expecting you, or someone like you. I've forgotten, in my advanced age, how frightening it was for me." She set the pen down. "Would you care for some tea?"

Chelsea continued to stare, unsure what to do. *What if she's in on it? She seems to know something. What if the book is a trap?*

"I won't bite, I promise. Come along, dear." Eliza walked around the counter, past Chelsea, and then continued into the shelves of books without looking back.

Well, either I have to follow her or just keep standing here like a dummy. Succeeding on my own power. I can do this. Catching up to the older woman was easy. Chelsea followed as Eliza moved through the bookshelves and to an employee break room.

Chelsea lingered in the doorway as Eliza dropped bags of tea into two ceramic mugs then poured in hot water from an orange-trimmed carafe. Eliza turned once again to Chelsea holding both mugs and gestured to a table with two chairs. "Please, have a seat. I don't believe we'll be disturbed in here."

"How did you know my name?" Chelsea demanded, as she continued to stand.

"It's a long story. Please sit, love. I promise you will feel better in a short while. If you take my advice, that is." Eliza took a seat and slid one mug across the table in front of the vacant table.

Chelsea laid her two books on the table and sat. "Alright. What's your advice?"

"Well, dear, I can't start there," Eliza began. "A long time ago, I think maybe it's been nearly sixty years now, yes sixty-one in September. I was a lot younger then, of course, twenty-two. About your age?"

"I'm twenty-five."

"Yes, then near. But it was different back then. I was an old maid, and women just didn't go to college, at least not the women from my hometown. I was … dejected. There was a boy … it's always a boy, isn't it, dear?"

Chelsea nodded then took a sip of tea.

"Well, you don't need the details. He chose to marry my best friend at the time. And there I was, alone, unspeakably old and unmarried, and of course childless, though it would have been worse if I had a child out of wedlock." Eliza once again pierced Chelsea's soul as she spoke, "I attempted to take my own life."

Chelsea's heart beat faster, and her normally pale cheeks flushed with color.

"You see where I am going?"

"No—" Chelsea started to say, but the ribbon woven though the piercings on her back suddenly tightened, causing her to gasp.

Eliza nodded then took a long sip of tea as Chelsea attempted to recover.

"I sat in a bathtub full of water and slit my wrists. My brother found me and took me to the hospital. It was there that I dreamed about the bookstore."

"You've seen it too? It's real?"

"Real enough and so was the tattoo. Imagine that. Only sailors had tattoos, not good girls who wanted to get married. I hid it as best I could, and tried desperately to find a way to remove it. I dreamed nightly about Ezra and his bookstore. We talked for hours and hours, but he refused to tell me why I had the tattoo or how to be rid of it, always just saying 'perhaps there is a book on the subject.' I looked and looked in every bookstore, but it seemed useless, and that damn pinwheel just kept spinning. Once, I asked Ezra if I could look in his bookstore, but he told me that the book wasn't in his shop, and warned me not to look at any of his books."

"Did you ever pick up another book?"

"No. I was a good girl, despite my earlier indiscretion."

"Well, you're lucky. I've touched two books so far, and it isn't working out too hot for me."

Eliza nodded. "One day, I was looking in a bookstore yet again, and I wasn't paying attention. I bumped into this man, and he dropped his stack of books. One of them had a picture of a pinwheel and my name on the cover. Needless to say, I was shocked. I asked the man if I could look at it, but he said it wasn't one he had in the stack he dropped. His eyes were kind, and he acted the gentleman despite the fact that I ran him over. I bought the book, and a year later I married the man."

"What was in the book?"

"It was what I needed. That's all I will say." Eliza sipped her tea again and folded her hands.

"So, do you still have the book? Did the title change to 'Chelsea?'"

"No. The title didn't change, and yes, I still keep the book. It is one of my most cherished possessions. As I said earlier, dear, I see almost all the books that come and go here. I found the 'Chelsea' book yesterday. It simply showed up on the help desk, just suddenly there when nothing had been there before. I bought it, and I've been waiting for you, love. I must admit I expected a longer wait."

"Well, apparently Ezra doesn't warn people about looking at books anymore. I had a bit more motivation to find the book."

"I see," she replied then she stood. "Well, the book is at my house, and I must go back to work. You are welcome to come over tonight. If you follow me back to the information desk, I'll write down my address."

Chelsea took the slip of paper and went looking for her friends. She found Persephone first in the New Age section.

When she saw her friend approach, Persephone said, "Look at this, a Manga Tarot. Isn't that crazy? I think I have to get it to add it to my collection. It's new, so it should be safe. Did you have any luck?"

"Actually, I did. I found these two books that looked good, but even better, this woman has a book with a pinwheel on the cover. She said I could come to her house to look at it. I think it might be the one."

"Really? Could it be that easy?"

"I hope so." Chelsea glanced down at the pinwheel as she said the word "hope." The pinwheel spun so slowly, it was nearly still.

"Let's find TJ. I bet he's in the fantasy section."

The girls managed to pull TJ away from the stack of second edition *Advanced Dungeons and Dragons* game books he was leafing through then they all made their way to the checkout.

After killing time until the end of Eliza's shift by eating at a diner, TJ programmed the address into his cell phone then gave the directions to Persephone. According to the Sonata's clock, it was nearly ten thirty.

When they arrived at the house, and all three went to the door. "Come in, come in. I have a pot of tea and some biscuits ready. Do make yourselves at home."

The plump woman turned back into her house. TJ entered last and closed the door behind him as they made their way to Eliza's living room. A pot of tea, four cups and four plates full of biscuits sat on the coffee table.

"I know you are the rightful owner of the book, Chelsea, but before I let you see it, I want to hear your story. Please, sit."

Chelsea nodded, looking to her friends for support.

"Don't worry, love, I'm only curious. I thought I was the only one, so you see, I simply want to know more for my own sake, dear."

Feeling a little more at ease, Chelsea sat and took a cup of tea. The story came in slow sputters at first, but as Chelsea told Eliza about her three trips into the bookstore, the words came easier.

"So, how is Ezra? I haven't seen him in so long," Eliza asked when

Chelsea finished her story.

"He seemed fine to me, a little grouchy, so we didn't talk much."

Eliza nodded.

"So, will you let me see the book?" asked Chelsea.

"Let me ask one more question first. Have you learned anything?"

"Yes, yes, oh, of course. I need to be more hopeful," Chelsea replied eagerly, setting her tea on the table.

Eliza studied her for a long minute. "No, love, I don't think you've learned the lesson the book was meant to teach you yet."

"Oh, please. I want to know. What is the lesson?"

"I will give you the book, and maybe it will help. But before I do that, I need to offer your friends some accommodations. The three of you look about ready to fall over you're so tired. There is no way you can head back to Grand Forks tonight. You need sleep. Come with me."

The woman led them down a hall. She pointed out the three guest rooms and the bathroom. "Your book is on your bed in the blue room. Try not to stay up too late reading. I will be in my room upstairs if any of you need anything."

With that, the woman turned and left the three friends alone. They nodded wordlessly to each other and headed into the separate bedrooms.

Chelsea found the pinwheel book exactly where Eliza said it would be. The cover was identical to the cover of the tattoo book in her dreams, except the book's title was "Chelsea."

She opened the book and watched, almost like a movie screen, as scenes from her life played out on the page. Over and over again, she saw herself saying, "I hate my life" at even the smallest inconvenience. Then she saw the evening before her first bookstore dream. She sat on her bed crying and holding a handful of pills. The water glass next to her bed was full. She stared at the pills for a long time as tears flowed down her cheeks. Then Chelsea watched as the movie-like book showed her placing the pills back into the bottle and saying, "I don't think I have enough. I'll get more tomorrow."

The weight of the words hit her, as the ribbon crawled against her skin, not tightening, but clearly sending a message.

The images on the page changed again, this time showing her happy childhood and teen moments, the look that TJ gave her that she never noticed before was full of love. The book went on to show what her life could be … a bookstore on the beach, the three happy blond babies she and TJ would have, a charity she ran to encourage children to read. Tears welled in her eyes as Chelsea realized what she almost threw away.

As the tears flowed, Chelsea found her body giving over to sleep. She curled into a ball and hugged the book close to her heart.

Once again, she was in front of Librorum Taberna, but this time she was in shorts and flip-flops. It was summer and bright daylight. She opened the door and entered the store.

Both Eliza and Ezra were waiting for her.

"Did you read the book, dear?" asked Eliza.

"Yes. I understand now. I'm so sorry. I didn't know … didn't realize …,"

"Do you really? Or are you going to go on throwing your life away?" snapped Ezra, his empty white eyes boring holes into Chelsea's soul.

"Yes. I get it. I understand," Chelsea began to cry, though this time with joy. "I will succeed, but no one is going to do it for me. I have to do it on my own power."

Chelsea held TJ's hand as the needles pierced her skin.

"Too late now, you're gonna be stuck with a pinwheel on your arm forever," TJ joked.

"Yup, that's the plan," Chelsea replied.

She thought back to the morning in Eliza's house. The piercings, ribbon and tattoo were all gone. At first, Chelsea had been relieved, but lately, she missed the tattoo.

"I want the reminder," Chelsea continued, "so I never forget again. I *can* succeed on my own power, and if I forget, I only have to look at my arm to remember."

TJ squeezed her hand, and his eyes sparkled as he said, "Yes, you can succeed on your own power, but it never hurts to have a friend."

The universe is full of injustice. No matter where I go, there is always someone hungry for power, not caring what it costs to achieve. I love it when someone fights back. EF

Mutiny in the Marketplace
by Todd A. Walls

The dual personalities of the suns cast schizophrenic shadows; one buttery, one brassy, causing overlapping multi-hued shades. The two suns made up a binary system in the constellation of the Phoenix. The heat of the day was at its highest during the hour of the sunflower, when the angles of the shadows were perfectly mirrored.

The lost human starship colony mimicked that flower by blossoming with activity and basking passionately in the welcome warmth and stillness. Winds would whip and tear the land with the setting of the first sun. For now, the marketplace bustled.

"Ten coppers say I disarm you first," Tarry said to a leather-clad girl who had announced her name as Spirit.

Her garb was loose and unrestrictive, but awkwardly short, flapping in just the right places to tease a man's imagination without being too obvious.

"What are you going to do? Bore me until I throw my sword down to shut you up?" Spirit crinkled the sparse freckles across her nose just enough to soften the taunt. Her fingers shifted position on the sword as if they had never held a blade before. The blade bore marks of character from historic battles, being older than all of the onlookers combined.

"No need to be rude. What I have in mind won't be boring at all," he retorted.

Tarry was tall with a severe sharpness to every edge of his frame and personality, though his clothing invited acceptance. A layered silk rainbow of earth tones wrapped richly about him. A red silk sash tied around his waist suggested power and influence. Hard, heavy, expensive boots protected his feet, while unkempt black hair belied all codes of grooming and appearance by waltzing out of control in every direction. He was, by any measure, a pig in a wig.

Spirit was barely a woman, petite, and fluctuated often between a jaded hardness and a soft inviting friendliness depending on the needs of the moment and which of the two souls within her was in charge at the moment. Supple and sure-footed leather shoes were her only other adornment.

The two circled with caution, swords at the ready, each reading the skills of the other. It had started as a dare but swiftly became a bet.

The spectacle of an influential local man and an attractive stranger circling each other with swords drawn was a welcome distraction from the everyday business of the marketplace. A dozen people, many of them Tarry's business associates and childhood friends, ringed the two fencers in the dusty lane fronting the old bookshop.

The bookstore was made of the same blue granite as almost every other structure in town because the local trees were too willowy and slender for serious construction. The surrounding hills afforded enough shattered and weathered stone to trip up an army of giants and made for easy building materials. The granite was also the genesis of the town's name, New Boulder.

The only wooden component of the bookstore was the sign that read, Librorum Taberna. The sign had its own hard-won history, evidenced by charred edges and softened features caused by frequent sandblasting from the nightly windstorms. In this town, the wide wooden boards of the sign were an anomaly.

For that matter, books were an anomaly as well and in high demand by those who could read them. Many who could not read often stopped by the bookstore on Sunday afternoons for lessons, causing no end of conflict with the affluent, who wanted to keep the masses ignorant. This bookstore, at this particular time and place, had the opportunity to influence the development of a society.

Market Street, where they stood, was wide and flat. Generations ago, an entire narrow row of buildings had been demolished to leave a wide area for commerce. The road was paved only in sandy dirt layered with many years' accumulation of castaway filth.

Ezra watched the unfolding scene, leaning against the doorway of his bookstore. The soft murmur of local businessmen caught his attention as they filed out of the Boar's Blanket Inn next door. The timing was perfect. They represented the New Boulder merchants' association, the most influential men in town, and their luncheon meeting had just ended. The crowd grew. The tall man checked his pocket watch as the faint sound of flipping pages came from somewhere in the shop behind him. It was important to stay here for a while longer. He could not move yet.

Ezra watched and he waited.

"Only ten coppers, barrister?" yelled a heckler from the crowd. He was medium and brown and dressed like a commoner.

"Yeah," another voice yelled from the gathering, "she's just a girl."

"You can take her, Tarry."

"What does she give you if you win?"

Many in the crowd laughed, mostly men.

Spirit appeared uncertain, tossing long blonde hair clear of her striking tarnished-copper eyes while holding her sword like a stick. "Ten silvers, and … I guess it's a bet."

"You haven't got ten silvers. Just look at you. But you know, I'll take a little something else instead, say about an hour of your time?" Tarry punctuated his proposition with a less-than-sincere smile.

Without breaking eye contact, she loosened a pouch from somewhere within the folds of her tunic and shook it. The clinking belied a tidy sum, even if they were all coppers, which they were not. The bag was full of iron shards from a broken cooking pot.

"Still interested?" Spirit flashed him a smile that probably worked on most rich young men. She looked about as harmless, and as beautiful, as a mermaid out of water.

Ezra snapped his watch cover shut with one pale, bony finger. It was time. He stepped out of the doorway and made his way down the stone steps. The crowd unconsciously shuffled aside to let him pass.

Tarry answered, "What do I need with silvers? What I want is you," he tilted his head and cut loose his most striking, roguish grin upon the crowd. A grin he had practiced many times in front of a mirror.

The growing throng closed ranks behind the proprietor of the bookshop. Ezra looked conspicuous wearing his crisp white linen shirt and black wool vest. Most of the townsfolk wore simple brown wool clothing or were heavily adorned with colored Elderworm silk, depending upon their wealth. He also smelled different. The crowd was all sweat and perfume, while the cool scent of musty old books clung to Ezra's gaunt frame.

"It looks like you need someone to hold the pot," he said with just enough volume for the crowd to hear and no more. His voice rolled out with the hollowness of a man chained at the bottom of a deep muddy well.

Tarry looked at Ezra with a sneer. "I bet you'd like that, wouldn't you. Go pack your bags, old man. I'll own your building before long, and you can be sure you'll be the first to find yourself on the street. Or in the stocks more likely, with rotten celery draped across your face. Your books and your lessons are cruel heresy against the people of this town."

Several people in the crowd snickered.

"You can hold mine." Spirit tossed Ezra the clinking leather bag without making eye contact.

"All right then, we'll do it your way," Tarry said. The well-to-do solicitor began to untie his own heavy money pouch as he spoke to someone nearby. "You can give it back to me in a minute, Gudder. After I show these fine townsfolk why they should support me as their new trade minister."

"Right," Gudder said.

A faint murmur filled the crowd at this political announcement, especially among the businessmen present. Tarry tossed the bag to Gudder, but a stranger's hand caught it inches before it found its target.

"You are a smile to the wrath of God," said the stranger. He nodded his head in blessing and bowed to kiss Tarry's bag of money, and then dropped the pouch into Gudder's hands.

Tarry sized him up. The stranger was tall, bald, and wore the brown robes of a monk. Only a keen eye would have noted how the wrinkled hands contrasted with his younger face. Tarry was far too distracted, and Gudder not nearly bright enough, to notice.

"Of course I am," Tarry said.

Turning back, Tarry struck a solid overhand blow without warning. Spirit parried clumsily and twisted to one side, untouched.

"What's wrong, girl? You didn't think I'd go easy on you just for money, did you?"

"I suggest you try again." Spirit looked up at her taller opponent, meeting his eyes in clear defiance.

"Certainly, if you prefer business to pleasure. I'll soon have your silver or whatever worthless baubles you carry in your pouch."

Swords clanged. Spirit fought back with exactly the skill and precision needed and no more. When the man fought with more accuracy, more speed, and more strength, the results were the same. They moved back and forth, but ended up in the same positions as before.

"You've been taking lessons, I see." Sweat beaded on his forehead and pooled in his eyebrows, more from embarrassment at his inability to dominate the young girl than from the physical activity. His demonstration of superior swordsmanship had developed into a real contest, and his carefully cultivated image was at stake.

"No matter," he jeered, on the edge of losing his cool. "If you don't have the full ten silvers I'll take the rest of it out of you in my own way—at my pleasure. You can bet it will *not* be at yours."

Some sniggered, but most of the crowd fell silent. Tarry was ruthless and unforgiving, as most of the local businessmen were, and his threats were never idle. They often measured success by the number of trampled adversaries. Image was everything.

Cruelty trumped compassion in this frontier of the galaxy, and money trumped the law. Tarry could likely do anything he wished with the poor girl and get away with it, but no one from the working class would dare show her sympathy for fear of being caught up in the barrister's cruel game.

To everyone's surprise, Spirit laughed and lowered her sword. The time was right. Tarry had wrapped the rope of public opinion around his own neck, and all she had to do now was tighten the knot.

"Come to your senses?" He asked.

"You have no clue what's about to happen, do you?" Spirit answered with a mischievous smile. "I'm about to give in."

It was half question and half statement. She approached her opponent slowly, swaying her young hips, flipping her sword to hold it by the blade then holding it loosely before him. She dropped it at his feet. Defiance and doubt drained away from her expression and were replaced with nonchalance and a warm, disarming composure.

"Nice." Tarry snapped his teeth together in anticipation of victory.

Before he knew what was happening her sword flashed up between them, propelled by a practiced flip of her foot. In an instant, she smacked his sword fingers with the flat of her blade and yanked the weapon from her grip.

"Or am I about to win?" She held both swords high and answered her own question, "Sorry, I guess I already did." She grinned impishly at the crowd, and then took a deep breath, clearly aware of her narrow escape.

The crowd took a collective double take. The girl had not been disarmed. Rather, she had voluntarily dropped her sword and then picked it back up. It was a valid win.

The crowd cheered, every single one of them. Laughter soon replaced the cheering, first by the business owners, then everyone else, all at Tarry's expense. They laughed and whooped a second time when Gudder poured out the contents of his bag to count out ten silvers and saw that it was filled with cheap lead.

The rumors would not be kind, especially among Tarry's political opponents. The slightest show of weakness in this town would set the jackals snapping at Tarry's heels. Money trumped the law, but reputation trumped all.

Ezra made a mental note to brew up a batch of his best spiced cider that evening for his visiting friends, who made a living from performing sleight of hand, juggling, and sword tricks in public markets.

He pocketed the girl's worthless money pouch and headed back into his store, wondering who would be generous enough to publicly lend the disgraced businessman the money to cover his debts.

Ezra did not pack his bags, or move the store. He still had work to do in this town.

It was a bloodless coup.

Love is a fickle thing. I have seen what it can do to mens hearts. Love can both hurt and heal. But understand it? Not even I can do that. EF

Shards of Reality

by Sangita Kalarickal

No. There was not even an inkling of a premonition.

Hot air rose from Lucknow's brown soil, creating mirages, but none of those contained a wisp of an image of the future she would have chosen.

She sat with her back to the sturdy trunk of the old mango tree with half closed eyes, watching the shimmering air hover above the ground, creating the illusion of a rain-washed tarred road. Suddenly the warm air shifted, and a cuckoo crooned from a distance. Though her mind was slowed down by the lull of an oncoming siesta, she noticed something strange in the landscape. A tiny building had emerged overnight adjacent to the huge Nirmala Nagar lawn, a mere skip away from her college. The board proclaiming the name of the structure squeaked loudly in the quiet afternoon breeze.

A few moments and a large helping of intrigue transported her to the front of the suddenly materialized structure. A Latin sign hung huge from the low roof. 'Librorum Taberna' it screamed, with white letters painted onto the scorched wood. A gigantic display of books adorned the windows. Hand written tags with the newly adopted sign of the Rupee announced the prices of the hardbacks and paperbacks arranged in what appeared to be an ordered chaos. "It's a shop!" she whispered, eyes growing round with incredulity. A shop springing up overnight was indeed astonishing.

Then a glint met her eyes arising from among the assortments of old and new hardbacks. Her brown eyes narrowed as she peered harder through the dusty glass. An old dagger winked at her in the sunlight, heightening her attraction to the store. Though unassuming, the weapon had a nice thick spine with a slow taper away to the blade. Despite the years it had obviously seen, the blade shone with sharpness. Its beautiful leather sheath lay innocently underneath. Her brows met in the middle of her forehead as she scrutinized the weapon through the film of dust, and studied the motif on the sheath. "The Y Ddraig Goch!" she exclaimed and promptly her hand flew to her mouth as she looked around, hoping no one caught her during her embarrassing dialog with herself. The Welsh red dragon with its spear tipped tongue looked majestic on the faded leather. She had only seen that pattern in books. Her interest in medieval European literature and history pressed her on, and she opened the door of the store. Bells chimed deep, yet sweet. The cluster of ceramic bells that hung on the doorknob trembled for a while after the door closed. *What a wonderful idea to let the owner know that someone has crossed the door!*

A few moments passed before she encountered the proprietor. *Oh my God!* His thin figure, his straw colored hair, and his white pupil-less eyes sent waves of panic through her entire body. Her heart beat as though it wanted to jump out of her body, and her legs sprung into action, jerked and almost carried her out of the store. *But, Y Ddraig Goch! How many stores carry this pattern on a dagger set out on display?* To top it all, the immense number of books in the store added another dimension to her curiosity. She staggered and maintained a straight spine.

"Do … do you have more Arthurian items?"

In response, all she received was, "Interested in that dagger, are you?" in a low, rough voice.

She mustered up her courage and looked straight into the pallid face housing milky white eyes. "Yes of course! Wouldn't anyone? Why else would you have it there? How old is it? Is it still sharp?"

The proprietor guffawed at the barrage of questions. "Young woman, you ask a lot of questions. First things first. My name is Ezra. And yours …?"

"Varsha."

"So, Varsha, you are interested in medieval literature. Anything in particular?"

"Arthurian legends. That's why the dagger looks very interesting to me."

"Ah yes, of course, if you are interested in those times then you'd recognize Carnwennan, yes?"

What! Her eyes grew wide with bewilderment and disbelief. "It can't be. It can't. King Arthur's dagger?"

No reply. Just an irritating chuckle. Ezra strode to the display window and picked up the dagger, pushed it gently into its sheath. "You are welcome to look around at my books. But I am not running an antique store, you know. This dagger was a gift and is not for sale." With that his fingers closed on the sheathed weapon and he carried it into the back of the store.

Carnwennan indeed! What a gimmick! The motif of the Welsh dragon certainly feeds his tale. But he's got a lot of books, a lot!

"Well, the dagger is nice, but I was really looking for books," she managed to retort under her breath, almost drooling at the sight of the stocked shelves.

The next days went by in a flash. To say that the store was large would have been an understatement. Ezra had enough books on Arthurian times to keep Varsha occupied for a couple of lifetimes. She never even knew such volumes were ever written. Fables, fiction and history intertwined, all in one place. She spent all her money on the books she could afford. During that time the most important thing she did, however, was to break Ezra's sarcasm ridden, negative, cantankerous façade. She figured he was nice to her since she was his biggest customer, of course. He no longer complained when she just sat and read the books, especially those that were old enough to be expensive.

All through her reading and research, one figure started reaching out through history and mythology to her, appealing to her sensibilities and romance. And it was neither Arthur nor Merlin. The character emerged as a collage of descriptions across fact and fiction, capturing all her attention and driving her study to obsession. The character of Lancelot. A man capable of honesty and bravery at the same time. A man whose life fate had filled with hopeless, unfulfilled love and yet who never gave up his morality to attain that love. A super human. That character struck her heart, created his home there, and made every male she had met look smaller in stature.

And so it was, during that harsh summer in northern India, when the heat sucked out even one's very desire to move, that Varsha sat under a slow, squeaking, rotating fan in Librorum Taberna, read, and fell in love with a legend.

Two Saturdays after she entered the store, she came across a peculiar book, as she scoured the stacks for something with a better focus on Sir Lancelot. Ezra ambled along, carrying a stack of books to shelve. She must have been lost in part thought, part dream, for he cleared his throat rather loudly. He raised one of his bushy eyebrows until the yellow eyebrow hair almost intertwined with the straw colored mop on his head. "If you've finished chewing up your fingernail, you may want to reconsider whether you really want to buy that one."

Varsha looked down at the cover of the old book she held. 'The Pilgrymage' it declared. She nodded.

"Sure, are you?" Ezra queried of her.

She nodded again and pulled out the last of her money. Color filled her light complexion as she counted the cash. "But I don't think I'm having enough money." Words stumbled from her tongue. All the English grammar that she had learned flew out the window as she realized with great embarrassment she had reached the bottom of her money purse. She'd probably have to borrow from her friends until the subsequent installment of her meager inheritance came in next month. The money in her purse was a hundred rupees short of the price.

"I … I cannot buy it after all." Regaining her composure, Varsha turned to place the book back on the shelf.

"Well, it is likely the best book you will find for what you want. Tell you what. You've been a delight to have around the shop, and a good customer to boot. Forget about the hundred rupees, the book is yours. But I must warn you, the text is not what it seems. It is what you *want* it to be."

Varsha's ears had stopped hearing words after 'forget about the hundred rupees'. She quickly grabbed the book and handed over the money. Pocketing the cash Ezra said, "Be careful what you wish for, little girl. This is no Harlequin Romance book. But if that is what you want it to be …." He terminated his sentence with a shrug.

A quizzical sort of guy, this man. Who knows if he's in his right mind, even. All the words that emerge from his mouth seem so randomly placed.

That evening, excited, she even skipped her favorite meal of *rajma chaawal*, the rice and kidney bean curry dinner they had served in the hostel cafeteria. Sitting on the edge of her bed, Varsha took out 'The Pilgrymage' and opened it. Chaucerian language stared back at her. Verses about Arthurian times floated out of the book. Time flew by, until she turned the hundred and seventh page and found the parchment that would change her life.

But there was not even an inkling of a premonition.

An old yellowed piece of papyrus with browning edges lay pinched between her forefinger and thumb.

The black ink on the three visible words had faded into a hue of brown. "Vita Phantasia est." Varsha laughed out aloud. *Sure. Sure. Life was one long journey of fantasy.*

It was late and her eyes hurt, burning with the strain of having read for a long time. She rubbed them and chuckled at her discovery of the parchment. She'd always wished she lived another life. Not the one she had, with no parents to go home to, where she had to make up excuses of summer projects so that she didn't have to vacate her hostel room as other students did to return home. Anything to keep from going back to her guardian, her uncle's house. She wished her life were a part of the world she had only read about and imagined. "Ya, of course." She yawned and spoke out aloud to the walls of her hostel room. The second hand poster of the Princess Bride she'd picked up at a sale loomed large on her wall. She'd never seen the movie but the faces had beckoned her into their world. Varsha smiled at the characters on the poster, dreamily. "Vita Phantasia est, indeed."

Time became hazy to Varsha. She felt a tingling sensation in the pit of her stomach. A feeling of being squeezed through a bell jar accompanied it. Her vision blurred and the posters on her wall danced around her table lamp before blending into trees—strange tall trees—complete with cold weather and musty smells. When her vision cleared up again, she stood barefoot in an old forest. Breathless and perplexed, she looked around. Tiny beads of perspiration appeared on her forehead and neck as she realized that this was no ordinary tropical forest. No, the trees looked very different. Tall, tall trees with vines clambering up the barks. She heard birds that she could not identify. She looked down at her clothes, which had turned into a long gown of cream-colored cotton. *A night dress? What's happening?* All she could recognize in that place was the book she carried in her left hand and the papyrus piece in her right.

Then came the sounds of footsteps. Startled and terrified, she sprang into the juniper bushes nearby and almost screamed out in agony as the branches scratched her arms through the light fabric. She peered out of the bushes only to rest her eyes on a man who limped along, with a far away look in his face, hair long and matted, beard grown bushy with time. His eyes wildly scanned the skies between the trees. A sudden feeling ran through her, cool through her spine yet warmth spread through her limbs. Varsha stood up straight and caught his glance. She looked into his light green eyes. A most beautiful smile then lit up his face. Varsha's heart missed a beat. Several beats in fact.

People speak of love at first sight, but what do they know?

Varsha sighed loudly. It was a sigh that almost became a sob. She did not completely recall the days after the encounter with the mysterious man in the old English woods. All she knew was that he was a knight. He was roaming around teetering on the dangerous precipice between sanity and madness. Rejection from his lady love had driven him into a rebounding passion for the dark lady with the raven hair and brown eyes. She did not remember his name. After a few days of being with him, she realized that in her, he saw not Varsha but the lady who had spurned him. Her mind plunged into a chasm of anger and depression. She ran to a nearby pond and flung the book that brought her to this place into the deep green waters. All that remained was the parchment with the Latin words she had slid into the folds of her clothes near her bosom. Tearfully, she pulled out the yellowed paper and scowled at it. "I don't want it! Vita Phantasia est? I don't—"

The next thing she knew was the piercing pain that brought her back to the room in the hostel she had left behind. Shards of reality had pierced her very soul. Nothing was to be the same again.

What could have been construed as a dream or a trip into mythology, ceased to remain so. She realized this after a couple of months as she stared at the positive pregnancy testing strip. Varsha was forced to flee from Lucknow to Mumbai, the big city which absorbed everyone, asked no questions, and silently collected any sadness into its folds. She had to change her name and start anew to stop all the accusing questions.

An unwed mother had a difficult life in India.

Varsha Choudhary became Ananya Bhatnagar and created a new life for herself. In a way, it was fortunate that she was an orphan, that she was raised by her uncle who was more than happy to have most of her inheritance left to him. She had walked out on a promising, easy life, to face the battles of motherhood alone. All that was left behind to bind her to that incident was the name she gave her son.

Sapan.

Dream.

That was what it all was. A dream that had bled into reality.

Sapan lay on the road, his green eyes blinking at the spots of light dancing in the air, the back of his head hurting slightly where it hit the pavement. Above him, he could discern a sliver of sky visible between the tops of the buildings around him. He turned his head. His cell phone was a few feet away from him.

"You are okay, no?" A pair of eyes peered from behind glasses and a hefty hand shot out at him to help him back to his feet.

Sapan nodded and then winced. A sharp pain shot through his ankle. *Serves me right. Ma always told me not to text while walking.* Somebody picked up his cell phone from the road, shoved it into his shirt pocket and patted him on his back.

"Th … thanks!" he murmured to all in general. The hefty hand had disappeared. He didn't even see who returned his phone. People in Mumbai were a busy lot. A helpful lot mostly, but busy. No one had the time to stand around to acknowledge niceties like 'thanks'. He dusted off his shirt and pants and tried again to put weight on his foot. Arrows of pain shot up the ankle. "Fuck, fuck!" the words exploded from Sapan's lips.

Tch! Tch! Kids nowadays!" a high pitched voice reprimanded as a woman brushed past him.

Sapan frowned. *Kids! I will be fourteen next week. I can curse all I want, you old prude. You would too, if your ankle hurt like this!* He sank onto the sidewalk and sat on the dusty stones. *The pain will subside if I wait a bit.* He thrust his hand into his pocket and drew out his favorite new toy and examined it. *Phew! Just a scratch.* The cell phone lay mute in his palm. The battery had moved out of its socket and the screen had gone blank. Sapan quickly adjusted the battery and switched on his phone. The screen flashed bright at him in a few seconds. The words "wot hpnd?" appeared.

"nutn. bc ltr" he typed. His mother would have rushed into a tirade of how language is being butchered by texting teens. He pushed the thought to the back of his head. He loved his Ma, but what did she know about the importance of using as few keys as possible and also inventing new spelling? Then he propped himself up and decided to brave it. After all, it was just a ten-minute walk home.

The painful ankle made each step he took more difficult than the previous. Sapan looked around. Large billboards vied with each other for space, advertising everything from butter to TV shows. Another turn into a by-lane and he would be home. He hoped his ankle hadn't sprained too badly. The pain was getting more intense by the minute.

A wizened hand rested on his shoulder. He looked up at the owner of the hand and almost jumped back a couple of feet. The man's eyes were white as milk. Hair the color of dusty gold shone in the sunlight. *Wow, how weird. He's like a villain from old Bollywood movies. A caricature. Can he even see properly? Maybe he's a kidnapper.*

"Want to sit for a while?" The rasp in the Old Uncle's voice grated on Sapan's ears. The boy shook his head, and tried to give a polite smile of thanks despite the pain in his ankle. But he was sure he did not want to take up the offer of a man who had, for all he knew, materialized from nowhere. The hand on his shoulder moved and gripped his forearm instead. Sapan attempted to twist out and flee. But try as he might, Sapan could not wriggle out of the bony, yet strong, hold. He had no choice but to follow Old Uncle a few steps down the alley between the Akash Ganga and Tarun Society buildings. Then it appeared before him.

A small store in the place of what used to be a dilapidated cottage.

"Hey! That building was never here! The house there was owned by that grouchy man with a rifle, no?" Sapan exclaimed, the soreness in his ankle pushed to the back of his mind for a moment.

The Old Uncle's shoulders shook as he chuckled in silence. "But how?" continued Sapan, nonplussed. "I heard he threw out or shot any contractor who wanted to buy his house and turn it into a housing complex."

"This is not a housing complex," came that rough voice again. "This is my bookstore, Sapan."

Sapan got another jolt. He looked up sharply and almost got a crick in his neck to match the hurt in his ankle. "My name. How … how?"

"I know you, child. My name is Ezra. And don't even think of calling me Uncle or anything like that. Just Ezra."

This unnerved Sapan immensely. First, could this man read his thoughts? With those eyes he sure looked like an evil wizard. Second he was taught never to address his elders by their names. That was the way to respect their age. All men were uncles and all women were aunties. Plus, this man must be as old as the Sahyadri Mountains.

"We'll have a look at your ankle and I'll let you go. I promise," Ezra said as he opened the door to his store. Bells chimed, and Sapan noticed the cluster attached to the doorknob. The bookstore sign swung to and fro and squeaked slightly. It hung from two metal hooks, with the words painted a faded white. Deep gouges like claw marks marred one corner. Sapan took a good look at it. "Librorum Taberna," he read aloud. "Wow, it's like a sign I saw in Prague last year. All the lettering and everything."

"In Prague, were you? When?" The milky whites of his eyes sparkled.

"Oh, last year. I went with my mom for a conference."

"Prague. Yes. It was nice last year," reminisced Ezra.

This man seems good enough. With trepidation diminishing in his heart, Sapan limped through the glass door. *Very strange. No locks. No metal detectors.* This man must not have things worthy enough for thieves and was not worried about terrorists.

"Librorum Taberna. I have seen the words Ex Libris on several books in our library. Must have to do with books, no?" Sapan looked at Ezra's face for a response and got none, except for a faint nod.

Ezra pointed him to a low wooden stool. Sapan sat down and looked around, his jaw dropping in amazement. Behind the old man, lay the vastness of a bookstore the size of a stadium. He was used to interiors of stores looking very different from the exterior. Shalimar Electronics next to his home was in a plain square yellow building but the interior, nicely lit and flashy, looked very futuristic. But this Librorum Taberna was unlike the rest.

It somehow was larger on the inside than the outside. And there was no doubt that it sold books and nothing else. No toys or music or coffee shop like Crossword Books down the street. Sapan glanced around again. *Yes. Just books. Are there really so many books in the world?*

On display by the window lay several volumes with old artifacts. One of these, a dagger, looked ancient but still sharp. Beside it lay a leather sheath with a red dragon embossed on it. Sapan hobbled over to it, enthralled.

"Fascinated by the dagger, are you? Like mother, like son," Ezra's voice boomed.

At the mention of his mother, Sapan looked up with a hundred questions in his face. But he did not get any elaboration from Ezra. Instead he got barraged by numerous questions himself.

"So, Sapan Bhatnagar, how *is* Ananya? Isn't that what she calls herself now? Still interested in medieval history? Is that why she went to Prague?"

"How … how do you know Ma's name, Uncle?" The words tumbled out of Sapan's mouth.

"I told you, no 'Uncle' business! Address me as Ezra! Can't you remember that simple instruction?" Ezra roared.

Sapan glared at the old man. He hated being ordered around or shouted at. "Ezra, Ezra. Okay?" he retorted. Anger gave him the guts to continue. "What kind of a name is Ezra, anyway? You must be a Jew or a Parsi. How do you know my mom?"

"Parsi! Jew!" he growled. "Shows what you know. But me? I know a lot of things. 'Knowing others is wisdom; Knowing the self is enlightenment; Mastering others requires force; Mastering the self needs strength.' One of my friends from China used to say that."

The pupils of Sapan's eyes reduced to a dark point in surprise at this sudden departure into philosophical dialogue, and his eyebrows flew to his hairline. *Whatever. Throwing all those words at me. He is definitely wacky.* "But you didn't answer my question, Ezra Uncle." 'Ezra Uncle' seemed to Sapan an acceptable compromise.

Ezra frowned but other than that, didn't react. Instead he pushed the boy back onto the stool, knelt down and inspected the sore ankle. "Well, this doesn't look to be a big problem. You'll be fine soon. I'm sure some ice will help." He stood up to his full height.

Sapan looked up. This man was probably no taller than Palkar sir, who was one of the taller teachers at school. But Ezra was thin. The whites of the Old Uncle's eyes grew milkier and he peered deep into Sapan's. *Extremely unnerving.* He thought he'd never get Ezra to answer his question.

"My mother?"

"Your mother," the old man sighed. "It's a long story. Ever wondered how you got that fair skin and the light green eyes, child?"

Sapan wanted to bark out something rude at the old man before him. He knew he looked different from his friends at school. So what? His mother told him that he had some Anglo Indian blood in him from some generations ago. Mostly, people never commented on it. Other than Palkar sir, who often called him a <u>firang,</u> especially when he failed to complete his homework. "I have green eyes. So what?" He raised his chin in defiance.

Ezra shrugged. "I can tell you about your father, if you like. He had green eyes like you too."

Sapan drew back. He suddenly felt there was something terribly strange about this old man. His Ma had told him about his father, a soldier who died a few months before Sapan was born. She never wanted to talk about her marriage. She hadn't even kept any old photographs. Sapan deduced that his father hadn't been a nice man. Why else would his mother try so hard to push the memory away? Clearly it was all very painful to her. This old man claimed that he knew his father. He even sounded proud to know him! Sapan squirmed and tried to stand up. He suddenly didn't want to be in the bookstore anymore. It felt like being in the enemy camp. He and his mom were a team. Always.

Ezra gave him a squeeze on his shoulder, pushed him back on the stool. He ordered, "Wait here" and disappeared among the huge stacks of books.

The musty odor of books grew stronger in the single minute that Sapan waited for Ezra to show up again. Humid Mumbai air always made books smell different. Damp. A heady sort of damp. Quite unlike the bookstores in, say, Delhi or even airports.

God knows he and his mom had scoured every city they visited for bookstores. Why, she had even been really upset when he told her about the bookstore in Prague with the very similar sign. They had boarded their plane to leave the city by then, and he had just mentioned in passing how he saw an ancient looking bookstore. "Why didn't you tell me before?" Her voice shook just for a moment. Sapan had been shocked at her reaction. He knew she was keen on seeking out bookstores and their owners but he had rarely seen her upset at him for failing to point one out to her. To him, the look in her eyes was that of disappointment in him, and he expected her to reproach him publicly.

Luckily, the flight attendant had interjected with glasses of water and jolted his mother back to reality.

Maybe Ma would like *this* store. But then, she must have already been here. Ezra seemed to know her quite well.

The proprietor returned with an ice-filled ziptop bag in his left hand. With his right, he thrust a thick book in Sapan's ribs. "Here. Take this. Read and return. I usually don't loan out books. After all, this is not a library. But in your case I'll make an exception. I owe it your mother, I think. This book is not for sale in any case. Besides, you don't have enough money to pay for it, even if it was."

Sapan looked at the book. It was old. *Probably as old as Ezra.* It was leather bound, the binding hand sewn with a thick sturdy waxed string. The title was faded and Sapan squinted to read it. "The Pilgrymage," the boy chuckled a bit. "The author doesn't even know how to spell. Ma would have a fit."

"Well, it was written a long time ago. Though not that long ago, considering. It holds the secret to your father's life."

Sapan held the book gingerly. His finger slid under the thick cover ready to flip it when Ezra slapped his hand. "Not now," he whispered. "Take it home. Read it in your room." The whites of Ezra's eyes seemed to gleam.

Ezra bent down to attach the ziptop bag to Sapan's ankle with a string. "No need to show this to your mother. The last time she had her hands on it, she tossed it away. She'll want to read it again, though. If she doesn't want her life churned over again, she shouldn't." He smiled, his yellowed teeth resembling sweet corn Sapan had seen in the market.

The old man inspected his attempt at first aid and nodded, apparently satisfied. He handed Sapan his sandal. "Go, now. You have reading to do." With this, Ezra stood up and walked away towards the book stacks.

Sapan stood up, the book balanced between his palms. He felt the cold traveling up from his now numb ankle up his body. For a long, stretched moment, he stood deciding whether to take the book with him. The man was decidedly bizarre. *The things he said about Ma!* He even insinuated that she changed her name recently. Sapan decided he did not like Ezra. His hands slowly stretched to leave the book on the stool.

But the things Ezra said touched Sapan somewhere deep inside. All his life he had wondered about his father. Maybe the old man was right, and there was information about his father in the book. Maybe there was something in the moral of an old story that would give him a clue to his father. *Maybe.*

The boy's hands retracted, and he looked down at the book again. His fingers closed tight on the leather cover.

As he turned to the door, he felt as if clammy hands were squeezing his chest. A chilly breeze kissed the back of his neck and Sapan shuddered, trying to shake off the strange mixed feeling of excitement and a faint premonition of impending doom. Bells chimed again as the door moved. He turned and almost broke into a limping run, his questions chasing him. Ezra's chuckle matched the staccato of Sapan's steps in his head as he shuffled home.

Be careful what you wish for. I need to have a sign made. I gave the young man what he really wanted, and look how it turned out. EF

Accidental Opportunity
by Kari J. Wolfe

"Those who do not learn from history are doomed to repeat it."
— George Santayana

The oil painting sat on the easel in the window. Jack couldn't see any alarms surrounding it. No sneaky wires hid in the glass to send a signal to the police if the window broke. A red velvet rope separated this section of the window from the remainder of the bookstore dimly lit by a light or two in the back. The window itself was lit by floodlights, and though he tried to find something vaguely resembling an alarm, he failed.

The longer Jack studied the storefront, the more he forgot that he had to piss.

The Van Gogh was simply just *there*. No guards, no alarms (that he could see anyway), no glass box surrounding it, *nothing*. Obviously, it wasn't enough for him to see the painting was unguarded. He needed to look around, scout out the place, and perhaps give it a bit more thought before jumping into something he might regret later.

If he did this—if he actually stole the painting and succeeded—he'd be rich beyond his wildest dreams. It would be the pinnacle of what little thieving career he had. For years, he had taken things that didn't belong to him—watches, purses, a car here and there—but nothing compared to this.

He knew who he would talk to after—a friend of a friend—in order to find it a new home and to pay him *beaucoup* bucks in return. That was the important thing. Going through the trouble to steal a painting he couldn't turn around for cash would be a complete waste of time—and taking that huge risk of being caught—for absolutely nothing. "Nada. Nuttin' honey," as Susan liked to say. That was before he accused her of sleeping around on him.

Of course, she didn't say it the night he caught her and her chimney sweep lover *in flagrante delicto* in his own bedroom. He chased them both out of the apartment, flashing a gun, maybe even shooting it a few times. He told everyone he didn't remember. Rage had a way of shutting off the memory synapses. At least according to his lawyer. The jury believed him and that was all that mattered. The bitch was buried in the cemetery on the east side—her bastard lover on the west. Second marriages weren't worth the paper the certificate was printed on.

He had moved to Colorado to get away from all of that. It didn't work.

The light from a car's headlights caught his attention and he walked away from the bookstore, hands in his pockets, his heart beating to the rhythm of some thrash metal group. A hot flood of liquid spread from his crotch, as he couldn't control his bladder any longer.

As the car passed, he tried to look normal, just out for a walk—*never mind it's 3:00 in the morning, never mind I've just pissed myself*—just a little stroll before bedtime, what the hell. He glanced at the car out of the corner of his eye—if it was a police car, it was undercover, no markings. He watched its taillights make a right turn a few blocks later.

"Shit!" Jack muttered. The front of his pants were soaked. He should have just whipped it out and pissed behind a tree. It wasn't like anyone would really have noticed him this late at night. The passing car was probably some guy driving home from his girlfriend's house and not an undercover cop. He glanced back at the bookstore. Around the block to his car, then several miles to the hole in the wall he called "home." But a few more minutes wouldn't hurt. Besides he wanted—no, he *needed*—to figure out whether he was going to do this or not.

In a bookstore—a freaking *bookstore*, of all places. The shop must have been newly opened. He didn't remember seeing it before. The streetlight near the building—*definitely a potential problem*, he noted—only partially lit the sign as it swung back and forth, the chains holding the sign creaking with each movement. He could barely read the words "Librorum Taberna" painted in white calligraphy on the wood.

Whatever the hell that meant, Jack thought. *Name of the bookstore probably. Doesn't matter.* He would be away from this stinking hellhole in a couple days and he'd never have to see it again.

The store itself was on a corner. The entrance was under the sign, one of those doors with a glass panel so you could see what was on the other side. Two signs hung from a chain attached to the open door shade, the one on top reading "Ezra Finfrock, Proprietor" and the bottom saying "CLOSED" in the standard neon orange, black and white. The door opened inward,

Jack noted for future reference. Straight across from the entranceway was a wooden counter with what appeared to be an antique register on the far end.

On the other side of the building, Jack couldn't see any other windows. Some sort of advertisement had been painted on the wall a long time ago but what it advertised, Jack couldn't tell. The paint had peeled and flaked off in more than enough areas to obscure whatever item it was selling.

The street itself was now deathly quiet. He barely heard the rumble of the cars on the interstate—what they were doing out at this time of the night, he had no idea. *Maybe going off to fuck their lovers in their "sacred" marriage bed. Whatever.* It didn't really matter—as long as they weren't bothering him, he'd not be bothering them.

The nearest streetlight flickered and went out, leaving him in darkness.

"What the hell?" Jack said under his breath.

The streetlights down the street were still on. Must have only been this one. But that would be far too much of a coincidence, right? He hadn't considered actually doing it tonight and, only *maybe*, tomorrow. He needed to do a lot more research, scouting out the neighborhood, making sure the police weren't watching this area too.

But … it really was convenient, you know? The whole corner of the block was dark. Quiet, even. All Jack could think of was that line from *The Night Before Christmas*, "Not a creature was stirring, not even a mouse."

He walked back to the front door of the building and took a closer look at the lock. It was an older door—wooden frame, big plate glass window in the middle. The lock was as old as the door, not very sturdy. There was a dim light on somewhere in the back of the store. He could probably slip in and out before anyone knew what had happened. His car was close, right around the block—not too far to go, even with a stolen Van Gogh in his arms.

He slid a credit card—*Visa, it's everywhere you want to be*—out of his wallet and held it, looking at the door. After this, there would be no going back.

Sliding the card between the frame and the door, he heard a click and felt the door open as he firmly pushed on the thin plastic. *Hurry, Jack.* He eased the door open, making sure it didn't bang anything behind it, and stepped into the store. The smell of dust, mold and mildew greeted him, a mix of freshly printed pages and ancient ink, a scent he remembered from the libraries of his youth.

Closing the door carefully behind him, he allowed the lock to slip back into place. To his right, the Van Gogh sat there, calling to him.

After the painting was sold, Costa Rica was out there—that had always been his dream—and as long as his heart didn't give out from the massive pounding it worked on his chest, he'd be there in less than three days. Maybe even two, depending on how quickly the buyer could get the money to Jack. Stepping closer to the painting, once again he looked for anything that could possibly set off some type of alarm. Seeing nothing, he reached out and took a hold of the painting's frame.

"Hello Jack," a deep voice came from directly behind him.

Jack's entire body went into flight-mode. He let go of the painting, his hand snapping back to his side. It crashed to the floor, mimicking the sound his heart made as it tried to make a run for it out of his chest cavity. Ready to run away, anywhere, Jack turned around, the nerves along his skin tingling. *My name! How did he know my name?*

The voice didn't really represent the man it belonged to. At least, Jack would never have imagined such a strong voice could come out of such an old and frail body. The man stood there, oily, yellowish-white hair lying on his shoulders, hands held together in front of him, only the fingertips touching. Only the whites of his eyes showed. *Maybe he's blind.*

"Did you drop something?"

Jack swallowed, the adrenaline coursing through his body capturing his voice. "H-how d-did you—?"

"Come now. Pick up the painting and put it back on the stand. Check the frame for any dents or scratches," the deep voice said, in contrast to the ancient body in which it dwelled.

As Jack bent over and picked up the painting, he heard the front door open and then shut firmly. An audible click let him know that the door was locked. For a blind man, this guy had no problems getting around. Hands shaking, he carefully placed the painting back on the easel where it had been and checked the wooden frame for damage. Footsteps told Jack the man moved from the door to stand behind him. *Why didn't I hear or see him before?* When he turned back around, the proverbial cat finally let go of his tongue.

"Oh, you must be the owner! I didn't know anyone was …," The words came stumbling off of his tongue, but once they left his mouth, others began to flow. He felt his mouth relax, breaking into what was hopefully a friendly—albeit somewhat toothy—smile. "I saw the door open and I was concerned that someone might come in and rip off the store, so I decided that I would—"

"Piss your pants and steal my painting?"

Jack flushed a bright red, his smile faltering slightly. "No, no …. I was going to lock the door for you. When I came inside, I thought I'd get a better look at that painting you have in the window. By the way, is that really a Van Gogh?"

"What do you think?" The man took a couple of steps closer to the painting, his head angled as though he were studying it.

"Probably not, huh? No alarms, no guards, no protection …."

"Then why did you try to steal it?"

"I wasn't—"

"Jack. As surely as I stand here facing you. You were about to abscond with my painting." The old man's brow furrowed, drawing his bushy eyebrows together. "Were you not?"

Until then, Jack's gaze had been focused on the floor, his mind racing to figure out how to get the hell out of Dodge. With this last statement, Jack raised his head, looking Ezra—*this guy sure looks like an Ezra, so he must be the owner*—in the eyes. There was no mistake. Ezra stared back at him.

"I'm sorry," Jack muttered, the flush along his neck and face growing hotter as the childlike apology came out of his mouth.

"I know." A faint smile crossed Ezra's face, his fingers remaining steepled in front of him.

Neither man moved for a few moments, although to Jack, it felt like an eternity.

"I'm lost." *Where did that come from?* Jack heard his own voice, felt his mouth move, but the words that came out didn't feel like his own.

"I know that, too."

"Would you help me find my way?" *Where the hell did THAT question come from?*

"Certainly. Come with me." With that, the old gentleman walked toward the back of the store. Jack took a quick glance out the window for what felt like would be the last time and followed the elderly man down the bookstore aisle.

"I wasn't always a … thief." The word wasn't fair. Jack didn't think so, anyway. But there it was. And it was the truth.

Ezra and Jack were in a room on the second floor. Like the main floor, books graced the shelves covering the walls. Unlike downstairs, there were more books and papers scattered about on the floor, some open pages filled with illegible handwritten scribbles, others full of antique script, and yet more looked to have been printed on traditional printing presses.

Jack sat in a comfortable leather chair while Ezra—there had been no introductions, but who else could it be—peered over the books and papers lying atop the massive wooden desk. Despite his mother's insistence on weekly trips to the library during his childhood, Jack had never been what one would call a big "book person," but he had a feeling, if he spent a couple hours in this place alone, he would have been converted.

"No, you weren't," said Ezra. "What happened?"

Jack took a deep breath. "My wife died."

"You killed her." Ezra's voice was matter-of-fact.

"I didn't do it. I meant my first wife." *He knows about Susan? How could he know that…?*

"How?"

"She was pushed. In front of a subway train." Jack's eyes began to sting. His mouth went dry and he clenched his hands together. "They never found the bastard who did it."

"Blamed you, did they?" Ezra handed him a tissue and a glass with a small amount of golden liquid inside. Jack took both and wiped his eyes with the tissue. Whiskey, by the smell. Even though Jack had given up drinking some time ago, he downed the liquid in one gulp, the familiar burn of the alcohol giving him the courage to talk.

He nodded, leaning forward to set the cup on the only empty spot he saw on the desk. "Said I did it for the insurance money. Hell, I didn't even know she had life insurance. We'd been married for six years and, from what they told me, she'd taken out a life insurance plan on both of us. Five hundred thousand dollars. Each."

Ezra raised his eyebrow as Jack gave the dollar amount, but remained silent.

"We met at the subway station near work. It was Friday night … we always had dinner downtown on Fridays." Jack paused, remembering. "When I saw her, I gave her the bouquet of roses I bought. I thought it would help make that night special. It was our anniversary." Jack stopped speaking, his throat tightening. After all this time, it was still difficult. Ezra lifted a bottle from behind his desk, unscrewed the cap and poured more of the precious golden liquid into the glass.

"I used to drink a lot." Jack picked up the glass and swirled the amber liquid around the bottom. "After."

"So did I," Ezra said, setting the bottle back in a drawer. "I keep it around for special occasions."

"We called it 'liquid courage.'" He drank the rest and set the glass back where it had been on Ezra's desk. "Where was I?"

"You gave your wife roses in the subway station."

A wistful smile crossed Jack's face. "Roses were Darla's favorite flower. I just wanted to make her feel good, you know?"

Ezra nodded in the same sage-like way he had since the beginning of the story. "I do."

"All of a sudden, this man ... Hell, I don't even know if it was a man. Everything suddenly blurred in front of me. A hot breeze rushed by, and this overpowering smell of piss lingered around me, followed by some sort of animalistic howl. I remember seeing the roses fall. I heard shrill screams, screams that sounded like Darla's. I remember thinking, 'Why is she screaming?' And then the train's brakes grinding, the wheels screeching on the tracks ... the smell of soot and oil ... a loud, wet thud like a huge chunk of meat being dropped onto a butcher's table. People pushed me in every direction as they swarmed around. I lost sight of her. When the train finally stopped, I realized a crowd had gathered at a section of the tracks, on the very edge of the platform. I pushed my way to the front. Darla...."

Ezra had already poured a couple more fingers of whiskey into the glass—Jack's hand shook noticeably this time as he took a hefty sip. "Darla... what was left of her... was on the tracks. Blood had sprayed everywhere when the train hit her." He downed the rest of the drink in one last gulp.

Ezra rose and gestured to the younger man. "Come. Walk with me."

Jack followed, the men walking the aisles of the bookstore while they continued to converse.

"After that, I pretty much fell apart," Jack continued. "I was accused of murder and then found 'not guilty,' but all this newfound money ... every time I bought something, Darla's face haunted me. I started drinking to get rid of the ghosts. Then Susan came along...,"

In the History section, Jack found himself wanting another drink, but they had left the whiskey bottle back in Ezra's office. *Probably a good thing.* There were books as far as Jack could see. The aisles of the store itself were a maze, twisting every which way, sometimes doubling back. He wasn't sure if he could find his way to the door at this point.

"I believe we have all been there at one point or another." Ezra stopped and looked at him with those weird eyes.

An uncomfortable tingle started in Jack's neck, sending a shudder through his back. *Am I really that bad of a person?* Jack lowered his head. a shudder growing inside him. "I'm sorry." The driving need to apologize and be forgiven returned the flush to Jack's cheeks.

"I know." Ezra gently picked up a book that had fallen to the floor, looked at the title on the spine and shelved it in silence. Jack shifted his balance from one foot to the other, not knowing what to say.

"Didn't mean to burden you with my stuff either," Jack glanced at the books on the shelves. Scanning the titles, he recognized little of the subject matter. History was never his forte. He could never remember all those dates and wars and names. "History could be taught a little better in schools," he declared suddenly.

"Instead of memorizing the trivial?"

"Yeah, seems to always be taught in the most dull and boring way."

"Well, that depends on who is doing the teaching. One with real experience is far more informative than one who learned his history from a textbook."

"This is the tenth anniversary of my wife's death," Jack blurted.

"I'm sorry, Mr. Dooley," Ezra's sightless-seeming eyes looked at Jack. "If you don't mind my asking, what would you have done differently?"

"I don't know, in all honesty. Maybe I could have stopped whoever it was from pushing her." Tiny hairs on Jack's neck and arms stood and his skin became alive with goose bumps as he looked back at the man. He tried not to stare. People with physical deformities didn't like to be stared at. But it was late and he was tired.

They made eye contact. Jack tried to look away and couldn't. Around him, the room stretched away from him, the aisle warping both directions larger and longer, everything else distended except for ....

Those impossible eyes.

Ezra's white, pupil-less eyes hovered before him, remaining the same distance from his own, their gaze locked with his, as the room, bookshelves, and even the rest of Ezra's body warped and sped away from him as though repelled by some opposing force.

Jack was pulled in every direction like he was on an amusement park ride taking him through improbable curves every which way at the same time. Sweat broke out on his forehead as his stomach lurched, trying to shove something hot and acidic up through his throat. He tried to reach up a hand to cover his mouth but nothing moved. Everything felt so heavy, so weighted down.

After what seemed like an eternity later, it was over.

Jack jerked away from Ezra, tripping over a short stack of hardcover books on the floor behind him. The books scattered as he landed on his rear. "What the hell was that?"

"Books. You are in a bookstore after all," Ezra replied, as though nothing had just happened.

"You know what I'm talking about!" Jack picked up one of the books. *Somewhere in Time* by Robert Heinlein. He threw it across the aisle where it thunked on the floor—a flat, somewhat pleasing sound—and stood up. "What the fuck just happened?"

"Mr. Dooley, I have decided to give you a second chance."

"Wait, what are you—"

"You wanted the chance to save her." Ezra interrupted Jack with a gesture towards the front of the building. "So, go."

Puzzled, Jack walked straight to the front of the store, wondering how he could have missed the path earlier. It had been night when he entered the building; now, the sun shone as he looked out the window. People walked back and forth on the sidewalk; cars and trucks passed in the street.

He stepped out onto the sidewalk. The overwhelming smell of the city— burning oil and hot blacktop—hit him in the stomach as he looked around. He wasn't in Colorado anymore. The buildings were far too tall for that. Beads of sweat formed on his forehead, the humidity making itself known. Sunlight reflected in the windows of the skyscraper across the street from him while the noise of car engines and horns blared.

"Watch where you're going!" said a little man with a bald head who quickly shuffled to one side after almost running into Jack. He scurried off, his black suit reminding Jack of a funeral attendant.

Jack turned around to say something to Ezra before he left. The bookstore was gone. He faced a huge park surrounded by green trees. A concrete path led to a fountain in the middle where children were playing in the water.

"What the hell …?"

A newspaper box caught his attention as he looked around, trying to get some bearing as to what was going on. He walked over and pulled on the handle. It wouldn't open. On the top of the box, it had a small rectangular slot that said INSERT COIN HERE.

A coin? Who carried money like that these days? It was all plastic now— if you were lucky, you could even pay using your freaking smartphone. He bent to look at the front of the newspaper.

SURVIVORS PLAN TO PAY RESPECTS
AT 50TH ANNIVERSARY OF HIROSHIMA

The date read: August 4th, 1995.

Jack stared at the paper and blinked a few times. August 4th, 1995? That was the day Darla died. He looked around and, as a taxi passed by, he read aloud, "New York Taxi Cab Company." The building across from him was Trump Tower. The park was Central Park. With a bit more spring in his step, he walked to where he could see the street sign: COLUMBUS CIRCLE.

Holy shit. Ezra really did it. I can save her!

He had no idea how he got here—much less in the time-sense than the physical-sense—but he didn't care. He could save Darla and change his life—they could live out their lives together as they originally planned. A lump caught in his throat and he swallowed a few times as he walked down the street, both accepting and disbelieving this new reality. A sea of people continued to flow up and down the sidewalks, hurrying to wherever they were going, never noticing anyone else around them.

Of course, this was the way of life in New York City. One and a half million people on Manhattan Island alone, never mind the other four boroughs. Jack theorized that the huge number of people crammed into such a small space was the main cause for the majority of the problems the city had. Darla would roll her eyes at him when he would tell their friends his idea.

However, even though people still lived in their own little worlds, in the 1990s, the city had started to clean up its act. When Jack appeared in court the first day of Darla's murder trial, Mayor Giuliani himself stood on the courthouse steps, talking with the press. As Jack walked by, he would have sworn—on the Bible, in the courtroom—the mayor stared daggers into him, angry he had taken the spotlight from the cleaning up of New York City and placed it back on the criminal element that lay beneath.

In the mid 90's, Jack worked near the American Museum of Natural History. City construction was his bag. Sure, the pay wasn't great, but he and Darla didn't need much. They were young and just starting out, and he did the best he could. They had all the time in the world—or, at least, they thought they did.

Until that Friday.

Later today. Jack kicked a soda can that had been lying on its side on the sidewalk and it skittered into the street. He could save Darla this afternoon. *So, okay, what to do now?*

Go see her. Ten years had passed since he heard her voice, her laugh, seen her smile—except in photos and photos never did anyone justice. A niggling voice in his head told him he shouldn't try to talk to her. She would never have believed him anyway. He wouldn't have believed himself either. But he could see her, at least. From a distance.

With a bit more spring in his step, he headed off in the direction of their apartment building.

A short walk and a subway ride later, Jack stood across the street from the entrance to the building he and Darla called home during the few years they were together.

The entrance was exactly the way he remembered it. *How could it* not *be?* Don Welch, the doorman to the apartment complex next door, sat asleep in a chair between the two entrances, his feet propped up on the empty concrete planter. Don worked days—8:00 am to 5:30 pm—every day but Sunday.

Counting the windows up the front of the building, he could see the corner window to their apartment with the rust-colored terra cotta flower box Darla had hung outside. He could see a couple of scraggly vines, but from this distance, he couldn't really make out specifics. The window itself looked onto what passed for a living room in the tiny apartment. Living in New York City, they were lucky to get the space they had.

At least they had a bedroom. They had friends who lived in one-room efficiencies, their beds folding into the wall, a set of doors hiding its location from visitors. He and Darla had scoured the city looking for an affordable apartment with a separate bedroom.

A loud giggle came from above him. *Was that Darla?* The apartment was air-conditioner-less and during the summer, they left the windows open hoping for a breeze to flutter by. Occasionally, he would put a box fan in the window, trying to pull some of the air in, but Darla would complain about the noise. That and it blocked her view of the city.

He crossed the street, eyes focused on the open window. Ten years was a long time. Here, she was still the same Darla he knew, and after tomorrow, she would always remain the same.

Welch slept in the doorway, but Jack's nerves tingled anyway. He didn't really want to be seen and, perhaps, recognized by anyone—there was no way in hell anyone would have understood. Hell, he didn't understand himself.

He opened the main door and walked inside, the smell of mold, fresh paint and that strange underlying smell of decaying body odor causing him to flinch. Familiar, oh yes, though he hadn't smelled it in years. After the trial ended, Jack never returned to the apartment. Not even to get his things. He chose, instead, to move as far away as he could with the insurance money and start his life over.

His second wife, Susan, never knew about Darla. He met her a couple of years later at a single's club late one night. Things clicked for a year or so. After that, it was all downhill. Susan would've used Darla's death—and the failed prosecution of him for Darla's murder—as a metaphorical knife to continuously stab him in the guts, the back, and anywhere else he could be hurt.

Susan was on top of her dark-haired lover when he found them, her naked torso moving up and down, her medium-sized breasts jiggling just so. Things had never really gone well with them after they married, and Jack had suspected her of cheating on him for several months. Hints had been dropped—little things here and there. He had come home early from work when he found them. When he opened the door to the bedroom, like the song went, *Whoomp! There it is!*

The gun was in the chest of drawers beside the door and the loud rap music hid any noise he made in opening the door, sliding the drawer open and grabbing the gun. He remembered shouting something and the gun fired into the ceiling as the two lovers scrambled to get out of bed and, as they covered themselves, the guy—covered in sweat and wearing nothing but a towel—moved towards him.

Jack remembered Susan's scream as the gun went off again, this time, not into the ceiling. And he remembered the silence after it fired a third time.

But none of that mattered now. If he could, somehow, rescue Darla from being murdered, from being pushed in front of that subway train, Susan would never enter his life. The trial that caused him to leave New York City, and ended his career, would never have happened. He could change it all, right here, right now.

In front of him were the five flights of stairs leading up to his apartment. His and Darla's apartment. The small hexagonal black and while tiles that covered the floor of what the tenants had affectionately called the "lobby" continued to climb their way up and over the steps, heavy black railings giving the room its only contours.

That slight niggling doubt re-entered his mind, probably placed there by numerous science fiction shows he'd watched in the past. But it wasn't like he was going to marry his grandmother or sleep with his mother, like that silly country song talked about.

Another giggle—this time, he was *positive* it was Darla—emanated from the stairwell. His heart pounding, Jack pushed the remaining doubts aside as he began walking up the stairs.

Every Friday, instead of going back to their 35th Street fifth-floor walk-up, he and Darla met near the entrance to the subway to catch a ride downtown to have dinner and, possibly, a walk on the boardwalk at Battery Park. She loved the view of the Statue of Liberty from the dock and they had spent plenty of evenings basking in the deepening pink and purple sunsets while watching the ferry to Ellis Island travel across the water.

Jack looked at his watch as he reached the fifth floor. Two and a half hours left until they were to meet. It wasn't quite time yet for Darla to be leaving. He couldn't see the door from this vantage point—it was on the far end of the hallway, another selling point when they first looked at renting the apartment. A corner apartment gave them the luxury of a bit of privacy by not having someone living on both sides of them, and, in New York City, that was a big deal.

Darla's laughter echoed down the hallway, coming from the direction of his apartment, and Jack's heart skipped a beat. *She's alive!* This time, he could hear the sounds of a deep male voice. He couldn't make out what the man was saying, but whatever it was, it made Darla titter like a schoolgirl. The rising scent of his own urine from his earlier accident burned his nose as he heard another giggle drifted down the hallway. The man's voice, again, saying something. The hallway echoed with the click of a shutting door.

Who was the man Darla was with?

No one was in the hallway as Jack walked to the apartment door. The floor creaked in a few places as he stepped. He and Darla complained time and time again to the property management company but they did nothing to fix it. Closer to the door, he heard muffled voices. It was definitely Darla and some man.

By the sound of it, they weren't just getting ready to talk either. The talking voices had given way to different sounds, sounds he usually only heard when he either was involved in the act or watching badly filmed movies with stupid soundtracks. The ones nobody watched for the acting.

There was a smacking sound, made by two sets of lips kissing, he imagined, and then Darla moaned softly.

Jack's world spun on its axis, and he crumpled to the floor, still hearing the ramped-up sounds of his wife's pleasure, ten years dead to him, yet alive and well in this day and time. *With another man.* But he wasn't listening anymore.

Cheating bitch.

When Jack opened his eyes and realized where he was, those were the first words that popped into his head. He remembered hearing Darla's voice moaning in passion. He remembered sitting down next to the door, the voice escalating in volume and intensity.

He didn't quite remember how he got here. The smell of burnt oil and the sound of the trains as they flew by gave away where he was even before he looked around.

The subway station.

He leaned against the route map near the stairs to the urban jungle above. The station was filling with people. Once on the concrete platform, they maneuvered to their places to wait for the trains to stop, eyes downcast, trying not to trespass on anyone else's personal space even as others invaded theirs.

The crotch of his pants was wet again.

The clock attached to one of the steel rafters running along the ceiling read 4:35. Around 5:00, Darla would be down here, and he would give her roses. The naive, innocent "him" that didn't know his wife was fucking around. Roses that symbolized his undying love for her.

Darla cheated on him.

He wondered how long she'd been fucking this other guy. Hell, he didn't even know who it was, which was a blessing in a way. There was absolutely no doubt as to what happened—those vocalizations coming from the apartment held no secrets, no double meanings that he could ascribe to them.

He looked down at his ring finger on his left hand. The indentation from his wedding band had faded over time but, even after Susan was killed, he could still feel the piece of cheap tin on his finger as though he had just taken it off and tucked it into his pocket.

It was easier to ignore when he thought Susan was faithful. When he walked into his bedroom and saw the glare of the streetlight through the window glisten off the sweaty sheen of her naked back, and then realized she was riding "cowgirl" on someone that was not him, his stomach started to sour with a guilt only a second marriage could bring out: *He should have been with Darla. She, at least, had been faithful. She had loved him with all her heart.*

Bullshit.

Tears filled his eyes. As he blinked them back, he caught sight of a young man in his early thirties walking through the crowd, a bouquet of roses in his hand. Jack didn't need to be close enough to count the roses to know how many there were. He remembered spending the last little bit of cash he had on those roses, thinking about Darla's face, her wonderfully expressive eyes, those thick red lips.

The same love he felt when he purchased those roses filled his heart now. The tears he had been trying so desperately to hold back flowed down his cheeks, dripping off his chin. He saw the man's face—his own, but years younger—happy and patient, his eyes eagerly scouting the crowd to find his "one and only." Suddenly, his eyes widened, and a smile spread across his face.

Jack looked in the same direction his younger self was looking and there was Darla, her blonde hair perfectly styled, her lips his favorite color of red. As she made her way through the crowd, for one brief moment, she stopped and looked directly at him, dropping a wink and a kiss.

It was at that point Jack snapped.

Jack smiled as Darla finally reached him. He wasn't as good at waiting as he told everyone he was. His heart pounded with excitement upon seeing her as she walked down the subway stairs. Six years, and he still had the same schoolboy thrill shooting through him, that electric impulse that caused him to breathe a bit faster and the blood in his brain to rush to another organ that stiffened slightly.

She was so beautiful, even in the typically harsh fluorescent light of the subway station. Nothing could tear away his gaze, not even the squeal of the brakes on the train entering the station. When she was within arm's length, he pulled her into a kiss, holding her tightly in one arm, the roses in the other.

"What are these for?" Darla asked, breaking the kiss and pulling back slightly to look at him. In the background, Jack heard someone shouting something as waves of movement began to rock the crowd. He wrinkled his nose slightly as he caught the smell of urine nearby.

"You. Just for being you," he said, still aglow with the warmth and passion of the kiss. "I love you."

"I love you too," she said, a pleased smile on her face, the bouquet in one hand, the other touching the tops as she looked at the roses.

The crowd shuffled behind them, and a man came bounding out of it. His eyes and Jack's met and, for one brief moment, Jack thought he recognized something familiar in that stare. But that couldn't be. Before Jack was able to pull Darla away, an anguished snarl escaped the man's lips, the cry of an animal in horrendous pain.

The man jumped at Darla, throwing his arms around her tightly, and both of them fell onto the subway track at the exact moment the train passed in front of Jack. A loud meaty thwack followed by the loud screech of metal on metal sounded across the platform.

The bouquet of roses fell forgotten to the ground in front of him while the crowd screamed.

Dragons have always impressed me with
    their drive to collect and protect
the world's treasures, never mind the motives.
Some even gather books, bless their hearts.
It's nice when I can return the favor. EF

A Dragon's Tome

By A.M. Burns

The wooden sign creaked faster in the slight breeze that blew down from the mountains. Alex Carlson looked up at the sign, which hadn't changed since the last time he visited the shop several years ago, right before he met Tal O'Duirwood, and his life changed forever. As they passed under the wooden plank, he caught a faint whiff of smoke. Looking up, he spotted the weathered burn pattern around the edges and the old gargoyle perched on top. The burn marks didn't reach the white letters "Librorum Taberna".

"Well, it is an out-of-the-way place." Tal looked impressed, nodding his approval. "I wonder how I've never found it before now."

"It seems to be hard to find. I've given folks directions to it many times. Some people find it, others don't. When I really need to find it, I come right to it." Alex opened the door with his good right hand before Tal could reach it. His left arm hung in a cast to protect a shattered wrist.

Tal glared a bit, but Alex only smiled at him. "I can open doors for myself. I still have one good arm."

"Next time, just remember to watch out for trolls," Tal snapped as he yanked the door the rest of the way open.

The soft tinkle of the bell announced their arrival, and the heavy smell of old books rushed out to meet them. Alex found the smell comforting. He loved rummaging around in used bookstores. They were almost as much fun as magical supply shops.

"You know there are places in this world that people can only find when they need to," Tal said as the door shut behind them, his displeasure at Alex apparently forgotten.

"I've heard that. Do you think this is such a place?" Alex scanned the rows of shelves, catching sight of several other patrons in the shop.

"Possibly."

Alex stood at Tal's side while they waited for the elderly shop keeper to finish selling a couple of books to a young goth woman. Alex recognized the cover of one of the books, a little-known tome by Aleister Crowley. Alex tried to scan the young woman, but something blocked his magical senses. He almost said something to Tal, but the woman walked away, and his partner stepped up to the counter with the five books he wanted to sell.

"You realize that everything is possible somewhere. Welcome back, Mr. Carlson." The old man's pale lips curved in a tight smile that didn't quite reach his pale, pupil-less eyes. He turned to Tal and said, " My name is Ezra Finfrock. How may I help you, gentlemen?"

"I have some books I'd like to sell." Tal laid the books on the counter.

"Very old," Ezra said, picking up a volume to examine it closely. "This is a first edition. Where on earth did you find it? I've heard rumors of course, some nonsense about a dragon's horde or some such." The wizened man looked up at Tal with those unreadable white eyes.

Alex suddenly felt drawn to look about the store. "You guys hash this out. I need to look around."

Tal raised a dark eyebrow then nodded.

The stacks went on for a good distance before the row ended, forcing Alex to head off to the right. Something in the store called to him. He recognized the pull of magic and continued on. He recalled the previous time he'd been here, looking for some books on magic for his studies, but couldn't remember the specific subject.

Alex thought about Tal, standing up at the register dickering with Ezra over price for the books. Now he had access to the knowledge that Tal had accumulated over the centuries. Tal was half dragon. He'd lived a very long time, and his human form didn't age. He'd changed Alex's life in ways the young mage couldn't have dreamed of before they met. The amount of magic they had brought into each other's lives was mind-blowing.

The nearness of the magic brought him out of his reminiscing. Not sure what he was looking for, he scanned the shelves, until a dark red leather spine caught his eye. There on the lower edge of the spine, barely perceivable due to age, a series of spirals were embossed on the leather. It was the mark of a druid, encircled by the mark of a bard.

The draw of magic stopped as he removed the massive tome from the shelf. It tingled slightly when he touched it, a flicker of magic. It weighed nearly ten pounds. Juggling it with his left arm in the sling was awkward, but he managed to get the book open. It reminded him of some of the spell books crowding the shelves in Tal's library. It looked handwritten, with small illustrations decorating the margins of most of the pages. The fancy script and ancient language made the book difficult to read, but it looked to be a tale of the last dragons. Alex decided to buy the book and wondered how Tal would react.

Hefting the book under his good arm, Alex headed toward the front of the store. It felt like it took forever to carry the heavy book to the counter. "How can such a small store feel so big? The pain killers must be affecting me worse than I thought." Alex wondered aloud as he rounded another row of shelves.

Ezra and Tal were just closing their deal for the five old books when Alex walked up toting the dragon book. The store clerk lifted a bushy eyebrow as Alex placed the book on the counter. "So, you found that quickly. Or did it find you?"

Alex wondered what he meant. He'd been gone for at least twenty minutes, finding the book then bringing it back up to the counter. "Not sure, but it looks like it might be interesting."

Tal glanced at the cover of the book. "I've never seen this one."

Ezra flashed a smile, showing yellowed teeth. "Consider it the last part of my payment to you for these treasures, Tal of Oakwood. I believe you will find the book enjoyable and, perhaps, a bit revealing."

Alex carried the heavy, leather-bound book from the small desk of the motel room to the large bed where Tal already reclined on thick fluffy pillows. He paused and looked at the lean form of his lover. They'd been together three years, but he never tired of looking at Tal. The sleek muscular body was contoured in just the right ways. Not for the first time, Alex wondered how Tal would've towered over people at the start of his life. Two thousand years ago, Tal would have been at least a foot taller than most people, even though today his five-foot, ten-inch frame was the norm.

"I could have gotten that for you," Tal fussed slightly, and started to get out of bed.

"No, you stay there, I'm fine. It's just a couple of feet," Alex replied. He sat down on the far side of the bed and laid the book between them.

The dark red cover looked a bit brighter in the light of the hotel room than it had in the bookshop. A large dragon's head decorated the cover, carved so delicately into the leather that it was almost invisible except at certain angles. There wasn't a title on the book's cover or spine, but old texts, especially magical texts, often didn't have titles on the covers.

"Let me see that." Tal reached for it.

As his delicate fingers came in contact with the book, the leather glowed, and the dragon's head lifted from the cover to become three dimensional. The magical hologram hung over the book. The image of a large black head, that could have been Tal in his dragon form, stared at them. Only the horns were different, curling in like a ram's, where Tal's were straight and pointed like an oryx's.

Alex paused in his slide onto the bed, his green eyes wide in wonder. "Wow. It didn't do that at the bookstore."

Tal stared at the ethereal dragon. "I didn't touch the book in the store. In fact, the old man was very careful to bag the book before handing it to me. This is the first time I've made contact with it." He lifted the book carefully into his lap. The red leather contrasted nicely with his grey sweat shorts.

"Maybe it's a special book for dragons?" Alex moved in closer to his lover.

Tal nodded, a small lock of black hair falling across his forehead. "The magic of it could be keyed to only activate when a dragon touches it." He turned the book over in his hands; looking at the back cover, studying the spine, tracing his fingers along the spirals on the lower edge. The symbol glowed with a faint blue light as his finger passed over it. "It's been blessed by both Druid and Bard. It doesn't feel malicious."

With a slow hand, Tal opened the book. The magical holographic image of the dragon smiled before a landscape replaced it.

"When I opened it, all I saw was old script and some dragons drawn in the margins," Alex said, settling his head on Tal's shoulder.

As they watched, the image began to move. A young man with unruly black hair and a thick black beard walked up a steep hillside heading toward a small village at top of the tor. A strong, rich voice began to speak in a thick Scottish brogue. "I am Taliesin and this is my tale, the tale of the greatest love of my life."

"Father," Tal whispered as he paled.

"That's your father?" Alex asked.

"Appears so." Tal sounded distant and troubled.

Alex reached for the book, and the image paused in mid-step when he touched it. "Do we need to wait and do this at home? Would it be safer to do this inside our shields?"

Tal shook his head. "No, I've waited long enough to see this. But we do need a bit of protection, this may take a while." His right hand moved in a series of sigils, and Alex felt a magical shield coalesce around the room.

Reaching for Alex's hand resting on the edge of the book, Tal caressed the freckled fingers before claiming the hand, and lifting it. The magical hologram of Taliesin resumed walking up the hillside.

"Like many a young druid before me, I spent my
journeyman years roaming the vast world. I carried news
from one village to another and gathered knowledge
everywhere I went. This particular day, I journeyed to
Snowhaven, a small village deep in the highlands of
Scotland. I'd been on the road for several weeks, with
the last village more than a fortnight behind me. Even
a druid can tire of the constant wind and sparse snows
that come upon the highlands in autumn. I've heard tales
that winter is even worse. I hope that I never have to
experience that.

"Snowhaven sat atop a large tor, in the middle of one of
the loch valleys. It was important because it was the main
commerce village in the area. I was carrying news from
the coast that the Norsemen had been raiding again but
had failed to gain a foothold, so Scotland could expect a
peaceful winter."

The magical image changed as Taliesin entered the village. The tiny huts
looked nothing like what Alex expected a village of the time to look like.
For the most part, they looked like yurts; small, squat and round. Somehow,
Alex thought they would look more like little houses.

"At that time, the people of the isles still held proper
respect for the druids. I received a warm welcome and
was swiftly brought before the clan chief. Even now,
I remember Tearloch MacFrost. In his prime he was
a massive man, standing well over five rods high, and
heavier than fifteen stones."

In the image, the big man stood more than a head taller than Taliesin.
His shaggy red hair dropped well past his enormous shoulders. A large
battle axe hung from his waist.

Alex whistled, "Wow, he's a big one."

"Back then, the clan chief was the most powerful warrior in the clan," Tal
explained. "I'd be surprised if he wasn't the biggest guy in the area."

"MacFrost and I walked around his village, and he
explained to me that he had a problem. He'd been waiting
for a druid or a wizard to appear to assist him. We
walked down the trail leading north of the tor. Below us
lay the pastures where the clan raised their sheep. The
field was full of the white, fluffy animals. The clan chief
explained there had been many sheep lost over the past

few months, and his shepherds could find no sign of what had befallen them.

"I advised the chief that as a journeyman, my knowledge was not yet complete in the ways of monsters, but I would try my best. He agreed, and offered the comfort of his own home while I worked on the problem."

The scene shifted to a moonlit pasture. It reminded Alex of the grassy meadow down the hill from their mountain home. It looked relaxing.

"For several nights I sat meditating in the pasture, with only the sheep for company as I requested the shepherds stay in the village to avoid any distractions. The first couple of nights were uneventful. Only a few wolves happened by, and they were easily scared off by my magic. On the third night, I felt a magical disturbance sweep over the pasture. It moved from the east. I looked up and saw a massive form blot out the moon. Huge wings cast an enormous shadow across the pasture."

"I tried to rise but some magical force held me in place. I could only watch in wondrous fear as the shadow swooped down and snatched up two of the sheep. The frightened animals made no sound at all. The hunter struggled back into the sky with its burden, like an eagle trying to lift a large hare. Finally it regained the skies, and I felt myself able to move again. I watched as the shadow again blotted out the moon and flew toward the east. Curiosity chased my fears away. I wished for the power of flight myself so that I might be able to follow the thing. But alas, at the time I was only a journeyman, and not a master druid.

"I used my magic to contact one of the nearby master druids. I quickly created a message ball with all the facts, as I knew them. In my mind, I pictured Euan, the druid of Cromwell. I magically pushed the message to him. Then I sat back to wait as the sheep renewed their soft nighttime noises.

"Euan's return message arrived as the sun broke over the eastern hills. His ball of blue energy bounced in front of my face until I accepted it into my hand. 'It appears you have a dragon, my boy. This is most wonderful news, as it has long been thought that all the dragons on the

isles were slain many years ago. Advise Tearloch McFrost
that I shall arrive this afternoon, and a party of warriors
will be there within a fortnight. We will make quick work
of this dragon.'

"I hurried up the tor to find the clan chief, and gave
him the news."

The view down from the tor became better lit as the sun rose, and a large
bird soared across the edge of the enchanted image. "Your dad must have
been one for detail," Alex noted watching the magical bird enter the scene.

"He developed a flair for theatrics over time." Tal flashed him a bright
smile.

Alex chuckled at his lover. "So you got your dramatic side from him?"
Tal's father continued, interrupting the playful conversation.

"A large eagle owl appeared on the southern horizon
that afternoon, and as it swooped down into the village,
it became the master druid Euan. I met him in the center
of the village and escorted him to the McFrost. I was not
permitted to stay as the two conferred, so I wandered the
village for a time.

"It was during that wandering that I met Oleta. She'd
been haggling with a traveling vendor over the cost of a
roll of blue cloth. The blue was the same color as her eyes,
an almost unworldly sapphire. I stood there, enraptured
by the raven-haired beauty. Never in all my travels, had
I encountered a woman who stopped my heart as this
one did. I approached cautiously. I wanted to know her.
I got close enough that I could make out her voice from
the merchant's. It sounded as soft and musical as any
songbird's."

The magical image showed a stunning woman with waist-long black
hair, fair skin, and Tal's blue eyes. The rolling hills, simple huts, even the
merchant's bright fabrics dulled in comparison.

"She looks so different here than her spirit." Tal's voice sunk to a near whisper.
"I wonder how much of it is my father's memories, and how much is the fading
we all undergo after we die."

"'Can I be of assistance?' I asked, wanting to be helpful
to the fair maiden.

"The woman turned to me and her face softened as
our eyes met. I fought the urge to take her in my arms
there in the middle of the village. I had no idea what her

husband would say, for surely such an attractive woman would be married.

"'Only if you can explain to this man that his prices are entirely too high,' even her voice gentled as she spoke to me.

"I cannot recall the details of the rest of the transaction with the merchant, but in the end, I assisted Oleta with her purchase, then carried her cloth to her hut. As we walked, she thanked me for my intervention and told me her sad tale. She recently joined the clan at Snowhaven after her husband was killed in the Norsemen's spring raids. He had been a distant relative of MacFrost, and her inclusion into the clan didn't create a hardship for MacFrost because she was childless and knowledgeable in herb lore. The current clan's healer was not likely to survive the winter and Oleta would make herself useful.

"Her hut lay on the east edge of the village. It was small with no yard or gardens planted yet. The mud in between the field stones showed only recent signs of drying."

The hut was small and dingy in the image, with just foot-packed earth around it.

Alex shifted on Tal's shoulder, trying to make his broken wrist feel better. "Not the best house in the village, huh."

"She offered to fix me a bit of mutton stew for dinner. Since the sun hovered on the western edge of the loch below the tor, I accepted. We spent the next couple of hours discussing the news, which villages were thriving, which needed rebuilding after the spring raids. Oleta had a quick mind to go with her radiant beauty. My heart was saddened when I heard my name being yelled in the village center.

"I left Oleta that night with the promise that I would return the following day, once my duties to Euan and Tearloch MacFrost were finished. Over the next fortnight, when I wasn't in council with Euan and MacFrost, I sought out Oleta. As a druid, I was wed to the land as surely as any priestess, so I was forbidden to take a wife. But for the first time I felt love building in my heart. We enjoyed walks on the highlands, quiet meals as she told me of her life, and I told her of the world beyond. After several joyous days, she even took me to her bed."

The ethereal scene changed several times, showing the pair getting to know one another, but it kept returning to linger on Oleta's blue eyes.

"She does have your eyes." Alex looked at Tal then reached over and ran his fingers along the dark-stubbled cheek.

"It was one of the few things my father ever mentioned about her." Tal caught the freckled hand and kissed it lightly.

"During this time, few sheep disappeared from the flocks. Euan surmised that the presence of two druids in the village helped scare the dragon away. I wasn't so sure. Tearloch MacFrost and his shepherds couldn't recall the previous pattern of disappearances. Then the warriors came."

Thirteen rugged men with huge swords strapped to their back rode massive horses across the highland landscape.

"They certainly knew how to make an entrance," Alex noted.

"Warriors back then rarely went anywhere by themselves. In reality, this is a small band called out to deal with one dragon. They probably spent their springs and summers as mercenaries selling their swords to the villages that needed defending from the Viking raiders."

"When the warriors arrived, they conferred for two days before coming up with a plan to trap and kill the dragon. One of them, a massive brute named Duncan MacDale, had a pike that was taller by half than the man himself. He claimed that he'd killed several dragons with it during his roaming the world. He said that a great wizard from the east had cast a spell on the pike so that the slightest touch of it was death to any dragon.

"Euan announced that he had figured out a counter spell to the dragon's freezing powers, so the warriors started sleeping out with the flocks. The first few nights nothing happened, then on the night of the full moon, when I sat in the pasture along with Duncan MacDale and two of the lesser warriors, the dragon came.

"As before, the beast came from the east, its body blocking out the moon. Again, an eerie silence filled the night as the sheep stopped their grazing and froze where they stood. It came quicker this time, almost like it knew of the danger awaiting it on the ground. It grabbed the first sheep it could, then labored to get back into the air.

"MacDale hurled his pike at the thing, and it managed to dodge enough so that the weapon fell harmlessly to the ground. The beast turned its head and looked down at us with eyes that flashed a sapphire blue in the moonlight. I felt sadness in that brief glimpse, then the dragon flew away into the night."

The scene focused on the eye for a moment before the dragon disappeared over the eastern horizon.

"The Euan and the warriors had planned for this. On silent wings, an eagle owl followed the dragon as it flew back toward its lair. MacDale called for the other warriors, and they brought horses for all of us. We rode out in pursuit.

"We lost sight of the dragon quickly, but kept riding, knowing that Euan, in his owl form, would be able to keep up with the beast, and would come back for us. Before half the night passed, the owl returned and resumed the shape of the druid. He announced that the dragon's den was not far away, but we must hurry to attack. The dragon would be in a stupor for a short time after its meal and that would be the best time to strike.

"The cave was on the side of the next tor east, hidden from easy view by a large rock fall. We left the horses at the base of the tor, and continued on foot. Euan and Duncan went first, the druid ready to block the dragon's spells, and MacDale with his pike held in front of them. The cave was fairly shallow, and almost immediately we could make out the shape of the dragon, a deeper black than the natural shadows.

"I felt Euan cast his spell to keep everyone moving in the presence of the dragon. It was a simple spell, more of a shield than anything, but it worked. The warriors moved forward, led by MacDale. One of them must have kicked a pebble or something, for the dragon raised its head from the remains of the sheep and glared at us. We blocked its escape. It flung the carcass of the sheep aside and roared its displeasure.

"The dragon cast some kind of spell. I felt something magical move over us, but couldn't tell for sure what the effects were. It may have been the spell that froze living things in its presence. It may have been something else. But whatever it was, it didn't seem to affect us. The beast charged, trying to get past and out into the open again. The warriors tried to block its path. It swatted the swords away, sending them clattering against the cave wall.

"Then Duncan MacDale stepped forward. He planted his pike in the path of the beast's charge. It swerved to miss the weapon, but the cave was too narrow, and the tip of the blade tore at the delicate membrane of the dragon's wing. The beast's screams sounded like a woman's.

"The warriors charged around the dragon trying to get to their swords. It slashed at them, sending two of them hard into the wall where they slumped unconscious. I heard Euan call fire to him. The fire danced around the dragon, unable to penetrate its magical defenses.

"Duncan spun his pike around, trying to get another strike. Again he caught its wing. Again the dragon screamed."

The scene followed the attack, dragon blood splashed outward only to fade several inches from the book.

"So are you sure your Dad wasn't the first special effects artist?" Alex reached up to wipe his brow and checked his fingers. "I almost expected to get blood splatter from that one."

"Well, I did say he developed a theatrical flair as he got older. You know some of the first special effects artists were mages. They did the effects with magic first, then figured out ways to explain it away." Tal's voice sounded lighter, but Alex could still feel the tension in his body as they watched the scene unfold.

"Then the dragon caught my eye in her sapphire gaze. I heard Oleta's voice scream in my head 'Taliesin help me! I carry your child!'

"I reacted instinctively. Magic flowed out from me in a massive wave of force. Warriors crumbled to the ground. Only MacDale remained standing. Something about that damned spear protected him from my power.

"'Why boy?' Euan asked as he struggled to his feet.

"I caught the older druid's gaze. 'For love,' I said, as my fist caught him in the temple. He slumped to the cave floor. Oleta caught the pike in her taloned grasp. She tore it from MacDale and smashed it against the cave wall. My next magical leven bolt dashed the warrior against the cave wall.

"'We should kill them all. They know you betrayed them,' Oleta said, walking toward Euan's unconscious form.

"I moved between my beloved and the druid. 'No. I will not kill another druid. It is bad enough that I struck him.'"

Alex hugged Tal. "Now I know where you got your sense of honor. I can thank your father for that. You know that's one of the things I love about you."

Tal ran his delicate hands through Alex's red hair before leaning in to kiss the crown of the other man's head.

"She reached around me, her massive clawed hand easily nudging me aside. She placed one claw alongside Euan's temple, where a heavy knot had already begun to form. I felt a strange energy pass between them. She lifted the claw away. 'He won't remember you ever being in the village of Snowhaven. When he wakes, he will return to Cromwell without reporting back to MacFrost.' She stepped forward to leave the cave. 'We should go before others come.' With a flick of her tail she smashed MacDale into the cave wall hard enough to ensure he wouldn't be getting up again. 'Please get the pike. We'll need to destroy it to break its magic.'

"I followed her out of the cave. The horses at the base of the trail fled in terror. The moon approached the western horizon. 'We must hurry. It will no longer be safe for us in Snowhaven,'" she said scanning the skies.

"In that moment, I knew I would follow her anywhere in the world. 'Where would you be safe?' I wanted to ask her about the child, but felt it prudent to wait.

"'It does not matter. Soon I will be restricted to one form until the child comes. As a human, I can blend in wherever I am.' She sounded sad. I knew she had only just moved to Snowhaven. When the dragon flexed her wings, a look of pain crossed her dark reptilian face. 'I cannot fly far. But I should be able to get us beyond

MacFrost's lands. You will need to be on my back so I can carry you.'

"Oleta knelt in front of me so I could swing astride her as I would a horse. I settled into a small spot between ridges just above the base of her wings. We flew to her hut on the outskirts of the village where she instructed me to retrieve some of her belongings. She explained that the energy for her to change back to human shape would leave her too weak to change back into dragon form so we could make good our escape."

The images showed them flying through the night sky, until they passed over a large wall as the sun began its rise over the horizon.

"I love moon-lit flights. They're always awesome," Alex said. "But I'd hate for you to have to do it with an injured wing."

"Wing injuries are the worst, and they take the longest to heal. If the wing membrane isn't set correctly, it can cripple a dragon for life."

"As the sun rose the next morning, she landed on a hilltop just south of Hadrian's wall, next to an abandoned Roman tower. Her breathing was labored as the first light touched the deep black scales of her head. An aura, the likes of which I had never seen before, bathed her. As I stood and watched, she shrank in on herself, and soon my beloved Oleta stood on two shaky legs where the dragon had been moments before.

"Her blue eyes fluttered and she sank toward the ground. I rushed forward to grab her before she hurt herself. 'Oleta, are you alright?' My heart beat so loudly in my ears that I almost couldn't hear her whispered response.

"'I just need a couple of minutes. My wing injuries are worse than I thought,' she said, cradling her left arm.

"I gently lowered us both to the ground. I laid her head in my lap and stroked her raven hair. 'What now?' I asked, looking around at where the forest was beginning to reclaim the land near the wall.

"She reached up with her right hand to stroke my arm. 'The ruins have been deserted for years. We can stay here through the winter. Game is plentiful, and we have time to gather mushrooms and such from the forest before the first frost.' She reached up and pulled my head down toward hers. Our lips touched, and I knew she would be mine for as long as I lived.

"The tower was in better repair than I could have hoped for. We managed to trade with the small village of Duirwood for a few of the things we couldn't find in the forest. Oleta's pregnancy progressed normally. I often questioned her about how I could have gotten her pregnant. She explained that since I was a powerful druid, I had enough magic to impregnate her. Human-dragon matings were not unheard of. Apparently, in the kingdoms far to the east, the rulers there often mated with dragons to keep magic flowing through their line. She said our son would be powerful both as a human and a dragon. By remaining human during most of her pregnancy she ensured that he would be born human.

"Her left arm never recovered from the damage the magical pike caused. Even after we used our combined magic to destroy the weapon, the arm continued to wither. She assured me that after the child was born she would be able to change into her dragon form and repair the damage. No matter how often she assured me, something nagged at me. But it gave me an excuse to dote on her.

"She was the light of my life. Never in my existence before or after, have I experienced the love that I had with Oleta. Through the coldest parts of winter, we spent hours curled up under bearskins on our straw mat near the stone hearth of the tower. We spoke of our love, and the love we would show our child."

The snowy image changed to one of young green shoots and flowering trees. The tower looked cleaner and in better repair. Gone was most of the rubble, and in its place, several garden plots grew. There was even a fat little goat enclosed by a wooden fence next to the tower door.

"I wonder how much of the sprucing up they did with magic?" Alex pondered aloud.

"Knowing my father, very little. He always said, 'why do something with magic when you can do it with your own two hands?' Unfortunately, it was that mentality that left people with as little knowledge of magic as they have today," Tal replied.

"As spring came, even though Oleta was now heavy

with child, we spent time wandering the forest around the tower. We found a small spring where ice-cold water bubbled up. She found it refreshing, although it was colder than I could tolerate. She said the water brought her temperature down, something she needed to help ensure our son would be born easily. As she sat in the freezing pool, I would lay next to her and stroke her long, lovely black hair. We would talk of what we would need to teach our son, both human things and dragon things. The human things would be easy enough for me, but the dragon things? Oleta would have to teach him how to change his shape, how to fly, and how to breathe fire. It made her happy to explain these things to me, and I enjoyed listening to her soft, melodic voice.

"In her human form, Oleta wasn't very good at hunting. With her injured arm she couldn't wield a bow, so she relied on magic. She would call prey to her and kill it with her knife. She could literally charm the birds from the trees. As the season turned around to Beltane and her time drew closer, I managed to get her to stay in the tower when I went out hunting.

"The magic of Beltane hummed in my body as I moved through the forest. I followed the spoor of a small boar as it moved about in the underbrush seeking roots and grubs. I had just spotted the boar when I felt Oleta's scream echoing in my mind. I slung my bow back over my shoulder and sprinted for the tower.

"The tower appeared as it had when I left it. I threw open the door and raced up the stairs toward the main room on the second level. Halfway up, I heard Oleta's heavy breathing. The fire on the hearth glowed lightly, casting long shadows across the room.

"I saw Oleta lying on our bed. 'My darling, what's wrong?' I ran to the bed, throwing my bow and arrows toward the table that sat near the fire.

"She turned toward me. Her eyes looked glazed. 'He comes, my love. Our son comes,' she panted.

"I knelt beside the bed. I stroked her sweat-soaked brow. 'What can I do to help?'

"Her good hand reached for me. I took it. 'Just being

here my love. The power of Beltane calls to our son, and he answers. Already he calls to the magic,' she gripped my hand as a contraction came on her. When it ended, her grip eased. 'I thought this would be easier,' she started to laugh, but it turned into a scream. Her body heaved again. 'He's close.'"

The scene showed a dark room with Taliesin holding the damp form of a crying baby. Oleta lay in the sweat-soaked bed with tangled blankets under her. Black hair lay plastered to her head, her face pale and drawn.

Alex stared at the magical projection. "Wow, you never told me you were born human. I'm not sure what I expected." He smiled up at Tal. "You were cute even then."

"Like the story said, that's why my mother remained in human form during the pregnancy, so I'd be born human. It's the form I'm most comfortable in. She must have paid dearly by staying human so long."

"Moments later, I held my son in my hands. He appeared normal in every way. Dark hair covered his tiny head and he had all ten fingers and toes. There was no sign that he was anything other than human. 'Look at our son my love.' I brought the baby closer so Oleta could see him. 'He's perfect.'

"She smiled at me, and her sapphire eyes cleared. 'Yes he is. Our Tal will be a great force in this world.' She closed her eyes and shuddered as the afterbirth passed from her. I handed over our son, so I could wrap up the bloody remains to bury in the forest later.

"Oleta's voice sounded sad and weak as she handed Tal back to me. 'You must take him to a wet nurse. I gave birth to him, but I cannot nourish him.' An odd look crossed her face as she leaned up and kissed the baby lightly on his head. 'Take care of him Taliesin, he is too important to our world. He may very well be the last of dragon kind.'

"I stood there holding our son and stared at her in horror. 'You are still here, so he's not the last dragon.' I tried to understand what she was saying.

"She shook her head. 'It has taken all of my magic to keep the poison of the pike from him. My time is done, but I will be at peace knowing that you are both safe and sound. Do not be sad, my love. We will meet again, in

another life. You will be the greatest druid the isles have
ever known, and our son will go on to be even greater.'
Her voice grew weaker with each word.

"I felt the magic of her life leaving her. I couldn't let
her die there inside the stone tower. I placed little Tal in
the basket she had woven for him. I went to Oleta, and
lifted her into my arms.'Let me get you outside. The
sky is clear, just the way you like it.' She weighed almost
nothing as I carried her down the stairs and out into the
afternoon light.

The image showed Taliesin laying Oleta onto the soft grass outside the
tower next to one of the newly sprouting garden plots, tears in his eyes. The
life-giving earth welcomed the body. The spectral woman reached up and
ran a shaking hand through Taliesin's long, black tangles.

Alex turned and saw a matching tear roll down Tal's cheek. He tried
to recall if he'd ever seen the other man cry in the three years they'd been
together.

"Oleta smiled at me as she smoothed my hair.'Thank
you my love. Remember me to Tal. Remember everything
I told you that he must learn. You can teach him what I
cannot. You are a good man Taliesin, and a better druid.'

"Tears ran down my cheeks and splashed down on her
face.'I will do right by our son. He will make you proud.'

"She smiled at me as the last of her energy faded into
the Earth beneath her. I sat there as I heard Tal begin
to wail in the vacant tower. He needed me now. Oleta
had passed back into the arms of the Goddess. I knew it
would be a long time before I would hold her again. My
arms would be different, her eyes would be different, but
we would be the same, and we would know each other.

The magical hologram of Oleta faded away slowly as Taliesin stood up
and walked back into the tower. Then the magical image faded away.

"So, I took our young son into the world to teach him the ways of men,
before the boy learned the ways of dragons." Tal's voice cracked as he read
the final page of the book to Alex.

"Wow." Alex wrapped his good arm around Tal's shoulders. He felt a
sadness coming from Tal he'd never felt before.

"I never met my mother," Tal sighed, laying the book aside and snuggling closer to Alex. "I mean physically. I've spoken to her spirit many times. But I never really got to know her. My father didn't like speaking of her when I was young. It was almost like it was too painful for him. Now I know why. He must have been three or four hundred when he wrote this book. The script's shaky in spots. I wonder why he never gave it to me. There's so much love in this tale. I guess it was the right time for the book to find me. Before I met you, I never would have truly grasped the meaning of a love as strong as what they had." He reached up and traced the line of Alex's jaw, and his blue eyes met his lover's green ones. "I can only hope that I honor their love well enough through my love for you."

"I'm sure they both would be thrilled with the man you are and your capacity for love." Alex bent slightly to kiss the man he loved.

"Call me Ishmael." It always sounded
better when Melville said it.
        Still I think old Herman would
be proud of these boys. EF

For Hates Sake

By Larry J. Cope

It was freakishly hot for the first of May in Savannah, Georgia. The bell rang, and I floated along with the rest of the seventh graders rushing out like the tide to start their weekend. I really wasn't looking forward to the days off; at least at school, I had two meals a day.

Next to me in the human tide was one of the prettiest girls in the school. She wore a pink skirt with a white sleeveless blouse. A pink ribbon bound her jet-black locks into a single ponytail spiraling down her back. She spoke on her heavily be-dazzled cell phone, and I pretended she was my girlfriend walking beside me. All too soon she made a quick left turn and disappeared out of sight.

Walking outside was like being smacked in the face with a hot wet rag. It was the kind of weather I'd expect in the middle of July in a really hot year. The old tee shirt I was wearing instantly clung to me like a second skin and each breath was like trying to inhale with someone sitting on my chest. It was calm, without a hint of a breeze. The moss, draped over the big cypress trees, hung lifeless in the oppressive heat.

I stood there on the steps of Jefferson County Middle School and looked into a cloudless sky, praying for one of those cool afternoon showers that somehow magically drops the humidity and cools the air to a tolerable level, but no such luck. Even in the middle of the afternoon, the sun was white and scalding with no sign of relief.

I wandered down the concrete steps with my tattered red backpack slung over one shoulder. Inside were several apples and granola bars I had garnered from the lunch lady to stave off hunger through the weekend. The only thing in our refrigerator at home was a partial case of beer my mother lived on. I walked under the big red oaks that were just filling out with the new leaves of spring and pondered my pathetic existence and how to end it. My mother and I tolerated each other, and I only had one friend. Thanks to the school bully, he was unconscious in the hospital.

Lost in thought, I kicked a rock like an idiot, and hurt my toe through my worn out shoes.

"Hey Dumbo – You owe me a buck. Give it to me, and I won't pound your face."

A burst of adrenaline sent a wave of heat up my face and into my very large ears. That gift from my grandfather dominates my head and draws quite a bit of unwanted attention. I had been wandering aimlessly and hadn't noticed the devil himself walking up to me. "You know I don't have any money, Butcher." Francis liked to be called 'The Butcher'. Because he was big for his age, bigger than anyone in seventh grade, nobody dared call him by his real name. I heard his dad was in the Special Forces and gone most of the time. "Why do I owe you a buck?"

"Lets call it a stink tax – you have to pay us to put up with your horrible smell." Francis Cobb was a typical school bully. He traveled with an entourage. These were average kids that just wanted to hang out with the big guy so they wouldn't get beat up. Butcher hit his growth spurt early and already had facial hair. He was a good head and shoulders taller than everyone else in class and spent a good portion of his time lifting weights. Today he wore a ball cap with the brim turned to the side and a gray t-shirt with the arms ripped off, making his arms look huge, especially compared to a wimpy runt like me. He had a round face, and his hair was cut so close to his scalp that he looked like a peeled onion. The only thing that did not fit his athletic build was his fat belly. I would not say that Butcher was fat, he just had a big belly. It kind of looked like he was pregnant. If I had the balls, I would have poked fun at him for it.

"You know I don't have any money, what'd ya expect me to do?" I then turned to the right to walk away, and Butcher stuck his arm out in front of me.

"I don't care if you ain't got it. Get it! Or I'll rip those big fat ears right off your head."

"Jus smack 'im Butcher and lets git 'for we git cawt," said Billy. Billy was Butcher's sidekick, always tagging along telling Butcher how cool and great he was. Billy had darty eyes and never looked at the same thing for more than a second. He was just as skinny as me and had a shock of red hair that curled outward in every direction. "Sides, he stinks something tear-ble. Don't you ever bathe, boy?"

I suppose I could have had Butcher kill me and put me out of my misery, but the prospect of being beaten to death did not excite me. If I check out of this vile world, I want to take him and his stupid sidekick with me. "Leave me alone," I said, my knees rattling together.

"Hey Billy, think if we threw him off the roof of the school he'd be able to fly with them wings he has attached to the side of his head?" Butcher tried to flick my ears but I was quick and dodged his attempt.

I looked around trying to find an escape route. To my left grew the thick forest of Cypress, Oaks, and heavy underbrush. If I went that way and they caught me, there would be no witnesses when he beat me to a pulp. To my right was a busy road. Running out there would be suicide, which wouldn't be a bad option unless they just maimed me instead of killing me. Not a good prospect. No way I could tolerate being a cripple on top of my other problems. I couldn't go around Butcher and his gang, so back toward the school was my best option. I was just about to turn around when he stepped on my toe and pushed me down. I fell backward, landing hard on my rear end in the dry dirt next to the sidewalk.

Anger flared inside me like never before as Butcher, Billy, and the rest of his gang laughed at me. I grimaced, grinding my teeth as my fingers flexed into fists in the soft dust. I don't know what possessed me or where my courage came from, but I hurled both fists full of dirt right into the face of the unsuspecting Butcher, filling his mouth and his eyes. I even heard a rock thump into his thick head. It sounded like a knuckle rapping on a ripe melon.

Billy and Butcher weren't the only ones momentarily stunned by what I had done. *Why had I done that?* The world and time seemed to stand still as a scream of pain and rage emanated from the depths of Butcher's large belly. I swear I lost ten years of my life from fear. Butcher raised his foot to stomp on me, and he would have succeeded if I hadn't woken out of my coma, scrambled to my feet, and sprinted away.

"I'm gonna kill you, punk!" Butcher yelled. "I'm gonna rip your arm off and beat you with the bloody limb. When I get done pounding on you, they'll need a spatula to clean up what's left."

He was still shouting at me when I neared the intersection on the other side of the school. I turned around and saw he was still rubbing his eyes as he ran, closing the half block lead I had gained on him. Terror fueled my flight as I chanced a busy intersection without waiting for the light. A car's honk and a screech of brakes let me know just how close I had come to having my wish to die granted. I ran as fast as my shaky legs would carry me. My heart thundered in my ears as I sped down the sidewalk along Sixth Street, with no idea where to go. A quick look back showed Butcher had cleared his eyes and was gaining fast, but I still had a good lead.

"I'm gonna rip you open and feed your guts to the birds, punk!"

My foot caught on a chunk of raised concrete and time slowed to almost a standstill. I looked down and saw the split in the sidewalk where the root of a huge maple tree had heaved the concrete. Magnolias and a brilliant dogwood filled my vision as I flew through the air and crashed into a bush filled with pretty purple flowers.

By the time I got to my feet, Butcher was so close I could see the rage in the whites of his bloodshot eyes, "You're mine, punk."

Terror filled me so much, I hardly felt the pain from the fall, but something was wrong with my shoe. I heard a clickety-clack every time my left foot came down. I spared a glance down and realized I had nearly torn the sole off my only pair of shoes. In a panic I looked for any place of refuge. I knew this street and knew there was nowhere to hide. Dread filled my bones making it even harder to run. I could feel Butcher's hot breath behind me, and I didn't dare turn around.

I was just thinking about jumping out in front of one of the speeding cars coming at me when I cleared the forest and almost stumbled in amazement. An old and worn, red brick building stood in what I would have sworn was an empty lot just yesterday. There were several windows spread evenly down the side with white faded storm shutters flanking each side. The roof was gabled with worn cedar shingles spaced haphazardly across the expanse. An old carved wooden sign sailed over the sidewalk as if it belonged there. With Old English, painted white letters, the sign read, "LIBRORUM TABERNA."

I had no idea what it meant, or even how to pronounce it, but it appeared to be my salvation. I slowed down long enough to hang a hard right through the open door. The strangest man I had ever seen stood there like a stone statue while I crashed onto the floor next to him.

Butcher came through the door with much more grace than I had. The evil smile on his face reminded me of a wolf's snarl before killing a helpless animal. Billy stood behind him, panting like a dog, not even bothering to come in. I instinctively crab-walked backward until I bumped into a glass showcase.

"May I help you?" the man asked Butcher. Somehow he managed to stand between me and the bully, even though I never saw him take a step.

"Get out of my way, old man," Butcher said, trying to push his way around the frail-looking man blocking his way.

I looked around for a place to run, but statue man wasn't as weak as he looked. He grabbed Butcher by the collar, dragged him over to a couch by the front window and set him down firmly. He exchanged soft words with

Butcher, so quiet that I couldn't hear what was said. He turned around and waved at Billy with a shooing motion, and Billy took off running like he had been shot with a BB-gun.

When his white-eyed gaze met mine, I thought I would wet myself. I had backed myself into a corner made by two glass cases filled with very old looking books displayed on white satin shelves.

He glided over to me without seeming to even take a step and said, "Hello there, young man. My name is Ezra Finfrock. To whom do I have the pleasure of addressing?"

The temperature seemed to drop instantly, raising gooseflesh along my bare arms. Every now and then a musty breeze that smelled like an old book ruffled my sandy brown hair and assaulted my nose. "M-m-m-m-my n-n-n-n-name is Rupert," I finally stammered.

"I am pleased to meet you, Rupert. What brings you into my humble establishment on this fine day?" he asked through a perfectly straight, yellowed smile. Ezra's dirty yellow teeth matched the dingy color of the hair that hung to his shoulders and the bushy eyebrows that stood out on his face like a pair of caterpillars glued to his forehead. He was bone thin, and his face looked like a rubber balloon pulled tightly over a skull, making him look like he was at least a thousand years old.

I was so mesmerized by his eyes that I couldn't form an answer. They had a hypnotic effect and I couldn't stop staring at them. I wasn't sure this ghost in front of me was any safer than the wolf sitting stiffly on the couch. *What in the world had he done to Butcher?*

"I do pride myself on being an excellent judge of people and their character," said Ezra through thin, bloodless lips. He had a strange accent I had never heard before. It wasn't quite English, Australian, Irish or Scottish, but maybe all of them somehow mashed together. "I find it gives me incredible insight into the true nature of their problems."

I looked over at a Butcher and started shivering. Hugging my arms tightly to myself, I figured it prudent to stand up if my shaky legs would allow me. "I-I-I-I'm s-s-s-sorry to b-b-bother you sir."

Ezra shot a malign glance at Butcher. Without taking his eyes off of the bully he said, "Sometimes the obvious problem isn't the real issue now is it, Rupert?"

I saw that Mr. Finfrock and Butcher had locked eyes. For the first time I could see fear and not hatred in the bully's cold brown eyes. "You didn't just stumble into my precious store by accident, my boy."

Ezra Finfrock placed a skeletal hand on the glass case. He stroked the top gently, like a man would caress the face of a lover, or a favored pet.

"Everything that happens here, happens for a purpose." Without waiting for a response he closed his eyes and continued, "She will help you, Rupert Washington. Surely, she will."

I didn't remember giving him my last name. How did he know that? I was just about to ask him when a disheveled woman came through a gilded archway decorated with elaborate carvings all the way around. Her red lipstick was smeared across her face, and her brown curly hair was messed up, like she had just gotten out of bed. She was holding her torn white blouse together because there were no buttons left, and her skirt was inside out, showing the tag in front. Just looking at the woman should have given me a clue as to what I was in for, but not in my wildest imagination could I have guessed.

She stopped and backed up when she saw Ezra, looking at him with such malice that for a moment I thought she could be Butcher's mother simply by the similarity of their expressions.

Ezra took the time to straighten his black wool vest over his crisp white linen shirt before saying, "Ah, Mrs. Turner. I take it the book gave you everything you needed?"

"You didn't tell me it would be like that."

"I told you that which you needed to know. How are your feelings for your husband now?"

The woman dropped her head and looked at the book she was holding. With a slight hesitation she handed the book to Ezra and said, "I think I should get home and get dinner ready before he gets home from work."

"As you say," Ezra nodded his head and gave her a slight bow. "Good day to you, madam." I watched her stumble through the front of the store and out the door.

"Now, where were we, young man?" He looked at a gold pocketwatch attached to a chain hanging from the middle of three gold buttons on his vest.

He cocked his ear as if listening to something. I had big ears and very good hearing, but all I could hear was the sound of air rushing every few seconds, kind of like something breathing. There were no other sounds. I looked around, searching for a back entrance or something and saw only beautifully carved and gilded wood that looked like it had been aged for centuries. The crown molding was made of cherry. The massive bookshelves and even the wainscoting on the wall were made of the same expensive wood. Each entrance to a row of books was marked with a different carved animal at the top. Ezra disappeared into an archway with none other than a wolf at the top.

A few seconds later he poked his head out and said, "Come along now."

For some unexplained reason my feet would not move. I felt as if I had grown roots into the knotted planking of the floor. He glanced at his pocket watch with impatience and said, "Now if you please?"

Somehow I took a step. My legs felt like I was walking through the thick mud down by the river. Each shoe seemed to have an extra twenty pounds on it. Every time the left foot came down I heard the double clickety-clack as the front of my loose sole slapped my foot and then the ground.

Ezra had almost disappeared down the long row of musty old books. It surprised me how far he had gone. He looked too old to move that fast. I curiously wandered down the row without a clue as to where I was or what I was doing. Anything had to be better than what awaited me if Butcher followed me outside. Ezra seemed like a hundred yards away, and the rows of books just kept going. I don't remember the building being *this* long, but I had been running pretty fast. I shrugged it off, thinking my mind was playing tricks on me from the stress of the chase.

After walking several minutes I finally caught up with Ezra who was examining the bindings on a shelf about the level of his head.

"'Oh, my captain! My captain! Noble soul! Grand old heart, after all! Why should anyone give chase to that hated fish!' Starbuck, chapter one hundred and thirty-two," Ezra said.

"What?"

"Maybe this one," Ezra said, pulling out an old leather bound book, "'Towards thee I roll, thou all-destroying but unconquering whale; to the last I grapple with thee; from hell's heart I stab at thee; for hates sake I spit my last breath at thee.' Best remember that if I were you. Remember as well, what happens there, happens here.

"Yes, I think this is just the thing." Without another word he walked two steps to an alcove and set the book lovingly on an antique cherry desk. Ezra opened the book as if he knew exactly which page he was looking for.

"W-w-what is?" I asked. Even though he had seemingly saved me from Butcher, he still terrified me.

"Moby Dick, by Herman Melville. First published in eighteen fifty-one. That Melville," Ezra's wry smile touched his eyes and his mouth twitched upward as if remembering someone. "He was a cheeky fellow."

"W-w-why?"

Ezra's thin purple lips pressed into a strained straight line as he first looked at me and then at his watch again. "That is something you will have to figure out before this night's over. Now I suggest you get started."

"I s-s-s-saw the m-m-m-movie at school already." I don't have a clue where my bravado came from.

"You haven't read this book. Now sit." He said the last part with much more force than his frail body should have had.

Without another word, I sat in the plush black leather chair behind the desk and glared up at him. The chair and desk were a matched pair and more expensive looking than anything I had ever seen in my life. The red grain of the cherry on the top of the desk looked so deep, perfect and amazing that I thought my mere presence would stain it somehow.

"I should think you will be able to stop reading when she thinks you have learned what you need to learn." Ezra turned on worn black leather boots that looked like they hadn't been shined in centuries and strutted back to the front of the store.

I looked at the words in the book without reading them. "Why do I always get stuck with the nutballs, and who in the world is this *she?*"

Just then, a cold, foul air blew across my face dropping the temperature at least ten degrees. I shivered more from fear than anything, and decided I had better figure out what *she* wanted me to learn, so I started reading – thinking maybe Butcher was safer after all.

Within moments, I found myself on the deck of an old sailing ship with men darting all around me. It wasn't just my imagination. I was really there. The smell alone nearly knocked me to my knees. Just the body odor from each man was indescribable; add to that a fishy smell that made the docks by the bay in Savannah smell like a rose garden. Men yelled, ropes creaked, sails flapped, and a very large scary man with one leg yelled orders. I had been somehow magically transported onto an old sailing ship in the middle of the ocean.

The rough-looking sailor looked right at me and yelled, "Ishmael, get on the boat!"

They called me Ishmael!

"But my name's Rupert," I whispered.

Stubb, the second mate, knocked me hard on the back of the head and yelled, "Get on the boat, Ishmael. Have you taken leave of your senses, man?"

How do I know that's Stubb? I suddenly realized I knew everything about where I was. I knew the difference between a *mizzen* and a *main mast*; a *topsail* and a *forecastle*. I looked at my hands as if for the first time. They were the hands of a man, a grown man. I made a muscle and realized I was strong and tall and powerful. Rubbing my face, I felt a full beard that tickled my neck. I smiled and yelled my happiness to the world, and even did a little dance around the main mast. I was Ishmael, a schoolteacher, aboard the whaling ship Pequod and I was a man. *Not a wimp!* It wasn't my imagination; I was really there... here. In the novel, Moby Dick.

Just then I heard a scream and a holler as a little black boy fought with Starbuck, the Chief Mate. Starbuck held him aloft by the back of his shirt as he kicked and fought. The child couldn't have been more than seven or eight. "My name's Butcher, not Pip. Quit calling me that and let me alone."

He then started crying great tears as Starbuck tossed him down the hold and said, "You'll stay down there without food until you learn your manners, boy. What's gotten into you anyway?"

I was jubilant as I jumped over the smooth wooden side of the Pequod into Stubb's whaleboat and took up an oar. I manned that oar much longer than I ever thought possible. The strain felt good, and I didn't complain or even stop smiling. I was the man and Butcher was the wimp. I could make his life as miserable as he made mine.

The whale breached right beside our wooden rowboat scaring me clean out of my seat. My mates laughed at me as I wiped the salt water out of my eyes. The massive sperm whale was bigger than I could have ever imagined. It had crinkled gray skin and small scared eyes on a head that melded right into the body without any semblance of a neck. The small flipper on its side looked puny in comparison to the rest of him, but that flipper alone was as big as our little boat. In one instant, our eyes met and I felt he looked right into my soul, at the same time Stubb's harpoon flew into his thick hide. I felt his pain through our shared gaze. Now his stare was accusing, and I could do nothing but turn away. I knew it was our job, and we had to do it, but my heart broke for the life we were about to take.

When finally Mr. Stubb punctured the great beast's heart, the sperm whale let out a cry of pain and a geyser of blood from its blowhole soaked us with thick red ooze.

We towed him back to the Pequod. My arms had long ago lost feeling. The intense pain in my back and my undying thirst told me this was no imagination, but quite real. I was fascinated by the myriad of sharks that had already gathered around our little oasis in the sea, diving, swarming and already feeding on our catch. They feasted as we rowed into a red sunset that was reflected on a sea so still it looked as if the water were on fire.

I lay exhausted on the deck when we finally tied the whale to the Pequod. I would have slept where I lay, but our job was only just beginning. We had to literally strip the flesh right off the leviathan. The water, if you could call it that, had turned into a sea of blood filled with a writhing mass of sharks that looked like a great mass of slimy maggots devouring the carcass. It was now a race to see who could get more of the whale – us or them.

If I fell overboard and was devoured by that demonic horde, would I wake up safely back in the bookstore, or would I die in both worlds? Ezra had said something about that, hadn't he? For the first time in my life, I wanted to live!

I continued on with the crew of the Pequod for what seemed like months, taking every opportunity I could to make Pip's life miserable. Queequed was a heavily tattooed Polynesian and my best friend on the boat. The harpooner never liked it when I messed with Pip but always held his tongue, which made me feel guilty for what I had done. At Queequed's request, I finally left Pip alone.

Lying in my hammock one night, I pondered what Ezra had said. Something about being able to stop reading when I learned what I was I supposed to learn. *But what was that? Was it how good it felt to be the bully for a change, because that sure felt good. Kind of. Was I supposed to learn how to fight? Honor? Respect? Courage?*

I was sure it was courage. I had always lacked courage, mostly because I was small, an outcast, and a wimp. But here, I was big, strong, and part of a crew. *How can I learn courage?*

The next day, I ran up the rigging with the sail crew. I took a turn as a lookout on the main mast. It was scary, but at the same time exhilarating, better than any amusement park ride. I took my turn on the whale carcass, killing sharks with a whaling-spade. One slip and I would fall into a flesh-eating machine more terrible than any meat grinder ever conceived, yet I remained a fixture on the Pequod.

Queequed, my best friend in the whole universe, got sick one day and declared he was going to die. Lying in his hammock, he even looked like he would. I was horrified at the prospect of losing him and wondered if that was the courage I was to learn. He called the ship's carpenter and had a coffin made. When it was finished, he even tried it out. Something broke inside of me, seeing him lying in his coffin, as if he was already dead. I cried like the child I really was. I cried and begged him not to die, as if he had a choice in the matter.

The very next day, Queequed decided he wasn't going to die, and by high noon declared himself fit for duty. I was ecstatic. For some reason he wouldn't explain, Queequed placed some basic supplies in his coffin and had the lid sealed with pitch and nails. As much as I begged, he never revealed his reasons; he just continued to carve figures in the lid that resembled the savage tattoos all over his body.

Captain Ahab became increasingly neurotic about killing Moby Dick. He would rant on and on about how the fish was the devil himself. Funny, because I always thought that Butcher was the devil himself. The first mate,

Starbuck, would somehow always calm the captain down but could never talk him out of his quest for the white whale.

When we finally caught up with the beast, Captain Ahab's blood lust was worse than any shark I had ever seen. We chased that whale for three days. Each day we fought Moby Dick, and each day he destroyed another of our small whaleboats.

Finally, with only one boat left, the whale had had enough. He turned and fought with Captain Ahab – man to beast. The great white whale looked like a porcupine with scores of harpoons jutting out from his thick albino hide, sadistic trophies of the many battles he had won against his human foe. I stood there on the little whaleboat and watched as Moby Dick rammed the Pequod with his thick blunt head, shattering her thick hull as if it were made of matchsticks. The ever-present sharks circled in a frenzy as if Moby Dick had somehow told them dinner was on the way.

I watched in horror as Moby Dick disappeared under the restless waves, and the Pequod followed. Slowly at first, and then faster and faster, it slid beneath the endless sea. It was then my attention darted to the Captain as he spoke his famous last words of hate. He sounded just like Ezra Finfrock.

"Towards thee I roll, thou all-destroying but unconquering whale; to the last I grapple with thee; from hell's heart I stab at thee; for hates sake I spit my last breath at thee." He had barely finished speaking when Moby Dick rammed us from underneath, sending our little whaleboat sailing through the air as if the hand of God had tossed it. I fell out of the flying boat and landed quite a distance from the breaching whale intent on Captain Ahab.

Just as I climbed the surface of the water and took a gasping breath, Queequed's coffin flew out of the water like it was shot from a cannon. It settled and bobbed right next to me. I scrambled on top of the coffin, as it was the only thing of decent size left floating for as far as my water-soaked eyes could see. My fingers clung to the hideous figures carved into the surface so I wouldn't slip into the dangerous waters. Desperately, I spun around trying to spot any of my shipmates. "Queequed!"

Then all of a sudden, I spotted a figure struggling not far off to the west, directly into the sun. It was Pip, or Butcher, coughing and clinging to a bit of flotsam, barely keeping his tiny head above water. Between us lay a field of tearing, ripping, fearless machines bent on nothing but filling their mouths.

If Pip died here, then would Butcher die in my world? If I just held on to my safety spot on top of the coffin, would I finally finish this story and get back Rupert's life? In those moments as I watched Pip struggle, time stood still. Hundreds of thoughts ran through my mind. On top of it all I kept hearing Ahab's last words, "For hates sake I spit my last breath at thee." Then it hit me. I was like Ahab. My hate for Butcher was just like Ahab's hate for the whale. I had just watched Ahab's hate end in utter destruction, not just for him but also for the entire crew.

"Butcher, it's me Rupert," I yelled at the top of my lungs. "Quick, swim here, and I'll save you."

"I knew it was…," his little black head dropped below the surface and I made up my mind. I jumped into the shark-infested water and swam over to where he had sunk beneath the waves. My hand latched onto his tiny body. Several sharks swam all around us, but none attacked. *Not one of your best ideas, Rupert.*

I kicked off of the body of a particularly large shark, propelling me toward the surface. Butcher coughed and puked water out of his lungs as I drug his limp body toward the haven that was my best friend's coffin.

The sharks were getting curious and came in closer as I neared the coffin. "What was I thinking," I said to myself. But I knew I had to do this, not just to save Butcher, but also to save myself. I really wanted to live!

Butcher regained consciousness and screamed as the rough hide of a shark brushed along the side of his leg, scraping off the skin just as if he had slid down a concrete sidewalk. "Why are you doing this?" he asked me.

"No time," I said breathlessly, "Get up there already!"

The blood from Butcher's leg inflamed the monsters around us. I shoved with all my strength and literally tossed Butcher out of the water and onto the coffin. Now it was my turn. I sprang to the surface just in time to be seized by, not one, but a bevy of hungry mouths. The screams that filled my head hurt my ears until I realized they were my own, and then everything went black.

I woke up suddenly, as if I had been slapped, but I didn't hurt anywhere. On the side of the book, covering the top left corner, lay a puddle of drool from where I had fallen asleep. The words 'THE END' filled my vision. *Was it all a dream?*

The sweet scent of flowers, mixed with the clean smell of a pine forest after a gentle rain caressed my senses. Soft light from a candled sconce danced around, casting playful shadows all around me. "Was it really all a dream?"

I rubbed my face with both hands, trying to push away the frightful nightmare that had so fully taken me. All I felt was the soft flesh of youth. Missing was Ishmael's itchy beard. "It was only a dream."

Wiping off the drool with my forearm, I closed the book and headed to the front of the bookstore on shaky legs. Gone was the powerful strength I had gotten used to. Gone was the respect I had earned. Gone was the friendship I had garnered with Queequed. I cleared the row, only to find Butcher standing there waiting for me. Looking around, I realized we were all alone. Now he could beat me to a pulp without distraction.

I stood there frozen to the polished cherry floor like I had been nailed down. My whole body shook as he got off of the couch and headed toward me, slowly at first and then at a run. It seemed he couldn't wait to finish what the sharks had started. I closed my eyes in anticipation of the inevitable blow that would send me to the next world.

Instead of a punch, I felt arms wrap around me and gentle sobs shook his body. I didn't know whether or not to return the hug or just stand there as Butcher cried on my shoulder. *Why?* "You're not going to pound me to a pulp?" I asked. *Shut up, stupid. Don't remind him.*

He pushed away and his face was a mask of sorrow and regret. "Why did you save me?"

I was confused. "Save you from what?"

"You saved me from the sharks," he said, sniffing. "I saw them eat you, Rupert. You sacrificed yourself for me, after everything I've done to you. Why?"

I was shocked he was in my dream. Then he'd used my name, which was a first. But really, I didn't know why I sacrificed myself for him. I shrugged. "I guess I didn't want to become like Captain Ahab."

He hugged me again and said, "Thanks dude, I owe you one."

Together we walked out of the bookstore and back toward the slums where I lived. Not until I got home did I realize I still had Moby Dick firmly tucked under my arm as if it were a life preserver. I hadn't meant to take the book. I had just forgotten to put it back on the counter when we left.

I ran out the door and all the way back to Sixth Street. I ran down the sidewalk as fast as my legs would carry me. I had to get the book back before the store closed. I rounded the tree line, and two things hit me. The first was the new pair of shoes I was wearing. *Where did those come from?* The second – the bookstore was gone.

There are times when being a "collector"
of rare books can be more of a bother than
it's worth. Still, I would prefer some tomes
to stay here with me, where I can keep
them safe. EF

Charisma

by Patrick Hester

Charisma loved that she could change the playlist of her iPod without taking her hands off the wheel. Modern technology was wonderful. The first words to Peter Gabriel's *Steam* blasted through her speakers. *"Stand back! Stand back!"*

"Must the volume be so high? And why the infatuation with Peter Gabriel? I've never understood that." The disembodied, British voice came courtesy of a small earbud snuggled deep inside her left ear. The device allowed her to communicate with someone on the other side of the world courtesy of satellites and the tiny microphone and speaker.

"You know your culture from your trash, your plastic from your cash."

With her thumb, she ticked the volume down. "To be fair, I only enjoy his more commercial songs," she replied, her own British accent showing her Northern upbringing. "I don't care for the artsy stuff. Do you have good news for me, Thomas? Were you able to contact Ezra? I'd rather not hold onto this any longer than need be." She spared a glance for the ancient book resting on the Poltrona Frau leather upholstery of the passenger seat. In her opinion, the metal clasps and raised demonic iconography clashed with the pale interior of the car. Not to mention the fact that, in the wrong hands, the book could open the gates to a hell dimension. Since unleashing an army of Demons on an unsuspecting human populace was strictly frowned upon in civilized culture, she would prefer to have the book safely locked away.

"No. Mister Finfrock does not answer his phone, nor does he have voicemail. I couldn't find a website, so I doubt he has email either. You would think someone would answer when you let the phone ring three hundred times. I counted."

"Short of walking in through the front door, I think phone is going to be your best bet. Or mail. You could overnight him a note to answer his phone at a specific time. That could work." Ezra was, at best, quirky. Understatement, she knew, but she had to ease Thomas into this life. One had to be careful with new facilitators if one wished to keep them for any length of time. Thomas had been with her for two years now, and showed a lot of promise with the amount of business opportunities he'd found for her. Alfred had been with her nearly fifteen years. She missed Alfred. There's just something about coming home to fresh baked pie that appealed to her inner child. Damn the man for getting himself killed!

"If it's so dangerous, I don't understand why you didn't just burn the book."

Honestly, she tried. The book refused to burn. Some of the more ancient tomes were like that. Stubborn. Irksome. Rather than answer the question, she decided to change the subject. "Zharkov loved the emerald necklace, by the way. Said it really brought out my breasts."

Thomas choked. Charisma laughed, shifting the car into high gear as she hit the straightaway. Pressing her foot down, she watched the speedometer climb over one hundred mph. The night was cool and clear, the scents of the desert rushing in through the open windows. She wore a low-cut black dress, stiletto heels, had her dark hair up in curls, and sported the emerald necklace with matching earrings this evening.

"I'm making excellent time. I should be through Vegas before sunrise. Try Ezra again. The sooner this book is behind lock and key, the better— No!"

"What?" Thomas asked. Charisma had no time to respond. The car's headlights showed a little girl standing in the middle of the highway. She spun the wheel right, foot slamming on the brake. The car dipped into the ditch and shot up at an angle. Everything began to spin before the car bounced and rolled over and over. Her airbags exploded with a whoosh, slamming into her face, driving the breath from her lungs. The seatbelt locked but gravity pulled and tugged her while the car spun. Glass shattered and swirled around her. Darkness flooded her vision.

"You're so very pretty."

Charisma groaned. Every part of her body hurt. Her tingling wrists were bound above her, feet below her, and every stitch of clothing seemed to be gone. If the scent tickling her nose was any indication, she had been tied to a Ponderosa Pine, common in the deserts in this part of the world. The light of a nearby bonfire cut the darkness. The heat of the blaze was unable to keep her skin from prickling in the cool air of the desert night.

With her back to the fire, the little girl from the highway stood, face shrouded in shadows.

Her hair looked pale as moonlight and fell straight down on either side of her face. She wore a blue and white dress with a matching blue ribbon in her hair that made her look disturbingly like the very famous Alice. Dark, shiny shoes and a simple silver bracelet on her right arm finished out her outfit. If pressed, Charisma would've placed her age at about ten.

"I don't believe we've been properly introduced," Charisma offered.

"Names are funny things," the child giggled. "Dangerous things, aren't they, *Charisma?*"

"Ah. I assume this means you won't be sharing yours?" When the little girl made no comment, Charisma nodded. "Well, I can't go around calling you 'little girl', now can I? How about *Alice*, then?"

"Alice?" she purred. "If you must."

"Alice it is, then."

"You let someone draw on your skin."

"I took the liberty of baking some cookies," Thomas whispered in her ear. She very nearly cheered at the sound of his voice. With all of her clothes and belongings gone, she took some solace that they'd missed the wireless earbud. He would be able to hear almost everything she heard. "Plan B was enthusiastically motivated by chocolate chips with walnuts. They are en-route and moving quite fast, but we need time. Stall."

"*Draw* on my skin?"

"Yes," Alice said. "There." She pointed at Charisma's tattoo, the one above her heart; a Dragon clutching the moon. There were six more. One on the inside of each wrist, twins on her ankles, one across her back and the last on her scalp beneath her hair. That had been the most painful, and not just because they'd had to shave her head. She'd had it done before the more modern custom of needles and ink were in practice. Just remembering the *tap-tap-tap* of the wooden mallet made her shiver.

"Unavoidable," she said. "I needed certain protective magics in my line of work. The tattoos seemed the easiest way to offer a permanent solution."

Alice grinned, her teeth gleaming from the shadows of her face. "I can't see your mind."

"The book," said a new voice. A tall, thin man walked into the firelight. He had a dark fringe of hair circling an otherwise bald head. His eyes lingered on her longer than she would've liked. There was a hunger there she'd seen before.

"You shouldn't take things that don't belong to you. That's stealing." Alice looked very cross, even with her face cast in shadows. "Isn't that right, Mister Norman?"

"The others have arrived."

"Oh, goody!" Alice squealed. "The others have arrived, the others have arrived, the others, oh, the others, oh, the others have arrived!" Alice began to do a little dance, bouncing around the fire. Mister Norman licked his lips, then closed the distance between him and Charisma, raising his hand and clamping it down on her left nipple. He squeezed until her eyes watered, that hungry look in his eyes turning into something more feral.

"I told you not to touch," Alice said, her voice low. Charisma screamed as the child leapt into the air and latched onto the man's back. Her head cocked awkwardly, Alice ripped into his throat with her teeth. Norman staggered back, hand releasing Charisma's breast. Alice's mouth moved like a squirrel's, rapidly nibbling away at his neck, blood gushing out, splattering warm against Charisma's skin. They spun round and round the fire for a moment or two, Mister Norman obviously shocked by this turn of events. He fell to the ground with a hollow thud.

Alice stood in a hunch, blood staining her lips, chin and front of her dress. Her head still cocked to the side, bones pressing against the taut skin of her neck. It was an unnatural position, to say the least.

"What are you?" Charisma whispered.

Bones popped and cracked as her head righted itself. Alice smiled brightly, skipping away without answering.

"How long til Plan B?" she whispered.

"Twenty minutes," Thomas answered.

Charisma wasn't sure she had twenty minutes.

The *others* wore hooded robes and chanted in Latin, never a good sign as these things went. The upside was that it took them nearly fifteen minutes to get whatever magical ritual they were performing off the ground, and they weren't chanting in Greek. Greek, in her experience, is bad. Much worse than Latin on the magical spectrum of incantations. Something about the inflections. The downside was that they'd opened the Grimoire of the Magi Medes, the very book she'd hoped to lock away at *Librorum Taberna* where it could do no harm. They were also pointing at Charisma from time to time, while checking the book and readying what appeared to be an altar mid-construction. More than likely, they meant for her to be some sort of sacrifice. The fact that they'd stripped her naked lent credence to this assumption since all the ancient spells were written by dirty old men.

Alice appeared to be quite firmly in charge.

Charisma wracked her brain trying to figure out what thing could be inside the child's body. The list turned out to be quite long. Given the way these others bent their necks to her, whatever creature inhabited the child must be incredibly powerful. That usually meant *ancient* as well.

Times like these, she wished she could live the life of a simple bookstore owner, like Ezra from *Librorum Taberna*. He never seemed to leave his store, let alone find himself tied naked to a tree in the middle of the desert about to be sacrificed as a component for some dark ritual.

Running her tongue along the inside of her mouth, she found a loose crown. Ezra probably had decent dental, too.

"Almost time." The voice was small. Alice's voice. At some point, she'd come up beside Charisma without her realizing it. "We're going to have a party. I like parties. I wish we had cake."

"I know what you are. It isn't a child."

"Don't be rude! If you're rude you won't get any cake."

"You just said you didn't have cake."

Her voice changed, became deep as James Earl Jones without the asthma. "No, but we have a Charisma piñata. I shall dance among your entrails."

Alice walked back into the circle of firelight.

"Plan B has arrived," Thomas whispered in her ear. "Shall I release them?"

"Yes."

Suddenly, a hundred tiny horns sounded in the darkness. The Brownies had arrived.

A pair of Brownies wearing patchwork camouflage scrounged, no doubt, from the desert floor, appeared on the branch above her. One of them belched loudly. She couldn't tell which.

"We shall release you!" To her eyes, it appeared as if a cigarette butt pierced by a pine needle were speaking. A flash of steel, then another, as the cigarette butt and the tin-foil gum-wrapper beside it, took turns hacking away at the ropes securing her hands.

Around the bonfire, chaos reigned.

Tiny arrows, each no longer than a toothpick though sharp as a razor, flooded the air in waves. The robed people were dancing around like spiders on a hot plate, knees pumping, arms flailing around their heads. The good news? They weren't chanting anymore. The bad news? Alice stood stock still, face aglow, eyes burning with hatred. Those eyes were fixed on Charisma.

"You need to hurry," she told the cigarette butt. "I must have my hands free."

"Yes ma'am!" the cigarette butt replied. Or maybe it was the gum-wrapper. Brownies and their asinine rules about staying hidden!

When she looked at Alice again, the child closed the distance between them in the blink of an eye. That same moment, the rope snapped and the weight of her body slammed down on shaky legs. She stood only a second before her legs gave out and her knees hit the sand.

"*Impedi!*" Charisma shouted, hand outstretched before her. Alice tried to move forward, slamming into the shield.

"Your magics are weak and pitiful," Alice said with that same, deep voice she'd used before.

"Enough to stop you where you stand."

"Is that what you think? That you've stopped me? With these insects?"

"No, I stopped *them* with insects. For you, I figure I'll use magic. *Incendi!*"

Alice swatted the fire away with her left hand, punched through the shield with her right, and sent Charisma tumbling backwards down the hill onto the desert floor.

"You were foolish to place yourself in my path."

Charisma groaned. She'd managed to roll with the blow, but now coarse sand congregated in every orifice and crevice of her naked body. Rocks had cut jagged slashes along her skin that burned brighter than they should have. The sounds of battle were muffled here, and the only light came from the pale moon on the far horizon.

Alice glowed like a ghost. She stood fifty paces away, yet her voice sounded as close as if she stood beside Charisma.

"As I recall, you were the one standing in the middle of the road. Technically, you were in my path."

Charisma reached up and pushed her black curls away from her ear, using the movement to check if the earbud were still there. It wasn't. Silently cursing, she knew there would be no help.

"Mortal children playing with fire. What did you hope to accomplish here? Sneak the Grimoire to that ridiculous little bookstore? Did you believe that would protect it? Keep it out of my reach?"

"Bigger, scarier things than you have tried to breach those walls. The book would've been safe enough. Still will be, when we're done here and I finish what I started."

"You don't even know what I am, mortal."

With a roar, Alice's head snapped back, mouth wide. Darkness sank down upon her as if leaking from the sky above. Deeper and deeper it grew until a shape a hundred feet tall began to take form. Massive curved horns on a jet-black head above a thick neck. Muscular arms spread wide, ending in three-finger-clawed hands. Cloven feet stomped the ground while a snake-like tail whipped and slashed at the air. As the creature reared up, a set of wings expanded from its back, beating at the wind. A foul smell washed over Charisma, a combination of rotting meat and sulfur. The stench of the thing made her eyes water. It bellowed and the sands vibrated beneath her. The only color in the otherwise black form, were the pulsing red veins in the wings, arms and legs, and the yellowed eyes and claws.

"Am I supposed to be impressed?"

The creature roared again. It took one step forward. She saw no choice. Charisma stood up on shaky legs, threw her own head back and managed an octave higher than the beast.

Silver mist rose from her mouth, expanding quickly in the sky above her. A shape began to form here, too. Silver scales stood out upon an elongated serpentine body. Clawed hands and feet were dwarfed by the long tail and wings. Her head was narrow, reptilian eyes set below a proud ridge and above a wide nose.

The dragon bellowed, and the mountains shook. Alice lay where the demon left her. The dragon bent down, lifted Charisma from the ground and placed her beneath a ragged tree for shelter.

"Dragon-kin," breathed the demon. "We need not be enemies. Long have our kind cooperated. The human world can be shared between us."

"You mistake me," the dragon said, her voice a melody on the wind. "I am human first, dragon second. Ever shall I stand against those who would do this world harm."

The demon looked down at Charisma's human body. "You marked the body not to keep me out—"

"—But to keep me *in*."

The dragon opened her mouth and spat ice and snow at the demon. Enraged, it fell back, skin sizzling like bacon in the pan. Holding its hand out to the side, a sword of fire formed. With a quick motion, it raised the sword high as if to strike. The dragon leapt into the air, wings beating with the force of a tornado. Sand and dirt slammed into the demon like a wall, staggering it back. Again the dragon spat ice and snow, concentrating the blast on the demon's head and torso, burning away the black flesh, enraging it.

Turning, the demon took several steps before leaping into the air, wings flapping frantically to gain altitude. The dragon shot up after it. Spiraling at a thousand feet, the demon sent a line of fire down the length of its sword, slicing down, forcing the dragon to veer left and away. Pulling her wings in, she dove to gain momentum. The desert landscape rushed up at her. She arched her back, snapping her wings out and gliding a hundred feet off the ground. Balls of fire began to rain from above. One slammed into her shoulder. Shrieking in pain, she danced back and forth to avoid the rest.

As quick as she could, the dragon began to climb. "*Tempestas*," she muttered, pushing her will out before her. Clouds formed and rolled, filling the sky around her in a heartbeat and shrouding her in darkness. "*Simulacrum*," she whispered. A dragon-shape sped off in a straight line through the clouds. Pulling her wings in again, she dove through the cloud cover until the desert floor appeared again. She corkscrewed and retraced her flight, keeping just below the clouds.

There was no way to know for sure if the demon fell for her ruse. Pumping her wings, she went into a vertical climb and didn't stop until she broke through the cloud cover. Spinning round, her eyes searched the sky. The demon had continued along her previous flight-path, raining fire down upon the wisp.

Again she climbed, rising higher and higher until she leveled off a thousand feet above the clouds. The winds helped keep her aloft as she glided along, closing the distance to her adversary. When her instincts told her she was close enough, she dove. Folding her wings in against her body, she shot forward like an arrow. Her eyes locked onto the target easily enough, its broad, dark shape contrasted against the clouds. Bright flashes announced another blast of fire slicing down at her doppelganger.

Waiting for her moment was difficult. Too soon would announce her presence and possibly get her killed. Too late and she could miss the mark entirely, which could also result in her swift death at the hands of the demon. The wind rushing in her ears, her mouth and eyes—so long since she'd taken flight, soared far above the earth, she allowed herself a moment to enjoy it. If she were honest with herself, she missed this.

Banishing such thoughts, she knew the moment had come. Unfolding her wings by half brought her underbelly up. Her claws and fangs glistened in the moonlight. The demon became aware of her too late to act. She roared as she slammed into its back, driving her claws deep into muscle and wing. Her teeth dug into the soft flesh of its neck, jaw working them deeper and deeper. Thick, oily blood filled her mouth.

The demon cried out in rage and frustration as they tumbled down, locked in a bitter embrace. The dragon kept hold with one clawed hand and two feet, while using her free hand to tear and rip at the beast's wing and back. She used her barbed tail to stab it in the torso, over and over. They spun together, demon trying to break free while dragon refused to be shaken. She raked her claws down its arm, forcing it to release the fiery sword. She bit deeper into its neck, causing it to bellow in pain. She shredded the tendons and muscles at the base of its wing, robbing it of flight forever more.

Spinning brought the desert floor into stark focus, rushing up at them faster than she thought possible. Seconds now, heartbeats, and they would be broken upon the sands. Rending away a mouthful of flesh and muscle, she pushed against the demon, releasing her grip and pumping her wings. *Too late! I need altitude.* Before she could gain any, the demon's good hand grabbed onto her ankle. The weight pulled her down as the ground rushed up. Her tail whipped, slamming into its shoulder again and again, digging into the wound there, and forcing it to release her.

She extended her wings to their full length, trying to glide, to soar. The demon smashed into the desert floor feet first, flames exploding out with a hiss, licking at everything nearby that could burn. The dragon glided and pumped, trying to move away. For a moment, she thought she had succeeded—her wings carried her away from the ensuing volcano of fire and heat. Her angle was off, though, her momentum too great. She plowed into the desert sands, and the world melted away.

"We have brought you the Vessel."

The dragon opened one eye. The Brownies had constructed a litter. Charisma lay on top. She looked so peaceful lying there, empty eyes staring up at the stars. How long ago had she fallen in love with the child? A hundred years? A thousand? The dragon tasted the air, a quick flick of her tongue. Charisma had many wounds. Such was the delicate nature of the human body. Still, given time, the dragon could heal these wounds, just as she always had. Her own would take far, far longer. She longed to reach out to Charisma, stroke her hair, but the strength eluded her.

"Thank you," she said to the bottle-cap standing before her. "And the other?"

"Buried per your instructions, Great One. We also brought this." An assembly of leaves, twigs, plastic bottle caps, and cheese wrappers brought the Grimoire before her. "The humans all fled before us."

"What of the demon?"

"Gone, Great One. It burned as bright as the sun for many hours, then it was no more. It left a blackened hole where it fell."

"Nothing will grow there for a generation or more," she said.

All the Brownies grumbled at this. She smiled despite herself.

"You have done well," she said. "Now, give me a moment."

"You heard the Great One!" the bottle-cap shouted. As she closed her eye, she assumed they would leave her alone. Never easy, this part. Opening her eye again, she stared up at the stars, so crisp, so bright. It would be a long time before she soared among them again. Too much work to be done.

With a deep sigh, she began the incantation, speaking the words that would change her once again.

Charisma woke with the sun. Every part of her body ached. She could still feel the rush of the wind in her face, the roar of it in her ears. The part of her that was the dragon rested now. Thinking of it too much pained her, as it always did. She contented herself in knowing that they had done great good here this night.

Rolling onto her side, she saw a box lying a foot or two away. On it sat the Grimoire. On that sat her earbud.

She set the book and earbud aside, opening the box. Giggling with delight, she pulled the clothing out and got dressed. The sun was just starting to peek up over the horizon, but it would soon be very hot, and one did not walk around in the desert naked unless one wished to become some form of jerked meat. Blue jeans, shirt, socks, and boots. Not the most fashionable attire, but what could one expect from Brownies?

"Thomas?" she asked, fitting the earbud back in place.

"Oh thank God!" he replied. "Those little—"

"Ah-ah-ah," she interrupted. "Language."

"Fine. *Plan B* refused to tell me anything except that you were safe."

"Which I am. The book as well."

"They demanded fruit punch."

"Oh, good *God!* The flat will be rendered uninhabitable for weeks." She sighed. The little buggers would throw themselves a week-long party, thoroughly trashing the place. They had probably saved her life, so she could live with a *little* inconvenience. Besides, this sort of situation is exactly why maid services were invented. "Any word from Ezra?"

"No."

She sighed again. Turning round, she wondered aloud, "Which way to go?" The sun caught the glint of metal. Crossing a dozen feet, she began to laugh.

"Is that amusing?"

"No," she said. "Brownies are amusing." Staring down at the giant metal arrow made of bits and scraps scrounged, no doubt, from the desert floor, she shook her head. "I guess I'm heading north. Keep trying Ezra. I want this book under lock and key as soon as possible."

"I'll have a car waiting for you at the nearest town."

"Something sporty, I hope."

"You are in the middle of the Nevada desert. I don't think we have a lot of options."

"Do your best. I'll also need a new iPod loaded with my favorite songs from the server. I'm in a *Wilbury* mood."

"Are you ever going to tell me what happened out there?"

The sun, already hot and bright, rose in the sky. The day would be long. Smiling to herself, Charisma began to walk. "I think these jeans really accentuate my butt."

Thomas choked.

With Peter out of pocket for a while,
  it is good to have young Justin around.
I am not as young as I once was.

  Ha! I am as young as I wish to be.
Having an extra pair of hands is convenient,
though. EF

A Poor Fellow Soldier

by J.T. Evans

Justin trudged against blowing snow. Only four blocks separated the University of Chicago's Regenstein Library and his small apartment, but the march against the wind made it feel like miles. An early October storm had moved in three days ago and showed no signs of letting up. Even in the best of times, the graduate student hated the trip home. Barely able to afford his tuition, the skinny young man from south Texas shared his apartment with five other students. His parents told him it was part of the "college experience." *They don't understand the challenges of life in twenty-seventeen! They graduated college in the last millennium, after all!*

With thoughts of his upcoming thesis topic bouncing around his mind, Justin kept his head down and wished the teacher's assistant stipend would somehow triple. If that miracle happened, he'd move out in an instant and find his own apartment.

Maybe I should just get another job.

The laughable thought competed for attention as he reminded himself of his research paper on the former Templar stronghold of La Couvertoirade in southern France. A specialist in Templar architecture, he had chosen to write a paper about the little-known fortress city built during the twelfth and thirteenth centuries. Justin felt like a fool for selecting such an obscure and sparsely populated region for his research. The historical texts and modern accountings of the area were almost nonexistent. The main reason he picked the location over all others was because his father had proposed to his mother at the town square.

Justin's stomach rumbled as he crossed Woodlawn Avenue. Slapping at his slender frame through the thick jacket only resulted in another growl issuing forth. The student shook his head at his plight. He knew he would find no food at the apartment, and he did not relish warming up in a nearby diner only to have to face the blowing winter again. Besides, he couldn't afford the meal.

Continuing homeward, Justin decided to risk finding a slice of three-day-old pizza that would have the flavor of cardboard and the consistency of chalk. The nourishment, no matter how horrific, might put him in a better mood. Stumbling through the snow, his feet finally carried him the last block to the corner of Kimbark Avenue and 57th Street. His apartment stood at the intersection over an abandoned bookstore.

Looking up to ensure he headed toward the right door, he fumbled for his key card. Three steps short of the narrow green door, Justin stopped. The faded sign that once proclaimed, "57th Street Books," had been replaced with a new sign painted with the holographic paint that had become all the rage for advertisement in the past two years. Oddly enough, the store's proprietor chose to depict black, wooden boards aged with weather and time instead of three dimensional moving neon characters. Old English script covered the boards, and a lifelike gargoyle perched on the corner of the sign.

Squinting through the snowflakes bombarding his blue eyes, Justin made out the phrase, "Librorum Taberna." Ignoring the squall attempting to tear his feet from the sidewalk, he mentally ran through the phrase. His historical and archaeological studies put him through a series of Ancient Greek and Latin courses. To no one in particular, he said, "Librorum is 'books.' That's the easy one. Taberna is strange. I think it means 'hovel' or 'small store' or something like that. Not commonly used. So, I'm looking at a 'book hovel' or a 'small bookstore.'" Eyeballing the doorway leading to his apartment and the new bookstore's entrance, Justin made the easy choice and entered the shop.

A small bell hanging from the door frame chimed warmly as Justin crossed the threshold. He couldn't help but crack a smile at the anachronistic charm of the sound. So many people now used remote sensors, heads up displays, and motion detectors to signal when a customer entered an establishment. Technological advances in the early twenty-first century felt so impersonal to the young graduate student. His studies of history in real ink-and-paper books offset the steady intrusion of technology into everyday life.

Justin closed his eyes as the door swung shut behind him, and he breathed in deep through his frozen nose. Smells of the slow decay of ink, paper and glue soothed his ragged nerves. The warmth of the shop helped as well, and he stopped shivering almost instantly. The exposed skin of his face sensed the perfect levels of humidity and temperature used to keep the deterioration of the books to a minimum.

"Ah, a customer! Taking refuge from the storm, young man?"

The grating sound of a two-pack-a-day voice startled Justin, and he stepped away from the counter on his left. With wide eyes, Justin turned to the person greeting him. An ancient man with yellowed hair peered down from behind the raised counter. He lifted a finger to scratch his crooked nose as he arched a bushy eyebrow in the direction of the student. "Well? You freeze your tongue off out there?"

After a long moment, the Justin stammered, "Y-y-yes. Well, no, that is. Sorry."

"No need to apologize." Thin lips spread in a smile that revealed large teeth the same smoke-stained yellow color of the man's hair.

Feeling like he was an intruder in the hallowed shelves of the bookstore, Justin asked, "Do you mind if I look around?"

The elderly man waved a bone-thin arm in the direction of the stacks. "Help yourself. That's why you're here, isn't it? Take all the time you need."

Justin took a step toward the rows of bookshelves, and noticed two small signs on the counter between haphazard piles of books. The first read "Ezra Finfrock, Proprietor" handwritten in neat calligraphy on parchment. The other sign featured red and white paint on a thin sheet of plastic stating, "Now Hiring."

Justin stopped in his tracks.

The old man arched his eyebrow again. "Having trouble walking, there?"

Shaking his head, Justin looked up and asked, "May I please speak with Mr. Finrock?"

"You may, and you are."

Justin pointed at the "Now Hiring" sign. "I see you're looking to hire someone. I'd like to apply for a position."

The eyebrow arched again. "Oh? Any position? There are a few available, but I get the feeling you'd be more interested in the clerk position than the janitorial one."

Despite his appearance, something about Ezra's attitude put Justin at ease. "Yes, sir. I'd love to work in a bookstore selling paper-and-ink books."

A puzzled look crossed the proprietor's face. "Are there any other kind?"

Where has this guy been the past decade? Justin kept composed and didn't show his confusion. "I wish ebooks were never invented. Sure, they're easy to search and facts can be found very quickly, but there's nothing like the feel of a solid book in your hands. I think my favorite part of holding a book is the smell and knowing the ink sitting in the fibers of the paper will eventually fade to nothingness if it's not properly taken care of. Digital data can be created easily, but never seems to be lost the way ....'

Ezra's wide smile caused the graduate student's rant about the coldness of ebooks to fade away.

Justin cleared his throat. "Sorry. I just get so passionate about books."

Ezra stepped out from around the counter and down to the main floor level. Justin realized the short man appeared to be nothing more than a bag of bones and sinew. *A light breeze would blow this fellow away.*

Ezra extended a thin arm and Justin accepted the handshake. He kept his grip firm, but not tight enough to crack the old man's bones. Justin felt each and every joint in the scrawny man's hand. After releasing his grip, Ezra said, "You're hired. I need people like you in my store."

With furrowed eyebrows, Justin asked, "Don't I need to fill out an application, do some paperwork for taxes, have references checked, and stuff like that?"

The owner of the store waved a dismissive hand. "I don't operate like that. You'll work what hours you can. I'll cover the rest. At the end of the week, I'll give you double minimum wage for each hour you work. It'll come from the till, and we'll call it even. How does that sound to you?"

Justin felt like he had just struck it rich with tax-free income so close to campus and his apartment. He fought to resist the urge to jump up and down. With happiness shining through his smile, he said, "That's fine with me, sir."

The owner waved his hand in the air again. "Please. Just call me Ezra. Now, tell me what hours you can work, and I'll put it into the schedule."

After entering the details of Justin's hours into a ledger, a lengthy tour of book placement within the stacks followed. Each time the graduate student thought they reached the end of the store, another turn revealed more rows of books. Being an archeology student, Justin had a great sense of space and direction. He created a mental map of the store as Ezra explained where things went on the shelves. The layout Justin put together in his head didn't make sense. The sections of the store fit together just fine, but the size of Librorum Taberna seemed too large to be true. It must have consumed most of a city block, but from the outside, the store didn't look to be much larger than most of the coffee shops dotting the neighborhoods around the University of Chicago campus.

Putting aside any misgivings about the layout, Justin focused on Ezra's explanations. The proprietor offered no reasoning for where things went, but moved through the books as if each were a shrine to some lost god. Reverence and awe filled Ezra's voice as he described each section of books.

As the two men made their way back to the front of the store, Justin asked, "Do you also purchase books from people that bring them in?"

"Of course! While I get many treasures from the sale of private collections and at auction, I also find the rare gem in the trove of tomes brought in through the front door. If someone wishes to sell a book to us, we offer one-quarter of the cover price in cash. If the book is rare enough or old enough to not have a proper price printed on the back cover, then offer what you think is fair. Make sure to leave some room for profit, though."

Astonished at the authority given him, Justin blurted, "So you trust me to buy books on your behalf?"

"Most certainly! You seem to have a real passion for an almost forgotten art. I trust you entirely to do what you think best for the store. I wouldn't hire you otherwise."

Pride filled the young man's chest and warmed his frozen core. Once the tour finished, he shook the shop owner's hand again. "I'll be back bright and early tomorrow morning to start work."

Flashing his yellowed teeth in a wide smile, Ezra answered back, "Excellent! A worker who truly wants to come in and work on a Saturday morning. I'll see you then."

Justin worked through Saturday and saw very few customers. Many of them sought refuge from the raging storm, but a few bought books. The free time between guiding customers through the stacks gave him a chance to work on his thesis. He hoped for a steady influx of customers to keep him busy and take his mind from his worries, but at the same time, Justin felt thankful for the time to get his paper done. Even though he knew the date, he kept checking the calendar on his smart phone. *Only twenty-one days, counting today, until I defend my thesis in front of Professor Kline and his department. I can do this. I know I can.*

When Sunday rolled around, the same pattern of customers and gawkers continued. During a particularly slow time, Justin's smart phone chimed to inform him of a new email. He pulled the phone from its belt holster and read the email. As his eyes scanned the tiny text, he began to sweat and tremble. When finished, the young man dropped the phone to the counter and fell back into a nearby chair. "I can't believe Professor Kline would do this to me. He just shaved a week off of my schedule. I defend on the twentieth, not the twenty-seventh! I hope his family emergency isn't just some lame excuse to leave in the middle of the semester."

To no one in particular, Justin complained, "I've also got some mysteries to resolve surrounding the missing top two floors of the stronghold in La Couvertoirade. If I could find the right resource...."

For the next ten minutes, Justin rolled around many different plans of action in his head. He decided to skip returning to the library for more research, because he felt Librorum Taberna could offer him as many resources on the topic of Templar buildings as any other source. He just hoped Ezra didn't mind his thumbing through the merchandise during the down times.

Bounding from behind the counter and almost running through the stacks, Justin came to the area dedicated to the Freemasons and their buildings. Knowing the stories and rumors that the Freemasons owed their roots to the Knights Templar, Justin started in this section. After looking through the tomes for close to an hour he came up empty, so he moved on to the Templar section of the store. All the while, he kept part of his attention focused on listening for the bell on the door.

The large collection of books on the Templars astounded Justin. It seemed as if Ezra had an intellectual fetish for the mysterious religious order. Three entire bookcases held nothing but books about The Poor Fellow-Soldiers of Christ and of the Temple of Solomon. Justin began his search through the massive number of tomes in hopes of finding more details about the stronghold at La Couvertoirade.

He skimmed the spines hoping for something to jump out at him. Titles scrolled past his eyes to no avail. Numerous leather-bound books contained no title at all. Justin mentally marked where each one resided and promised himself to return to them if the more modern texts provided no information. He occasionally pulled a book from a shelf, checked the table of contents and index, and returned the book to its resting spot with a heavy sigh.

Lost in the research and smell of the musty tomes, he lost track of time until he heard Ezra's polite cough behind him. Turning to face the proprietor, Justin presented the book in front of him as if to shield himself from an angry tirade. He had only been on the job for two days and felt like he was about to be fired for dereliction of duty.

A smile crept over the older man's face revealing his straight, yellow teeth. The smile turned to a grin and eventually to a deep-throated, raspy laugh. "I say! You are most engrossed in what you are looking for. Don't worry, I ... assisted ... the two young men. Is this why you so eagerly asked for a position here? To plunder my knowledge? Or are you just that much in love with my small collection of ink and paper?"

Justin stammered for a moment. "I'm so sorry, I didn't hear anyone come in. It's just that I'm in a tight spot and need to find a reference for a remote stronghold the Templars built in La Couvertoirade. It's in southern France."

"Ah. I see. In a bit of a pickle are you? Is this for your research paper you mentioned?"

"Yes, sir … er … Ezra."

"Well then. Things are quite slow right now. Perhaps I can help you with your search. The best sources are those written by people that were actually there during the times when the building was used for its original purpose. I'm sure anything modern, like the book you're shielding yourself with, is nothing more than a tourist guide or a visitor's accounting."

Justin looked down at the book in his hands and realized Ezra spoke the truth. In his desperation for information, the young man had grabbed anything from the shelves that looked promising. "What do you suggest? Do you have a book that may help me out?"

Ezra patted the student on the shoulder with a spindly hand. "I can do better than that for you. I have a collection of rare books coming in to add to this section. They will arrive in a few days. I'll be out of town, so you will need to catalog and shelve the books. Feel free to pull any of interest to you for your research and use them for as long as you need."

Astounded at the generosity, Justin blurted, "My paper is due in under two weeks. When will these books arrive?"

Ezra arched a bushy eyebrow. "You'll have plenty of time to write your thesis based off of the books. Trust me. The collection will be here on Friday." The proprietor paused and then asked, "You're not the superstitious type are you? That is Friday the thirteenth after all."

Justin laughed at the implication. He knew the story of the origins of the Friday the thirteenth legend. It all started with the day King Phillip of France arrested and imprisoned a vast majority of the Knights Templar, October the thirteenth, 1307. Justin realized that this very same day was coming up next Friday, but removed from the original event by seven-hundred and ten years. Justin responded to Ezra's question. "No. I'm not superstitious at all. I'll be here on Friday to receive the books and get them into the store. You're sure they'll help me?"

"I'm positive."

Justin worked the rest of the week in a daydream. He spent many hours at Librorum Taberna. The pace of the customers picked up with the abatement of the storm. He itched to get back to the Templar section of the store, but restrained himself. Deep down, he somehow knew Ezra's promise of help arriving on Friday would bear fruit. Between guiding customers through the maze of the over-sized store and stocking books arriving via courier, Justin had just enough time to work on his thesis in preparation for the miracle help arriving in a few days.

Finally, Friday the thirteenth rolled around. Justin found himself hesitant to leave the front counter in case the courier arrived. The day wore on and the young man found dismay and disappointment growing in his chest. *Perhaps Ezra was wrong. Perhaps the courier was delayed. Maybe nothing is going to show up at all. My thesis is due in a week!*

As a customer left with his purchase, the young man heard the distinctive clip-clop sound of horseshoes on pavement. Chicago was one of the few major metropolitan cities to maintain a mounted police force in this day of advanced technology, so Justin felt compelled to walk to the front door to watch the amazing animal march by the store.

To his surprise, two men mounted on a large horse stopped at the front door of Librorum Taberna. Both wore white tunics, leather breeches and black riding boots. As the man in the rear dismounted, a flash of red caught Justin's eye, but only when the other man on the horse turned, did Justin see the emblem of the red cross on the left breast of his tunic.

He looked around to see if anyone else reacted to the strange sight, but the street was empty.

How odd. There's always someone *out here.*

The dismounted man pulled a heavy set of saddlebags from the horse's back and walked around the steed to approach Justin.

The man spoke with a thick, French accent. "I believe these are the books you are waiting for?"

Still not sure what was going on, Justin robotically held out a hand to take the saddlebags. The incredible weight of the books and leather satchel caught the young man off guard. He stumbled a step and then caught himself physically and mentally. "Yes. I have been waiting for these. What do we owe you for the books?"

The man dressed as a Knight Templar knelt on one knee. "Just promise to me, oh kind sir, you will use the knowledge within to bring glory to Christ and restore the good name of the Poor Fellow-Soldiers of Christ and of the Temple of Solomon. Both have been smudged in the books of history over the past seven centuries. Can you do this?"

Not knowing how to properly respond, Justin did as he had read about in his history texts and motioned for the knight to rise. "I promise to do everything within my meager abilities to bring truth to the world through the knowledge you delivered today."

The knight rose to stand before Justin. "That is all I can ask of you. Go with God." With the final declaration, the man strode back to his place in the rear of the horse and mounted with the help of the other rider.

Justin stood in the fading sunlight of the cool October evening and watched both riders advance down 57th Street toward the University of Chicago campus. After a few moments, the glare of the setting sun caused the young man to look away. When he shaded his eyes and looked again, the two men and their mount had vanished.

Shaking his head at the strange turn of events, Justin hefted the saddlebags with a smile. Ezra had come through after all, though in his own strange way. With hope lifting his spirits, the young man walked back into the bookstore to see what he now held.

With great care, Justin untied the laces on the bags and opened them to find four thick tomes waiting. Unsure of the age, quality or value of the books, Justin left them in the saddlebags and ran to the washroom to clean the oils and dirt from his hands. After the quick but thorough washing, the young man returned to his prizes and slipped them from the bags. He laid them all out next to each other with wonderment in his eyes. The smell of ancient leather and thick paper coupled with the distinctive odor of mold wafted up from the books. Justin was not put off by the scent. The faintness of the smell meant little damage to the papers themselves had occurred. It was most likely in the folds of the binding instead.

Two of the books were identical in appearance with no titles on their covers of light tan leather. Small clasps of brass, tarnished to green held the tomes closed. Justin decided to leave those two for later since the covers of the other two books held embossed titles.

The third book bore the title, "*Occulta Veritas Monastica.*"

Justin said to no one in particular, "Interesting title. Either the Templars truly were a cult, or this is some hidden truth about the order revealed in the book. I bet it's the second one." The student squinted at the cover as he translated the Latin.

After a few moments, he came up with a probable translation. Justin mumbled, "The Hidden Truth of Religion. Yes. I think that's right."

Moving to the fourth book, Justin read the French title of "*Le Dernier Patron*" but couldn't translate it. He borrowed on his Latin expertise, but it only helped with the word "Patron" which Justin thought to mean "father" or something with a similar connotation.

Justin closed his eyes and ran a hand over the covers of all four books in hope of some divine guidance on which one to open first. God refused to whisper secrets in his ear, so he took the plunge and pulled "*Occulta Veritas*

Monastica" closer. With deliberate movements, he opened the cover. The creak of the leather binding, combined with the soft crackling of dried glue, made him pause after a few inches. He'd heard worse from other books, and his desperation for help on his thesis drove him forward.

After laying the cover wide open on the counter, Justin peered at the beautiful illumination of two men astride a single horse surrounded by the text, *"Non nobis Domine, non nobis, sed nomini tuo da gloriam."*

With a little concentration, the young student translated the saying and whispered the words, "Not to us, Lord, but to Your Name give the glory."

As if he were handling a newborn babe, Justin turned each page of the book. The paper revealed prayers in Latin on the left and, presumably, the same prayer in French on the right. The clear and precise text matched anything created since Gutenberg invented the printing press, but Justin knew the inscriptions and illuminations in the books were done by hand, using quill, ink and handmade paper.

Amazed at the sight before him, the young man couldn't help but turn page after page even though none of the information, chants, benedictions or rituals within would help him with his thesis. Despite knowing the book would provide no further help, Justin couldn't help himself. He gaped at the beautiful illustrations, the gilded edges of the paper and the precise notations of text throughout the book.

While he had never been particularly religious, Justin was forced to stop and stare at a powerful rendition of the crucifixion of Jesus Christ which depicted angels singing in Heaven through a cloudy sky and the rays of a setting sun. The crying figure of the Virgin Mary lying in a pool of Christ's blood struck Justin with the greatest impact of everything else he saw in the picture. Shaking off the awe, the student swallowed hard and continued to gently work his way through the book.

With the final page turned, he closed the tome and exhaled hard. He had just looked through the official prayer book of the Knights Templar. The collection of paper, ink, leather and glue before him was priceless to historians, religious experts and especially the Vatican archivists.

Riding on a high of adrenaline and wonder, Justin pushed the prayer book aside and pulled *"Le Dernier Patron"* closer to himself. As he lifted the cover listening for the tell-tale groan and crack of an ancient book being opened, he felt the strong whoosh of a hot breeze blow across his hands and arms. He dropped the cover closed and recoiled from the tome. A puff of smoke expelled from the pages as the leather binding fell shut.

What is going on? Was this book somehow sealed or caught in a fire at some point?

Braving the book again, Justin used an extended fingertip to pry open the cover. Again, a strong wind blew out of the book along with a steady stream of smoke and small flakes of ash. Maintaining his ragged nerves, he continued to lift the cover until he opened it halfway.

At that point, a loud cough exploded from the tome and the cover flew open to its fullest extent. Justin leaped from his chair, knocking it over backwards, and moved away from the book. Smoke, burning ash and small bits of flame poured from the book and collected on the floor instead of rising into the air. Afraid for every scrap of paper, parchment and novel stashed within the hallowed halls of Librorum Taberna, he looked around for a fire extinguisher and found none within easy sight.

Particulates and embers flowing from the book coalesced into a smoke-hazed form. The human-like shape built up from the floor to a height of about six feet. The smoke and fire flowed into the form as it gathered itself into a more solid appearance.

The smoke-shrouded human forming before his eyes shook and shuddered several times as more burning embers and flames flowed into the body. In under a minute, the book stopped expelling hot gas and the last of the fire poured into the man standing before Justin.

The shocked graduate student forced himself to break his gaze away from the smoky form and glanced at the front door. Contemplating running from the shop, Justin shook his head and decided to stand his ground. Ezra entrusted him with the safekeeping of the store and its contents, and Justin would not break that trust despite how strange things became. Steeling himself for anything he could imagine, Justin squared his shoulders and stared hard as if issuing a challenge.

He had a sense he had seen the man before, but could not place him. The long, curly, gray hair flowing from around a balding pate complemented the man's mustache and forked beard. Piercing brown eyes glared at the young man as a smoky cough exploded from the man's lungs. A simple tunic and cloak of unbleached cotton bearing the red insignia of the Knights Templar covered the man's torso. He wore a thick leather belt from which a sword hung, and Justin saw bits of chain mail peeking out from beneath the man's clothing.

The Templar scrutinized Librorum Taberna before mumbling something in what sounded like French. It felt to Justin the man's gaze went through him, as if he weren't there at all.

Justin cleared his throat to gain the man's attention. "I'm sorry. I don't understand what you just said."

The man turned his glare to the young graduate student and repeated his statement.

Justin shook his head and furrowed his brow to show he didn't understand what was just said.

The smoke-built man switched to Old English and repeated his statement.

Justin picked out a few words of the sentence, but could not follow the rapid-fire speech of the Templar. Hoping to be able to communicate with the strange man that appeared from within the book, the student said in a loud voice, "Do you speak English?"

The Templar sighed before very slowly speaking in Latin. "Do speak the tongue of the Romans?"

Justin patted himself on the chest and said, also in Latin, but a little too loudly, "I'm Justin Louvier."

The Templar winced at the volume of the student's voice, but at least they had established the common language of Latin through which to communicate.

The knight's response to Justin's loudness forced him to lower his voice and continue in a more conversational tone. "Who are you?"

With a flourish of his cloak, the Templar intoned as if from a ritual, "*Je m'appelle Jacques ... Pardonez-moi,* I am still accustomed to speaking with the beauty of my native language." The man cleared his throat as if preparing himself for something painful before continuing to speak. "My name is Jacques de Molay, Grandmaster of the Poor Fellow-Soldiers of Christ and of the Temple of Solomon."

Justin nearly fell over in astonishment. Through the sudden rush of adrenaline hammering through his body, he managed to stay upright with one hand on the counter to steady himself. He was unable to respond to the Grandmaster in any intelligible manner, so he settled for swaying on his feet and staring with wide eyes at the man standing before him.

"Is this how you greet your guests?"

Justin recovered his wits, but still stared at de Molay. "My apologies, Sir Knight. I was not expecting a visitor of your stature or ... method of arrival." A million questions burned through his mind, but the young man decided not to bombard his newly-arrived guest with them. There would be plenty of time for them later.

"Apology accepted. Now, provide some details, *s'il vous plait.* Where am I? When am I? How did I get here?"

Justin motioned out the front windows of the shop. "You're in Chicago, Illinois, which is a large city in the United States of America, but of course you wouldn't know where that is. The New World wasn't even discovered when you were burned at the stake."

"New World?" The obvious puzzlement in the question made Justin realize the need for further explanation.

"The New World is, well, another set of continents across the Atlantic Ocean from Europe and Africa."

"I see. Go on."

Justin replayed the questions in his head and started answering the next one. "The year is two-thousand, seventeen." After a moment's pause, he added, "In the year of our Lord."

"Do you mean to say that I've been in Purgatory for the past seven hundred years?"

Justin nodded.

De Molay looked astonished at the length of time that had passed since he was slow-roasted to death over a fire. "Well then, my last question for the moment is this. How did I arrive at your fine establishment?"

Justin shrugged. "You were delivered by two men dressed as Templars and riding a horse. There are three other books over there on the counter that came with the one you exploded out of. When I opened the book entitled, *'Le Dernier Patron,'* you ... you ... well ... smoke and fire came out and turned into you!"

"Merveilleux!" roared the Templar Grandmaster.

Suddenly looking around, as if looking for eavesdroppers, de Molay spoke in just above a whisper, "My order has done well and brought our greatest treasures to you. They were under orders given by me just before my arrest to keep these four books secreted away until such a time they believed they could find someone to restore the good name and purpose of the Templars to the world. Glory go with Christ! They did it!"

Justin wondered what the Grandmaster was talking about. He glanced down at the four books lying on the counter and back at the Templar. Amazement crept into Justin's voice. "What? Where? How? What can I do to help you?"

Laughing with a deep bellow, de Molay answered, "You can help restore the good name of the Knights Templar, of course. You must be a scholar of some sort in order to work among books. Let me tell you a tale of how we came to be."

Shaking his head, Justin cut off the Templar. "I don't know how I can be of any help. I just study ancient architecture and archaeological sites important to the Templars and write papers about them."

"Ah. I see." De Molay twisted one fork of his beard in his hand and looked at the ceiling as if pondering a great decision. After a long pause, the Grandmaster spoke. "Perhaps we can work out some sort of arrangement."

"Arrangement?"

"Yes. Of course. An arrangement. A deal. A bargain of sorts. As you surely know, the Templars are about more than just protecting pilgrims in the Holy Lands. We finance a great number of ventures and are powerful enough to create kingdoms, empires, guilds and so much more than mere armies."

Justin nodded in agreement.

The Grandmaster continued. "I will give you pertinent information about a site of your interest, and assist you in revealing the powerful truth about it. Then you put quill to parchment about a topic of my choosing. We'll alternate in this way until we're both satisfied the full truth about the knighthood is known to your modern world."

Justin's mind flashed to his unfinished thesis and the abandoned Templar stronghold. A smile spread across his face. "We have an agreement, and I know just the site I want to start with."

De Molay returned the smile and reached out his hand.

Justin grasped the Templar's forearm in the traditional manner of the knight's times.

After they released each other's arms, Jaques de Molay smiled. "Where do we begin?"

The young man returned the Grandmaster's smile. "La Couvertoirade."

The Grandmaster brushed past Justin to the counter holding the charred remains of *"Le Dernier Patron"* and the other three tomes. De Molay reverently picked up *"Occulta Veritas Monastica."* He turned through the pages and smiled as if greeting a long, lost friend. Lips fluttered and twitched as the Grandmaster read through the prayers. After several long minutes, the Templar crossed himself and stepped back from the book. He turned his back on Justin, sniffed hard and appeared to wipe a tear from his cheek.

Not wanting to intrude an obvious personal moment, the student stayed silent until de Molay recovered himself.

Turning back to face Justin, de Molay said in a thick voice, *"Pardonez-moi."* The Grandmaster cleared his throat and continued, "I've not seen or heard those prayers in many long centuries. I missed them."

This was when Justin realized just how long seven hundred years could be. "What was it like being trapped in the book?"

De Molay answered with a smile, though his eyes shone with passion. "Lonely. Honestly, I can't say I remember much. Like a quickly fading dream where I just felt ... alone and abandoned by my church. I can understand King Phillip's actions, but I never imagined Pope Clement was so deeply within the king's grasp. For seven hundred years, I've heard the whispers of people each time my knighthood was mentioned. The chatter became louder and louder with each passing century until it overwhelmed my senses. I hoped this day would come soon, and it has. I'm here. Let's talk about La Couvertoirade now. What about the fortress did you wish to know?"

Justin thought about the gaps in his thesis research for a moment. "The main keep now stands only a single story high. I've uncovered information about the second and third floors, but they are long gone. Were those floors intact during your time?"

"Very much intact. I assume you want me to tell you the secrets of the lost floors of the keep?"

A flash of panic jolted through Justin and he wiped his palms on his pants.

The Grandmaster saw Justin's jittery motions. "What is wrong?"

"The problem is that I have to have verifiable resources for all of my references. I can't claim to have interviewed a man that was burned at the stake seven hundred years ago!"

De Molay turned to the two unlabeled books. "I have a solution for you. These books contain the written histories of my knighthood. Surely you can use them as a reference and leave my name out of your writings?"

"If what you have to tell me is contained within those writings, I can use them."

Turning to the remaining two volumes, de Molay picked up the first and thumbed through it with great care. After skimming several sections, he closed the book and placed it back on the counter. "I believe what you are looking for can be found in the second volume." He then turned to the other book and carefully turned page after page.

Justin shuffled his feet back and forth in an effort to contain his nervous energy and subdue his excitement at what was about to be given to him.

"Ah! Here is the section on La Couvertoirade. Before I turn the book over to you, let me tell you what I remember of the beautiful countryside and the keep built to protect it."

The Grandmaster took a deep breath. "The first floor, as your studies have probably told you, housed the stables, barracks, dining hall, kitchens and other rooms to support a cadre of a dozen knights and close to three hundred pages and staff."

Justin nodded and remained silent with rapture.

De Molay looked up at the ceiling as a far-away look crossed his features. "The second floor was the bane to the staff. We were close enough to what remained in the Muslim lands in Hispania we dared not practice our movements in the open. You see, the wall around the fortress was still under construction and left us exposed. While the flooring was thick enough to support the stomping of men, it resounded throughout the lower levels of the keep like the worst thunder of a horse charge. The servants used the phrase 'tonnerre roulement' to describe our movements. Our rolling thunder gave a great deal of inspiration to our troops before entering battle in the Holy Land."

Justin raised his hand as if he were in a class and wanted to interrupt the professor, but didn't wait for permission to speak. "La Couvertoirade is a large building. Are you saying you used the *entire* second floor for troop movement and practice?"

"Everything except our horsemen. We discovered the hard way the floor was not sturdy enough to support a war horse." De Molay broke into laughter, and when he quieted his mirth, he said, "You should have heard the threats of the head cook. The horse fell through into the kitchen and in fright, pissed and shat all over everything. Had we not gotten to the kitchen when we did, we would have been feasting on that horse for a week!"

More guffaws followed his explanation and Justin couldn't help but laugh along with the Templar Grandmaster.

Once the two men gained control of themselves, Justin asked with a great deal of eagerness, "What was held on the third floor?"

De Molay glanced around the store again. After a moment,, he grabbed Justin by the collar of his shirt and pulled him close. In a quiet whisper that could barely be heard across the inches separating lips and ear, the knight said, "The Grail."

Justin's eyes flew wide open and he reeled back from the Grandmaster. Before he could blurt out what he had just heard, de Molay clapped a calloused hand over the student's mouth.

"Sshhhh …." When Justin recovered his wits, the knight released his hold.

Justin shook his head as if clearing cobwebs from its insides. "But? How? Where did it go? Why was it there? Why an entire floor?"

De Molay waved a hand in an effort to abate the flood of questions. Justin stopped talking, but his breathing still came in quick bursts as if he had just run a mile in heavy armor.

With another glance around Librorum Taberna, the Grandmaster said, "We hid the Grail there to keep it from falling into the hands of our enemies. La Couvertoirade was a small, almost unimportant, fortress. As for where the Grail went, I do not know, but would give almost anything to discover. As far as why it took an entire, large floor to contain a simple cup. Well. There was a maze of the deadliest traps and contraptions you could think of surrounding the Grail."

The Grandmaster smiled. "I'm certain you've heard tales the Freemasons gained their roots in the destruction of the Templars?"

"Of course. Who hasn't?"

"The truth lies much deeper. The roots of the Masonic Orders are intertwined with the discoveries the original nine knights made in the Temple of Solomon. Even I don't know everything about what was uncovered in their years in the temple, but I do know many relics of Christendom were found there. The Nail of the Left Hand, pieces of the True Cross, the Holy Grail and other things were found buried beneath the temple."

Justin couldn't wait to get back to his paper and write about everything he was learning on this day, but he continued to listen to avoid missing any important details.

The Grandmaster continued. "The original nine Templars knew they would have to build strongholds against attackers, infidels, heretics and perhaps even the Church itself to protect these relics from being destroyed, perverted or lost to time. They garnered their funds and the gold of many nobles along with the blessing of the Church to form a protective group for pilgrims in the Holy Land. This was all a guise. Their true purpose was to gather the greatest builders from the known world and create strongholds in which to keep their treasures."

With the silent mouthing of the word, "Wow," Justin waved for de Molay to continue.

"Craftsmen from all over the world were gathered back within the confines of the Temple of Solomon, where an open and free sharing of information was exchanged. All of the knowledge was gathered into tomes and scrolls for future generations to take advantage of. A secret brotherhood of builders from Egypt, Hispania, Italy, Germania, France, England, Scandanvia, Prussia and even as far as India and China were formed over the course of several years within the temple. This, my friend, is the start of the Order of Masons.

"We spent the next couple of centuries protecting these Relics from harm through guile, gold and construction. Alas, I feel we failed in our mission with our fall to King Phillip." De Molay hung his head as if the fall and shame of the Templars fell solely on his shoulders.

Justin reached out and patted the other man on the back in consolation. "It's not your fault men of power wanted more power and became greedy.

We've made an arrangement, remember? Once I finish with my thesis paper, we'll start rebuilding what the Templars once were. We'll find those lost Relics and restore them to their proper place. It won't be easy, but I think we can do it."

The Grandmaster raised his head and looked Justin square in the eyes. "If it is possible, then I wish to succeed. If it is not possible, then I will die trying."

Justin extended his hand to the Templar. "That's a motto I can get behind, but first I really need to finish up my thesis and defend it. That's only one week from today. Can we focus on my paper first?"

Jacques de Molay, Grandmaster of The Poor Fellow-Soldiers of Christ and of the Temple of Solomon, roared with laughter. When his mirth finally settled, he said, "Of course. We can handle your research with ease, and bring the glory of Christ back to the Templars!"

I don't like having to chase people all over creation just to make a point. Don't they know I have better things to do? Damn musicians never change. ET

Thief of Dreams

by Frances Burke

Johnny Cunningham stood smiling in the dim corridor of the motel, one arm slung over the top of a battered pay phone. He cradled the receiver against his shoulder as he brushed a lock of curly blond hair from his green eyes.

"Sure thing, sugar." He chuckled. "I'd love to stop by to pick you up, but you know how it is on tour. All we got is the van, and it's full of the guys' stuff. Why don't you come on down to the club? We can take your car and swing by a Denny's for something later."

He listened for a minute, his grin fading. "Sure, bring her along. Um, she's the one in jeans with the camouflage tank top?" The young man scowled as he mouthed, "Shit," while the girl on the other end of the conversation responded. "Yah, great personality." With an audible groan of disgust, he said, "No problem, maybe we can fix her up with Jojo." Silently he added *Connie and Jojo have a lot in common. They both looked like the dinners in Alpo ads.* He listened to the girl giggle as she held her hand over the receiver to pass this bit of information on to Connie.

His mouth twisted into a sour grimace. "No, the drummer's name is Bobby Ray. Jojo isn't exactly with the band. He, er, works for the club." Before she could ask, he continued, "Hey, sugar, I gotta go. We got a hot offer for a gig in Vegas, and we gotta work out the scheduling. Yeah, see you tonight, bye."

He hung up thinking he could lose Connie and the bouncer and then ....

"Johnny, we got to talk." Misty Rose leaned against the door of their room, her arms folded across her really excellent chest. Misty looked a lot like a shorter version of his niece's Barbie doll. *If blonde jokes were based in fact, she would have the IQ of a fruit fly.* She had an equally impressive voice, but even if she couldn't sing, she would have been a hit in the clubs they played.

"Now Misty, it's not what you're thinking. She's ah, she's got connections to—"

"Don't wear yourself out with plausible deniability, Johnny. That's not what we have to talk about. Well, not exactly." Misty nodded to their room. He followed, his mind searching for an excuse he hadn't used before.

A relative, she could be some sort of cousin. Did I use that one in Durango? No, that one was Mexican.

Misty sat on the sagging bed, pointing with one long red-tipped finger to the bench that still held his bag.

She doesn't quite look mad, just sort of determined. Maybe she only caught the end of the conversation.

He tried out his boyish grin, working the dimple to the max, as he shoved his things off and sat down, hands clasped between his knees like a kid in the principal's office.

"This is the end of the road, honey," she drawled. "You're gonna have to find yourself another roommate."

His mouth fell open in astonishment. "Misty, sugar, I can explain, honest!"

She actually laughed. "Better zip up your mouth, honey. You never know what might jump into it in a fleabag like this." She indicated the threadbare carpet and drab, formerly yellow walls.

She's laughing. It can't be too bad. She's got to be kidding. Relief began to surge.

"I'm quitting the band, Johnny. I'll be twenty-seven the end of next month and my biological clock is telling me it's time to git on back to Alabama. Find me some sweet young thing just back from Iraq and settle down to real life. I already got my old job back at The Beautiful Hairs Salon. I'm goin't git me an SUV, have a couple of kids and sing in the church choir."

The color drained from Johnny's face, the dimple forgotten. "But what about your career? What about us!"

"Oh, honey, I don't have a career. Sure I can sing, and I got the looks, but so do about a million other gals, n' looks don't last forever. What I don't have is ambition. It's been fun. You've been a kick, but it's time I move on with my life." Misty blew out a deep breath of relief.

Panic choked Johnny. "But what about us, baby? You know how I feel about you. We've been good together. You're my girl. You can't just walk away from this, what we have together."

At that she let out a peal of deep bubbling laughter. "Darlin', we don't have anything 'together' and, as for this, take a good look where we are. This dump is about half a click up from a cardboard box under a bridge. If Teller knew how to book us into a box, that's where we'd be tomorrow night." Her smile took on a look she might use with a not-too-bright child. "We've had a lot of fun together, and I just love you to death, but it's been a 'you scratch my itch and I scratch yours' kinda thing from the git-go. You know that's all it's ever been. What my daddy used to call sowing wild oats." She stood up to leave, smoothing down her tight black skirt. "I wouldn't have missed any of it for the world. But my mama didn't raise no stupid children. Well, maybe Cullen," she said with an impish smile.

Without Misty, the band didn't stand a chance. It would fold, and his career would go down the toilet. "Give me another chance." He gulped air like a gaffed fish. "I'll … we'll get married!" *Oh, shit, did I really say that?*

Misty walked to the door. "Now that would about the dumbest thing I could think of. When a girl marries, she's taking a mighty big gamble. With you, it wouldn't even be that. More like shooting craps, hoping to make thirteen." She came back to stand before him, put her hands on his shoulders and leaned down to kiss his forehead. She tilted her head and gave a slight frown. "You know, honey, I've never been able figure out if you really believe all that garbage you talk, or if even you just don't know where the bullshit ends and truth begins." Misty's pretty brow wrinkled still more. "If you really do mean what you've been saying, darlin', you're not just a dreamer, you know, you got a serious problem with reality."

She straightened, her eyes squinted in a smile. "By the way, I collected what you owe me for the last five or six rooms we shared from Teller. Consider everything else a gift. I'm catching the bus south first thing in the morning. Got my ticket, and I'm going home." Turning on her spiky red heels, she walked out.

Johnny slumped, his head in his hands. "Well, shit."

Later that night, he sat at the bar in the Watering Hole nursing a beer with Jojo.

"You know she's right, Johnny. I seen a lot of bands come through here. This ain't no life for a nice girl like Melissa," the bouncer said.

"Melissa? Who the hell's Melissa?" Johnny sipped his drink while he kept one eye on the girls entering the club.

"Johnny, you are one big shithead, you know that, man? Misty's real name is Melissa, Melissa Pulaski. She's supposed to be your girl, and you don't even know her real name?"

"Well, how the hell am I supposed to know? She's always been called

Misty."

Teller, the bass player, who also managed the band, came over, gave the beer in Johnny's hand a disapproving look and sat down. He didn't like band members drinking before they played. "I guess you heard from Misty. She wanted to tell you herself."

Johnny traced a finger in the sweat on his bottle. "Yes, I heard from her." He shot Teller his darkest look, knowing full well dark looks weren't really his strong point. "And why the hell did you give her half my paycheck? I need that money. My deal with Misty is none of your business."

The older man shrugged off Johnny's irritation. "She's a nice girl, and you're a shithead. You'd never get around to paying her back. Besides, the band is folding. This is our last gig. Misty's going home, Bobby Ray is hooking up with what's left of Road Kill, Trent Marshal's old band, and I got an offer to do backups with Shockwaves."

Johnny let his beer bottle slide out of his hands to thump on the bar. "Backups with Shockwaves? No shit! You think maybe—"

"Forget it. They got a guitar, and you aren't in that league by a long way. Good enough for this." He waved his hand around at the dingy little club. "But if I was you, I'd catch a clue from Melissa. Go back to school. At least get a day job."

That depressing bit of wisdom still hung in the air as its recipient spotted the little redhead from the night before. He noticed with some satisfaction that her girlfriend, Connie, didn't seem to be with her.

"Put it on my tab," he called to the bartender as he got up to meet his date.

"No more tabs, Johnny. Max says you got to settle up." Erica, the big blonde bartender, had a friendly smile, but women like Erica intimidated Johnny. She seemed immune to his dimple.

He looked at Teller, who just grinned and shrugged.

"Well, hell," He reached into the back pocket of his tight jeans for his wallet.

Johnny felt the hand on his shoulder. *Ah, the little redhead found me. What a strong hand she has,* he thought as he stood to turn, working the dimple. The hand belonged to a very big, very buff guy with a military buzz cut. His other hand rested on the redhead's shoulder. "Ashley just wanted to stop by to say thanks for keeping her company while I had to work last night."

The girl peeked around her boyfriend to wiggle her fingers at him. "Hi," she giggled.

The boyfriend leaned down to whisper, "Now piss off, shithead," as he settled himself on the stool Johnny had just vacated.

The young, almost unemployed, guitarist walked away muttering, "My name is not shithead."

When he woke up the next afternoon, Johnny's temples pounded, his stomach hated him, and his eyes felt as if they had been sandpapered. *No Misty, no money, no job. God, my life has become an old Willie Nelson song. What the hell am I going to do now? Without Teller's connections, I am so totally screwed.*

He rolled over and tried to go back to sleep, but that didn't work either. *No hope for it, I have to call Jamie.* He scooted deeper into the threadbare sheets. He hated calling his sister. She could always be counted on to bail him out, but he'd have to listen to a boatload of sisterly crap.

He reviewed his options, *Can't call Dad, his last words were something like, "Don't phone home until you can afford the price of the call." Mom would fret, then put Dad on the phone. Luke?* He moaned, trying to dodge that one. His brother hadn't spoken to him since that little incident with the car. *No, it'll have to be good old Jamie. She should be good for a couple of hundred. Five would be nice, but Jordan the jerk, probably wouldn't hold still for anything over two.*

Wishing Misty had stayed around at least long enough to make him a cup of coffee, he sat up, waited for the room to settle down, then scraped together enough strength to search for his jeans. Bending over to pick them off the floor did evil things to his head, so he collapsed onto the bed again until the sledgehammer let up a bit.

Something sticky had spilled on his pants. He tried to remember what it might be, but came up blank. He did remember sitting at the bar talking to Erica. She had been much nicer to him, almost human for a change, but then what? Something about Bobby Ray. They must have gone someplace. He reached into the sticky pocket and pulled out his wallet. Wiping his fingers on the sheet, he counted out his money, looked in the wallet again, counted the money once more, then tried the pockets in the hope that maybe he had stuffed some loose bills in there.

Damn, how much money did Misty take, anyway? He remembered Erica made him settle up his bar tab. Had he paid the drummer his share of the gas money for the van too? He counted the money again, hoping that it would magically multiply in the process. *One hundred and twenty seven dollars. That's not going to cut it. Jamie'll just have to cough up more than two hundred, or I'll have to get a job.*

Johnny went into the dingy little bathroom. He really did miss Misty. The place looked even more depressing without her crap all over. *How could she say they didn't have anything going between them? The heartless wench actually laughed when I proposed. I'll have to mention that to Jamie. A broken heart should be good for another couple of hundred at least.*

He showered, shaved and brushed his teeth. *Christ, she even took the mouthwash.* For some reason, Johnny felt he should look his best when he called his sister for money. He recognized the absurdity of this, but he had always relied on his good looks to get by. Checking his watch, he tried to calculate Sacramento time. If he called her before her husband got home, he should have it in the bag.

Johnny practiced his guitar for an hour and half while he waited. He hated playing without amps, but if he couldn't run a bar tab, there wasn't much else to do.

At five-thirty on the dot Sacramento time, he walked down the hall to the pay phone and called his sister. Listening to the ring, he worked his dimple without realizing it. When he heard Jordan's voice, his toothpaste-ad smile faded. "Hi, Jordan. How's it going? Is Jamie home yet?" He listened to the low rumble of his brother-in-law's voice saying something as he handed Jamie the phone.

"Hi, Johnny. What's up? Where are you?"

"I'm in Denver." For some reason that sounded better than Colorado Springs, more impressive. "How're you and Lilly? Bet she's getting pretty big by now."

"We're all fine. Jordan's business is really taking off. He's going to have to hire three new guys."

The pride in his sister's voice annoyed him even as it boosted his estimate of how much he could ask for. "I'm glad to hear things are good for you guys." He took a breath and plunged into the deep end. "Listen, James." Using his kid name for her usually softened her up. "I'm having a rough time. Misty left me. I asked her to marry me, and I guess she just couldn't take the commitment." He managed to sound sufficiently choked up by his loss.

"Oh, Johnny, I'm so sorry!" she cried, putting her hand over the receiver to mumble something to Jordan. "How long were you two together, almost a year?"

"Yeah, she just up and left last night. The thing is, without her, the band'll have to fold. I gave her some money, you know, to see her safely home." He thought that sounded really good, caring and forgiving, even though she broke his heart. "And that left me a little short. I was wondering if you could see your way to helping me out. Just until I can hook up with another band. Just a loan, you know." He deepened the dimple. "I'll pay you back as soon as I get my feet on the ground again."

Shit, she's talking to Jordan, the jerk. That'll knock off at least a hundred. Then he heard his brother–in–law's voice.

"Hi, Johnny. I'm sorry to hear about Misty, but I told Jamie five grand's the limit. You went over that the last time when you missed the van out of Phoenix."

He couldn't believe his sister had actually discussed a limit to sisterly love with this moron.

Jordan went on, "You know the old saying, 'give a man a fish and he eats for a day, give him a job and he can buy his own damn food,' or something like that."

Johnny bit back a sarcastic comment. *He's giving me a goddamn sermonette instead of the money.*

"I'm telling you, make it here by next Wednesday, and you can have a job as a framer. The pay is good, and the work is steady. You can pay back your sister what you owe, go back to school, whatever you want. I don't think we'd really be helping you by giving you any more money. Most of the musicians I know have regular jobs. That's it, Johnny. Make it back here by next Wednesday, and you have a good paying job for as long as you do the work, but no more cash."

Johnny could tell Jordan would have had a lot more to say if Jamie hadn't been standing right there listening. *What an arrogant bastard. I've got to talk to Jamie. Maybe set up a time to call when the jerk isn't around.*

"Hope to see you then. Bye," said Jordan. He hung up.

Johnny stared at the phone as though it had betrayed him.

His sister had never let him down before. He tried to think what to do next. Nothing came to mind.

Bobby Ray came out of his room whistling. "Hey, Johnny. Man, you don't look so good. Too bad about Melissa. You guys were together for a long time, weren't you?"

The Misty, Melissa connection took a minute. "Man, I am so screwed." He hung his head and slammed the pay phone. "Even my own sister has turned against me. Her moron husband won't let her send me any more money. Said I could go to work for him as a lousy house framer if I can get back to Sacramento by next Wednesday." Johnny smiled his best hangdog smile and added hopefully, "Hitching a ride with all my shit isn't easy and, even if I picked up good rides, I couldn't make it in time."

Bobby Ray gave no indication of having caught the hint. "Bummer, man."

"I don't suppose you could see your way …." He pulled out all stops on his grin.

"Save it for the ladies, man. You still owe me five bucks from three weeks ago." The drummer laughed. "But framers make bank. You know Ryan Pacheco, the bass for Fallen Angels? He does construction around Salt Lake sometimes. He's got a wife and kid someplace. Playing clubs doesn't cut it for him." Bobby Ray picked up his bag and walked down the hall. "C'mon," he called over his shoulder. "I'll buy you a beer if you help me pack up my shit and load it in the van."

Great, now I'm doing flunky work for beers. "You think I could pick up work with some local band 'til I get a good gig someplace?" he asked as they muscled the equipment down the stairs.

"Maybe, but they don't pay shit here." Bobby Ray grunted, trying to keep his drums away from his suitcases swinging in Johnny's hands. "You should try Denver."

Together they stowed everything in the back of the van and headed to the Watering Hole. The drummer shoved his hands deep into the pockets of his thin jacket and pulled them together in front of his stomach to compensate for the broken zipper, "You really should take that job with your brother-in-law. To tell you the truth, Johnny, you're a good enough guitarist, but in order to get ahead in this business you got to have something extra, you know. A real need to make it. I get the feeling, for you, this is just a way to score with the chicks."

Johnny pushed through the doors into the club. Even for a Monday night, the place looked dead. Jojo sat in his usual position shooting the breeze with Erica.

Erica listened to them discussing Johnny's sad situation. Jojo commiserated. Then Erica said, "Why don't I get Casey to check on the web for cheap flights to Sacramento? If he can find something, you only have to hitch a ride to Denver."

"Not even that, man," interjected a beaming Jojo. "My sister is loaning her car to my little brother. If you can pick it up in Monument and drive it up to Denver, he'll probably take you to the airport. That'll save me having to drive all the way up there and the bus ride back." Jojo clapped his big hairy hands, rubbing them together as though washing away a vexing problem.

Erica looked around the room, and then told Jojo to watch the bar while she ducked into the tiny office to check with Casey on the flights.

"Listen you guys, I gotta go." Bobby Ray paid Jojo for the two beers. "Good luck making it to your sister's in time to get that job," he told Johnny as he headed for the door.

Johnny asked, "Where the hell is Monument, and how am I supposed to get there?" Thinking it sounded like one of those desert places he had read about once.

"Oh, no problemo, man. It's just up the highway from here, right on your way to Denver." Jojo seemed so happy not to have to make the drive, Johnny wondered about asking him for a small loan.

The bouncer noticed a young man sitting in the shadows of a back booth. Jojo walked over to the man and, in full muscle twitching display, bent down to get right in the guy's face and whispered something to him. The young man shot the bouncer a nasty look, but he got up and left the club.

When he returned to his place at the bar, Jojo said, "Small time pusher. Gives the place a bad rep with the cops. Told him he'd be working without thumbs if he doesn't stay away." The smile of anticipation on Jojo's face persuaded Johnny maybe he shouldn't ask for details.

Erica returned with a printout of flight prices. "Where's Bobby Ray?"

"He had to take off. Lots of miles to cover tonight, I guess," Jojo said, looking a little uncomfortable.

She sighed. "Look, you can get a flight out from Denver tomorrow evening that gets you into Sacramento early Wednesday." Handing him the paper, she tapped a red-circled line.

Johnny's brief bubble of hope collapsed when he got to the price. "Shit, nothing cheaper?" he asked.

Jojo said, "You gott'a be kidding, man. That's a great price! You ain't going to find anything cheaper than that."

"Yeah, well that's just eighteen bucks more than I got." He flashed his dimple hopefully at Erica.

She didn't even seem to notice. "Bummer," she said with a certain disinterested sympathy. "But once you're in Denver, you can probably find something to tide you over 'til you can afford the flight."

Johnny hung his head. "Maybe you're right about that, but you don't understand. I have to be there Wednesday or no job. And how would I get to Monument anyway?"

The bartender rolled her eyes at the whining. "Hitch. It's not that far."

Jojo said, "Okay, here's the deal. I'll drive you up and leave you at a strip mall just off the highway. My sister will drop the car off at the coffee shop there. You find some way to scrape together enough for the plane ticket. Ricardo will take you to the airport, and you're golden. If you can't come up with the money, at least you're where you have a better chance of finding work."

"Golden!" cried Johnny. "How can you call getting a job banging nails into two by fours all day long golden?"

"Oh, come on, it's a day job. Every musician I've ever known has one. Besides, you can probably make enough for the ticket by playing on a street corner." Erica scrubbed an already clean glass. "Being a musician isn't all about dimwitted groupies and going platinum, you know." She tossed the towel down in disgust. "Don't you ever listen to those, 'crying in your beer' songs Melissa's been singing? Being an artist is about knowing pain and loneliness and regretting missed opportunities."

"Hey now," Johnny shot back. "If those girls are old enough to be in here drinking what you're selling them, then they're fair game, and I don't make any promises to take them home to meet my mother, you know. They're here for a good time, and I figure I'm part of the fun. They just want to go back to the pizza joint or wherever they work and tell the girls all about the guy from the band."

"How do you know what they want? What any woman wants? You know what? You are such a shithead, Johnny." Erica slammed the glass down on the bar and stormed off.

"Who peed in Brunhilde's corn flakes?" Johnny asked staring after her.

"Watch your mouth, man. Erica's real good people." Jojo shot him a frosty frown. "She sort of had a thing going with Bobby Ray."

"Bobby Ray? You got to be kidding. The guy's practically a midget. He must be at least five inches shorter than she is."

Jojo shook his head. "She's right about you being a shithead, you know that, man? Looks aren't everything." The bouncer leaned in for a closer inspection of Johnny. "Maybe that's something you haven't had to learn yet. Trust me, you will if you ever grow up."

The guitarist thumped the beer he had been nursing down on the bar. "Okay, I get the message. I'm a shithead, and it's better to be a personable dwarf than a good-looking shithead, right?

A voice behind him said, "Now that you got your lines down, maybe you should practice them in the mirror when you're shaving your dimple."

Johnny turned to glower up at Teller. *God*, he thought, *it's a good thing we're splitting up. These guys are no fun anymore.*

"What time will you be picking me up tomorrow?" Johnny asked the bouncer.

"Better make it around nine. My brother needs the car to get to work."

"Right, see you then." He cut Jojo short, downed the last of his beer and left.

The next day, Jojo arrived right on time. Johnny put his duffel bag and guitar in the back seat and slid in next to the bouncer, *He sure looks different in the daylight, almost human.*

"How you coming with promoting the twenty you need for the ticket?" he asked as they drove north to I-25.

"Great, I got it covered," Johnny lied. He slung one arm over the back of his seat trying for an air of relaxed confidence.

Jojo glanced over at him. "You suck at lying. You know that, shithead?"

Johnny crossed his arms over his chest, slouched in the seat as far as the seat belt would allow, and looked out the window. "Yeah, well, I'm working on it. I got some calls out."

"If that's the truth, I pity the poor girl you're scamming now. Do you ever see women as anything besides cash-cows, you know, like a person or something?" Jojo asked in disgust.

Of course I don't see women as cows, cash or otherwise. With a grin, he replied to Jojo's taunt. "I love women. In fact, I love them every chance I get."

Jojo laughed and punched the guitarist's arm. They traded highly colored stories of their conquests the rest of the way to Monument.

When they pulled off the highway, Johnny felt the tension in his neck muscles relax.

The bouncer didn't have time to wait for his sister. As soon as Johnny closed the car door, Jojo grinned. "I hope you make that flight …," he paused and Johnny could see the words "Shithead" hanging in the air over Jojo like a cartoon bubble. "Man," Jojo added with a wicked grin.

This whole "shithead" thing is really getting old, he thought, as he unloaded his duffel bag and guitar case from the car.

A coffee shop occupied one corner of a little strip mall right next to a hole in the wall shop with a ratty looking sign. As he passed, Johnny stopped to catch his reflection in the window and noticed the pile of books that looked less like a display and more like someone had walked off leaving them behind. *Some funky new advertizing gimmick, he thought. They look old enough to be something Adam and Eve were reading beside a cozy fire in their cave.* He checked the sign again. Librorum something. The thing looked like it had been left over from a fire sale. "Odd," he muttered.

A bell tinkled as Johnny walked into the coffee shop. Three customers glanced up at the newcomer then went back to their steaming mugs. He took a seat as far from the counter as he could. The rich aroma of coffee, fresh-baked breads and cookies had him salivating. He fingered the change in his pocket.

Even if I get even the cheapest thing they have, I'll only have to come up with more cash later. It'd be bad enough missing the plane because I'm eighteen dollars short. It would be a major pisser if I missed it because I had one overpriced cup of coffee.

To get his mind off the rumbling in his stomach, he examined the wall tiles. They looked like nice, a basic gray slate, with a little rusty earth tones thrown in. If he concentrated, he could imagine scenes in them. *Kind of like finding animals in clouds as a kid. That one looks like the things that fade in and out in a dream. Or maybe it's my rosy life as a musician fading away into the gloom of becoming a goddamn house framer.*

A chair next to him scraped, interrupting his train of thought. An older woman having the mother of all bad hair days and dressed in expensive looking black slacks and a hot pink silky blouse clinked her coffee down, folded her newspaper and got up to use the bathroom. On the back of her chair hung a large, gaping purse. There, wedged between a pack of cigarettes and her glasses case, he could see a fat, red wallet. He darted a quick look around. No one was looking. His fingers actually itched. *It's like a sign from God*, he thought. His hand seemed to be levitating in the direction of the purse when the bell over the door chimed again, causing everyone to look up.

The levitation wilted. "Well, shit," he muttered.

A lumpish dark-haired woman in faded jeans and a slightly too tight t-shirt scanned the room. She smiled when she saw Johnny and walked over.

"Hi, I'm Theresa. You must be Johnny, Jose's friend," she said.

He didn't think someone who constantly called you a shithead qualified as a friend exactly, but he stood up. Working the dimple, he wondered if anyone went by their real names anymore, and how much his good friend Jojo had told her about him. He took her hand in a warm, caressing handshake. The awkward way she let his hand drop put a damper on any hope of hitting her up for the money.

"There it is, in all its glory." She nodded to a total heap with two differently colored fenders and a primer gray hood parked just outside. She smiled at his alarm. "Don't worry, it runs a lot better than it looks." Reaching into her back pocket, she pulled out a folded paper. "Here's the directions to Ricardo's apartment. You can't miss it. It's right on Colorado Avenue just a few blocks from the highway."

He took the computer printout. "Thanks. Looks easy enough," he said after scanning the map for a minute.

Theresa looked out the window as an older Honda pulled into the space next to the heavemobile. "There's my ride. Good luck with the job." She handed him a set of keys on a "Jesus loves you" key ring, waved to the guy behind the counter, and left.

The owner of the purse returned, and Johnny stood looking at the key ring. "So much for a sign from God." He sighed.

"See you later," the man behind the counter called as Johnny headed for the door with his things. He turned to wave goodbye and, to his chagrin, he noticed the man behind the counter seemed to be sporting the shithead bubble.

"Snap out if it," he told himself, stowing his things on the passenger seat. "I bet lots of people wait here for a ride. I've got to stop thinking these negative thoughts. I'm not a shithead," he muttered.

A balding man wearing a hardware store work shirt gave Johnny a fishy look as he climbed out of his pick-up and headed into the coffee shop.

"Well, shit on a biscuit," Johnny muttered.

Much to his relief, the junker turned over on the first try. He turned on the radio and got a garbled blast of scrambled stations. Relying on the old tried and true, Johnny gave it a good smack. This left him with a stinging hand and no sound at all from the radio.

"Piece of crap," he grumbled as he drove back to the highway.

That purse had been such a sweet set-up, his mind began to run through all the places a woman might leave one untended for a few critical minutes. *In a locker in a health club? But where would I find a health club and how would I get into the woman's locker room unnoticed?* He dumped that idea. *A supermarket, yeah, that's promising, or maybe a cheap department store.* His head filled with images of open purses left in the kid seats of pushcarts. That morphed into a truly ugly scene of a large woman, bearing a striking resemblance to Erica, beating him over the head while screaming for the cops.

He winced and the car swerved towards a small blue and white rest stop sign.

With a yelp of laughter, he cried, "Yes! Thank you, Jesus! That's perfect. I'll just sit there until someone has to pee real bad and rushes off without locking up. I won't even have to leave the questionable comfort of this mobile junk pile."

He pulled into a parking space closest to the walkway leading to the public restrooms, unbuckled his seat belt, reclined his seat, slipped on his sunglasses and waited.

Like a spider waiting for a big fat fly.

After an hour and twenty minutes, the only patrons of the facilities were two burly truckers who looked like they would break him in half for even thinking about their wallets. Another forty-five minutes dragged by before an old couple stopped by to eat sandwiches. Half an hour later, he began to feel a growing need to pee. *Must be what comes of thinking of about peeing for over two hours.* He sat, debating his chances of making a quick trip to the men's room when an older red Neon pulled in right beside him.

He opened his mouth in what he hoped looked like a convincing sleeping man pose. From the very corner of his eye, he watched a slim woman slide out of the car's front seat and make a beeline for the bathroom. She vanished into the bunker-like building. Johnny jumped out, had her car door open and a large floppy tote bag in hand in less than a minute. He dove back into his junker and roared out of the rest stop in a dense blue cloud of smoke.

"I did it. I actually did it!" He pounded the steering wheel in glee.

His elation lasted for a few miles, to be replaced by a burning curiosity. "Christ, what if the damn bag is her knitting?" His sister used a tote like that just before she had Lilly. She must have knitted a dozen baby booties, and the kid never wore one of them.

Sweat slicked his palms as an even worse thought popped into his head. *What if she has medicine she needs in that damn thing, Insulin or one of those pen things for allergies?* A twist of fear gripped his guts as other disasters occurred to him.

A drug mule would have the mob after him with Uzis.

Starving babies shriveling from hunger as their single mom tried to tell them that some shithead stole their rent money.

I'm not cut out for this. If I don't stop soon, I'm going to toss my cookies. For what seemed like hours the road rolled on over sweeping vistas of grassland and low, stone-topped hills fringed in scrub oak before he spotted a turn off.

The little country road appeared to be blissfully deserted. He pulled over onto the dusty shoulder. Ripping open the bag, he heaved a sigh of relief. The only thing that could be considered medicine was a half empty bottle of Tylenol. Next he rummaged around in the wallet and found thirty-eight dollars and nineteen cents. A euphoric tide of relief washed over him. He leaned back in his seat and closed his eyes, the better to bask in the sensation. This glorious release reminded him that he really did need to pee so he got out and relieved himself onto a fencepost.

I made it. No one will die. No one's going to try to kill me. I didn't get caught. And I will never do this again, so help me God. He never stopped to wonder if this was a prayer, or a realization that he didn't have what it takes to be a criminal.

Riding this happy crest, he zipped his fly and got back into the car so he could see what other goodies he had scored. Breath mints, a small brown bottle with a dropper top labeled Kick-Ass Immune Activator. He held it up and laughed, then put a drop on his tongue, ran the flavor around in his mouth and decided it tasted a lot like hedge clippings. Dropping it back in the bag, he continued his exploration of what he thought of as girly stuff, some grocery receipts, a dollar twenty-six in change that he stuffed in his own wallet along with the rest of the cash, a checkbook with a balance of three hundred dollars and nine cents. Another sigh of relief. *No drug mule here.* The bag also contained two books. One of the books, a romance novel, he dropped in the discard pile. The second held his interest.

The journal had a tree design stamped deep into rich brown leather on both the front and back. He liked the feel of it, heavy, good quality. Johnny had seen something like this in a bookshop in Dallas. He would have gotten it then, but choked at the price. Opening it, he found the actual book could be removed.

"Well, thank you very much. I'll toss the filler and get my own book."

In a little side pocket of the tote, he discovered a baggie with two, what looked like homemade, chocolate chip cookies. His mouth watered at the sight. He tried to remember his last meal. Maybe the previous night, but, if so, he couldn't really recall it. He wolfed a cookie, wishing he had something to wash it down with, and decided to keep the other for later. The next likely food on his horizon wouldn't be until he got to Jamie's.

Hoping for another break, he reexamined the wallet and found nothing but the usual assortment of cards, a Visa, health insurance, driver's license with a really botched picture, both a King Soopers and a Safeway card and a few pictures. One picture showed a pretty young woman with light brown hair smiling up at a soldier.

If she went blonde, she'd be a babe, he thought, then reconsidered.

Her mouth had a soft sweetness that gave her the all-American girl look, and the eyes had an oddly appealing hint of seriousness. For one stabbing moment, he deeply wished some girl would look at him like that.

He winked at her. "Just to prove I'm really not the shithead everyone seems to think I am, I'm going to mail all your crap back to you." Johnny checked the name in the checkbook, and added, "Malia Scott. I could bounce your checks all over Denver and run your credit card into the dirt but, since I am a nice guy, I'll only keep the cash, because I really need it." He stuffed the journal into his bag, "And I'll keep the cover as a finder's fee."

He shoved everything else back into the tote before jamming it into his duffel bag. Being a good guy, scoring enough money for the ticket and having gotten away with his heist without any unfortunate consequences, made him feel better than he had in days, maybe even months.

This house-framing gig might not be such a bad deal. Having a little more money in my pocket is a definite plus. I guess I'm ready for a change, he thought.

Finding the address on Colorado Avenue proved easier than he expected. Ricardo sat on the hood of an old pickup with two flat tires and, Johnny suspected, serious internal problems, waiting for his car. He appeared to be about nineteen. *Only a few years younger than me.* The young man had his sister's good looks and the beginning of his older brother's impressive build. For a fleeting minute, the musician considered trying to promote a few beers or, better still, a burger. That hope died a fiery death when Ricardo blasted him with, "Where the hell you been, man? You were supposed to be here," he checked his watch, "over two hours ago. I should'a been at work by one." He took the keys from Johnny's hand and slid into the driver's seat.

"Come on. Jose said I got to drop you at the airport, and I ain't got all day, man."

Johnny climbed into the passenger side. Before he could buckle his seat belt, Ricardo roared off in a cloud of burning oil fumes.

The trip became a blur of speed, bilingual cursing, and creative driving that left Johnny wanting to kiss the concrete when they finally pulled to a stop outside the terminal.

Johnny thanked Ricardo, silently adding, *for not getting me killed,* as he ran to the back of the car to catch his guitar before it bounced to the pavement next to the duffel bag Ricardo had already tossed out of the trunk. Knowing what was coming, he scooped up his bag and held his breath before the blast of blue smoke engulfed him.

Denver International Airport had the bright and shiny industrial cheerfulness of a corporate business lobby. He checked the time. His flight didn't leave for several hours. *Well, first thing first,* he thought, *better get my ticket nailed down.*

Two hours later, he had explored all the airport had to offer a young man with no money to spend. He had hung out in a snack shop reading the magazines until he thought the store manager might be about to report him as a suspicious character.

All the fast food places wanted way too much for their burgers, and the incessant reminders to keep all personal possessions within sight at all times made it impossible for him to try a repeat of his earlier success at petty theft.

Just as well. It would be stupid for me to get busted now when all I have to do is wait for the damn plane.

To kill time, he did one more lap of the shops selling traveler gift items, stuffed buffaloes, Rockies ball caps and neck pillows. From somewhere a slight breeze sent an antique sign swinging. "Librorum Taberna," he read loud and stopped to look at the dusty window display. The same wobbly stacks of what looked like seventeenth century books sat there, like someone had left in the same abandoned way.

Must be some kind of new chain store. But with Amazon putting pressure on places like Barnes and Nobel, how can anyone think something so funky has a chance, he wondered. A shadowy movement caught his eye and the figure behind the books seemed to gesture for him to go in. "Not my thing," he mouthed to the shopkeeper and walked on.

He knew the airline wouldn't serve any real food, but even a bag of peanuts sounded pretty good to him. Pulling out the ticket, he checked to make sure he had the right departure gate.

The waiting area had the deserted feel of a club hours before opening. He took out his guitar and played for a while, but the PA system ruined the atmosphere. *Dinner time,* he decided, taking the crushed cookie from his bag. No cookie had ever tasted as good. Definitely homemade, with big chunks of chocolate and walnuts. "God, what I wouldn't give for a decent cup of coffee." He moaned, finding he could perfectly remember the smell of the coffee shop from earlier in the day. Closing his eyes, he took small bites to make the cookie last longer. When he finished, he went in search of a drinking fountain to wash it down.

Once back in his seat, he hoped for some self-defense napping. Reaching for the bag to create a headrest, he noticed the journal poking out of the ripped pocket. *Must have torn when Ricardo tossed it on the concrete.* He slipped the book out. Memories of sneaking a peek in his sister's diary as a junior high kid flooded him. He flipped the journal open.

Instead of confessions of undying love for Robby Riley, he found an ink drawing of a swallowtail butterfly with a few little practice details of the wings in different positions. Johnny knew nothing about visual arts, but even he could see that the sketch had a lively delicacy that captured the small creature perfectly. Thumbing through the journal, he found many more sketches. The cramped, unintelligible handwriting bordered on cryptic, but from the line layout, he guessed a lot of it must be poetry. Some drawings were in ink, others in colored pencil. Mostly they were of animals or insects. A few seemed to have been done from life, the subject having taken off before she had time to finish. The head and shoulder of a squirrel with his body only lightly roughed in looked to Johnny like he wanted to climb out of the page. She avoided cuteness by adhering strictly to detailed anatomy while conveying a love for her subjects and their idiosyncrasies. He stopped at one of a few stems of grass. It had an appealing simplicity and delicacy. He wondered how much something like that might be worth. For a moment, he considered ripping it out of the book to keep, but the idea of destroying the journal didn't feel right, something akin to desecration.

Well, what the hell, I'll just keep the whole damn book, he thought. Looking up, he caught his reflection in a blank arrivals monitor screen. The handsome face flashed him a dimple and mouthed the word "shithead."

Almost reflexively he said, "I am not a shithead."

"Oh, yes you are," the image in the monitor laughed.

"Christ! They've got me talking to myself. Next thing I'll be on Oprah spilling my guts to the whole world about what a shithead, sexist, chauvinist pig I am."

Johnny stuffed the journal back into the bag and took out his tickets to read the very fine print on the back, in hopes of boring himself to sleep. But his tired mind wouldn't give up.

This sucks. When did thinking get to be so depressing? I've always been a pretty cool guy. At least I thought I was. Now the shithead balloon thing seems to be dogging me like some damn Batman shadow, big and menacing.

Moving to a seat facing away from the screen, he tried to concentrate on the good parts of his personality. *I'm good-looking, and I play the guitar well*, adding, in a rare moment of honesty, *when I really try*. A few minutes went by before he could add, *I shower regularly.* That sounded pretty lame. "Well, damn! I have lots of great qualities. I'm just too tired to think right now."

He rested his head on the bag and shut his eyes. *I have really got to work on this whole shithead thing. Something like this could be the kiss of death with women.*

A carry-on bag landed on the floor next to his. He looked up, surprised to notice the waiting area had filled up.

I must have dozed off, he thought.

A lean young man dropped into the seat next to him and nudged Johnny's guitar case with the toe of his boot. "You play?"

"Yeah, but the band broke up." If he weren't so tired, he might have trotted out the line about a big gig in Vegas. Then he remembered the plane they were about to board didn't stop in Vegas. The truth had its advantages. He didn't have to remember so much crap.

"Bummer, man."

Another guy leaned over to ask, "You famous or anything?"

Johnny barked out a dispirited laugh. "No. We had a really good singer, but she wanted to go home, get married and have kids instead of having a career." He slid up in his seat. The young men settled down to pass the time in friendly conversation.

When the call came for passengers holding seats in rows thirty-four through forty-six to please have their tickets and boarding pass ready, Johnny picked up his bags and pulled out his paperwork. As he walked down the long loading ramp, he realized that he couldn't even remember the last time he had had a real discussion. They just talked about music, job prospects, girls, and travels. He told them about some of the crazy things that happened while on the road. They had laughed and said he should give them a call when he got settled. Maybe they could go out for beers. The really strange thing about the encounter was that he had stuck pretty much to the truth.

The old guy in the seat next to Johnny didn't want his bag of snack munchies and gave it to him. This still left him hungry enough to chew a wing off the plane, but he managed to get some sleep, dreaming about his sister's spaghetti and meatballs.

On landing, he considered his options. At this hour in the morning, Jordan would not take kindly to a phone call to come pick him up. Same for his parents. A taxi would cost too much. Catching a bus into town would only leave him stuck in Sacramento in the middle of the night, not a particularly appealing idea, or he could just find a quiet corner and wait until morning to begin his new life as an exhausted, rumpled mess.

The constant reminders to watch luggage and not to smoke in the airport, the announcements for people with strange names to go to a white telephone, and the sleep he had on the plane all combined to keep him awake. Somewhere around six, he decided to find a men's room and do something to clean himself up. By seven, he broke down and bought an overpriced egg sandwich. At eight on the dot, he thought Jordan would be at work and it might be safe to call.

He held his breath until he heard her voice. "Hi, James. I made it. I'm at the airport. Got in really late and didn't want to wake you or the baby, so I just hung 'til I figured you'd be up."

When she said she could be there in less than an hour if traffic cooperated, he breathed a huge sigh of relief.

"Any chances you could bring…," he almost said "some sandwiches," but that would delay her, and he had already seen more of airports than he could stand. "Lilly. I haven't seen her in ages. I bet she's big. I really miss her."

The pause on the other end of the line had him thinking that he had gone too far. But his sister laughed and said, "She's two, Johnny. I'm not about to leave her home alone just yet."

Jamie picked him up forty-five minutes later.

Sitting in her cozy kitchen breakfast nook with California sunshine and the smell of lemony floor wax, he downed a huge breakfast while they caught up on each other's news.

He had no intention of going into the whole shithead thing, but his sister had always been one of those people who could drag things out of him as if by osmosis.

"I'm really not a shithead, but you don't think a guy could be one, and everyone else would know it except for him, do you?" He downed the last of his coffee looking at his sister over the rim of his cup.

"Johnny, everyone thinks the way they are is just how everyone else is too. Only the lucky ones stop to think, 'maybe I really am a shithead. Let's see, how do I treat other people?' Think about that, and then ask yourself if you want to change. You're what, twenty-three now? Maybe it's time you grow up."

If this had come from his father, he would have thrown his napkin down on the table and stormed out of the house.

God, I did that enough times to know the drill.

From Jamie, it stung to know she considered him both immature and a shithead, but she had smiled at him with such love and hope when she said it, he couldn't take that easy way out. Instead, he heaved a great sigh, flashed the dimple and asked, "When do I have to report to Simon Large?"

Jamie flicked him with her dishtowel. "Jordan isn't the villain in this, you know. He's giving you a chance a lot of men in your position would kill for."

"Yeah, yeah, yeah, a regular knight to the rescue," he said, getting up to leave.

"I mean this, Johnny," her voice serious now. "Jordan is giving you a chance. Maybe your last one." She reached out and laid her hand on his, then gave it a little squeeze. "I love you. So do Mom and Dad. Don't screw this up."

Johnny couldn't think of anything clever to say in response to his sister's obvious concern for him.

She shook his arm and said, "New house rule, clean up your own mess." She looked pointedly at the litter of dishes on the table.

"Sheesh, a regular tough love boot camp you're running here." He laughed.

His sister didn't. "Something like that," she said as she walked out to check on the napping Lilly. "You're to be at Jordan's office at noon. You can take my car." Jamie turned in the doorway. "You're bright and talented and too charming for your own good, and you're my baby brother." Her smile had just a hint of sadness. "Please, just this once, try to stick to the plan."

While rinsing his breakfast things, he thought of all the times someone tried to get him to stick to a plan. His parents, teachers in High School, Christ, even Thad Barlow's dad in his first and only year in college. Now, his big sister decided to have a go at it. While taking a shower, he remembered how funny it seemed at the time to yank their chains. Now he thought of all the time and effort people had spent trying to help him.

Wiping steam from the bathroom mirror he caught that boyish grin with its ready dimple. This time, he turned away in disgust. "Shithead isn't the half of it. This time, Boy-o, you are *not* on the fast track to being a total screw up."

At ten to noon, he arrived in Jordan's disaster zone of a construction trailer washed, shaved and ready to give it a real try. His brother-in-law wasted no time in pleasantries.

"Okay, so here's the deal." Jordan tapped a pen on his desk. "You can stay at our place 'til you can get your own apartment. I'm figuring about a month, when you get your first paycheck. You can use Jamie's Toyota until you can line up wheels of your own, maybe another month. You will show up on time and do your work, no screwing off."

He narrowed his gray eyes and set his jaw.

"I'm running a business here. I've got a wife and a kid, and a crew of good men who depend on me for a living." He nodded to the blueprints stacked on a long table against the far wall. "This is it, bud. I can't afford to do charity work. You pull your own weight and, in time, you can move up to a more skilled position with a damn good pay scale."

He seemed to lose a little of his steam after the hardball stuff. "I'm not looking to give you a hard time, man. I just want you to know how it is."

Then the steel flashed back into his eyes. "I'll be taking two hundred every other week for what you owe us. You'll have medical, paid holidays and accrue vacation time. Talk to Ruben Hernandez, he's my foreman. He'll fill you in on everything else you need to know."

Jordan reached for a stack of invoices. "You mean a lot to Jamie, and she means a lot to me." He gave Johnny a look drill sergeants would envy. "I swear to God, Johnny, if you try any of your scams, you'll be out of town so fast you'll pull G-forces." To indicate that the interview had ended, he nodded to the door.

Johnny stuck to the plan, the apartment, the truck, he even found he liked being a house framer. The crew he worked with were fun, if a bit rough. He got a killer tan and had more money to spend, even after Jordan's deductions, than he ever had in his life. The honeymoon period lasted about three months.

Somewhere around the fourth month, Johnny began to feel restless. The guys he worked with had a rather limited range of interests—girlfriends, a few beers after work, and their pickups, maybe saving for a better house or a bigger TV.

One day, while waiting to use the saw, one of the crew started laughing. "Hey, man, you do a mean air guitar."

It took a minute for that to sink in. His fingers had been feeling for the chords to the song that had been running through his head. "I used to play with a band, old habits die hard." He tried to shrug it off, but the thought of playing his guitar sent an almost physical pain of longing through him.

That night, he sat having a pizza and beer in the little storefront operation just around the corner from his apartment, trying to decide if he was a musician just doing the day job thing, or a house framer who could play guitar.

It took two weeks to find a gig playing in a little coffee shop, very much like the one in which he hatched the plan to steal a purse. The first night he found the answer to his discontent. For better or worse, he was a musician, and that surprised him.

Two days later, while stuffing some dirty clothing in a washing machine at the laundromat, the stolen journal tumbled out of the pillowcase he used as a laundry bag. While he sat in the linty dampness trying not to make eye contact with the winos or weary-looking women pushing carts full of bundles, he attempted to make some sense out of the handwriting. It took a while for him to discover that all d's, b's and p's were interchangeable, r's could be either v's or u's, some letters were just left out of words altogether, while others were reversed. The list of possible interchanges included most of the alphabet. He considered the possibility that the woman might be an idiot savant.

Would she have been allowed to drive, and didn't she have a checkbook? The drawings showed a sense of humor, and I seem to remember autistic people don't get humor. The journal intrigued him enough to see if he could decipher one or two of the poems. By the time the dryer buzzed, he had become totally engrossed in the puzzling handwriting, the poems and the woman who wrote them.

On his way home, Johnny decided to stop and pick up a lined notebook to copy her work into real English. He almost passed the shop before noticing the weathered Librorum Taberna sign creaking slightly in the wind. He stopped abruptly. The same scorched look and the same pile of antique books sat stacked in the same grimy window. Definitely not a friendly neighborhood bookstore.

Sometimes, once you notice something, it seems to pop up all over the place. But this is getting freaky. What the hell? He pushed the door open. The dusty smell of old books made him sneeze. Dim lighting revealed only what seemed to be an endless labyrinth of shelves.

"Hello, anybody here?" *This might be some specialty library or a graveyard for dead books.*

"Yes, indeed I am here. . . now," came a slightly accented voice from the shadows.

Johnny jumped at the sound. The voice was not unpleasant but it seemed to imply something vaguely creepy.

The man had not moved into the light, but Johnny had the feeling no one had been there just a moment ago.

"Hi, I'm looking for a notebook. You know, kind of a copybook thing." Johnny turned to reach for the doorknob, sure this place didn't have anything of the sort.

"A notebook, yes I see," said the shopkeeper. He moved from beside a stack of fat, leather-covered volumes. "But you wouldn't be interested in any of these." He caressed a display of expensive looking journals with long spidery fingers.

The guy passed behind a tall shelf to arrive at a table covered with disordered piles of dark cloth bound books. The geezer patted them fondly. They emitted a rustling whisper of dust.

Johnny read, "The Shadow Book of Deliverance Mather," on the cover of the one on top. Other titles were written in different languages and even in strange alphabets, some with stick figures of letters.

Now at close range, Johnny noticed the thin proprietor was. *And having a really bad hair day.*

"Ezra," he said," Ezra Finfrock's my name." He looked up and flashed a nasty yellow smile. Unfortunately, the smile did nothing to distract from the man's eyes. Almost hidden behind bushy, haystack eyebrows, they were solid white, or maybe only the palest blue imaginable.

The man chuckled at Johnny's discomfort. "Notebooks are very interesting things." He slid away to yet another stack. "They are pure possibility until you actually write in them. Then they can take whatever character you create for them. Kind of like a soul. Don't you think?" He quirked one bushy brow at Johnny.

"Um, yeah. I guess so." Johnny started to work out an exit strategy in his head. He didn't really need the damned thing all that much.

The old geezer chuckled again as he picked up a volume. "Ah! Here it is. See that spider web design? That, my young friend, is a dream catcher." He traced the pattern with a long yellow fingernail. In the dim and dusty atmosphere, the web seemed to shudder slightly. "Books," he breathed the word, "are the repository of all man's dreams, desires and drama." The eyebrow twitched again. "You seem to be a man to looking to *catch* a particular dream. All these books," he waved his skeletal hand to encompass the entire store, "can teach us so much." Again came the knowing chuckle.

Johnny wanted to ask, "Teach what?" but checked himself before letting the words out. "Great. I'll take it. How much?" He reached for his wallet, willing to pay whatever just to get away from Spiderman's grandpa and his disturbing shop.

Once out in the fresh air, notebook firmly in hand, Johnny tried to work out why the shop had creeped him out so much. *Must be that moldy smell*, he thought. *That stuff's bad for you. No wonder that guy looked like he had been marinated in tobacco juice.*

While he walked, Johnny thought of the passage he managed to translate while waiting for his washing to finish. As far as he could make out it just read, "Somewhere behind my eyes, or in the deepest recesses of my memory, there is this sanctuary. This landscape of my soul."

That night, after putting away his laundry, he went back to work translating the journal. Now that he had opened the door to Malia's mind, he found something quite extraordinary. A mystery, a challenge his life had been lacking. Though he didn't bother to put a name to it, he suspected that it might be contact with a woman who shared his artistic nature. He felt a twinge of guilt for not sending her belongings back.

He had thumbed through her journal before, many times, but now he decided to ration it out, like a secret treat, one page, or part of a page, at a time.

After a week, he worked out three more poems, odd poems to be sure. Johnny took a new and peculiar delight in this secret life. By day he framed houses, and two nights a week he played guitar at the Cracked Cup. Most nights he spoon-fed himself crumbs of a pretty young woman's dreams.

Johnny liked women, loved them in fact, but the loving had always gotten in the way of really getting to know them as people. Now he had the voyeuristic pleasure of exploring a fascinating woman's unconcerned mind without the intoxication of lust fogging his perceptions. For the first time since sixth grade, he was getting to know a female personality.

For one thing, she had dyslexia, and not just the garden variety, crappy-spelling, slow reading kind. He picked up on a feeling of solitariness in her work. Not lonesomeness exactly. So far, he found no references to people in any of her poems or drawings, but the picture from her wallet that he used as a bookmarker showed her with a guy. *Could the difficulty with reading and writing cause a person to go off into their own little world?* That picture bothered him. He had taken to only sliding it partway out of the pages, so only her face showed. That way he could imagine she smiled that soft serious smile only for him.

One rainy Friday night, he sat in the Cracked Cup playing to the few who had braved a gutter-flooding downpour. One older couple seemed to be having a low-key argument, while another couple happily shared an artery-clogging dessert, which boasted about a billion calories. Dim, watery light from the sign on the antique shop across the street filtered in through the rain streaked front windows. Smells of damp overcoats blended with that of the coffee.

In the good old days there would have been a smorgasbord of girls out there ripe for the picking. Now, no one even seemed to be listening. On the other hand, I can play whatever I damn well feel like. He started in on an arrangement of *Für Elise*. The wet night seemed to lend itself to something quiet and classical.

Max, the counter guy, nodded his approval. Johnny shut his eyes, drifting away with the music. Imagining Malia would like this, he improvised, trying for the comfortable solitariness of her. Something like being in a familiar forest for an evening walk beneath a high blue sky, alone and content in his own company. He let the feeling guide him through the notes. Time stopped for him, and when he finished the piece, only Max sat in the dark coffee-scented shop.

"Man, I didn't know you could play like that," the counter man said. "It was weird, like music geek space aliens abducted your head or something, you know. You were really in the zone." A hopeful flash flickered across his face. "Or you're on some really good shit."

Johnny laughed. "No way, man. I got enough heat from my brother-in-law already. Something like that would cost me a pretty good job." He packed up his stuff and checked the tips jar. The twenty-five bucks surprised him. Someone had actually been listening. *Probably the happy dessert couple.*

That night, still riding the crest of his musical rapture, he decided to move his exploration of the journal into what he had come to think of as the last frontier, the personal stuff. If the poetry had been a mess to try to decipher, the personal stuff degenerated into total chaos. The poetry might have been written with the idea of reading it again. The personal stuff seemed to have just escaped willy-nilly onto the page.

Flipping the book open to the first page, he propped his head up with a pillow, laid the dream catcher pad on his stomach, and read.

"My gob eaten is messing ir auction"

A mental image of the man in the photo messing his pants popped into his mind, only to be yanked away by the significance of his mental replay in standard English.

"My God, Ethan is missing in action. What am I going to do? Mom says I should come home, but I have to be here. I have to stay, so I will be here when there is some news. I am so afraid I can't think. I just hurt so bad. I want him back and I don't know what to do. The chaplain from Fort Carson who married us stopped by, and all I wanted to do was scream and throw something at him. I know he just wanted to help, but there is nothing he can do besides spew out the same old crap about what a good soldier he was and how God will watch out for him. I don't want him to be any kind of a soldier. I want him home with me. I want to wake up and find us back home in Auburn. I can't stand this not knowing. How the hell can they just lose someone, like some goddamn car keys. Half the time I can't believe he's really gone. I just know someone will call to say it was all some stupid mistake. The rest of the time I know I'll never see him again, and I can't stand it. I just want to die."

Johnny let the journal close in his hands, and the dream catcher notebook slid to the floor. A bad feeling settled in his gut, like when he ate too many greasy tacos.

I don't need this either. I don't really know this woman or her stupid husband.

But deep inside, he felt her loss as a terrible bitter ache. *I can just shut the damn book. What must it be like for her?* He'd never lost anyone important to him. *Hell, I never had anyone who I didn't walk away from sooner or later. Who would leave such a deep wound, maybe even deep enough to kill my soul if I never saw them again? And what would it be like not knowing if they were hurt or dead or … shit.*

He didn't want to feel like this. He tossed the book into his nightstand and slammed the drawer shut, then went into the bathroom. The really cool smiling young man in the mirror tried to flash his dimple reassuringly. "Shithead," Johnny told him. "Malia doesn't die. She goes on to do all those great pictures and to write all those poems." *Alone,* he thought, *she goes on alone. That's what I've been picking up on in her work.*

Knowing his sense of her had been right pleased him, but he also felt her loss, and that made his pleasure seem like a mean and selfish thing.

What I need is a cold beer and a break from all this depressing crap.

Bennie's Bar, just a few doors down from his apartment, still held a few die-hard patrons.

Johnny slouched on a stool at the bar and downed his drink, following it with another. The day had been a long one. He felt like shit.

I should go home and get some sleep. Either Jordan or Ruben or both will ream me if I show up hung over.

"Woman problems or money? It's usually one or the other." The bartender smiled with sympathy as he leaned on the counter.

Johnny ordered another. "A guy I know is missing in action," he said without thinking.

"Whoa, man, that's hard. Missing, huh? No closure there. He a good friend of yours?" Something in the craggy face of the bartender made Johnny want to talk.

This is crazy. These people are nothing to me. But his mouth said, "I didn't know the guy too well, but I kind of had a thing for his wife. Nothing ever happened," he added hastily. "I just like her. She's a nice girl, kind of quiet, and she's taking it pretty hard." He polished off the third beer and dropped a few dollars on the counter.

He walked out into the rainy night, wondering, what *the hell am I doing crying in my beer over a girl I've never even met?* As soon as the words were out of his mouth, he knew they were all too true. He felt more for the strange woman than he had for any of the girls who were in and out of his bed over the last three years.

You total moron. What have you done? I've got to get rid of that damn book. I'll send it back to her, or burn it, or just throw it away. But he knew he would do none of those things. That was her first entry, and the book was completely full.

How long had Ethan Scott been missing? At least a year? No, longer. I took the journal about six months ago, and there is one hell of a lot of work between those pages. Okay, this is just too stupid to be true. Of course I feel bad for her. She seems like a nice girl, and I'm not really a shithead. Of course I feel bad for her, who wouldn't? This just proves what a non-shithead I am.

As Johnny went back to his apartment to think things over he passed a shabby bookshop, unaware of a thin man with ratty, shoulder-length hair grinning at his concentration.

Before going to bed, he made a solemn promise not to open the nightstand drawer until he had his head on straight.

The rain kept up for the rest of the week. After lightning almost zapped a guy, Ruben called the framers off the job until the weather cleared. Johnny picked up a few more nights at The Cracked Cup. To pass the quiet time before closing, he sang songs he'd written using lyrics from some of Malia's poems.

The next week Max, the counterman, told him, "You know that guy who started coming in here the night you wigged out playing your own stuff, the one you thought was waiting for somebody all the time?" He handed Johnny a new coffee concoction involving a lot of chocolate, whipped cream and imitation rum flavoring.

"Yeah, I remember him. He always sits way in the back by the cup display, kind of a flashy dresser. What about him? He looks like a gangster of some kind." Johnny took the cup and sipped. Not all of Max's attempts went down well. He thought this one would be pretty good if he used real rum.

"He came in last night wanting to talk to you. He had this big black dude with him. You don't owe anybody money or anything, do you? I mean they looked pretty rough in a really cool sort of way. Oh shit." Max nodded to the door. "Here they are now. You think you could, like, leave, for a while? I don't want any trouble, man."

Johnny looked over at the two men. He didn't owe anyone anything, but some internal elevator headed for the basement. These were the kind of guys no one would want to spend time with in a dark alley. The one, the black man, wore a leather coat that had to have been custom to fit so well over his super-sized frame. The guy looked vaguely familiar.

"Hi, I'm Bryan Smith," said the shorter man. He held out his hand to shake.

Johnny had to wonder how he managed to lift anything so loaded down with rings. He'd seen jewelry store windows with way less bling than this man walked around in.

The dimple came unbidden to his cheek. "Nice to meet you. I'm Johnny Cunningham. Max said you were looking for me." He looked around for Max, silently damning the counter man for a chicken when he couldn't find any sign of him. "He seems to have ducked out to refill the whipped cream dispenser."

That sounded pretty good, like he'll be right back or something, He casually strolled over to stand closer to the window. "What can I do for you?"

The other man looked over the offerings on a menu hanging over the counter.

Damn, where have I seen that guy? Visions of Post Office wanted pictures flitted through his mind. *Ridiculous, I haven't been in a post office in months, and I don't think they even do that anymore.*

"I been telling my man," Smith nodded to his companion, "'Bout your songs. Slick Trick!" he called. "You c'mon over here. Get your mind off food for a minute. Slick Trick Jackson, I'd like you to meet Mister Johnny Cunningham."

"Holy shit!" Johnny gasped. "Slick Trick Jackson," he said, shaking the man's meaty hand. "I knew you looked like someone I should know, but without your do-rag and the chains I didn't recognize you."

The man smiled. "Yeah, that's my stage persona, you know, kinda homey. Me, I like a little more style, though." A diamond cross gleamed on a substantial platinum chain. His rich deep voice sounded like he could do some real singing instead of the rapping crap. For a guy who had done hard time for armed robbery and manslaughter, the rapper had a sort of goofy smile, high round little chipmunk cheeks and big square teeth.

"Let's sit down. You think you could get us some coffee? Where the hell did that guy go to get whipped cream, out to talk personally to the damn cows?" Smith headed for his usual table.

Johnny, who had never stepped behind the counter before, went in search of a recognizable coffee pot. He came back with three mugs and a carafe he hoped contained fresh brewed coffee.

"It's like this. Slick here's been picking up a lot of heat lately for of some of his work ever since that kid shot the cop in East L.A. He wants to do something crossover, you know, appeal to a wider audience? I tol' him 'bout that song you got. The one 'bout the guy who tol' fortunes with a deck of worn out cards. 'Bout how you just kind of talk it real soft like. A little Bob Dylan thing going on there. So how much you want for it?"

The swallow of coffee went down Johnny's throat like a solid brick. "You want my song?" He wheezed. Visions of a whole new career opened before him, one minus the hammer, replacing it with hundred dollar bills that fluttered around his head like so many green butterflies.

"Yeah, look, we got to catch a plane to Vegas here in 'bout an hour." Smith stood up. "Here's my card. I'll have my girl send over the standard contract. You can have your man look it over and get back to me. Where should she send it?"

In a daze, Johnny wrote his address on a paper napkin and handed it to Smith.

"See you round, man." Slick followed his manager out the door.

Max emerged from the back. "I had the phone in my hand the whole time, man. Any shots, and nine-one-one would have been right on it. So what did they want?"

The coffee brick finally slid the rest of the way down the stunned young man's throat. "You know who that was? Slick Trick Jackson! And his manager, some guy named Smith. Slick Trick wants to do one of my songs." Excitement flooded Johnny. He laughed and slapped the table until his hands hurt. "He wants to do one of my songs! I could be a goddamn millionaire." He reached over and shook Max until his head wobbled.

"Hey, cut it out!" the counter man cried. "I'm getting whiplash." He rubbed his neck. "I hate to bust your bubble, man, but what makes you think one song will make you rich? The way I hear it, a writer doesn't get rich on one of anything."

"Yeah, but Slick Trick is really hot right now. He could mumble his way through a car insurance policy, and it would probably go platinum. And then everyone and their dog wants to cover it and then, everyone and their dog wants me to do a song for them, maybe a whole goddamn album. I will never have to sweat my ass off on another shaky ladder again. C'mon, man, close up. Nobody's coming in now anyway. I'll take you out for a beer."

Johnny's euphoria carried him through until three twenty-six in the morning when he sat bolt upright in bed. "Holy shit! Hopping Christ on a cracker! I don't own the fucking lyrics!" he exclaimed.

Jumping from his bed as though he discovered a nest of scorpions sleeping with him, and began to pace the room looking for a way out of his dilemma.

I can go ahead with this and hope she never hears the song. No way. It won't be a rap song and will be in the top ten inside a month. She'll hear it and Slick Trick will break my kneecaps, at the very least. Forget that.

I could send her a letter saying I found the journal, maybe in a second hand book shop, and have a friend in the music business that is interested in recording it. That sounded better. But she's going to want her journal back, and God knows how many more songs are in there. Maybe I could get away with saying I only found the one page. Shit no! Then when I get an offer for another song, I'm right back here again. God, I am so close to making it big, I can taste it. There must be a way. Maybe I could just write some other words. But I wouldn't do it justice... I can't make it flow like Malia did.

He went into his tiny kitchen and threw instant coffee into a cup, added warm tap water and swallowed a big gulp without noticing how awful it tasted, then went back to doing rapid circuits of his apartment.

Just as his alarm went off, telling him he had better get himself in gear and make it to work on time, the only feasible answer occurred to him.

If I were not such a shithead, I would have seen it right away. I've got some vacation time coming. *I'll fly back to Denver and talk to her.* He flexed his dimple at himself as he shaved. There hadn't been a girl who could resist his charm since he left seventh grade. *What the hell, I'll even cut her in on the action, maybe a seventy-five, twenty-five split. No, no, we'll go closer to sixty, forty, that way we could collaborate in the future. Oh, yes, that's it!* He thought of the pretty, serious, gray-eyed girl and felt his world tilt slightly. When it came right down to it, he didn't want to scam Malia.

Leaning on the sink, he watched the foamy water swirling down the drain. The build-up of soap scum seemed to have taken on geologic significance since he moved in. For some reason, he thought of Lilly and of Jordan going to a nice clean home with Jamie and real food waiting for him. He looked through the open bathroom door at the stack of unopened junk mail on the kitchen counter and Coke cans under a chair brimming with dirty socks and boxers. For the first time in his life, the thought of domesticity didn't make him want to toss his cookies. Instead he winked at himself in the mirror and whispered, "Wish me luck."

Jordan never said anything about Johnny's sudden urge to visit Denver. The tickets were lined up by noon, and Jamie dropped him off at the airport the next day. His palms started to sweat the minute the plane took off. The woman next to him hogged the armrest and seemed impervious to both his charm and his discomfort.

Okay, he thought, tucking the pillow he got from a stewardess under his arm. *I'd better come up with a plan. Let's see, I always meant to bring back her stuff. I've been wracked with guilt over taking it and wanted to bring it back when I could repay her in some way for taking it. That's good. Wracked with guilt is good. I had to get back to Sacramento because my mother was dying, no sick. Um, no, I better leave Mom out of this. Better to stick to the truth as much as possible. Okay, so I had to get back because I needed work, and I read her journal when I had to spend the night in the airport with no money for food, much less a book. Make that a sleepless night. That's easy. So then, I realized the potential in her writing. Saw is better, I saw how great her work is, and thought a friend of mine in the music industry would be interested in it. He wanted me to compose music for it, and here I am.*

The armrest hog folded down her tray and began sorting documents on it, occasionally letting them spill over onto his lap. They looked like legal stuff. Johnny remembered he had no one to look over the contract Smith said he would send him. Maybe Malia knew a lawyer they could use. He didn't think Jordan's construction guy would have much experience with the music industry.

I wonder where Teller is now. He'd be able to look it over in a heartbeat.

The thought of Teller, *that smug little son of a bitch*, reading over a contract for one of his songs Slick Trick wanted, actually asked to record, delighted him so much he smiled at the Armrest Hog. She looked past him out the window.

What if my charm fails me just when I need it most? That thought rattled him. *No, this is a good deal for the both of us, and I am not scamming her. She'd be nuts not to go along with the deal.*

He spent the rest of the flight trying to come up with rebuttals to every possible objection Malia could raise. The trip exhausted him.

Once the plane touched down, he decided he needed a rental car, something nice but not flashy. He found a map of Colorado Springs in the glove compartment and marked her address. *Maybe the butterflies in my stomach might be hunger. I better pick up something at a drive-thru.* He found a Mexican place that looked promising, but after a few bites he realized his jitters were nerves with wings.

As he pulled out into traffic, he did a neck-punishing double take. There, a block ahead, he saw it. *As though the damn thing has a flashing red spotlight on it! The Librorum Taberna sign in all its grimy scorched glory,* he thought. *This time I'm going to find out what this is all about.* With a squeal of brakes, he pulled into the first parking place and got out. The display had the same pile of books, the same streaks of crud on the windows. *This damn store is following me, or am I losing my mind?* He pushed through the door and caught a lung full of ancient book dust. "Ezra!" he called.

The man materialized from the shadows. "Now, now, Johnny. Only one dream to a customer. You already chose yours, for better or worse. Leave a few for others." The nasty yellow smile flashed and Johnny caught a disconcerting twinkle in the milky eyes. "Well, would you look at the time. Time to move on." Ezra moved forward in a way that seemed to push Johnny back to the door.

"Why are you and this place always following me? Wait, I need some answers!"

"Don't we all?" cane the sly insinuation voice as the door closed.

Johnny got back into the rental. *Well damn it. I'll just come back after I straighten things out with Malia.* But even as the thought formed in his mind, he knew he would never find it again.

The closer he got to the actual meeting, the more nervous he became. *What if her husband showed up after I took the journal? What if she goes postal on me for stealing her stuff? What if she got depressed and gained fifty pounds? What if she hates rappers? What if she's already met someone else? Christ, I should have done this sooner.*

By the time he pulled up to a tidy little house in one of the town's older sections, he had to take several deep breaths before getting out of the car. The home had a well-trimmed front yard with tiger lilies and some feathery purple thing he couldn't identify growing along the walk. A big elm tree shading the front porch was festooned with hanging baskets of petunias. It looked just like he thought it would. He took that as a good sign.

This is it. It's just like an audition. I always do really well at auditions. He checked his teeth in the rear view mirror to make sure he didn't have any of the stringy burrito meat stuck in his teeth. He worked the dimple once for confidence, then walked up to her door, pushed the bell and waited.

In a moment, he heard the sound of someone coming to the door. Swallowing, he fixed his most charming smile in place, tried for something a bit more sheepish in a hopeful sort of way, and almost deflated when a frail old lady answered the door.

Shit, she lives with her mother, he thought. *Well, that's not bad. It means she isn't remarried or anything.*

"Hi," he said in his best all American boy voice. "Is Malia Scott at home?" The little lady looked a bit perplexed. *She has the same serious gray eyes as Malia.*

"Yes, I'm Malia Scott, how can I help you?"

He grinned. "I think I'm looking for your daughter." He decided it wouldn't hurt to work on the mom a little.

"I'm sorry, I don't have a daughter." She spread her age spotted hands in an apologetic gesture as though saying, this is all there is.

"A niece maybe?"

His hopeful expression seemed to disturb her in an odd way. Maybe he looked a little too desperate.

"Why don't you come in and tell me what you want?" She stepped back into her tiny entrance way.

The front room had a well lived in look. He recognized Malia's touch in the bright paintings that splashed color on the walls. The light that filled the room filtered through the shade of the elm just outside the window. The furnishings had been out of fashion at least twenty years, but they looked tidy and comfortable. A TV sat in a corner by the shaded porch window, enabling her to watch a show or look out at the neighborhood. The end table next to a cozy armchair held a litter of pills boxes marked Monday through Friday morning, noon and night. And behind that sat a picture of Malia and her missing husband. The sight of it gave Johnny an unexpected boost of confidence.

He sat in a rocking chair across from the old lady and nodded to the picture. "Malia, right? I'm looking for her."

The woman smiled in confusion. "Well you found me, young man. I'm Malia Scott."

"I don't understand. The girl I'm looking for is about my age." He got up to get a closer look at the picture.

She handed it to him with an unsteady hand. "I just turned twenty-three when that picture was taken. It's my wedding picture. Ethan, my husband, went missing in action less than a year after that."

The devastating effect her words had on Johnny made her reach out to steady a man who weighed many times more than the picture she could barely lift. "Are you all right, Mister ... I'm sorry I didn't get your name."

"Cunningham, Johnny Cunningham." He sat staring at the girl in the picture, the girl he had come so far for, in so many ways. The girl he had fallen in love with.

Even though she did it with some difficulty, Johnny never heard the woman get up to bring him a drink of water. When she placed it in his hand, he looked up into her soft gray eyes, pleading silently for her to say she didn't mean it. *Maybe she guessed why I came and wants to punish me for stealing from her daughter.* He prayed for anything but the truth.

"I think you should tell me what this is all about, Mister Cunningham," Malia said. A blend of curiosity and concern shadowed her smile. "There seems to have been a mix up of some kind. I never had any children. Ethan wanted to wait 'til he got home to start our family. He went out on a patrol in the Mekong Delta and never came back."

Mekong Delta, Viet Nam not Iraq! And Johnny suddenly understood

Confession is supposed to be good for the soul. He had gone beyond caring about what kind of a fool he might seem to this frail old woman.

Johnny sank his head into his hands, partly so he wouldn't have to look at this new Malia, partly in reaction to the most genuine grief he had ever experienced. "I'm a musician, at least I was up to a little over a year ago. Music, like a lot of things, came a little too easy for me. Maybe that's why I never took it, or anything else, very seriously," he began.

Cicadas shrilled in the elm tree beyond the open window. Evening had crept into the little room by the time he finished with, "I guess I thought I could come out here and, I don't know, convince the girl in the picture to collaborate with me." He made a helpless shrugging gesture. "She'd become the girl of my dreams." A bewildered sigh escaped him. "I fell in love with a dream."

The stark simplicity and sense of loss with which he spoke touched Malia. "I can tell you from bitter experience, dreams, even perfect dreams, make for a thin life. Reality, for all its warts and discomfort, is all we have to build with." A tear slid down her papery cheek. "It seems we have both stolen something from the other." She waved her thin hand to the pills on the table. "I'm not going to be around long enough to see how this all works out. You may keep the poems, but I want my journal back."

A wrenching fear at the thought of losing the only contact he had with his Malia shot through him. She saw it and knew all too clearly what it meant.

"You can make a photocopy of it, but I want it for now, and when I … no longer need it, I'll see to it that the journal is sent to you.

They talked on as evening turned to night and Johnny realized how weary the old woman had become. He kissed her cheek as he left.

In a daze, Johnny walked to the rental car, got in and gripped the steering wheel. *She's gone. When someone dies, at least you have a funeral or something, but this, this is … My God! It's just what she had to go through when she found out her husband was missing.* Sharing such a bond with his Malia comforted him a little. *I still have her poems, we can still collaborate.*

He envisioned the years of work he had ahead of him, and knew now he would have something to work for, a mission. *I'll have to get serious about my music.* He looked into the rearview mirror still tilted down to show him his reflection. *The blond hair will have to go. Something more subdued, just a little darker than my sandy color.* He definitely had a more mature air. A slight lowering of the eyelids as he sucked in his cheeks, *yes that's it.* The dimple quirked. *Only flashes of the dimple,* he decided, *like some bright thing glimpsed in dark water. That was good, dark waters run deep.*

The pain in his heart became a warming glow to this new Cunningham. Johnny seemed such a kid name now. *John Cunningham, Mister John Cunningham* realized he could never bring himself to talk about his tragic loss. The world could never understand such a pure love. *Of course I will love again, but never like this, no woman could measure up to my Malia.* He fingered his dimple, and sighed at his reflection. He couldn't wait to get back to Sacramento and see how long it took Jamie to realize how profoundly he had changed.

At some point, every writer needs a bit
of inspiration. A kick in the pants if
you will. I've seen most of them at one
time or another. I just hope the good
doctor is prepared for his. EF

Jack English, MD, Dragonslayer

by Richard E. Collette

Good thing Professor Google knows everything. You'd think after practicing medicine for fifteen years, I wouldn't need to look up the definition for Addison's Disease, but you'd be dead wrong. Of course, I never saw that working in Peds, but still, I'm almost certain I learned something in medical school.

The top result was some government website drafted to the lowest common denominator. No thanks. Then Wikipedia. Ugh. I would have given my right hand to still have a subscription to Up-To-Date. Finally, I reached a link to the Mayo Clinic. With any luck, it would tell me something I didn't already know. Scrolling down yielded minimal information, except a potential link to Celiac Sprue.

So, my character needed to have a healthy respect for gluten, check. He needed to be aware of what he ate at all times. That could influence how his whole life played out. If I changed that, I would be rewriting chapters and chapters. But right now he's emotionally flat as a pancake. That's a lot of rewrites, though. Bugger that.

I was getting nowhere, so I decided to check out some writing websites, hopefully shed some light on my mental deficiency, or writer's block, as many like to call it. The existence of such a thing is a topic of endless debate, but it cheesered me to know others had my same difficulties. That is, it made me happy. People still look at me strangely when I say things like that. I blame my parents and then tell them to bugger off.

It's a damn joke, of course, but usually all I get is more weird looks.

The screen flashed with an advertisement, and I was about two inches from clicking it away when it drew my attention. "Librorum Taberna – A bookstore from the ages," the ad read. It went on to list all the various and sundry big name authors who frequented the shop. I raised an eyebrow at the list. Stephen King. Danielle Steel. Michael Crichton. J.K. Rowling. Jules Verne. Ernest Hemingway. Apparently, the place had been around a while. Still, if it was in New York – the publishing capital of the world – and could lure authors from halfway across the globe, it must be at least decent.

Plus, maybe they had some books on writing.

1234 Fifth Avenue. New York, New York. How terribly cheeky. But I could use a trip into the city. Syracuse wore on me after a while. The constant motion in the Big Apple might get my brain working the way it should. I grabbed my phone and looked at the ad again. "212-555-1234" scrawled across the bottom. Incredible. It must have been difficult to get a matching phone number.

The voice on the other end crackled. "Librorum Taberna, this is Ezra. How may I assist you?"

"Yeah, hi. Do you have books on hand about writing?"

"Not in my hand at the moment, no." I hesitated, and the man barked a laugh. "But I'm sure I can find whatever it is you'd like in the store."

"So … is that a yes?" I asked.

"I have any book you need," the man said. That was a rather haughty statement. But something about his tone, maybe just his accent, spoke to me.

I decided to see what all the fuss was about. "Great. I'll be there this afternoon. What time do you close?"

"We're open twenty-four hours, my good man."

I waited. "That must be a joke, too?"

"No, sir. Come whenever you wish. Though I might avoid the subway after dark."

Where was his accent from? "Uh, okay. See you this evening then."

"Wonderful, sir."

Six hours, two ventis, and half a Dave Barry book later, I found myself walking along Fifth Avenue. I had successfully heeded Ezra's warning; the sun hung just above the trees of Central Park to my right, the skyline silhouetted above them. Summertime in New York City is a bit like being crammed into a hot oven with eight million other people.

And this time of evening is the most interesting. It's true what they say – this city never sleeps. It only changes hands. There were people in business suits running home, mixed with night clubbers in sparkly dresses trying to get an early start, and everything in between. The city's congested, it's noisy, it smells, and it's absolutely delightful. The sidewalks sing.

I counted down the addresses. How many blocks away was this

place again? I passed 1243 Fifth Avenue. Strange then, that even and odd addresses would be on the same side of the street. But who was I to question New York's city planners – they obviously knew what they were doing. The next building was 1221 Fifth Avenue. *How did I miss it?* I'd only passed some monstrous medical center. I retraced my steps. Yes, the massive hospital rose eight stories, tan upper floors blazing in the evening sun.

But it took up the entire block.

There had to be a street number on it somewhere. I found it quickly – 1235 Fifth. By this point, I was dumbfounded. Could it be that I remembered it wrong? A quick smartphone consult told me what I already knew. 1234. No way did I forget it. But all the street numbers here were odd, and the idea of a no-name bookstore in Central Park sounded absurd, even to me.

I looked into the trees just to say I did before calling and berating the clerk, and there it was. Well, I shouldn't say, "there it was," because all I could see was the sign. A rectangular piece of wood, *Librorum Taberna* scrawled across it in some pseudo-old English font, hung from what appeared to be just one of the park's many streetlights. Below it, an arrow pointed down. Was the shop *under* Central Park? They must be joking. But I'd traveled six hours and the thought of turning back now pained me.

So I froggered my way through the traffic of Fifth – a pretty easy prospect given the cars scarcely moved – and walked up to the sign. Made of several boards nailed together, the thing could have been constructed in the time since I left home, aside from the weather-stained wood. The arrow pointed down into the bowels of Central Park East, a dark and bottomless stairwell. How ominous. I considered calling my brother Michael, telling him the prank wasn't funny, and thanking him for wasting my entire damn day. But my ass couldn't bear the thought of sitting back on the bus.

So what the hell? I went for it.

The stairs fell down into darkness. My footfalls became the only sounds in the world. Musty earth supplanted exhaust and sweat. The light streaming down from above faded, and I hesitated, trying to find the next step. Lamps sprang to life around me. I paused in the orange glow. How good of them to light their creepy corridor with motion-sensing sconces. A lone spotlight illuminated the door at the end of the stairwell like the hard glow of an otoscope on the eardrum.

This day grew weirder by the moment, but at this point, curiosity beat out my apprehension. I grabbed the ornate door handle and twisted. Cold raced up my arm, but the door showed no sign of unlatching. Sighing, I glanced around for the hidden cameras and Ashton whatever-the-hell-his-name-is to jump out, but it was just me and the door. I pushed on it and, to my surprised delight, it swung open.

More electric torches flickered on inside, casting their glow over a reception desk, an old man behind it, and no more than two rows of books. The old man had to be at least two hundred years old, his nose previously fractured at least once, likely twice.

"Do you often work in the dark?" I asked.

The man raised an eyebrow. His eyes were white as milk.

No iris, no pupil. Solid white. Maybe he was blind?

"Of course not, that would be rather absurd." He held up a flashlight.

Must just be some fancy contact lenses. "Ah, so you're one of those lovely enviro-conscientious people, eh?"

I realized it hadn't been the phone crackling; this man's voice just sounded that way. "Right you are. I am Ezra, purveyor of fine books. And you are Doctor English."

Okay, honestly, what the hell? I moved a step further into the soft orange glow of the room. "How do you know me?"

"A name is no more than a string of letters used for identification. No, I do not know you."

I sighed. "Okay, how do you know my name?"

"Professor Google knows everything. Besides, English is a simple switch from Eglintoun."

My father changed it when they moved to this country in the 30s. This had to be a dream.

"I am glad you took my advice about the subway."

I nodded, eyeing the door. "How long have you guys been here? I've never heard of this place."

"Why, we're here when you need us," Ezra said, rather matter-of-factly. "Now, what brings you in today?" He swept his arm back with the dramatic flair of a Broadway actor ... over the two shelves of books.

Okay, I'll play along. "Er, right. I could use some writing references."

"Ah yes, for a medical thriller, is it? I believe you'll find everything you need down aisle two." He pointed to his left. I followed his finger and walked down the darkened lane, glancing back to see that the clerk had gone back to whatever he was doing in the dark.

More motion-sensors lit the corridor as I walked, keeping me in a perpetual bubble of light. Darkness shrouded the end. I glanced back again, but Ezra had been consumed by the darkness. This had to be a dream, didn't it? Books lined the shelves to either side – solid medical references from top to bottom. How very convenient. I pulled one at random, and it turned out to be an anatomy reference. I read a few pages, hearing my professor's voice in my head as I went.

The bones of the hand can be divided into three groups, it read. *The carpals, the metacarpals and the phalanges, in proximal to distal order. The carpals comprise mainly the wrist and upper hand, while the metacarpals stretch distally, forming the majority of the hand itself. The phalanges–*

I looked up. And found myself sitting in first semester anatomy class. Dr. Hillroy stood at the front, drawing a terrible rendition of a hand on the board as he spoke. Students all around scribbled furiously, trying in vain to imitate the prof's cockeyed drawing. Hillroy looked back over the rows of chairs, his bespectacled expression asking, "Any questions?" Then he kept right on rambling, as if he expected my sudden appearance in his classroom.

I shook my head, trying to wake up, but nothing changed. Though I'll admit, I found it amazing how well I remembered anatomy class. Everything down to the pencils strewn across Hillroy's desk was as it should be. Something told me to play along, though I couldn't say what. I felt compelled to take notes, even though I knew all the information being covered. I closed my textbook, reached for my pen, and the room vanished.

Total blackness.

My vision darted about without input, when the soft orange glow popped around me. I turned and there stood Ezra, those weird eyes staring at me. I leapt backwards and, through some act of God, didn't smash right into the shelves.

"Ah, sorry my boy," Ezra said. "Didn't mean to frighten you."

If that image – white eyes, smoker's hair, perfect, though yellow, teeth – didn't wake me up, this wasn't a dream. No way could my subconscious build such a person. I put a hand to my mouth and whispered. "What is this place?"

"A bookstore," he said, looking at me like I was a bloody idiot. "Do you still need more books? Perhaps a similar story to get the ol' juices flowing, yes?"

I nodded absently, and followed the old man further down the aisle. Well, at least I think it was further down; I couldn't be sure at this point which way we'd come from. I could walk for what seemed like forever and never see the exit.

"So how does it work?" I asked without hope of an answer.

"How does it work, sir? Well, it's simple really. They say a good book is transformational. Here, that is most certainly the case. Surely you can understand."

I surely didn't, of course. How could a book put you in that world? The thought was stark mad. But I couldn't very well tell Ezra that. I needed a diversion, something to relieve my overtaxed brain and get the gears turning. "Do you have any fantasy novels?" I asked, somewhat hesitant. Seeing a couple knights duke it out could give me a much-needed break.

Ezra only nodded, stained grey hair rustling. Within the space of two steps, dungeons and dragons replaced catheters and musculature on the shelves. The organizational system in this place could dumbfound a Nobel Prize winner. Every fantasy novel in existence hung out on these shelves. Dragons, damsels, swords, and vampires. Anything and everything imaginable. But how to choose? Again, I just grabbed one off the shelf.

The book I picked bore a dragon laid over a cover designed to look like singed leather. The pages appeared burned as well, and the book carried a smoky scent. I frowned. Maybe I should grab another?

"I assure you," Ezra said as if hearing my thoughts, "the book you selected will not disappoint. It is a very engaging read." He winked.

"Okay," I said slowly. I opened it to a random page and read.

The dragon just stood there, grinning with those teeth like a thousand swords, face menacing. Larak didn't believe it, so close to the castle and now the beast chose to show itself. He felt the magic rise within him, an uncontrollable torrent willed forth by the dragon's mere presence. All he had to do was —

I gripped the book in white knuckles. Even without context, these kinds of scenes always intrigued me. A strange green glow came from behind the pleather cover. I flipped the tome over. My hands … pulsed. Green light flared around them, as if I had been irradiated. A lot.

I looked up to see if this book had the same effect as the last. The dragon cocked his head at me, massive horns rising all along his head and back, spindle eyes questioning. The creature roared, shattering the silence of the rocky plains.

Oh, bugger.

I leapt behind the nearest rock as the fire seared past. I slid to a stop out of sight of the dragon, my hands shaking. Unsteady, I checked myself for burns or flaming clothes. I wore a simple brown robe, and it seemed unscathed. I was okay. Plus, all I had to do to end this was close the book. Oh, damn! I searched around frantically. I must have dropped it when I rolled out of the way. It sat on the ground some ten feet away, covers curled by the heat, but otherwise unharmed. The pages rustled in a light breeze, it was still open.

I just had to get to it. The fire still scorched the rock behind me, relenting intermittently so the dragon could take a breath. My hands still pulsed. Magic! These kinds of books almost always had some kind of magic in them. Perhaps I could use it against this animal. I channeled my inner Toby McGuire, trying to figure out just how to use this newfound power. A bevy of magical words ran through my mind, and I shouted them all… to no avail. Not only did I fail to lance any green fire from my fingers, I managed to make the moss-colored pulsing stop completely.

The rock cracked under the intense thermodynamic shift. A few more moments and it would shatter. And the fire would consume me. I looked around, trying to find an out. Nothing. I hid behind a brown rock sitting on a flat of more brown rock. Brown rock stretched away in every direction. Who the hell wrote this scenery? Dreadful.

My hands pulsed again. If only I could figure out how my magic worked, I might have a chance here. Another blast came, hard and furious, against my hiding spot. The flames came in about twenty-second increments. There was nothing for it. I counted it off in my head. Three, two, one. The fire stopped. I launched myself out into the open as the dragon inhaled.

My muscles responded like a PT patient. I stumbled onto the book and rolled across the rocks. Pain shot across my shoulders from the impact, but I managed to keep hold of the pleather cover. The dragon finished breathing in. I slammed the book closed and everything – dragon included – vanished in a glorious blaze of blackness.

I lay on the ground of aisle two in Librorum Taberna, breathing ragged and shallow.

"Ah, Doctor English," Ezra said, his face unreadable.

Did the man ever smile? You'd think he could make some facial expression since reading his eyes was impossible.

"Was the book as engaging as I said?"

I closed my eyes, trying to steady my frayed nerves. I hyperventilated. Try as I might, I couldn't breathe regularly. I must have looked like someone from a psych ward.

Apparently Ezra noticed. "Wait here, Jack. I'll be back in a moment."

Where am I gonna go? I lay curled up in a darkened hallway, not sure which way was out. Ezra vanished into the darkness. Why don't the motion sensors light up for him? I blinked in an attempt to clear my head, and pulled myself into a sitting position, back against the shelves. The aging bookseller returned after no more than thirty seconds, an enormous stack of books in his arms. They stretched up above his head, balanced with precision.

How could this emaciated twig of a man carry so many books – hardcovers, mind you – without even breaking a sweat? Or a hip. He loomed over me, face an expressionless mask. "I've gathered you a selection of medicine-related books. With luck, one will give you what you need."

I picked one up at random, flipped it open, and read.

"*The damage is bad, Doc,*" *the nurse said.* "*Double gunshot wound to the torso, one substernal, one right upper quad.*" *She paused, helping to slide the patient to the operating table.* "*What do you need?*" *In reality, a stiff drink and a good woman is what he needed.*

"This is no time to be reading, Doc!" the nurse yelled.

I looked up from the book. The nurse's nametag said "Kacy." She wore her long blonde hair loose about her shoulders – completely inappropriate for a scrub nurse – and her blue eyes and bright red lips bore more makeup than most models in magazines. The operating table stood behind her, a patient – my patient now, it seemed – bleeding atop it.

I set the hardcover down, and walked up to the table, letting the circulation nurse tie on my gown and hold out my gloves. The patient's injuries *were* severe. His shirt had been removed. Blood oozed around the holes in his torso, running down to pool on his stomach. Black sludge mixed with it; he likely had bowel damage. I racked my brain to remember my four-week surgery rotation in med school. The guy probably had sepsis. If he didn't get proper care in the next few minutes, he'd die for certain.

"I can't do this," I said. "I'm no surgeon."

"Doctor Dobson," Kacy said. "You're the only surgeon in-house right now!"

I looked around the room. Anesthesia already had the patient intubated, breathing regulated by a ventilator. The clock in the corner read 00:34. Middle of the damn night, of course there wouldn't be anyone else here.

"Okay," I said. "First we need to check for lung damage. Give me a scalpel."

Kacy looked at me like I'd grown a second head. "Lung damage? That bullet is way too low for that."

I looked at the patient again. She was right, of course. I sighed. But there was nothing for it. If I didn't do what I could for this man, death was a virtual certainty. I grabbed the scalpel from Kacy, and I cut.

The blip of the monitor turned into a static buzz.

"I need a crash cart!" the anesthesiologist roared. He pushed me out of the way. "Asystole. Two milligrams epinephrine IV push. Defibrillator." I stood in a daze behind him as he worked. The flat beep of the monitor didn't change. "Charging. Clear." Thud. "Again. Charging. Clear." Thud. The static beep never changed. The whole room reverberated with it, a constant reminder. "Time of death, twelve forty-five."

I reminded myself this was just a fiction novel, but the body on the table looked real enough. The anesthesiologist pushed past me again, the look on his face screaming at me without him saying a word. Blood dripped down the patient's arm and puddled on the floor as the technicians came in to clean up.

My feet felt as though they were glued to the floor. No matter how I tried, they wouldn't respond, my gaze pinned to the dead man on the table. But this was just a book, a bloody story. Surely Kacy's alluring good looks told me that much. No nurse looked like that, especially in the middle of the night. But it felt so real.

I blinked, trying to clear my head, and the room vanished.

I sat on the floor of Librorum, Ezra looming over me. The novel about that operating room sat closed a few feet away, the soft orange glow reflecting off its cover. One of the techs must have closed it.

"Still no luck?" Ezra asked.

"Luck with what?"

"Your own book," he said. "Why, that's why you're here, is it not? To come to your own epiphany?"

"I …." Why am I here? I had just seen a man die. But all I could think of was plot devices and character deaths in the scheme of a novel. I had *been there*. Why could I not bring myself to admit that? "I don't know," I said.

"Well, would you care to try again?"

I nodded tiredly, looking over the stack he set before me. "Why are you doing this to me?"

"Doing what, my boy?" Ezra asked.

"This," I said, sweeping my hand over the books. "Making me see these things."

"As I have said, a good book is transformational. You finish a different person than when you started. I am merely a facilitator."

"So this," I said. "All this is just to train authors? Who are you?"

"Ah," Ezra said, picking out a small book from the stack. "This one should serve you well, I think." He paused. "But I think you should start from the beginning. Better results that way, usually."

"Okay …." Still sitting on the floor, I took the book and opened to page one.

Doctor Dobson stood just over 5'11", with brown eyes, a strong jaw, and a nose just barely too large for his face. His brown curly hair was cut short, and try as he might to avoid it, graying at the fringes. And right now, he had a job to do.

Odd that the writer would describe me so well. Perhaps I was just that generic-looking.

"Where the hell did you find a book?"

I looked up and shaded my eyes against the sun, letting them adjust. A golf course stretched away before me, green and imposing. A bald man leaned on a driver with an expression that said, "What the hell are you doing?"

"I was, uh, just reading up on some new swing techniques," I said.

A quick glance at the scorecard said this man was named Frank. And now he cocked a brown eyebrow up toward his shiny head. "Right. Well, it's your shot."

Why did it have to be golf? Already this book had hit one major doctor stereotype. And was I the same Doctor Dobson as in the operating room? That's what Kacy had called me. But why would Ezra give me the same book? Maybe it was a series.

I could play golf about as well I could perform neurosurgery, but club already in hand, I stepped up to the ball. I swung and missed completely. "Practice swing," I said. Then I swung again. This time I connected, but the ball veered off into woods along the side of the course.

"What's wrong with you, Paul?" Frank asked. "Usually you're spot-on with your drives."

"Guess I'm just tired," I said, trying to sound weak. "Think I'll turn in for the day."

"But this is only hole four!"

"I know, but I'm not feeling well."

"Ah, don't be such a little girl," Frank said. Sweat beaded on his forehead, but it wasn't that hot outside. In fact, the temperature felt quite nice. He cringed.

"You okay?" I asked.

Frank collapsed. Apparently, he was not okay. I rushed over to him. "I feel like I've got a weight on my chest," he said. "Acute myocardial infarct."

Who would say that during a heart attack? Not even a cardiologist. But this guy was obviously a doctor, or at least written as a stereotypical one. Be that as it may, I still had an inexplicable desire to help the guy.

I checked his vitals. His pulse was irregular, his breathing at least semi-regular. I called for an ambulance, and it arrived in short order, driving right up onto the golf course. Classic.

Twenty minutes of zany book time later, I stood in the emergency room of Saint Sebastian – a fictional hospital located … twenty minutes from a golf course. How did the author get away with not telling us where we even are? If Ezra thought this book could help me with ideas for my own writing, he had to be mad. The old man was clearly insane. Nothing for it but to try, though. After all, what did I have to lose?

I approached the desk. "Hi," I said, "I'm here to see, uh, Frank."

The nurse behind the desk looked at me like the idiot I must have seemed.

"Golfer," I said. "Acute MI, just came in. I was with him at the time."

The nurse squinted. "Doctor Dobson? Is that you?"

"Yes, yes! What room is Frank in?"

"Twelve thirty-four."

"Thank you," I said, already moving past the desk.

The architect who designed this ER apparently had masochistic tendencies – the hallways ran at strange, curving angles, twisting back into the bowels of the hospital. The room numbers – those visible at least – had no discernible order. I passed 1375, then 1201 through 1205. Then 1245. I closed my eyes and sighed. I glanced back and could still see the nurse's station. So I kept walking.

The hallway stretched on and on, but eventually I reached 1234. Hang on, wasn't that the address of Librorum? How did Ezra find a book with such parallels? Of course, it wasn't the most original number, perhaps there were just more writers who used such dumb tactics than I thought.

I walked through the door and pushed back the curtain. Frank smiled up at me from beneath his stylish hospital gown. "How are you feeling?" I asked.

"Pretty good, Paul, although my chest hurts like hell."

"I believe it. They run any tests yet?"

"Nah," he said. "Just waiting to see Erickson now. Apparently they thought I was stable enough to let sit and wait." He grinned. "Damned ERs."

Erickson must have been the ER doctor. I nodded and Frank eyed me. "How are *you* feeling?" he asked.

"What do you mean?" I asked, setting down the book and rummaging through the sideboard looking for the television remote.

"You said you didn't feel well. What's up?"

"Oh right," I said. "No, I feel fine now. You sure you're good? You look a little pale." His face had developed a faded look, almost as if he were going vasovagal. I'd seen that plenty in my own clinic, but Frank wasn't sweating, and he seemed to be perfectly alert.

"Yeah, I'm good," Frank said with a look that added "idiot."

But the guy didn't look right. "Now that you mention it, I think I'm running a fever," he said. Then his skin began to turn from pale to green. His eyes turned yellow. Acute liver failure? But how would he show jaundice after just seconds? It made no sense.

"Nurse!" I yelled, stepping into the hallway. "Anyone?" Of course they couldn't hear me. This had to be the worst emergency room design on the planet. I pushed back into the room, looking for the call button. Nothing. Worst. ER. Ever.

The pull string in the bathroom would work, maybe. I ran in and grabbed it, noting that Frank's skin turned more green by the second. That wasn't normal jaundice. When pulled, the alarms rang out through the room, echoing down the hallway. Immediately, several nurses rushed into the room. How convenient.

The emergency doctor, presumably Erickson, strode in moments later, his air of self-importance radiating. He glanced briefly at Frank. "Acute Hepatitis, with patient presenting signs of bubonic plague."

I frowned. The nurses in the room looked at Erickson with unhidden adoration, eyes wide and praising. Plague? Was the man serious? But he didn't grin, he didn't break into a fit of laughter, he only stared at Frank, the gears behind his eyes churning. "Mask up, Doctor Dobson," he said. Suddenly, everyone in the room – including Erickson – had masks on, though for the life of me I never saw them grab the things. If only emergency medicine were so easy.

I fastened a mask behind my head. "You really think this is plague, Erickson?" I asked. "There's been all of one reported case in the last year."

"No question," he said. "Look at the raised pustules forming beneath Frank's arms …." He pointed. "And here, on his neck …." Sure enough, there they were. All the typical signs of plague – and by typical I mean the signs you read about in some medical textbook but have never actually seen. Save for on television, of course.

"Okay," I said, "but how do you explain the liver failure?"

"It's easy really," Erickson said, experimentally pressing on one of the pustules. "The plague bacterium infiltrates the liver, causing hepatic cells to cease their function. This is fast moving. Push IV Gent and Doxycycline."

This had to be the smartest ER doctor ever. A little *too* smart. No modern physician would have the first clue about the epidemiology and treatment of plague. Sure, it's antibiotics, but this was ridiculous. The guy came to a diagnosis and outlined the perfect treatment plan in less than twenty seconds. Is this really what the general populace thought about modern medicine?

I mean, I had watched shows on television, but I thought those were entertaining strictly as dolled up soap operas. No one actually believed medicine played out like this. Did they?

Frank's heart rhythm became irregular. His pulse raced like he'd just finished a marathon – or in Frank's case, maybe a 1k. "Let's push some adenosine," Erickson said, hands flying over Frank checking for advancing symptoms. He moved with superhuman grace. I shook my head. No one was this good.

As if hearing my silent declaration, the rapid blip of the monitor turned again to a static buzz. "Paddles," Erickson said. The nurses pulled in a crash cart. Erickson tried for ten minutes to revive Frank, screaming obscenities and phrases such as, "Come on, damn you!" and "Don't you die on me!" This whole story grew less believable by the second. Finally, Erickson called it quits. "Time of death, twelve thirty-four."

A smile crept onto my face. Whoever wrote this thought himself terribly clever. "Something you find amusing?" Erickson asked.

Maybe my smile touched my eyes, too, but then I realized my mask had disappeared. What a clever plot device. Creating tension out of thin air, a majestic trick. "No," I said. "But –"

"Doctor," a nurse interrupted. "Your face, it's …." She trailed off. Here again, she looked like a Victoria's Secret model wearing scrubs that could have come from a similar catalogue. But her smoky eyes stared at Erickson.

The man's face had taken on a slight greenish hue, and then he collapsed on the table. What was the incubation period for plague? I racked my brain, but the answer certainly wasn't ten minutes. Two days sprang to mind. Two to five, even.

One of the nurses laid a finger on the emergency doctor's neck. "He's dead," she said, already starting to edge toward the door.

I squinted and raised an eyebrow. Had Erickson been exposed previously? "Did Erickson see Frank at all in the last couple days? Like socially, maybe?" I asked.

"I don't think so," the nurse said. "Doctor Erickson hated Doctor Mati." Then two of the nurses showed symptoms, their skin going from tan to pale to green. The Victoria's Secret nurses appeared plague-immune, but others, ones I hadn't even seen before that moment, keeled over. How handy that the beautiful ones seemed immune to the effects of the disease.

Still, a book about an epidemic? The fastest spreading outbreak in human history.

This whole scene just screamed ridiculous. I couldn't help but laugh. Maybe that was it. I could write a book poking fun at what the medical fiction genre has become. Sure, it could turn out a clichéd mess, but at least

I could get some ideas down on paper.

Thoughts sparked through my mind. A medical thriller examining the way a true epidemic would be handled. Cut out the absurdities, and maybe even make veiled references to them, and I could have a decent story on my hands. There had to be a market for cynical satire, didn't there? Surely, the actual workings of medicine interested *someone*. Didn't it? And even if it didn't, I could make the book enough of a satire to appeal to the masses.

At any rate, I could write. I reached over to the bedside table, the gorgeous nurse looking at me in horror, and closed the book.

The room vanished.

Shade from swaying trees moved across my face and I looked up. I stood in Central Park East again, the massive medical center on Fifth Avenue across the street, the parallel smells of grass and exhaust in the air.

I glanced around for the Librorum Taberna sign, but it had vanished. Of course it had. Ezra's words rang in my head. *We're here when you need us.* Could it really be that simple? I still held the most recent book in my hands, and I looked at the cover. *Bubonic Pandemic.* Wow. By far, the worst title I could have envisioned based on what I'd seen of the story.

If this hack could get published, I certainly had nothing to worry about. Right?

It's not often that a patron truly understands what they are looking for. Rarer still when one appreciates my gift. But she will in time. EF

Scales

by *Amity Green*

The well-earned scholarship to study abroad for three weeks in London changed Tessa Marie Conley's young life. When her laptop chimed into the quiet of yet another eventless Saturday night, Tessa tore her focus away from her book. She scrolled the mouse to the tiny envelope and clicked on the email from Professor Sirmons. She expected the message to be yet another suggestion for studying, maybe an attached essay or a recorded podcast from some authority or accomplished author. Not expected was an invitation to set foot into the heart of London to tour the roots of British Literature.

Professor Sirmons was dear to her. This year marked the third she'd been studying with him, and he knew her story. Living in a "home for girls" did not lend much to life outside school, so Tessa delved into the only thing she had to enrich her life. She easily breezed through classes, and started acquiring college credits early with the grants she found available to children with no parents. The first class had been English Composition Two. Then she'd moved on to what they both considered "the good stuff"— British Literature and History.

His courses were designed perfectly for Tessa, spending what she considered adequate time studying the history of the authors themselves, as well as their works. Like her, some were orphans; some were the poor kids on the block.

Other students on the study abroad program had different focuses. While Tessa could appreciate the opportunity to legally go into a club in downtown London and have a drink at the ripe age of eighteen, she would much rather concentrate on the beauty of rich history, the roots of literature, and most of all, the ancient objects in the museums, theatres and antiquities shops. The thought of laying her hands on such wonders made her fingertips tingle in anticipation. And there wouldn't be just one old shop; each would be nestled cozily between others of their kind in SoHo.

After a tight itinerary of tours and workshops, the three-week-long course in London would come to a close in two days' time. Tessa had arranged her schedule perfectly. Her essays were written and emailed to Professor Sirmons. She'd be *danged* if she would blow her 4.0 average just to have a day of indulgence. The Professor's email contained a cheery explanation that she would finally, *blessedly*, have the last Sunday afternoon of the trip to herself. She would take the Tube to the Covent Garden stop and go in search of Cecil Court. It was her last day in London, and she intended to live it up a little.

She checked her reflection, adjusting a knee length skirt on her petite frame and slipped her feet into her favorite creamy, sling-backed, peek-toe pumps. A rose and beige cardigan completed the look, a practical necessity when perusing shops in the chilly London air. She added a quick brush of mascara to accent the almond shape of her soft brown eyes. *What the heck, maybe I will meet a nice boy.* Then she grabbed her backpack and made sure to lock the door behind her.

Stepping from the Tube stop into the cloud-covered afternoon, Tessa shouldered her pack and made her way along the bustling sidewalk. Her gaze swept the sides of brick buildings along the way, reading placards attached high above her head. To the left of a shadowed brick lane, her eyes came to rest on a plain sign fixed to the stone wall that read, *Cecil Court*. After traveling nearly six thousand miles, she now stood, fingertips tingling away, at the gateway to the best mix of old bookstores and antiquities shops she could hope for.

Taking a deep breath of sweet, damp air, Tessa scanned the court, ripping the vision like a CD to her memory. Tall buildings blocked all but a few hours sunshine in the brick lane, adding a chill to the air and a dark tint to the paving stones and storefronts. Converted gaslights lined the center of the narrow lane, flickering to life in the midafternoon. The musty scent of old things swirled atop the herby fragrance of potted lavender. Shingles hung on ornate wrought iron brackets anchored in stone and brick. Not many people strolled the sidewalk with her in the quiet court, so Tessa meandered freely. Catching the sound of her favorite heels clicking against the stone walk, she daydreamed. *I'm really here. I want to remember it, just like this, forever.*

History called to her from every door. The court was a small place of thrilling but murky times gone by, the buildings there each lending stories of seedy barber shops, unhealthy eateries, and houses of ill-repute to London's colorful past.

The next shop had an especially long sign that didn't match the rest. Rather than the typical brackets, the sign was held by a crouching gargoyle, one arm extending two-thirds the length along the bottom of the sign's wooden plank, the creature's chin resting on the top corner in an oddly human way. The thing's skin shone like a muted oilslick in the fading light of the narrow alley.

Old English lettering announced the name of the store below as *Librorum Taberna*, which Tessa quickly translated from her small knowledge of Latin as "small shop of books", or something similar. The elongated plank was darkened across the bottom portion, matching the upper half of the wooden storefront perfectly; both somehow winning the battle against the damaging effects of time, flame, and weather.

Tessa couldn't take her gaze from the storefront. Only a few intact facings remained after the fires, especially in Cecil Court, where arson had been a two-century long trend amongst the residents of Georgian and Victorian London. This one was in remarkable shape for its age, though all the way to the top of the two-story building, tell-tale burn marks licked at the right side.

The thick facing that surrounded the oversized double doors was expertly crafted. Ornate carvings twisted throughout the design ending a chest level. She ran a hand over one of the two male faces that protruded from the wood. Softened by time and weather, their wooden features were rendered subtle and smooth. With sightless eyes, they stared at the few passing patrons of Cecil Court.

Tessa's gaze drifted to the large door handle. A shop like this one could take hours to thoroughly enjoy, and Professor Sirmons would lay an egg if she came back late. *Screw it*, she decided. *I'll never have this chance again.* A defiant grin tugged at her dimples as she walked inside.

The heavy door clicked shut after she stepped through, taking with it a portion of the light in the room. Tessa stilled while her sight adjusted to the dim lighting, and her senses burst to life. The aromas of aged wood and leather blended sweetly behind a top note of Earl Grey steeped with a hint of nutmeg. The only sound that greeted her was the gentle hum of a dehumidifier that helped to preserve the old books. Tessa sucked in an exhilarating breath.

She stood in the open foyer, the store yawning before her like a cavern.

Leading beyond her sight, darkness swallowed the towering, shelf-lined walls so tall that wheeled ladders rested at the junctions. Occasional gilded wall sconces added muted light to delicate beams, casting perfect shadows. The section labels glowed in the soft light, announcing the names of British Literature's family of writers and playwrights and pulling her into the depths of the bookstore. She walked the aisles, perusing authors, her neck craned slightly to the right. She read title after title from leather-bound spines that lived on shelves so impeccably organized any librarian would feel envious.

She rounded an ornate, bull-nose corner to encounter a nook harboring two leather reading chairs. A small writing desk held a lamp and a box of tissues used for the delicate process of reading from old tomes without staining the pages. A solitary case stood against the back wall. Tessa froze when she read the illuminated sign on the top of the glassed-in bookcase. *The Works of Mr. Christopher Marlow*. A set of replicas for reading rested on a nearby shelf.

"Aw, you had to, didn't ya?" she told the empty room. Tessa skirted the desk and centered herself in front of a row of books, gaze coming to rest on her favorite closet play—Dr. Faustus. The banter of Faust and Mephistopheles called to her from between the tome's leather covers as she hugged the book to her chest and plopped into a chair.

A leathery, scraping sound, then a loud *slap* popped through the store. Easing up from the chair, she set the book down, listening hard. Raspy, scratching sounds floated eerily across the tops of the bookcases, chilling her skin.

"Hello?" The call resonated. *You're such a chicken*, she thought, chiding herself.

Scrape. Tap. Scrape. Tap.

Tessa followed the sounds through the darkened store to a reading nook far in the back. She drew in a breath to call out, but a voice from the darkness stilled her.

"Jack and Jill went up a hill ...," the voice trailed off, huffing with sarcasm.

Whoever recited the nursery rhyme had a seriously bad set of teeth from the sound of it. Creeping forward, Tessa allowed only enough of her face to clear the side of the thick wooden bookshelf so that one eye could see who was there.

On the floor, the gargoyle from the store's sign lay sprawled on its back, scale-like skin glistening in the dim light. One leg stretched out with a heel resting on a low shelf, clawed toes thoughtlessly flicking a hardback to and fro against a row of books. Canine in shape, its head rested on a pillow formed by two folded, segmented wings. Currently silent, the thing touched one talon of a four-digit hand to a forked tongue, moistening the tip to flip the page of the tome propped open on its chest. A long tail twitched, and then snaked up to scratch at the flap of a leathery, bat-like ear. The idle leg made rapid scratching motions against the shelf, almost toppling rows of dust-coated books. Relaxing once more, it settled back into its read, lyrical, boyish brogue rhyming out a cadence.

"To fetch a pail of water. Jack fell down and broke his crown, and Jill came tumbling after," the thing huffed again. "Pssssscht. Did Jill learn *nothing*? What a peahen." A reptilian palm slapped a furrowed brow as it sighed with gusto. "I'm so tired of this rubbish." Clapping the book shut, it sent the rejected tome spinning on the hardwood, the scarred leather spine coming to a sliding stop against the wall.

Tessa found herself mid scream. She stood in full view, at some point having stepped from behind the cover of shelving. The gargoyle shot to its feet in an instant, startled against the wall. With scaly hands clamped over oversized ears, it let loose with the most horrible, crackling, high-pitched noise Tessa had ever heard. Her scream diminished into a noncommittal, airy "aaahhh."

"What the bloody hell is wrong with you?" the thing spat. Chest heaving, it lowered its arms, one hand planted dramatically against its heart. Bright hazel eyes rolled in exaggerated hysterics. "Never, ever, do that again. Please." After a beat to catch a breath, it stepped away from the wall. "I'm Peter. Pleased to make your acquaintance." The thing bowed in a flourish of spread wings and sweeping tail.

Wobbling, Tessa accepted the fact that she suffered from brain overload. *I'm going to faint, this thing is going to eat me, and there isn't a measly thing I can do about it.* She gave an ironic snort before she collapsed in her own flourish of pink and blonde on the wood floor.

"Well, I, for one, like her."

The sound of the man's voice startled Tessa awake. Her fingers felt soft fabric beneath her. The smell told her she was still in the store. She stilled, keeping her breathing even so she could listen.

"She's a *girl!*" a familiar voice said.

"I think she'll make the perfect addition. She adds contrast to this place."

"Ezra, I just brought up the sign because—"

"Would you rather be a downspout?" the new voice cut in.

"No, it's just I asked for help holding the sign all day because I thought it might be nice to have some company around this place, and, well she's all ... soft and fluffy ... and ... and *pink*." The words "soft" and "pink" were audibly accompanied by a fresh spray of spittle. Peter harrumphed his disenchantment with the situation.

"You know as well as I, that you don't feel the weight of that sign when you hold it. This is more about companionship than your duty as my sign holder. You seemed charmed enough when you introduced yourself. You must admit, she will liven things up around here, Peter."

"Oh yes, she's a real live one." Sarcasm dripped from Peter's words, adding a hiss to the "yes" which he drew out long over his forked tongue. "I didn't know you planned to keep her."

Tessa felt their eyes on her. She hiccupped. *Keep me?*

"You'll learn to appreciate these things. Softness, and pink," the voice called Ezra stated. "It may be time for you to start reading something other than children's books."

One peek-toe heel fell to the floor with a loud thump. *Hiccup.*

"Please reconsider, Ezra."

A single set of footfalls sounded, leading away, followed by the solid click of a door shutting. Tessa chanced a look, but with only one eye open a slit. The gargoyle slouched in an armchair nearby, resting its chin on a fist in an all-too-human posture.

"I know you're awake over there."

Tessa kept still.

"You'll soon wish you'd kept walking."

The door clicked shut once more.

Tessa rolled upright, checking herself quickly. Her clothes were all present, save for the one pump, which she hastily retrieved. She'd become puffy or something while she slept. The shoe was tight and hard to slide her foot into but after a couple quick little stomps it was back in place. She wavered, lightheaded, beside an ornate, cloth-covered chaise in an even more ornate room. Obviously a study, the whole area was centered around a huge, impeccably tidy, mahogany desk. A tall, rose window made of stained glass was centered behind the workstation, candlelight glinting from its many beveled edges. Designed by a gifted craftsman, the glass rose petals blended from rich purple, through blue, and finally to red at the center, where a scarlet E had been set into the inner petals.

Ezra. The name Peter had called the other voice.

Tessa took a shaky step toward the door but stopped short when she heard the horrible creaking noise her pumps made when she walked. *What now?*

Bulging toes fought against neighbors for control over the holes that were meant to just show a peek of her neatly polished nails. She'd apparently walked a lot longer than she planned. *Note to self: wear sensible shoes next time out of the dorm.* Heels in one hand, she padded to the door. The rose window showed that it was after dark, so Professor Sirmons was likely laying an egg. Tessa reached to twist the handle and embedded the fingernails of her right hand into the solid wood of the door. She yanked them free, sending shards of wood darting to the floor. She held her hand up, eyes growing wide. Enlarged knuckles burned as if her hands had been rubbed down with Icy Hot. Elongated digits were tipped with pointed nails that were foreign, save for being painted with her favorite Strawberry Ice polish. A button shot from her cardigan, ricocheting off the solid wood before her. She squealed and ducked, covering her head with her arms. The burning sensation spread to her elbows and shoulders as the fabric of her sweater split along her collarbone, leaving bits of knit wool hanging limply from her wrists. The hook-and-eye clasps of her favorite lacey bra popped loudly across her back in unison to the waistband of the matching panties. Her skirt slicked across her thighs, revealing that her skin was coated with a viscous blue substance.

"Ewwww!" Tessa inhaled with a sharp snort and screamed.

She managed to bludgeon the door handle enough that it relented, allowing her access to the hall outside the study. The corridor was long, displaying huge, floor length portraits of dogs.

"Whu …?" she muttered, staring in confusion at the odd choice of art.

Tearing her gaze from the walls, Tessa gimped down the hallway, feeling heavy, foreign feet clomp on the thick carpets. Her whole body felt hot as terror grew in her chest. She launched herself toward the next doorway in the hall, pounding at the thick wood of the closed door.

"Please help me!" she wailed, "Somebody open the door!" The shiny doorknob landed on the floor with a dejected thump. *So much for trying to open the door.* Tessa yelled again, balling her fists. "Help me!" she screamed into the dark hall of proud, staring canines.

Silence. Not even an echo returned her pleading calls. She sniffled, head twitching with hysteric sobs, and ran as best she could down the dim corridor.

The hall ended, offering the choice of turning either left or right. Tessa peered both ways, shaking with such tremors that she put a hand against the wall for support. She decided to continue her flight down the hallway to her left. Incredible detail emerged around her; contrasting colors and shades of light took over her sight, creating an echo of visible, layered dimension to her surroundings as she ran.

She slowed, realizing she was lost in the labyrinthine bookstore. She hiccupped violently, and gave in to morbid curiosity.

Her hands were no longer hers. Violet scales covered the skin, reflecting purple and blue as she examined them in the light of a wall sconce. She trembled on elongated feet bearing claws for toenails, each tip glinting with crackled pink polish. Muscles bulged within the skin of her calves, tapering to her ankle. The fluid that coated her body was nearly dry, leaving behind glimmering, spade shaped scales that connected to form a tough, interwoven, plated skin. Her skirt hung loose around a tapered waist, length abbreviated far above her knees, more of a loincloth than the previous statement of fashion and modesty. Her cardigan was gone, apparently falling away completely in her frantic sprint from the study. Only a camisole remained, now blotched with sticky blue fluid, clinging to a flat breastplate that replaced the feminine features of her chest. Looking down once again, she saw a slender tail spiraled around her left leg, the pointed tip resting on top of her foot. The end twitched toward the ceiling as she stared.

Exhausted, the young woman fell to her knees and was forced face down onto the carpet. Something behind her stopped her body from coming to rest on the floor. Turning her head, she saw that curved wings rested atop her shoulders, the boney frames jammed into the carpet behind her. She grasped the bottom of one wing and pulled it free, repeating the motion on the other side. Resting on her knees, she was then able to sit back, wings stretched alongside her.

Saving what she considered to be the worst for last, she put a hand to her face to feel what changes had taken place there. Her chin jutted forward, forming an elongated jaw that rested under a pointed nose. Angular cheekbones protruded from the sides of her face. Her hair hung from a ponytail still thick with blue gel. She pulled strands from where it dried to the scales. Some of it plastered to her shoulders, some stuck in her mouth and other pieces were tangled across the top of her wings. When it was finally gathered in one clawed fist, she pulled it forward across a shoulder, letting it fall in a mass of swirling light- and violet-blue lengths across her ruined camisole. Tears fell to her thighs, and she wiped at her nose, which was oddly short, she decided. Not nearly as long as Peter's seemed when she'd first seen him. She gasped.

Peter.

"Peter!" she called loudly, noting the way her "P" was accentuated by lips stretched across elongated canine fangs. She leapt to her feet. Her wings fanned wide with excitement, smacking against the walls of the narrow hallway on either side.

"Whoa," she moaned, reaching back in an attempt to fold large, leathery blue wings behind her so she could proceed. When she tucked her arms to her sides, the wings followed suit, furling together on her back with the curled ends sweeping forward to rest against the outside of her thighs. Her legs shook as she took a hesitant step forward, learning her stride. Her knees remained bent a little, but she was able to put one foot in front of the other and make her way down the hall, alternating sobs and calling for Peter as she went.

She wandered halls, finding nooks filled with treasures that on any other day would send her into gleeful sessions of examining the old things the bookstore harbored on its age darkened shelves. Gem encrusted letter openers gleamed on dark shelves with thick magnifiers for reading.

Tessa continued to walk, shoulders slumping, and finally gave in to both physical and mental exhaustion. She tucked herself against the wall in the next corner she came to. She slumped down against the joining walls, gathered her knees to her chest and rocked in hysterics, soft mourning sounds erupting occasionally, against her will.

Peter cleared his throat gently but still managed to startle Tessa. She gazed up at his winged form through thickened eyelids and pools of unshed tears.

"What's happening to me?"

"You're becoming," he said, just above a whisper.

"Becoming what?" She snapped tensely at his cryptic response.

"Really? You have to ask that?" Peter held out his hands, pointing at himself with sarcasm. "Hellooo … maybe a gargoyle? You think I've been like this my whole life?"

"I don't understand," she said, averting her face. "And my body is so hot. I feel like I could throw up."

"That will pass," he said. He pulled up close and squatted on his haunches next to her as she sobbed into her hands.

"You'll grow accustomed to it. Grow used to it," he offered.

"How?" she yelled back. "Look at me! I'm disgusting! This … slime …," she spat as she held out a sticky arm.

"It's already drying," he said. "Then you'll just have …."

"What?" she snapped. "Scales?"

"Scales," he said at the same time as her.

"Nooooo," she cried.

"The blue is really pretty. Beautiful, actually. Almost purple," he said. He cringed when his words accomplished nothing more than sending her into a fresh bout of hiccupping sobs. "Oh, there now," he whispered. Peter crept close beside her and extended an arm over her shoulders and a wing over hers, hugging her tightly beside him.

She sobbed openly against his shoulder, finally stilling after a while. He held her close the entire time, occasionally looking down at her brilliant scales peeking from beneath the remaining pink fluff she'd worn into the store.

"Unbelievable," he mused. "I wouldn't think Ezra capable of doing this to another. I thought I'd gleaned an understanding of the old geezer by now," he sighed. "Really though, who has ever been able to put Ezra in a nutshell?"

The newly created gargoyle didn't answer. Her slow, steady breathing showed she was already asleep.

Tessa awoke to sunlight warming her face. A smile tugged at her features. Sunshine was a rarity in London. *And that's where I am … my favorite place on the planet … the museums … theatre … bookstores—*

"Crap!" she screamed, shooting to her feet.

Peter's head clunked against the wall. "Owww," he moaned. He rubbed his temple. "Careful, girl. That hurt." He blinked in the morning light, hazel eyes focusing on her.

"Whu …," Tessa muttered, patting her back-to-human hips. She looked over her shoulder, and then doubled over, looking under her skirt. *No tail!*

"What on earth are you doing?" Peter sat cross-legged, an elbow resting on his knee, watching her frisk herself.

"I had the craziest, most far out dream I've ever had," she said. She rested her rump against the wall, bent forward and placed her hands on her knees while her heartbeat thumped wildly in her chest. "I dreamed I turned into a gargoyle!" She giggled nervously. "And not just any gargoyle, a freakin' *purple* one! Ha!" She laughed, letting her head fall limply forward. After a moment, she glanced at the young man on the floor before her. "Wait. Who are you?"

"Peter," he said. "Pleased to make your acquaintance," he deadpanned. "Again."

She was silent, slowly coming to a standing position against the wall. "But you *are* a gargoyle," she stated quietly. She crossed her arms over her chest matter-of-factly.

Peter rose to his feet and slowly moved to stand in front of her. "I, most certainly, am a gargoyle."

Tessa gazed at the man before her. Familiar hazel eyes were lined with a fan of dark lashes. Boyish, yet strong features met her gaze. A full, pouty lower lip curled slightly in a small grin. His thick, black hair was pulled from his face in a long tail, part of which fell over a bare, muscular shoulder. A linen vest was the sole piece of clothing on his torso, hanging open across his wide chest. A pair of soot smudged, ratty, calf-length trousers hung off his hips, displaying two ropes of tapered muscle that descended below the waistband there.

She gulped audibly.

"Don't worry, Ezra will likely hand you a big book of something childish, like nursery rhymes, to keep your mind where he wants it," he said. Without taking his eyes from hers, he pulled a timepiece from the small pocket of his vest. "We have a couple of hours before the store opens," he said after a quick glance to get the hour. "I'm certain Ezra has a room ready for you by now, so we should head upstairs." He turned toward the hall.

Tessa was plaster on the wall. Thoughts whirled through her mind, making her feel faint, as if she stood in a surreal place, looking down at herself from some mystical, veiled place nearby while her body reacted to her new surroundings. Memories from last night assailed her. When Peter turned back to her, she looked up at him and a tear trailed down her cheek. Growing up the way she did had always lent her a tenacious quality when she needed it, but now, try as she might, she was unable to draw on the strength of that virtue. She blinked, trying to clear the feeling that her vision was narrowing. Her hands shook. She needed the wall in order to remain vertical.

"I'm a gargoyle," she whispered.

"I'm afraid so," he answered. "More so at night." He took Tessa's hand and pulled her along toward the stairs.

After dragging the young woman through the store and back to Ezra's study, Peter deposited her back on the ornate chaise. She looked up at him with doe eyes, shock still prevalent in her expression.

Peter gave her hand a squeeze. "I'll be back in just a moment, all right?"

"Mmmm hmmmm."

"You stay put, yeah?"

"Okay," she said, feigning preoccupation with the polished fingernails of her right hand.

When he turned to leave the room, Tessa asked, "Who's holding the sign?"

"I'm sorry, what?"

"I don't get it. If you're here, who is outside? Who is holding the sign?"

"It's not a *who*, it's a *what*, rather. My gargoyle holds the sign during the daylight hours."

She glanced away from her manicure and looked at him with exaggerated doubt. "Really? That's all you've got?"

"Look, this stuff is magic. I don't fully understand it either, although I'd wager *yours* is out there too, now," he offered. "It will be all the time. You won't realize it, or even feel that, at all. I'll ask Ezra if I can take you out for a moment to see for yourself."

"Okay." She was back to studying her fingernails, bare feet swinging from the chaise.

Tessa shot from her seat as an elderly man appeared in the doorway.

"Take her upstairs, Peter. She'll have a good look from there," Ezra said. He clomped past in a pair of thick-soled black boots, to sit in the chair behind the huge desk. After slipping on a pair of wired spectacles, he began examining a short stack of unopened post.

She eyed the gaunt, elderly man. *So this is Ezra.*

"I'd rather see from the sidewalk, if you'd show me out," Tessa said.

"Perhaps another time, dear," he said, and opened an envelope.

"I think just now is perfect." Tessa held her breath and bit down on the inside of her cheek. Tears welled up once more, and her face grew warm as urgency flooded her emotions with the need to run from the place. She wouldn't stop until her butt was firmly planted on a jet back to the States, if she could just make it out the door. She hid her shaking hands, clasping them behind her back.

"I'm afraid that is not a possibility today. It's quite sunny outside." He set his mail aside and looked over the rim of his glasses at Peter. "We wouldn't want any mishaps, dear girl." He turned his attention her way.

"My name is Tessa. I am not your *dear girl*," she said, in an exaggeration of a formal British accent. His accent sounded somewhat British, but there was something puzzling, something more to his lilt, the brogue far too deep than the typical accent of people in London. "And I love sunshine." She looked over at Peter, who was standing beside the chaise. "Please show me out."

Peter shook his head slightly and looked down, sliding his hands into the pockets of his ruined pants.

"Tessa." Ezra smiled up at her. "Tessa, I like that. So fitting for one with such spark," he said, rising from his chair. "You can't go outside today."

"Why?" She cried. Hot tears fell. She wiped at them hard.

"Why what?" he asked playfully.

"Why can't I leave?" She sobbed. "Why am I even here?" She waved a trembling hand in a quick arc indicating his study.

"Why?" Ezra stepped toward them. "Well, it's simple, Tessa," he hissed her name slowly. The man stood quietly in front of them, ridged, lips drawn tight.

No one moved. Tessa stared at the misleadingly feeble appearance of the man. There was no doubt in her mind of his ability to keep order. What she had mistaken for cataracts was a complete lack of pupils. She stared. The extreme white of his eyes accentuated the yellowed quality of his uncombed hair and crazy eyebrows. Oddly, he seemed physically well but weathered, his clothes perfectly pressed, right down to the huge clunky boots badly in need of a shine. Silence impregnated the room around them. Tessa shuddered.

Ezra's rare, playful demeanor returned. He tugged at the thick cuffs of his starched, linen shirt and straightened his wool vest. He smiled at her as though he was her long lost grandfather.

Tessa gulped. *He could use a couple hours of practice grinning at himself in a mirror before he takes that one on the road.*

"The 'Why' is very simple," he said. "Boy-goyle," he gestured at Peter with a thin, dry-skinned hand. "And girl-goyle." He turned toward her, smiling the smile of what Tessa supposed was typical at any asylum for nutjobs of equal caliber.

Tessa gaped at him. He seemed pleased as punch. She turned to get Peter's reaction. Eyes closed, the young man rubbed his brow with his fingers, snorted softly with half a laugh, and shook his head slightly.

"Well, no one asked me!" she yelled. "This is … you're … freaking crazy!" She jabbed a finger at Ezra.

"Now, dear girl, we can't always get what we want," he said, glancing sidelong in Peter's direction. "Now off with you both. We have a business to run here. I'll see you both at nine, sharp, ready to work." He looked at Tessa. "Smiling," he said, without one of his own. He tugged a silver watch from the left-hand pocket of his wool vest, checked the time, and shot a meaningful glare at Peter through narrowed eyelids.

Peter caught her elbow and gestured toward the door. She turned to follow him out, but wheeled around to face Ezra once more.

"It's that Rolling Stones' song. You know the one I mean." He hummed the melody to the familiar hit of the sixties. "It tells it how it is."

"You've gotta be kidding me," Tessa muttered, shaking her head in disbelief.

"I am," Ezra said, spreading his hands. "And I'm not. You can't always get what you want." He grinned at his own wry humor.

"Really, Ezra?" said Peter. "That's quite helpful, thanks." He took Tessa's elbow firmly.

Tessa was stunned. *Is this guy for real? Unbelievable.* She opened her mouth to say something but words wouldn't come. She let Peter pull her toward the door, Ezra banging out the beat on his desk, long stained silver hair flopping against his weathered cheeks as he sang with enough gusto and volume to reach the cobbled court outside. The old man belted the lyrics, ushering them from his study.

"He," Tessa said, jabbing a finger toward the study, "Is a first class nut job!"

"Yes, I can't argue that. Really, he just thrives on irony. In his defense, he knows everything about every book in this place," said Peter, as he opened the door to her room. "He really is quite brilliant. You'll see. This place is quite ... special."

Peter swung the door open and strode across plush carpeting to an oversized window seat, built into the wall around a double pane of aged glass. Sunshine shone through, casting a bright splash of light onto the royal blue pad on the bench below the window. "There, you see? We are both out there doing our duty, holding the sign," he said, beckoning her to stand beside him as he pointed.

She strode past a station that held a mini fridge, microwave oven and a coffee pot to a four-poster bed to her right. The thick comforter was quilted in rich beige and pink satin. Matching throw pillows were arranged in an inviting, over-stuffed looking wedge that ran up the cream colored wall behind the bed. A small, dark wood table stood beside the bed, complete with a reading lamp and a thick, leather bound book. Tessa tore her gaze away and peered out the second-story window to the sign below.

The same, dark grey gargoyle that held the sign yesterday rested there, long arm stretched across the bottom of the wood, nearly to the other side of the plank closest to the storefront. Where nothing had been yesterday, a smaller gargoyle crouched against the wall of the shop, a slight lavender-blue hue glinting from an outstretched arm holding the other end of the sign under the word "Librorum."

"And why couldn't we see this from the sidewalk?" Tessa turned to look up at Peter when he failed to answer her. She traced his gaze to her forearm where it rested against the windowpane.

Warm sunlight washed across the skin of her hand and arm, clear to her shoulder. A network of purple veins spider-webbed their way across her flesh, growing darker in shade against translucent muscle. She rotated her arm in amazement, eyes widening at the sight of bright blue bone peeking through sinewy, pale violet tendons and dark amethyst ligaments in her wrist. She flexed her shaking hand, bringing it close to her face. Once out of the direct sunlight, the skin there returned to peachy flesh that covered the inner workings of her hand.

She wobbled slightly. "What the heck has that freak done to me?"

Putting his hands on her shoulders, Peter gently lowered her to the cushioned window seat, being careful to keep her from the sun's rays. He reached above her and released a blind to cover the window.

"Now you see," he said, plopping beside her. "While the sun is up, we look just like we did before." He searched her face for understanding. She nodded, lip quivering. He continued. "We work at Librorum Taberna during business hours, helping Ezra with his patrons." He rose and strode to the small table, retrieving the large book. "At night, we are free to wander this place as our gargoyles. The store is huge, by the way. We can read, but only what Ezra gives us permission to read."

He approached, handing her the book. "I'll wager this is a big book of children's nursery rhymes. And don't get any ideas. Ezra is in control of what the pages of every book in this place contain. You won't be able to read anything he doesn't want you to."

"That's not possible, Peter," she retorted. "I was reading a bit yesterday and nothing was different in the books I looked through." She shrugged.

"It will be different now, trust me. I've been stuck reading children's poetry forever. Ezra keeps me reading nursery rhymes to control my focus. Keeps things simple. The power of the written word is amazing."

He turned to a row of wooden cabinet doors along the wall opposite the bed. Opening the first set of doors wide for her, he displayed a vanity table with lighted mirrors and a plush stool. The next opened on a student desk with outlets and a lamp to study by. Another set revealed a clothes armoire where hung two collared shirts. Peter pulled one off the closet rod and held it out for her to see.

She snorted. "I am *not* wearing that." Embroidered letters spelled out Librorum Tabera on the left breast. The shirt was, of course, pink.

"Come on, why not? Mine are plain white. At least you get some color," he said.

"You can have the pink ones, too."

Peter rolled his eyes and continued flipping open doors. "The book store opens in about forty-five minutes. There is a full bath and toilet at the end of the hall," he said as he opened the last cabinet door. On a low shelf, sat her backpack. Her clothes hung from the pole above.

"Hey! My bag. I'd forgotten all about it." She walked to the cabinet and grabbed her pack. "Wow," Tessa admitted. "He thought of everything didn't he? How did he get all this out of my dorm room?"

"Ezra has odd means of making things go in his favor, believe me."

She sifted through the hangers. Her shoes were neatly arranged on a cedar rack. Her shower bag rested atop a stack of towels and facial cloths. A quick inspection of a small set of drawers within turned up her underwear and sweats.

"Whoa." Peter took a step back at the sight of her neatly folded bras and panties. "I need to get to my room and shower. I'll be back in half hour to get you." He moved hastily toward the door. When he heard no response, he turned toward her once more. "Are you okay?"

"So, this is it?" She gestured with a limp hand. "I … I'm just *here* now?" she said, exasperated. She bit down on her cheek to stop her chin from quivering.

He gave a solemn nod.

"What about what I want? How will I ever do the things I want to do? I mean I have no one waiting for me in the States, no family, and it sucked and all, but …," she drifted into thought. *How will I break free now? And be in the lead for once?* "I wanted to be a British Literature teacher!"

"I know how you feel," he offered, trying to calm her.

"How can you say that," she said through tears. "You can't possibly know how terrible I feel right now."

"Well, Miss British-Literature-Teacher-Wannabe," he sneered. "You're not the only one with a tragic past, you know. As a child, my first word was 'sweep.'" When she was silent, he continued. "Let's see how well you know the works of Mister William Blake. I mean, since you're willing to attempt to make a living teaching about British history."

Studying him, Tessa eyed him doubtfully. "What are you saying? That you've been alive since the early eighteen-hundreds?"

"Born in seventeen-eighty-nine, sold in seventeen-ninety-two," he stated flatly.

Tessa was still. Her studies told her the horrible life of a child born into the terrifying age of child labor during England's Industrial Age. Peter was lucky to have matured to manhood. Lucky to be alive. A vision of him as a small child flashed vividly through her mind. She saw him malnourished and frail, skin blackened with soot stark against the snow … alone.

"I'm sorry, Peter," she said quietly. She didn't know if she wanted to apologize more for her anger earlier, or for the torment he must have endured as a child. "I really am."

"Be ready in half hour," he said, and clicked the door softly shut behind him.

Straggling shoppers meandered away in the fading light of the midsummer night. *That wasn't as bad as it could have been,* Tessa thought. Spirits slightly bolstered by a hot shower and hotter coffee, she'd emerged from her room wearing the collared pink shirt, her favorite jeans, and her running shoes, since she was sure she would be on her feet all day. Talking with the store's patrons helped to brighten her outlook, but not as much as she enjoyed watching Peter interact with them. He was quick to smile, and despite the fact that he was only allowed to read what Ezra decided was safe, Peter had an extensive knowledge of the shop's contents. Best of all was the way he allowed boyish charm to radiate throughout whatever task he worked at.

As Tessa came to the cash register with Peter, Ezra met them with a smile and handed over her iHome, three spiral-bound notebooks and a new package of pens.

"Thank you," she said tentatively.

"You're welcome, dear girl."

"Ezra, my laptop is missing from my bag. Do you know where it is?" she asked pointedly.

"I have it," he answered, as he pulled a set of keys from his vest pocket. "The notebooks will have to do, for now. Once you've done things to earn my trust, we'll talk about your use of the Internet here at the store. It's not wireless and you won't find any hotspots for your iPod."

Tessa swallowed the urge to protest. She realized his gift of music and the writing utensils was likely Ezra's version of a peace offering.

He was trying, at least. She nodded her response.

Ezra said nothing, and strode toward the back stairwell.

"What, no 'goodnight, dear girl?'" she taunted.

Peter snorted a small, sarcastic laugh.

Ezra glanced over a shoulder with a smile. "You and I are going to get on just fine." He winked and continued on his way.

"Shall we close it up for the day?" Peter asked.

Tessa followed him to the entrance. As Peter flipped the, "OPEN. Please come in" window card to read "Please call again at 9," she gazed out to the wooden sign above the sidewalk in her beloved Cecil Court. Their gargoyles were statuesque in the gloaming.

"What do you think?" Peter asked.

She sighed. "Better to hold a sign than be a downspout, huh?" she answered, and made an "O" with her lips.

He laughed, and made his lips round, as well. "No … this just isn't me either," he said, bending the words as he kept his lips in an imitation spout.

Tessa snorted a quick laugh. They stared out the window in silence for a moment, taking in the beauty of the London evening through the thick pane of glass.

"It's about time to change for the night," he said.

"I think I'd like to go to my room." She pulled her gaze from the beauty of cobbles and flower boxes at twilight. "I just need some time to let this all gel, y'know?"

Peter nodded and watched her go.

Safe in her room, Tessa stood examining her serpentine countenance in the large vanity mirror. The surreal feeling was back. She tried to think up one word to sum up her appearance as a gargoyle.

Demonic? She tilted her head in the mirror. *No, not evil*, she decided. She opened her puggish snout to display pointed fangs shining white against the dark purple smoothness inside her mouth. *But absolutely wicked, for sure.* She wiggled her upturned nose.

She lit one of the travel candles she had packed and the aroma of jasmine scented her new bedroom. Adele's "Rolling in the Deep" thrummed low from her iHome's speakers. Her mini fridge came stocked with fresh fruit and snacks, and after a considerable amount of crumbled failure she was now able to set a portion of a raspberry tea biscuit on the tips of her forked tongue, chew, and swallow. She stuck her tongue out in the reflection, moving the two tines separately. *Go figure*, she thought, ironically drawing dark similarities between the fork in her life's road and her current state of toying with the tines of her violet hued tongue in the mirror. The thought pulled at her heart, her chest growing tight with anxiety. She scrubbed at her cheeks, attempting to erase the evidence of her sadness. *What the heck did I have to return to, anyway?*

A light knock sounded at her door. Tessa took a sip from the straw hanging from a bottle of Pepsi. She opened the door to find Peter there.

"Come on in," she said, and closed the door after he entered. She looked up at him. "Look at you, all … gargoyle-ly."

"I just wanted to see how you fared against the transformation," he baited.

"It was quick," She walked to the mirror, checking for any remnants of the viscous fluid that remained from her change. "It seemed to dry faster this time, and the burning feeling wasn't as intense as last night." She gestured down at the stained skirt and camisole she'd worn the night before. "I put these on just in case. And I'm glad I did." She pulled at the skirt, attempting to get it to hang straight across the span of her thighs. She'd given up on the thin, satin cami and it rested unevenly against her plated chest. Her body was slender and sinewy, but bulging and muscular in places like her thighs and shoulders, reptilian.

Tessa huffed and crossed her arms tight over her chest. "I hate this." Her voice cracked as a fresh bout of tears threatened. "I can't help feeling that any second, I'm going to just, like, *wake up* from all this."

"I know this has been horrifying for you, so I thought maybe—" He sighed, tail twitching. "Want to, um … do something with me?" he stammered. It'll get you out of the bookstore. Sort of."

"We can't leave the bookstore, Peter. At least, I can't. Ezra would lay a golden egg or something." She dropped onto the bed, causing the frame under the mattress to squeak in protest.

"Were you planning to tell him?" Peter didn't wait for her to answer, just pulled her up by an arm and tugged her toward the door.

"Peter, I—"

"Shhh!"

Tessa did her best to walk in silence and keep up with Peter as the two made their way up a long staircase that led to the store's rooftop. She sucked in an amazed breath as she stepped into a bath of silver moonlight in the clear chill of the night. Shingled rooftops reflected dark metal hues below their perch atop Librorum Taberna, which seemed misleading from the look of the storefront. Clearly, the building that housed the bookstore was monstrous beyond the façade on Cecil Court. Tessa spun, taking in the full beauty of the London night.

"Thank you, Peter." She gazed at the sleepy city she loved, and stepped to the ledge to get a better view, gulping lungfuls of fresh air.

"We aren't there yet," he said, taking her clawed hand in his. He stepped to the ledge beside her. "You have to be silent when we do this, yeah?"

"Do what?" She looked down. Surely he didn't want to jump off the roof or something crazy. *I've had enough crazy to last me a lifetime.*

"I thought we could go for a little flight over the city. I mean, unless you're scared or something," he teased.

Tessa looked from the street below to Peter's face, testing him for sincerity. "You're messing with me."

"I would never." He winked.

Tessa jerked slightly as a series of gentle *pops* sounded just behind her. Peter unfurled his wings to an impressive span along the length of the rooftop.

"What do you think these are for?"

"I don't know, balance?" she said, trying to step back from the ledge.

"I knew it. You're scared!" he baited. "But that's okay. I mean you are a *girl*, after all."

He launched with silent grace from where they stood, staying level with the rooftop, gliding in a slow arc through the crisp night air. Tessa watched with amazement. He flew close and pumped his wings to gain altitude just above her, sending two bursts of cool air to buffet her hair. She spun around as he landed lightly on the roof. Tessa's mouth hung open a bit. She clapped it shut with a sharp snap of her teeth.

"Want to try it?" he said as he strode toward her.

"I don't know if I can. I mean, I can't even swim," she admitted, sending Peter into a brief bout of laughter.

"Where's the water?" he managed to say. He snorted.

"I mean, I don't float," she snapped. "I really don't see what's so freaking funny here."

"I'm sorry," he cleared his throat. "You're right. Not funny. But let's go anyway." He held out a claw.

Tessa looked from his awaiting talons to his face, then to the ledge. "Promise not to let go?"

"Promise," he stated, making a cross over his chest plate with a finger. "Unless you tell me to let go."

"Deal." She took his hand, and he led her to the ledge. He took two paces back. She followed suit without questioning the actions.

"Best to get a bit of a run at first, so we'll take two running steps then jump on three," he nodded for emphasis.

"Let's just do this thingy before I change my mind, okay?" she asked shakily. A loud hiccup racked her chest. She put a foot down on her tail to keep it from twitching.

"Deal." He squeezed her hand. "Look out there." He motioned to the open air beside the rooftop.

"Okay." *This is nuts, nuts, nuts. What if I pee?*

Peter leaned forward so Tessa did the same, despite the shaking in her legs. He announced the first step with a stern sounding "One." She matched his paces with her right, then her left foot, and on his count of "Three" she slammed her eyes shut, diving forward. "Crap, oh, crap." she said between clenched teeth. Cool air pushed at every inch of her body.

"Pssst," he whispered. "Open your eyes."

Tessa peeked. Her feet hung above the lane below, making it seem eerily small. Her stomach lurched as her eyes flew wide. She inhaled with a loud snort for a scream that resounded shrill around them. She fought through the air to grasp at Peter with her other hand and one leg, inadvertently pumping her wings, pulling him close, sending them both spiraling forward in a shrieking mass of iridescent purple and silver scales and wings.

"No ... oh, bloody hell!" Peter yelled.

He pulled her head into the crook of his shoulder to protect her as the two large gargoyles slammed into stone, fracturing the wall of a building adjacent to the bookstore. Shards of limestone shot into the air, peppering the cobblestone sidewalk below. They bounced into a free fall. Peter spun out flat in the air, grasping Tessa's flailing form with a large talon. He caught her hand, dragging her through the air as he pumped his wings, pulling her along until she regained a soaring position beside him and quit squawking.

"So much for quiet, huh?" he asked from beside her.

"Sorry," she yelled. A frantic feeling still owned her, and she tried shaking her head to clear the ringing from their impact into the wall. She caught her balance on the air, using her tail to maintain her place next to Peter. "I think I got this," she yelled.

"No need to shout," he said. "That's where the big ears come in." He shot her a toothy grin full of fangs, waggling his pointed ears at her.

She grinned back, beginning to feel the exhilarating effects of their flight. "I think you can let go."

"You sure?"

"Yep." She gave his claw a little squeeze for emphasis.

Peter released her, dropping back so she was in his line of sight. After a few moments, he pumped his wings hard. He circled silently above her, but remained close to the bookstore.

Tessa watched Peter's winged form as he eclipsed the moon with a wing. Moon glow shone through the membranous film spanning between the boney segments, creating a glittery halo around the celestial orb. His body gleamed dark metallic in the night, majestic on the air. She pumped her wings once, trembling midflight from the massive lift obtained from the stroke. One more beat against the air sent her back to his side. She smiled over at him. "Thank you."

"You're welcome," he said. "Tessa?"

"Yeah?" she said, still a bit too loud. She made breast-stroke motions beside him in the air.

"You're not going to try to run away, are you?" he asked.

"I don't know where else I'd go," she replied after a moment of thoughtful silence. "I mean, look at this." She gestured at herself. "I can't go anywhere. And besides, I feel like I've lost … *me*." She looked away.

"Well, I've found you."

The two soared a bit longer until Peter led her back toward the bookstore, where they alit lightly with not much faltering from Tessa. They rushed down the long staircase where they burst through the door, encountering Ezra on the other side.

Tessa hunched beside Peter. Judging from Ezra's state of agitation, he'd been waiting for them to return for some time.

Tessa's heart sank when she saw the way Ezra glared at Peter with his colorless, frigid stare. Peter gave her a reluctant smile. "It was worth it," he whispered.

"Go to your room, Tessa." Ezra didn't take his eyes from Peter.

"Did someone see us?" she asked.

"No," Peter answered. "We wear glamour at night as long as we are close to the book—"

"Now, Tessa!" Ezra thundered at her.

She gave Peter one, last, resigned glance and paced toward her room. The conversation between the two followed her down the hallway.

"Just when I'd considered letting you read something besides nursery rhymes …," Ezra began, "and you're going to pay for the damage to that building."

"Of course, Ezra."

Later, when Tessa answered the knock on her door, Peter was there, leaning against the wall opposite her doorway. She let the door hang open, so he could follow her inside.

"I'm sorry you got in trouble," she said, walking to her mirror. Adjusting to her new reflection was taking some patience. "And I'll help you pay for the damage we caused. I mean, it was my fault we hit the building."

Peter hesitated, then replied. "Okay, I'll let you. But only because it will be interesting having you around while I work off the damages." He toed the carpet. "And don't worry about it. I seem to have a knack for getting into trouble with Ezra. Hence, he makes sure I read only nursery rhymes."

She picked up her brush and began pulling through her knotted, pale purple hair. Turned out, flying was hard on the tresses. "I just can't wait to see what I get to read," she replied sarcastically.

"I have something for you here," Peter stammered. "It's not much but I hope you'll like it."

"Okay," she said gently.

He held out a length of shell pink ribbon. "I was just remembering what you said earlier. About losing yourself. You don't have to give up everything, Tessa. You're still you inside." Circling behind, he stepped over her tail and tied the ribbon around her neck. "You're beautiful, Tessa," he said over her shoulder, locking their gazes in the mirror. A dainty letter "T" dangled from the ribbon against her throat, shining silver against purple scales.

Peter let his canine chin rest gently against her hair. "Welcome to the world of scales."

"Thanks." Tessa smiled.

Some days I get so tired of this life.
The endless parade of lost souls coming
through my door looking to change the cards
they have been dealt. But the days I can
ease the passage? Those are not so bad. GF

A Page Lost

by Nicole Godfrey

Prudence let out an exasperated sigh and shoved the wretched cell phone, with its oversized buttons and large screen, into the bowels of her purse. Her granddaughter, Lina, insisted she carry the confounded contraption in the event of an emergency, but it only caused her headaches. Gone were the days of roaming around town in peace and quiet, and here are the days of constant phone calls. Apparently, if Lina didn't know where she was every minute of every day, that was an emergency.

Looking around, she realized she'd taken a wrong turn on her walk due to the phone's distraction. Her coffee shop should've been in view, but instead she found herself looking up at an unfamiliar wooden sign above a small shop. Despite living here all her life, Prudence was sure she'd never laid eyes on this particular store before.

The plaque was old, rugged and worn, and charred in places as if it'd been burned. The slight smell of acrid smoke made her nose itch, and she let out a little squeak of a sneeze. Thick wood, about a foot in width, sat flush against the old brick like it'd always been there. A faint, discolored section of brick above th sign made it look as though something sat on top at one time. Beveled corners, like gaping and toothless mouths, were the only hand-made feature on the wood other than the actual lettering. Thick white letters spelled out the name "Librorum Taberna" in a stark Old English script. The two words made her tongue tingle as she spoke them.

Between the smell and the charred edges, Prudence decided there must have been a fire that caused the store to relocate here. Her gaze drifted down to the narrow windows on either side of the slender recessed door. Delight completely eliminated the last of her sour mood with the sight of beautifully bound antique books displayed there.

A bell tinkled lightly overhead as she opened the door and stepped inside. Blinking rapidly, Prudence took in the expanse of shelves that stretched beyond her vision in every direction. Like spokes on a tire, they fanned out in a circle from the focal point of the entrance and invited the unknowing to lose themselves in their depths.

"Ahem." A low, melodic voice came from Prudence's right where no one had stood a moment before.

She jumped slightly, and then jumped again when she looked up a few inches into a pair of solid white eyes. The man's thin, pale lips hitched a centimeter in one corner, giving the slightest impression of amusement before he spoke.

"May I help you, madam?" His rolling accent was indescribable, or at least it was to Prudence, his words flowing over each other with vernacular grace.

"I…" she cleared her suddenly dry throat, "I would like to peruse your wares." She tried to bring herself up to her full five foot five inches so as not to feel intimidated by the man, but she only succeeded in getting closer to him then she wanted to be.

He stepped back, giving Prudence her first good look at him.

Taller than her, and made to look even taller by his narrow stature, the man stood with his back straight and shoulders squared. *Impeccable posture for someone who must be in his seventies,* she thought. His long legs were clad in thick black wool slacks, with a heavily starched, white button-down long sleeve linen shirt, and black wool vest to match. Three gold buttons held the vest closed and a silver chain hung from the left of two matching pockets, presumably connected to a watch of some sort. The outfit was rounded off by heavy leather boots that looked like they'd seen better days, perhaps during the Civil War.

In contrast to most of his outfit, the shoulder length white hair atop his head hung in thick, oily strands and were tinged a vile shade of yellow. Prudence wondered if tobacco was to blame. He pulled a silver watch from his pocket and raised his yellow-tinted eyebrows.

"I do not believe time will allow for the perusal of all my wares." He stowed the elegantly engraved pocket watch once more and looked back at her with those unnerving white eyes. "Perhaps we can narrow your search?"

Prudence looked at her own wristwatch and frowned at the 9:45 am reading. *Were there that many books to look at here?*

"Um," she wet her dry lips, trying to think of a title she wanted to find, but none came to mind.

"Any specific genre that interests you?" he persisted in that unknown accent, crossing his arms and shifting his weight to his other hip.

He was making her feel uncomfortable, and she got the feeling that he was enjoying it. His translucent pale skin was stretched tight over his gaunt face, his shaggy brows still arched high, and those thin lips pressed into a straight line as if he loathed the smile he hid.

She took a deep breath. "Historical romance, if you please, sir."

He did smile then, briefly, the straight row of yellowed teeth matched his tobacco stained hair.

"Please, call me Ezra. Ezra Finfrock. Right this way, madam." He swept a long, thin hand toward one of the spoke-like rows and lightly nudged her shoulder with the other to encourage her forward.

Once away from the door and its fresh air, the smell of an old forgotten attic set in, even though the shelves held no traces of dust. Prudence tried to keep pace with Ezra's long strides. The man could move like any youth she'd met, and she clutched her purse to her chest like a safety blanket. The book cases kept going on and on, making her wonder when the back of the store would come into view.

They passed an open area with a counter set in the middle covered in stacks of books. Without breaking stride, Ezra picked up a large stack on the corner and continued on. Wide-eyed, Prudence followed in silence.

After several more minutes, he stopped and pointed down the aisle while balancing the stack of books on one hand.

"From this point on is every Historical Romance from the early 1900's to present day. They are alphabetized by last name of the author. If you need anything, please do not hesitate to call my name." With that, he brusquely walked back the way they'd come and disappeared from sight.

A shiver ran down Prudence's spine, but she shook it off and looked at the beautifully bound books with awed excitement. There were titles she knew and loved and others that beckoned with their unknown pages. Her hand slid over the supple leather bindings with their engraved lettering, and a smile creased her face. This was the most exquisite collection she'd ever seen.

Scanning the names without much direction except to appreciate the sheer volume of books, her hand hesitated over a title she thought she'd never see again. The book had gotten her through some of her darkest days as a child and had been lost when her family had been forced to move unexpectedly. It called to her, pulled on her heart strings with its familiarity, and she couldn't help but take it from the cradle of the surrounding books.

The covering was different, better quality then her old beat-up paperback, but the curve of the script was the same. Its weight in her hands was comforting and she sighed happily before opening to the first page.

What happened next would never be clear in Prudence's mind. Later, the blur would be attributed to her first episode of dementia. She'd expected to see the main title page when she opened the book, but instead she found blank paper. Her consternation increased as she felt a pull from her mind, down her arms, and words began to appear where nothing had been written before.

Even stranger, the words that appeared were of things that only Prudence could know. Her first memories, her childish hopes and dreams spilled out before her eyes, and the further she read, the more new things appeared.

Her teenage years, with their carefree optimism, came next. Then came her first heartbreak in high school, and her first marriage proposal. She silently laughed at her naive belief that it would last forever. The birth of her children brought tears to her eyes. She was too young herself, and they'd been her world; it had expanded with each new addition.

Even the bad memories were present. How her first husband had revealed his true colors over time, and with his violence almost ended her life on several occasions. Then she read about the brief second marriage that only gave her one good thing; her youngest son. These torments tore at her chest with talons of regret and pain.

Finally, a light in the darkness arrived; her granddaughter. And with the memories of her grandaughter came the introduction of her third husband. Lina had been 5 years old, embodying everything that was good in humanity, when Allen came into the picture. They'd met too late in life to have children together, but they shared each other's family nonetheless, as well as their hearts and souls. He'd made her whole and given her many years of married happiness. She couldn't even be saddened by his passing; he'd been too wonderful for that. *And how I loved him.*

As events started to catch up to where she was today, she felt her arms get heavy and her knees get weak. Her head swam with images of the book shelves around her and she stumbled from the vertigo. *What is happening to me? Why are all these memories flooding back, now of all times?*

Strong hands caught her under her arms before she hit the ground, and Ezra's voice was a soothing anchor in the roiling turmoil wreaking havoc in her brain.

"Breathe, Mrs. Mirdoc, the feeling will pass," he crooned, his words her only haven, and she focused on them with all her will.

It took longer than she liked, but the feeling did eventually pass. She found herself sitting on the floor, leaning against one of the bookshelves with a glass of water pressed into her hands by long, pale fingers. Her head felt as if someone had tried to split it with an axe.

"Drink this slowly, it will help." His insistence bordered on pompous.

She wasn't in a fit state to argue, so she did as he requested, eager to have it done. She wanted to ask him what'd happened, but when the water was gone, he spoke before she could take a breath to do so herself.

"I had begun to think you would never arrive, we have been stationary far too long, you see, and I have never left a task unfinished. Your tale will be stored here for the enjoyment of the Elevated, but not until it has been earned. They have a direct link to all the books, and the individuals whose lives occupy their pages, from their home plane. Do not concern yourself with the details, you will not remember any of this when you leave here, but I believe in being well informed, and I try to extend the courtesy to others as well." He stopped long enough to take the empty glass from her white-knuckled grip.

"Why … what …?" She wanted to ask what the meaning of all this was, but couldn't form the right words.

"One at a time, Mrs. Mirdoc. Why can be answered by the extent of diversity you have faced throughout your life, and the fact that you became stronger for it. The what is a little more complicated. Just think of it as a biography made available only to a select few. They share experiences you've had that they never will. Your gift allows them to *feel*, something we mortals take for granted." There was no smile to make the impact of his words more bearable. He spoke with the certainty of a college professor, with all the cool detachment that goes with the position.

"And what do you get out of all this?" she finally managed to form a coherent thought.

"Why, knowledge of course. I have been given the ability to use the full capacity of my mind, and I have filled it with all the vast knowledge that comes from the history of our world. What more do I need?" He didn't sound like he wanted, or needed, an answer. His eyes gleamed brightly, the incandescent light catching the milkyness and making them glow eerily.

Prudence stared up at him, wanting to comprehend the fervor he felt but was unable to look past the fact that he believed in. . . well, she wasn't quite sure exactly what he believed happened here at his store.

He regarded her with his head tilted and rubbed his beardless face.

"It is not required that you believe now, Mrs. Mirdoc. You will see soon enough." He handed her the book that had pulled her life experiences onto its pages, and she flinched away from it. "Do not fear, it can only be imprinted once, and then it is finite."

Slowly, she took the book from his hands and gasped when it thrummed beneath her skin.

"This book will stay with you, no matter the circumstances, until your time comes. No one will be able to take it from you, for it is yours alone. You will not see me again, or remember any of what has transpired, until you return many years from now." His tone was severe, as if what he said held dire import.

Prudence looked at him, her brow creased as she clutched the book. Ezra looked at his silver watch and shook his head.

"*Tempus fugit, non autem memoria,* Mrs. Mirdoc." He stood then, and in a blinding flash, she found herself standing on the sidewalk outside of an empty storefront.

The rough bricks had worn edges and the windows were dingy. *Why did I stop here? What is it about this vacant shop that nags at the back of my mind, like a tickle of a memory that should be clear?*

Shaking her head, Prudence dug out the offensive cell phone Lina insisted she carry around and hit 1 to dial her granddaughter.

"Grams? What's wrong?" Lina's concern made her smile.

"Dear, I need you to come get me, please. I . . . don't know where I am . . . or how I got here."

After numerous doctors came to the same conclusion, Prudence finally accepted she had dementia. Her oldest son bore the responsibility of taking over her affairs as they slowly overwhelmed her, which happened more often as the days slipped by. Her granddaughter was far away, at her own encouragement. Lina moved with her fiancé when he'd gotten a job in another state. She didn't want her beloved grandchild to see her diminish with her condition.

Several years later, Prudence moved into a supervised senior community after she lost her driver's license due to one too many close calls. It was there that the disease took a stronghold. Her mind slipped as frequently as she was coherent, and she began to lose awareness of self. The other seniors housed there became familiar strangers that she did activities with and ate meals beside every day.

The months played out like the pages of the book that never left her side. She would flip through them, reliving the times that meant the most to her or had the greatest impact. The people she'd known, the ones she loved and loathed, all came to visit her at random times. Most of the time they'd make her smile, but others would make her cry and she would beg them to leave. It was on the bad days that she felt tired, worn down, at the end of her rope and grudging what the next minute would hold.

One night, she awoke to voices. It annoyed her at first, but then she recognized some part of the sound. Getting out of bed, she found a narrow door waiting for her. A charred, thick wooden sign perched on the wall above it with the words 'Librorum Taberna' painted in bold white letters.

Out of the door stepped a tall rail of a man with unkempt hair. His smile, only the second time she'd seen it, was warm for a change.

"Prudence Mirdoc, your chariot awaits." He swept his hand out in a formal gesture and bowed slightly at the waist, motioning for her to precede him into the store.

"Ezra Finfrock. A pleasure to see you again. What kept you so long?" Everything was clear for the first time in years. She knew this man, and his shop. All the memories, from the day she'd met him to the one she was walking through now, came back as well. She handed him her book as he responded.

"As circumstance would have it, you are quite the fighter and refused to let go. No matter, you are here now, and I am happy to announce that Allen is waiting for you, madam." His words were thick with emotional sincerity.

Her heart swelled; it had been far too long. Tears burned her eyes as she stepped toward the open door.

Her head turned back to the old shop keeper, and she smiled as tears streaked her wrinkled cheeks. "This is the side of you that only a small few get to see, isn't it?"

He nodded, his features turning stern once more, and he was the man she'd met that fateful day so many years ago. "Only those in transition."

Looking back to the doorway, her eyes slid closed, making more tears fall as she clasped her hands together. "My beloved," she breathed, and with the tinkling of a familiar bell overhead, she stepped into the light.

Why must people persist with lies?
Isn't the truth easier to accept?
Difficult as it may be at first, honesty
is far less damaging in the end EF

The Truth
By Ben Roc

Ever since that phone call two days ago, the memories Bob Smith thought he buried in the past, in the back of his mind, were resurrecting. Though it had taken him damn near ten years to finally stop the scenes that played out in his head like reruns of old and worn-out TV shows, they just kept coming back, as if he were stuck on the same channel.

The call that altered the trajectory of his life came from Kathy Yates, the wife of his old Army buddy, Lieutenant General Perry Yates. Softly and calmly she said, "Bob, this is Kathy Yates. Perry died yesterday from an unexpected heart attack. The doctor called it a widow maker. He told me many times that when he passed on I should call you. That you would come and deliver his eulogy. He was so insistent I call you and... well, it's time."

Bob didn't know how long he remained silent while Kathy patiently waited for his reply. She must have known that bad news delivered by phone takes a person by surprise. Like an ambush.

Bob froze, as he always did when he heard the snapping of a twig. It was instinct; it's what used to keep him alive. Finally, he recovered from the shock and corralled the rampaging thoughts coursing through his mind. When he found his voice, all he could say was, "I'm deeply sorry Kathy. Of course, I'll be there." She gave him the details of when and where the funeral would be held. He didn't recall taking the few notes she gave him.

The final approach into Ronald Reagan Washington National Airport afforded the right side passengers a view of the CIA Headquarters, the Pentagon, the United States Air Force Memorial and Arlington National

Cemetery, final resting place for over three hundred thousand souls.

A young-looking Army Captain greeted Bob when he exited the plane. Apparently, the officer recognized Bob from old Army photos. As they strode briskly to a waiting Army sedan, Captain Parrish introduced himself and briefed the older man on the details of the ceremonies.

The officer said, "Captain Smith, may I express my condolences upon the passing of your friend and comrade in arms, Lieutenant General Yates? I never had the privilege to serve under his command, but from what I've heard these past few days, he is deserving of all the honors he shall receive as we lay him to rest in Arlington National Cemetery."

Bob listened to the well-intended words of Captain Parrish and perfunctorily replied. "Thank you, captain, for your sentiments. They're very much appreciated. I just hope I can carry out my duties."

More than two and a half decades had passed since Bob had visited Arlington National Memorial Cemetery, the Nations' resting place for her Honored Dead. He felt that this tangible edifice, above all others, was the starkest symbol of the price our fallen comrades have paid for freedom. Bob flared red as he recalled those who considered their sacrifice as futile, a waste, or misplaced patriotism. The fact is, they died in service to their country and to argue the validity of political circumstances only demeaned their sacrifice.

Today another soldier will join the ranks of honored dead. Bob's duty was to offer the last words of praise. He didn't want this mission. *Where's the courage of old that seemed to appear from nowhere during combat? God help me,* he thought as he assumed the same spot vacated by the Minister from Perry's Baptist Church. *How can I add to the simple but moving words already spoken by this man of God, who understands how to sum up a man's life?*

As Bob planted his one real leg and one artificial leg by the soil that would soon be heaped onto Perry's flag draped coffin, he took in the sea of grave stones that waved like whitecaps on land.

With a deep breath, he began. "Lieutenant General Perry Yates and I served together in Viet Nam from 1967 to 1969. In the beginning of our shared Army life, he was a First Lieutenant, and I was a Second Lieutenant. Yates was the commanding officer of our platoon. I could name the company and battalion but it really doesn't matter now."

When he finished this preamble, he glanced at the three by five note cards that held the words he had labored to put to paper. It took almost five hours to conjure up what he felt to be a fitting and proper eulogy for a man that most people here probably only knew by name and rank. *How can they gauge the measure of the man?* All his prepared words seemed hollow and artificial, like his leg.

Slowly he pocketed the cards. "I cannot stand before you today and speak the words that I prepared. In no way do they portray a man that I knew well and admired. And in no way do they describe the man you should remember. Therefore, I want to tell you a true story."

Now was the time to bring back all those memories filed in the archives of his mind. It was time to lay down the past, so it may be forever buried with his friend.

"Lieutenant Yates and I led a platoon of eight men into the jungles of Viet Nam. Our mission was like many that some of you here may recall. We were to go in country to determine the location, size, weapon type, and troop strength of the enemy. Our reconnaissance march was fairly routine. Until all hell broke loose. Our platoon crossed the path of a Viet Cong patrol, and we found ourselves engaged in a deadly firefight. Death was the winner that day. Of the ten men who left the firebase, only Perry and I survived. However, in the scheme of war we were the victors, because our ten warriors cut down their fifteen. It was then that I caught a round in this leg, which was later amputated."

Suddenly, Bob felt a jolt of pain in the leg that was not there. The images of the rifle flashes as killing bullets spit at them, and the cracking sound they made punched him like they did in 1969. Years, which in reality only measured moments, passed before he continued.

"Perry had, miraculously, only been grazed on his arm. However, I was spilling blood in a foreign country. When the jungle finally became silent Perry turned his attention to my leg. I was in a very bad way and required a tourniquet that had to be tightened and then loosened every twenty minutes. I was fading in and out and could not walk. We were at least ten miles into enemy territory with no radio, since it had become a casualty as well."

Bob looked around at the faces assembled before the coffin of Perry Yates. Eyes wide and attentive, they were now realizing the courage of the man who they came to honor today. Others looked like they were reliving their own horror stories of war.

Bob continued. "On that day, in unbearable heat, after having fought a determined enemy to the death, Perry Yates bore me on his back and marched out of enemy territory. Every twenty minutes, he stopped to adjust the tourniquet on my leg. It took three days to pack me back to our firebase. So, as we say goodbye to Perry Yates; the soldier, the friend, and the husband, let us remember that his actions in life speak well of the man."

There was nothing more that Bob could say to convey the worth of the man that saved his life. With those final words, he returned to his seat and witnessed the folding of the flag of the United States of America as the Honor Guard of seven riflemen marched into position. Shots punctuated the quiet of this hallowed cemetery. Bob had not heard Taps for quite a long time, but now the remorseful slow notes washed over him. Without realizing, tears flowed down his face. *There can be no more sorrowful sound than a lone bugler playing Taps.*

Perry's comrades serving as pallbearers respectfully folded Old Glory. Everyone's attention turned to the five-star General, who solemnly carried the flag to Kathy Yates, bent over, and softly spoke into her ear. Bob could hear him as he whispered. "Mrs. Yates, on behalf of the President of the United States, and the people of a grateful nation, may I present this flag as a token of appreciation for the honorable and faithful service your loved one rendered this nation." Then he placed the flag in her reluctant hands, slowly came to attention, and presented her with a trembling salute.

The many military and civilian friends and well-wishers filed past Kathy and offered their heartfelt condolences. As Bob came up to do the same, she pulled him down and softly said, "Please wait with me until everyone has left. I want to talk with you."

Bob straightened and quietly strode to a secluded spot.

Finally, everyone had paid their respects to the grieving widow, and she walked next to Bob. Tenderly taking his arm, she led him down the gently sloping hill away from the grave. As they came to rest she looked at him with warm embracing eyes. "Bob. Perry told me about the battle you shared with us a few minutes ago. He was very troubled by it. For a long time, he couldn't make peace with himself. Then, almost imperceptibly, he seemed to be free from torture of those memories."

After a few uneasy moments she asked, "What really happened that terrible day in Viet Nam? I always felt he kept a secret that if spoken would crush him."

"I told all I recall," Bob replied. "I was drifting in and out of consciousness. I have no recollection of anything, except Perry telling me he and I were the only survivors. I recall him applying the tourniquet, then nothing."

Kathy continued. "For so many years, Perry was troubled about that mission. Before he found peace, he kept to himself in his study, and I think he wrote a few pages. Like his memoirs. Maybe a confession. I don't know. I was hoping you might be able to clear up the mystery."

Bob could only reply, "Perry and I never spoke of that patrol after I left for stateside to convalesce. I never pressed him. I think he buried the ordeal deeper than I did."

Kathy nodded. "I guess we'll never know the truth. The answers will be buried with my husband forever." She reached up and lovingly kissed Bob on the cheek. "Thank you for being his friend. And mine." She turned and walked to her waiting car.

Bob and his driver left Arlington Cemetery by way of the George Washington Parkway. He just told the Captain to "head south". Captain Parrish would look at Bob in his rearview mirror periodically, but said nothing. Sometimes men who bore the scars of battle often disconnected from everyone around them. So, they drove south on the GWMP, which paralleled the Mount Vernon Trail, passing Ronald Reagan Washington National Airport along the way. Land that George Washington, Father of the Nation, would ride from his beloved Mount Vernon home to what would become his namesake and the Nation's Capital, Washington D.C.

Bob's mind was dwelling forty years in the past when he heard a growl that seemed out of place. When he heard it again, he realized what it was. Looking to the front seat he asked, "Captain, did I just hear your stomach growl?"

With some embarrassment Captain Parrish said, "Yes sir. I apologize. I'll try to keep the racket to a minimum."

"When did you eat last?"

"Well sir, it was about oh seven hundred this morning."

Bob snapped out of his reverie fully and realized he too was in need of chow. "That was over eight hours ago. Let's stop in Alexandria for a bite to eat. We both have had a taxing day. We better feed the beast."

Ten minutes later, Captain Parrish was cruising down one of the historic streets of Alexandria, Virginia. He spied one of the local eateries in Old Town, in the southeastern part of the city. The place wasn't so upscale that it would take forever to get seated and served. He found a parking space nearby, and they exited the car.

The Captain led the way with Bob in tow. They entered the diner, were seated right away, and ordered within five minutes.

Bob and Captain Parrish ate without saying anything more than, "Pass the salt, please." Bob picked at his food while Captain Parrish inhaled his.

Bob could not hold back the memories. His thoughts jumped around like a pogo stick, striking solid ground then back up in the air where nothing had weight or substance.

When Bob rejoined the present, he showed a quizzical expression as he looked out the window. Bob was looking for something. A specific something.

After a moment of searching up and down the street, Bob said, "Captain, I recall seeing a quaint bookshop just around the corner. It looked like it may have been one of the original shops when Alexandria was first settled in the mid seventeen hundreds. I feel like a diversion. If you don't mind, order up a dessert and have another cup of coffee. I shouldn't be long."

Captain Parrish said, "No problem, sir. Take all the time you want. I'm attached to you until you fly out tomorrow morning."

With that, Bob walked up to their server and asked the waiter to take care of Captain Parrish and stated that he would be paying the tab when he came back in a couple minutes.

Bob turned left out of the restaurant then left again at the corner of the building. Five shops down his side of the street, in the middle of the block, he caught sight of the shop sign that sparked his imagination. It pointed towards the street, like an accusing finger. Librorum Taberna was written in all white lettering on a wooden plank that looked to be older than time itself.

He turned the knob on the door, and when he passed across the stoop, he looked up at a doorbell without a bell clapper. It made no sound when the door opened, nor when he closed it behind him. Then, even stranger, he noticed there was no lock on the door, no deadbolt. Nothing would block entry into the store.

Bob stood in the entry and let his gaze wander around the shop. It was narrow but long, and along every wall, from floor to ceiling, were shelves filled to the rafters with books. Some looked to be extremely old by the discoloration of the pages. Many, if not most, of the books seemed to be bound with leather instead of the rigid hard covers or flimsy paper of today's volumes. Along the floor were waist high bookshelves and they too were stocked to the gills. He seemed to have stepped back in time. *But, to what century?* At the rear he glimpsed a curtain that must lead to a backroom. As he stood still, he took in the size of the room, which seemed to expand. His logical mind knew this was not a large building, and yet he had the sensation of standing in a large hall. And while he grappled with that contradiction his nosed twitched. There was an overpowering smell of old burnt wood, mixed with an unmistakable smell of the sea. Then a musty odor of aging paper and book leather took center stage. It seemed that he was standing in a room that had alternately been burned, sunk under water, and then left to dry in an old barn.

As he attempted to reconcile these confusing sensations, he witnessed the appearance of a man that looked as if he too had suffered the same fate as this room. When Bob locked eyes with this apparition he could not turn away. The ancient man approached down one of the aisles separated by interior bookshelves. Bob could only see the man from the chest up. His upper torso glided without any of the usual motion a bipedal human makes. The smooth and swift gait seemed impossible for a man of his age. When the ancient one turned the corner, Bob could see him fully, head to toe, coming right up to him.

The apparition and Bob stood for what must have been a minute or longer, neither speaking, yet still communicating. Neither diverted their locked stare. This ephemeral creature was taking the measure of him. They were total strangers to one another. Yet Bob felt an overwhelming subservience to this man, this Svengali, this hypnotist, this Rasputin.

Then, with a quiet but commanding voice, the apparition said, "Welcome to my little book shop. How may I help you?" He spoke with an accent that Bob could only imagine originated somewhere in old Europe or maybe the Balkans.

All Bob could muster was, "Hello."

"I am Ezra Finfrock, proprietor. Is there something in particular you seek? Something that speaks to the past?"

Bob regained his composure a bit. "Well, Mr. Finfrock, I stopped in the restaurant just around the corner and caught sight of your shop as we parked the car. I guess my curiosity is piqued. Your store seems to be older than the others along the street."

Ezra made the slightest of grins with his paper-thin lips and arched an out-of-control bushy eyebrow. Turning his beanpole body and lifting a bony finger that was more skeletal than human, he waved a hand around the shop, declaring, "Here you see a collection from all parts of the world, from many eras and customs. They speak to the follies, the sacrifices, and the courage of mankind in combat. I gather by your uniform you have served in the Army."

"Yes, during the Vietnam War. I just attended funeral services at Arlington National Cemetery. Lieutenant General Perry Yates was laid to rest today."

"Ah yes, I heard about his passing. You have my sincere condolences, Mister …?"

"Smith. Bob Smith is my name."

Ezra took several more beats then turned to head down the center aisle with Bob in tow. As Ezra glided along he suggested, "Perhaps you would be interested in some of the more esoteric history of the Arlington National Cemetery, Mister Smith. I'm sure I have a rather informative tome about that renowned institution."

Ezra paused, scanned a few of the books, and pulled one down. "Here is one you will find most gratifying about the Arlington National Cemetery and in particular, the customs of a military funeral." He held the book between two bone thin hands with a reverence. "For example, the flag which drapes the coffin is meticulously folded twelve times by an honor guard of six, three on each side. Each fold represents a symbolic sentiment. Such as honor to the fallen comrade, respect for the mother and father of the fallen, and recognition of Hebrew figures of old. The twelfth and last fold is a meaningful symbol of eternity, and shows humility and respect by the Christian faithful to God the Father, the Son, and the Holy Ghost. When the folded flag is presented to the next of kin, the stars will point upwards as a reminder to all Americans of the national motto, In God We Trust. It takes the shape of a bicorne hat. The presenter will softly utter these words for a fallen Army soldier, 'On behalf of the President of the United States and the people of a grateful nation, may I present this flag as a token of appreciation for the honorable and faithful service your loved one rendered this nation.' All very somber, very respectful. Three volleys from seven rifles. All accompanied by a military band and escort platoon."

Bob replayed the scene earlier in the day and recalled exactly what Ezra just described. "Have you attended many such funerals, Mr. Finrock?"

Ezra paused and then looked about his shop. While opening his arms to encompass his books he replied, "Many, many times. More than you could possibly comprehend. In many places, on many fields of battle, in many honorable cemeteries."

Bob accepted the book as Ezra proffered it, and thumbed through a few pages. With a hesitant look, he met those disturbing white eyes again.

Then, Ezra glided further down the same aisle, offering more minutiae along the way. "Arlington National Cemetery is the only military cemetery that has the distinction of permitting horses to be used as a part of the ceremony. There are about fifteen funerals a day, around three thousand conducted each year, and it is thought that the cemetery will reach its full capacity in the year twenty-twenty."

Bob could only marvel at the mental agility of Ezra, the erudite recollection of the topic at hand. Again, Bob felt driven to ask, "Mr. Finrock, your command of the subject is impressive. I would guess you taught at a Military Academy, maybe West Point or the Naval Academy?"

Ezra looked around the shop at his books, lingering for the briefest of moments here and there. Finally, he met Bob's gaze and said, "I am a student, not an instructor. I've simply lived the experiences. I've been there, seen and felt the humanity. And the inhumanity." Then, Ezra made a beeline for another book.

Bob fell in behind, like in the days when he was a recruit learning how to march in unison.

Ezra came to an abrupt halt, spun around to face Bob, who almost ran up Ezra's heels. Stating as a fact-of-matter as much as a question, Ezra said, "I notice you have a slight, almost imperceptible stutter to your gait. I take it you were wounded some time ago."

"Yes," Bob said, startled. "It was a long time ago. In fact, Lieutenant General Yates and I were on a patrol when I was wounded so badly I lost my lower leg. I use a prosthetic, but I thought I had learned how to move without it being noticed. I haven't fooled you, though."

"I've seen many men wounded in battle before and after they have been tended to by physicians. In fact, here is a little book that might interest you. It describes some of the historical developments of medical care in combat."

Bob accepted this second recommendation and asked, "What will I find in this?"

Immediately, Ezra rattled off a few nuggets of wisdom. "Pain-killers are a relatively new development. In ancient times, the wounded that suffered their injuries were considered quite courageous. For example, during the third century, one Roman soldier is said to have received as many as twenty-three battle wounds, and so he was esteemed for such courage. Alexander the Great is arguably considered one of the most courageous warriors and leaders in all of history. In battle, he received many grievous wounds in his neck, legs, shoulders, and ankle as well as a serious wound to the chest. Fortunately for Alexander, he had the best medical care of his day."

Upon reflection, Bob interjected, "I lived because of my friend, my brother in arms, Perry. He carried me to our side after a very deadly firefight. He alone saved my life."

Bob took a few seconds to deal with the emotions raging through him. It was painfully evident on Bob's face, and Ezra nodded in understanding. Then, away Ezra raced to find one more piece of literature. Only this time, Bob stood still, feet firmly planted in the jungles of Viet Nam.

Coming back to Bob's side, Ezra gently placed a thin book in his hand.

Quietly, but with a firm voice, Ezra drew Bob back to Librorum Taberna, the little bookshop in Alexandria. "This book just arrived this morning. It's not a great literary masterpiece, but a simple anthology of personal stories written by the men who survived their own episodes of Hell. Perhaps you will find some solace in sharing their trials and tribulations. Men like you make sacrifices that only you and they can understand."

Bob listened but didn't completely hear all that Ezra said. All that came to his lips were, "Thank you, Ezra."

"You're welcome, Bob. Now, I have a client due in ten minutes. If you would like those books, it will cost you twenty-five dollars. I'm sorry, but I only accept cash. Credit cards and the like seem too much like voodoo magic."

Bob mechanically withdrew the wallet from his back pocket and pulled out a twenty and a five. Handing them to Ezra, he made eye contact one last time. "Here. You know, I would like to return sometime to scour through your collection. May I have a business card?"

Ezra gave Bob a quizzical look and shook his head. "When you need to visit again, you will find me. In fact, you'll probably see me when you least expect it. There is no need to give you a card."

Hesitating a moment, Bob offered his hand in farewell. It hung there with no movement from Ezra. All he got was a penetrating stare and some parting words.

"Bob, life and death are opposite sides of the same coin. They co-exist as one, inseparable and often completely confusing. But always know this—answers come forward when you least expect them. Embrace them and their messengers." With that, Ezra tucked the bills away with his scraggily fingers, made an about face and was through the curtain like a puff of smoke.

Stunned by the abrupt exit, all Bob could think to do was turn around and walk out the front door. As he stepped onto the sidewalk, he glanced up at the silent doorbell again. *Movement, but no sound. Strange.* He came to a halt a few feet from the door. His physical senses were registering opposite of what should have been. He was chilled in the warm sun. He felt light-headed, even though his heart pulsed with a slow rhythmic beat. No sounds registered despite the car and human traffic streaming in front of him. Seconds or minutes, he wasn't certain, passed before he seized reality, the dream-like state passing. He turned right and made his way to the corner where he made another right into the entrance of the restaurant. Bob walked the few paces to the booth where Captain Parrish sat with an unfinished dessert and a half-empty cup of coffee.

Bob took his seat opposite Captain Parrish and sat perfectly still, as if in a trance. His face showed no sign of recognition of Captain Parrish or even where he was.

The young officer indicated Bob's purchase. "I see you found a few books at that little shop around the corner. May I see them?"

Bob thought he heard a voice. He was disoriented. It was the same sensation he often felt when he crossed from a fitful sleep to consciousness, that threshold between the world of illusions and the physical, the tangible. The world that was measured by the finite and linear realities that were book-ended by birth and death, with only life filling the spaces.

Captain Parrish repeated, "May I see the books you have? The small one is titled, 'A Soldiers Anthology'. That's an intriguing title."

Bob lifted the booklet and scanned the front page, then handed it over.

Captain Parrish began to leaf through the pages and then turned to the table of contents. His eyes widened. He got Bob's attention and with a little excitement in his voice said, "Sir, there's a story in here called Danny Boy written by Lieutenant General Yates. That's amazing." Handing the book to Bob he said, "Take a look for yourself."

Still in a daze, Bob didn't fully process what Captain Parrish said. He robotically accepted the book. The Captain saw the confusion on his face, so he turned to the table of contents and, while lifting the book to within six inches of Bob's face, pointed to the last entry on the list.

Bob slowly regained his focus and trained his eyes on the selection. There was Perry's name next to the title *Danny Boy*. His Danny, the young soldier that died back there, in that place, in that time. What were these two names doing in this book? He looked at the author and title, and back to Captain Parrish's puzzled face.

"Maybe you should read the letter, sir," the young officer encouraged. "I never heard of General Yates ever writing any personal memoirs. He wrote military reports, and opinions, but nothing about himself."

Nothing made sense to Bob since he stepped foot in that bookshop. Everything was at sixes and sevens. *No up or down. Just unease. Wait, didn't Kathy say something about memoirs?* He paged to the last story in the book and began to read.

Bob's hands trembled with trepidation.

Dear Bob,

If you are reading this, then it is a safe bet that I am dead, and you have just given me a glorious send-off. Thanks buddy. Forgive the cryptic way in which you were given this letter, but I wanted you to understand something. I hope you don't mind recalling some unpleasant memories. No doubt you remember that bloody day when our platoon was caught in a firefight that took the lives of our comrades. Well, there is a truth that I never made you aware of.

Remember Danny? That's right, Danny Becker. He was

even younger than we were, so skinny and virginal. He's the subject of what I want you to read. The following is a poem I wrote a number of years ago that helped me come to terms with what I did then. I call this poem 'DANNY BOY'.

Our mission we marched in-country.
We were a team that knew each other so well,
That our steps we followed so closely,
Hardly, a footprint could the enemy tell.

Our lives we depended on each other,
To keep safe from harm and death.
Despite all the fears and the danger,
We knew we would escape its cold breath.

The jungle was full of pitfalls,
As we journeyed together that last time.
The enemy was shrewd and relentless,
Quiet and sure like the mime.

Then suddenly the anger of bullets,
Licked at our heels with flames of fire.
Some found their mark in your body, Danny,
As we sought a defensive position to retire.

The battle raged throughout the night,
Grim death was the winner.
So few of us remained,
Both the saint and the sinner.

Our patrol was a team of ten,
So gallant did we march that day.
After battles silent justice,
Only three were left to pray.

Bob, me, and you,
We survived the night.
But both your bodies,
Could no longer fight.

Bob's wounds were serious,
As best I could tell.
I'm no doctor damn it,
But he would get well.

Your cries of pain,
Were heard through the night.
The jungle full of danger,
Dear God, show me the light.

Life wept from your body,
Into puddles of red.
Your guts laid open,
Soon you would be dead.

Sobbing shook your body,
The pain you could not bear.
By the sound you made,
The enemy would know where.

With courage and love,
You knew the end was near.
Only one could be saved,
You pleaded through tears.

Stop my pain,
Save the two of you.
Dear God in Heaven,
If only you knew.

With bayonet point,
As I covered your eyes.
I heard your last prayer,
Then thrust where the heart lies.

Your death came quickly,
My hand found its way.
Peaceful silence,
Upon your face that day.

Bob and I survived,
One life you traded for two.
Your place is in Heaven,
May God's Grace shine on you.

Bob, I have sought God's forgiveness for the decision
I made that day in the jungle. I couldn't carry you both.
Danny would not have survived, but you had a good
chance. I think the choice was correct. I tell you this only
because I made a promise to Danny. As long as one of
us lived, the truth would be known till the last one died.
Well, I preceded you buddy, so please, in Danny's name
remember him and the sacrifice he made for the both
of us. I know this may seem like an unbearable burden,
but if you see the unselfish gift he gave us, then you may
rejoice in his memory as I have these many years.
    Be well, be happy and remember.
    Your friend,
    Perry.

Bob sat motionless as warm, salty tears made their way down his
cheeks. How could he possibly carry the weight of the truth? "No Perry, it
is unbearable," he whispered.

The fate had been cast to the wind and could never be recaptured. "I will
remember and will attempt to come to terms with the truth as you did, Perry.
On this day I bury two friends."

Captain Parrish saw the anguish in Bob's face and heard his plaintive
whispers. Something just landed a body blow to Bob, and it clearly was
the result of the letter, the words from a dead man. "Captain Smith, what's
wrong? You look like you just saw a ghost."

Bob jumped to his feet and reached for the three books. Pulling two
twenties from his wallet he sputtered, "Here, pay the tab, and then follow
me around the corner. I have to see that old man in the bookshop. Right
now."

In seconds, Bob bounded out the door and turned the corner, just as
he had done barely twenty minutes ago. His eyes instantly began to search
for that weather-beaten sign. When it didn't immediately come into view,
he slowed to a steady gait. He stepped to the curb to get a bead on all the
shops in this block.

He muttered, "Where the hell did it go?" A thorough scan up and down
the block showed that Librorum Taberna was not there. *It has to be. I was*

just there. He distinctly remembered that ancient plank extending from the outer wall, pointing to the street like a bony finger of a cadaver. Like the fingers of Ezra. Bob remembered it was five doors down, so he counted each with the concentration of a man with a purpose. One, two, three, four and now, standing squarely at the entrance of the fifth door, all he saw was a sign stating 'This Property for Sale or Lease'.

Captain Parrish appeared at Bob's side. He too stared at the realtors sign. The older man's face was a jumble of emotions; shock, confusion, even a tinge of fear. "Bob, what's wrong? Where's the bookshop? Is it just down the block?"

What can I say? This is where the shop was, but it's not here now. I'm going crazy. I've had a mental breakdown and you better take me to a Veterans hospital.

"I thought it was here." Bob stepped to the door and with trepidation turned the knob. Locked. He tried again but it would not move. *This isn't right.* He shook the knob, rattling the glass in the door.

The racket caught the attention of the shop owner next door who walked up and asked, "Can I help you? I'm Janice."

Bob wheeled on the intruder and blurted, "I was in this shop a half hour ago!" He proffered the three volumes and told the interloper, "I just bought these books. The old gentleman, Ezra Finfrock sold these to me. There was a sign hanging right above us. Librorum Taberna."

"I'm sorry, but you are mistaken. I've had my business here for nearly fifteen years, and there has never been a book shop here."

Bob was losing it. He held the tangible evidence in his hands. *They didn't materialize out of thin air. This is the place where I bought them less than half an hour ago.* He turned to Captain Parrish and asked, "Did I have these books with me when we first walked into the restaurant?"

"No sir, you just purchased them about thirty minutes ago. We stopped at the restaurant next door to eat and then you wanted to browse through a book shop that was just around the corner. This corner. You came back with the books in your hands. That much is certain."

Turning to Janice, the Captain asked, "Are there any antique book shops nearby?"

She paused to think and then replied, "The nearest bookstore, antique, contemporary or any kind is on the other side of Old Town, at least a forty-five minute walk from this spot."

Silence lingered heavy between the three. Bob finally spoke, "Then something happened to me that can't be proven, except by me. Captain Parrish, please take a minute to read this letter from General Yates."

The Captain pored over the poem and gasped when he finished. Looking up, he meet Bob's penetrating gaze. "Sir, I –"

"Captain Parrish, what is today's date?"

"May twenty-fifth, twenty-ten."

"And Captain Parrish, what is the date at the end of the letter?"

"May twenty-fifth ... twenty-ten."

Nothing to do about it now, but perhaps
I shouldn't have let that particular book out
of the shop. Mister Pylorius certainly knows
better than to attempt to use it. Ǝꟻ

The Door, the Lock, the Key
by R. Michael Burns

to the fond memory
of J.L.B. and H.P.L.,
with utmost humble gratitude

"…Leave behind…all divine enlightenment and voices
and heavenly utterances and plunge into the Darkness …"
—Dionysius

Douglas Cronan stared a moment at the mummified yellow page, the arcane characters there, his eyes wide, his mouth dry as crepe-paper. Then, gingerly, he closed the cover and pushed the tome away. Slower even than his great many years demanded, he settled into the wing-backed leather chair, pulling at his lower lip with a gnarled-as-driftwood thumb.

"By Astaroth, Myles!" Cronan whispered, still pulling at his lip. "Is that …?" He stopped, tried to gather the dark thoughts gusting through his mind, to make his tongue cooperate with his intentions. "*Is it?*"

Across the table from him, the man called Myles Pylorus offered a yellow sliver of a grin, his face reflected in the polish of the dark mahogany surface like an autumn moon. "I wasn't certain until now—this moment. But … yes, I can see it in your eyes. *You* recognize it, too."

Cronan took a long, shuddering breath, tugged at the tartan scarf draped across his bony shoulders. Even the blaze crackling in the Club's wide hearth couldn't seem to keep the London chill at bay. The damp cold penetrated him deeper with each passing year.

"Imagine," Pylorus said, steepling his long fingers and gazing at his old friend, his eyes black-bright in the firelight. "After all these years, I've discovered it. That which we knew *must* exist, but sought in vain ...."

Cronan could scarcely take it in—his gaze kept dancing from Pylorus' sallow smirk to the book's ancient cover, bound in something like tanned skin, something he felt sure wasn't leather. "Where ...?"

"Ah—that's something of an odd tale in itself," Pylorus said, reaching now for the snifter of cognac on the table beside him. "I purchased this ... treasure ... at an obscure bookseller's in the Strand—*Librorum Taberna*, I believe the place was called. But it's odd, you know—I've spent a great deal of time in that part of the city, haunting the shops there, yet I'd never before encountered this *particular* shop. And when I returned only days later to further enquire about the volume—to discover how the proprietor had come by it—I couldn't locate the place at all. I asked around at the various boutiques in the area, even broached the subject with several local officers of the peace. Yet none of the people I spoke to had ever so much as *heard* of the establishment." He paused, sipping his drink, seeming to savor it.

Savoring, too, his own words, Cronan thought, his ever-so-sophisticated diction. An affectation, Cronan knew—overcompensation for his lower class origins. If anything, his conversation had grown all the more elaborate over the years.

Replacing his glass, Pylorus went on, "After several days' fruitless investigation, I was forced to the conclusion that the place no longer existed—at least, not in that particular location. It's almost as if the great machinations of the world opened a window for the briefest of moments so that I might finally acquire this ... priceless item."

Looking at the book—and the man in the chair just beyond it—Cronan imagined he could feel the afternoon's drizzle chilling its way down his back. It made his joints ache.

"Myles," he said, slowly, a man testing the thin ice beneath his feet, "you, ah ... you have no intention of putting that ... *item* to use, have you?"

Pylorus set his snifter aside. Silent, he bent forward and traced with one long pale finger the obscure symbol engraved on the book's grotesque cover.

"I shall take it back to the Library, of course," he murmured. Cronan could hear the capital letter in the man's tone, the reverence with which they'd all once spoken of the Library. It hadn't been so long ago—no more than an eternity, surely—when the assembly and care of the Library had been their shared task, their mutual secret. Their purpose in the cosmos. "I shall study it," Pylorus went on, "plumb its depths, learn its secrets. Merely cracking its cipher will be the challenge of a lifetime!"

"But you won't attempt to *use* it, will you?"

"Douglas, my old friend," Pylorus said, sitting upright once more, bringing his fingers together under the point of his chin, "you mustn't worry yourself so."

"Don't treat this matter lightly, Myles," Cronan said, rigid in his tall chair. "Part of the reason we allowed the Order to disband—"

"The Order disbanded because the membership lost their faith in the search—in the very idea of the Library," Pylorus said, voice smooth and cool as polished marble, almost soothing in its stony implacability. "Nor was that the root of it. The truth is that those pretenders knew only too well that they could never rise to the level which *you and I* had attained. Our power intimidated them, Douglas—*frightened* them."

"Well it might," Cronan said, trying again to stretch his scarf until it kept the chill at bay. "We'd gone too far, strayed into dark places where we had no business. Our power far exceeded our wisdom, Myles—we were on a path to unthinkable disaster."

Pylorus' smile faltered, then twitched and returned to its full candlepower.

"Now, now. No need to employ such histrionics … Master Calchas."

Cronan glanced about him, assuring that no one was around to overhear them. Even given the privacy their environs afforded them, some things were secrets among secrets. "No one's called me that in ages," he said, "not even here at the Club." Yet despite the absurdity of it, he couldn't quite suppress the tickle of pride that passed through him at the mention of his Initiate name. "I think I've done very little of late to deserve it—if ever I did."

"One cannot un-become what we *are*, Douglas," Pylorus said, sipping his cognac with a self-satisfied smirk. "The others were merely playing at unlocking the secrets of the darkness which underlies all of existence—but not us. We two discovered the door, we crafted the lock … and now *I* possess the key."

"But you dare not use it," Cronan said, shivering.

Pylorus leaned close. "Think, Douglas," he said, eyes narrowed yet fervor-bright. "All the 'gentlemen' of this worn-out Club are so very proud of themselves, the great adepts of our age cloistered away behind thick walls and hidden doors, secretly working their great magicks, congratulating themselves on their ability to tug at the threads of Time's vast tapestry, to nudge world events this way or that. Just look at how they congratulate themselves on their great influence, on being the ghostwriters of history. But the very best of them is a second-rate Svengali compared with us,

Douglas—with what *this* makes possible."

Cronan shook his head. "Our day is past, Myles," he murmured, gazing into the dying fire. "We're the last two embers, the heat swiftly fading from within us. It's ... better that way."

Pylorus sighed. "It saddens me to see one as powerful as you so frightened, my old friend. Men such as we are should fear *nothing*. But perhaps I overestimated you."

"You won't persuade me with insults, Douglas," Cronan answered, pleased to hear a tone of firmness in his voice. "Not one of us has the wit or skill to use the Library wisely. The most intelligent thing we ever did was to abandon the project when we did."

Pylorus shook his head like a father disappointed with a slow child. "I might have guessed you were no more than a gifted dilettante. Why shouldn't you turn your back on all that we have accomplished over the years? It all came so easily for you, born into wealth, chasing ancient secrets as a hobby, nothing else to occupy your time, no other use for your funds. *I* had no such advantages. I fought for all that I have, and I made myself what I am through strength of *will*, Douglas. So perhaps you can understand why I am not so ready as you to abandon our work—*my* work. I am ... disappointed to see that you are so like the others."

He stood, picked up the antique tome and clutched it to his chest, idly stroking its cover. "It doesn't matter," he went on. "I am fearless, and I have worked alone for many years now—the solitary Librarian, last of the Order of the *Bibliotecha Obscura*. I've carried on our work—and with *this*, I shall *finish* it." He paused then, smile vanished, gazing like a raptor at the seated man. Cronan saw power smoldering in those dark eyes, not mere embers but bright coals bedded in a blacksmith's forge. "Now, you'll pardon me, I hope—I've a train to catch shortly."

He turned and strode away, into the deep gloom of the Wescott-Mathers Club's grand Elizabethan hall. Cronan half-rose, meaning perhaps to pursue, but the cold damp had settled deep into his old bones, weighing him down, and he sank back into his chair. The call he'd meant to utter came out instead as a muffled gasp.

Douglas Cronan closed his eyes, searched the darkness within for flickers of inspiration, sparks of enlightenment. He felt weary, *vastly* weary, as if the years had caught up to him all at once.

So—Myles had done it. He had finally found the item to which their scattered brotherhood had devoted so much searching, so much effort. The last piece in the great puzzle, the Philosophers' Stone, the Key to the Abyss. The final missing volume of the Hidden Library. Generation upon generation of secret societies had sought that tome, most of them unaware of the nature of that which they so devoutly desired. Many had hunted for it even before its creation, anticipating it, sensing its inevitability. The search had perhaps begun with the followers of Thutmose III in ancient Thebes, fifteen hundred years before the dawn of the Common Era. It had continued down the labyrinthine passage of ages, its true object unclear or misunderstood or altogether forgotten. It manifested itself in the crusades of the Knights Templar in twelfth century Jerusalem and in Geoffrey de Gonneville's Order of the Rose-Cross. It arose in the Kabala of the Spanish Jews and inspired delusions among the Bavarian Illuminati. So many men, stumbling partly or mostly blind through the corridors of history, all of them seeking, and not knowing what they sought, not understanding the manner in which it would ultimately manifest itself.

But the grand design of the darkness underlying all reality was woven into the very fabric of human existence, inscribed in the genome, perhaps, or whispered through the collective unconscious. And over the ages, the pattern *did* emerge—a scroll here, a tome there, a volume somewhere else. Those that were lost when the Library at Alexandria burned, those buried beyond reach beneath the Vatican by the voracious censors of the papacy, those suppressed or destroyed anywhere eventually emerged again elsewhere, their elements perhaps recombined but always contributing ultimately the same substance to the whole.

So while the alchemists forgot the real goal and wasted their time trying to cajole lead into becoming gold, while the Kabalists played number games and the befuddled Freemasons sought the True Word of God in the structure of King Solomon's long lost temple, the Order of the *Bibliotheca Obscura* had come together and begun to gather those unthinkably rare and far-flung volumes that represented the True and Hidden Library, the books which when assembled in a single setting of appropriate design, might reveal to the most ingenious of scholars the door to the luminous darkness underlying everything.

The clues were scattered throughout the True Volumes—secret arrows pointing to other True Volumes, past, present, and yet to come. And all of them hinted at that ultimate book, the one which would unite and complete all other True Volumes. The Grand Index, the nexus of all genuine arcana. The key that would turn the lock and spring the door wide.

The very thing which Douglas Cronan had seen today, in Myles Pylorus' hands.

Cronan uttered a guttural noise from deep in his throat, an inarticulate negation which nonetheless eloquently summarized his fears, the discontent gnawing at the marrow of his being. He pinched his eyes shut tight and pulled at his lower lip with arthritis-knotted fingers.

He had no certain knowledge when the Order of the *Bibliotecha Obscura* had come into existence—the Order had never kept written records of its own history and its origins were long since lost to the deep shadows of time. What he knew for certain was that the last Initiates of the Order—the last Librarians, as they'd called themselves—had disbanded almost a quarter of a century ago. An inevitability, surely, with so many brilliant, powerful men and women working toward their goal. Egos had swelled and tempers blazed; members bickered and jockeyed for rank. Several of the rising adepts had abandoned the Order in anger or disgrace.

Then the one who had taken the name Charon had vanished while on an expedition to Bangkok, and speculation over his fate had created an atmosphere electric with paranoia, bristling with static suspicions.

All the while, the sense of futility had infected the Order like a black plague. They would never find the lost volume, some insisted—it might not yet exist, might *never* exist. And in any case, the world was too vast a place to search for a single lost book—one might spend a thousand lifetimes and scarcely have begun.

Douglas Cronan hadn't for one moment shared their bitter pessimism—but he had done what he could, with whispers and omissions, to foment it.

The possibility of failure hadn't troubled him. It was the likelihood of success which had ultimately prompted him to provoke the final dissolution of the Order. The closer their goal had loomed—so vividly felt in the black depths of his being—the more tightly fear gripped him. In the waning months before the blessed parting of ways, he'd slept scarcely a wink and what slumber he managed, hideous nightmares inevitably ruined. The disbanding of the Order had come as the greatest relief in his too-long life.

He hadn't thought to wonder, at the time, why Pylorus had similarly pushed the others away, though he knew well enough that Myles Pylorus had never once doubted their ability to complete their great goal.

All those years ago, he'd allowed himself to believe—without conscious scrutiny—that Pylorus, too, had sensed the danger of it all, and opted to let the mission die rather than risk the consequences. His decision to remain in charge of the extant part of the Library had seemed only reasonable— the place needed a caretaker, after all. And a guard.

It hadn't occurred to Cronan then that Pylorus simply wanted the Library's secrets to himself. Thinking on it now, he could hardly credit his own foolishness. He could only attribute it to willful ignorance on his part, to his desperate desire to put the whole cursed affair behind him, no matter whose hands he might leave it in.

And now—now Myles had the final piece, the index, the Key. If he succeeded in unriddling its cipher, if he discovered its relation to the other True Volumes and found its precise place in the Library, then... Cronan shuddered against the pervasive London gloom, unwilling to follow the thought to its conclusion.

Except... Perhaps he and Myles had gotten it wrong, after all. Perhaps this new acquisition would prove to be yet another dead end, a false promise, like so many others before.

Cronan frowned, shook his head. No. Whatever instinct he had left for the occult and the arcane buzzed with the absolute certainty that what he'd seen today was the genuine artifact. Pylorus had found it, and he *would* use it.

"He must be stopped," Cronan murmured to the gilt-framed portraits above the mantel, the empty chair across from him. "Someone *must* stop him."

He glanced around him as if expecting to find the savior, some well-healed young adept skulking in the shadows, eager to play his part in this ageless comedy of the absurd. Yet none were left to send, none of those younger men whose constitutions might be worthy of the task, capable of the journey, and of doing whatever might need to be done. All of them, scattered to the winds, faded from his world. He sat alone in the hall, a relic among relics.

And that left only one choice, didn't it? A choice which was no choice at all.

With stone-heavy fatigue, Douglas Cronan lifted the tiny silver bell from the table at his elbow and gave it a twitch. A moment later, a bland-faced man clad in a black tailcoat appeared at his side, looking down at him with a practiced air of neutrality.

"May I be of service, sir?"

Cronan let out a sigh that shook him like a sob.

"Yes, Howard," he said, voice low. "I'll need to go to Venice. And kindly arrange for my usual accommodations."

Though Cronan hadn't used his "usual accommodations" in well over a decade, Howard merely nodded and, with a muttered, "Very good, sir," vanished again into the gloom of the club.

Cronan looked around the place with eyes still sharp despite all they'd taken in over so many years. He noted every detail—the butterscotch whorls in the marble of the hearth, the grain of the dark walls, the leaded casement window, fat pearls of rain rolling down the glass. . . Something at the core of him felt certain that he would never look upon this place again.

For the first time in a hundred visits over the course of his too-long life, Douglas Cronan took no pleasure in the venerable sights of Venice. The Piazza San Marco, the lofty Torre dell'Orologio spire casting its shadow over the façade of the Doge's Palace like the blade of a magnificent sundial, the soaring Rialto Bridge. . . What had always inspired a kind of deep, placid joy in him now provoked only trembles, despite the blazing sun. He watched unsmiling as his driver turned the water taxi off of the mooring post-studded Grand Canal and wended his way down a much narrower watercourse, beneath lines of laundry flapping like pennants, under low arched bridges, past buildings whose bottom floors stood a foot deep in dark water.

A few moments later, they moored at a flight of moss-slick stone stairs on the Rio dei Santi Apostoli, the driver hopping out of his seat to help the old man step safely to the walk. Cronan pushed a fifty euro note into the driver's hand, muttering "Grazie, grazie," without much thinking about it.

"*Signor!*" the driver called. Cronan turned to look down at the man. The mustachioed driver sneaked a glance at the cash in his hand, then looked up at Cronan with a broad, open face, and asked if he should wait there.

Cronan shook his head. He didn't watch as the water taxi zipped away on the gray-green canal. Bent over his brass-handled cane, he hobbled down the narrow street between crumbling brick buildings, tiny closed-up shops undiscovered by tourists, homes that looked stuffed with shadows, not lived in for ages. Shaking visibly now, and not simply because of the strain on his arthritic joints, he turned the final corner and stepped into the Campiello della Strega.

And stopped in his paces, his heart thudding in his thin chest.

He knew this place, knew it well, had come here dozens upon dozens of times during his years with the Order. His feet could guide him here if he walked blindfolded.

But the library wasn't there.

Cronan looked around the square again, unable to credit what he saw—and what he couldn't see. There, a tall house, only darkness behind its windows. Across from it, a tiny *osterie*, a faded sign reading *Chuiso*—"closed"—hanging in the curtained door. Beside that, a building that looked like a single large home carved into separate flats, doors all shut, blinds drawn, no wash hanging from the naked spider web of clotheslines. Across from that, a tall house, gloom pressing against its windows.

Cronan frowned, stared down at his black patent-leather shoes a moment, then looked once more, studying each angle, each view—house, wine bar, flats. Wine bar, flats, house.

"Wrong," the old man muttered to the still, dank air. "It's all wrong."

He pinched his eyes shut and shook his head, trying to silence the mad voices suddenly gibbering in his mind. The place didn't make sense—a square with only three sides, four perspectives yielding three sights.

"Ah," the old man whispered to himself, almost a chuckle, almost a gasp. "You've indeed become clever, Myles. Most clever, yes."

Under his breath, he muttered a few arcane and long-unused words, relics of a tongue dead and forgotten by all but a few. After an instant's silence, he opened his eyes and looked up once more.

The Library crouched where it had for ages, adjacent to the neglected homes, staring down the forgotten *osterie*. Whatever rite Pylorus had performed to obscure the place had worked well—even an old adept like Cronan might stare at it for hours without seeing it, the grand old building reduced beyond triviality in some distant but powerful part of his semi-conscious. Invisible to the alert mind.

He paused just a moment now to examine the place, the lines of its terracotta roofs, its lancet windows and squat brick towers, the misty-gray dome rising above all. It had been built as the *Scuola della Parola Nascosta*, the School of the Hidden Word, around 1486. Rumor held that the designer had been one Jacopo Bon, the late-in-life bastard child of the celebrated architect Bartolomeo Bon who'd built the celebrated Ca' d'Oro Palace. Clandestine histories reported that Jacopo had traveled to Germany in his late twenties or early thirties and joined with the Rosicrucian Fraternity, where he had combined the talent he'd apparently received from his father with the architectural gnosticism of the early Masonic lodge. Having reached the level of adept, he'd returned to Italy at age fifty-five and opened his own school where he might selectively pass on the teachings of his secret brotherhoods.

From the outside, the school looked no more impressive than any of a thousand small churches and *scuole* in Venice. The interior layout, however, was unique. The cunning floor plan represented the Kabbalistic Tree of Life—ten galleries for the ten spheres, twenty-two interconnecting halls and corridors for the twenty-two paths—such that traversing from chamber to chamber corresponded to moving among the different degrees of wisdom, the many levels of penetration into the splendid darkness. Surely no building on earth had better suited the needs of the Librarians of the *Bibliotecha Obscura*. Even now, with his toes on the very brink of the abyss, Cronan couldn't help admiring the grandeur of it all, the deep pulse of cosmic power that ran through the centuries and culminated *here*.

But all of that was delay, of course, a feeble and sorry excuse to stay a moment longer in the sunlight before admitting himself again to the shadows.

Drawing on whatever courage remained in his tired heart, he clutched his cane and hobbled up to the front door. Fingers trembling, he withdrew the ankh-shaped key from his pocket and fitted it into the slot in the large iron plate. Whispering the entrance incantation, he gave the key a turn.

Within the heavy iron lock, tumblers fell, a bolt withdrew. The door moaned open.

Not allowing himself any further pause, Cronan stepped into the darkness.

The atmosphere within the cavernous foyer hung dank and motionless to the point of stagnation. He shivered against the clammy touch of air never reached by the sun, a cool only slightly less damp and penetrating than the Club's London cold. Taking in the utter bottomless silence of the place, Cronan could almost imagine that no one had wandered these musty passages since the Order disbanded—or long before. Light though age had made him, the hushed whickering of his footfalls nonetheless echoed from the frescoed walls of the many-sided chamber as he shuffled to the doors opposite those by which he'd entered, ignoring the side passages which led to the building's more prosaic offices. He didn't hesitate as he noted the X carved almost secretively into the door's deep-grained wood, but mumbled another well-remembered invocation and pushed into the library proper.

The dry yellow mummy-spice odor of ancient paper enveloped him instantly, at once pleasantly familiar and vaguely sour. Books slouched forgotten beneath long years of dust, rising from floor to ceiling along the gallery's ten walls, candles flickering from sconces set into the corners. At his feet, Hebrew characters cunningly etched into the marble floor spelled out the name of the lowest sphere—Malkuth, the Kingdom of Earth. A name once believed to be the first rung on Jacob's ladder to God, but in truth, only a foundation upon which to build the first of many ladders, not all of which ascended to Heaven, nor even extended in that direction.

Standing here once again, Douglas Cronan felt his thin blood rage and race with a sense of grandeur and awe, of purpose and power.

He took a long, steady breath, swallowing his swelling pride and resolving himself once more to his purpose.

"Myles!" he called, and heard his voice rebound from chamber to chamber, down passages and staircases, doubling back on itself until the echoes seemed to trip over one another, lost somewhere within the library. "We need to talk, old friend!"

"Then, *old friend*, do come join me!" The voice seemed to emanate as much from the vaulted ceiling and the laden bookshelves as from the narrow staircases ascending from either side of the room, seemed to originate more in the floor itself than from the darkness within the iron-scrollwork staircase that spiraled away into the depths beneath.

Cronan frowned. Surely he'd never seen that staircase before. Of course not—a basement or cellar in Venice would swiftly become a cesspool. Yet as he peered down, he smelled no dank canal-water stink, heard no lapping of trapped waves, none of the ceaseless *plink … plink … plink. . .* of the earth's eternally dank places. Instead, he caught a flicker of firelight, a breath of free-flowing air. Gazing into the dark—chasing that phantom voice—he caught a glimpse of the elaborate fresco crafted in the molding. That he recognized—a tiny masterpiece by the great Rococo artist Giambattista Tiepolo: an androgynous yet beautiful figure clad in a winding scarf and holding aloft a marbled sphere. Beneath this, the legend *"Il Mondo."* The World. First of the twenty-two paths designated by its corresponding image from the Tarot deck. Yet it had no business there, set into the floor where one might see it while descending the wrought-iron staircase. It belonged in the wall, above a broad hallway to the next gallery. His mind might have dulled some since the days when he'd honed it with potent incantations, but he had no doubt of this fact. Which led to only one possible conclusion: the Library had been rebuilt in his absence. He gritted his teeth and shook his head at the impudence of it.

Frowning rigidly, he followed the metal spiral down into the gloom.

The dark loomed close, closer, as deep as a nightmare, impossibly deep. The staircase seemed to corkscrew toward Hell itself, down and down further.

Then at last light flickered from below and Cronan found himself emerging into chamber IX, the sphere of Yesod, Foundation. Here the books appeared older still, draped in tattered tapestries of cobweb, yet arranged upon the shelves with the utmost care, their order every bit as vital to unlocking the great secret of the Library as the order of letters to the creation of a meaningful word.

Yet here again the place seemed both familiar and unfamiliar at once, the well-known features somehow recombined in patterns he could no longer fully recognize. The passageways left and right—surmounted by representations of the Tarot figures of *"Il Sole"*—The Sun—and *"Le Stelle"*—The Star—respectively, seemed almost as if they belonged. But the hallway behind him looked as if it must extend from the opposite side of the room, or else it doubled back beneath the foyer and ended in a cul-de-sac. Yet when he stepped through the arch, it led on as it should, under the brilliant fresco of Temperance and into chamber VI, the sphere of beauty whose name was Tiphereth.

From this hexagonal room led many paths—*"Il Diavolo"* leading down in darkness behind him and to the left, *"La Morte"* into gloom behind and to the right; *"Il Papa"* and *"Gli Amanti"* ascending in steep, narrow flights on either side of the wide bookcase directly ahead, *"L'Eremita"* and *"La Giustizia"* opening at his immediate right and left. In the center of it all, a greater staircase still, twisting up and up to the tall rotunda above. In the gallery's six corners, books lay splayed open atop fluted pillars, pages carefully selected, displaying symbols and glyphs both elegant and awful. All around, countless other volumes crouched upon shelves alongside cubbies stuffed with silk-tied scrolls, etched stones, carved ivory plates. Upon every inch of visible woodwork, Librarians had scratched obscure yet vital formulae, empowering the place, preparing it for the day when its contents would at last be complete.

Cronan turned a slow circle, taking it all in—the books, the rites, the many paths. Everything where it ought to be, and all of it wrong—so utterly and fundamentally wrong that for a moment he couldn't identify where the problem lay. But of course, it was everywhere, all around—in stairs that went up where they ought to go down, in passages that ran straight where they ought to bend, in chambers whose relationship to one another couldn't possibly exist in any architect's designs.

"Lost, old friend?" Pylorus' voice came, from the mezzanine above and from all around, god-like in its omnipresence. "Gotten turned around in your old stomping-grounds, have you?" Something in that voice sounded terribly unlike the man Douglas Cronan had known for all those strange, wandering decades.

The old bastard gave a low chuckle that sank into Cronan's very bones, made his joints ache. All at once, the chill of the place seemed to treble, wracking him with shivers. So many years he'd held death at bay with just the right charms and rituals, but now the Library which had given him so much strength seemed inclined to leech it from him, freezing him at once from within and without.

Not wasting his breath on a response, Cronan took The Hermit's way into the Fourth Chamber. Here now the books and scrolls all around seemed more than mere objects, seemed to twitch and writhe at the edges of his vision like things alive—or in any case loathsomely *animate*. But of course, the whole of the Library had a kind of life, one that the man calling himself Pylorus might yet realize if ever he managed to untangle the code of that singular volume he'd unearthed in London only yesterday. Cronan let his fingers tickle their way along dry and broken spines, taking back a little of the power the place sought to steal from him, reclaiming it as the right he'd always imagined it to be. Moving straight ahead, he followed the first path, the way of "*Il Matto*," The Fool, and though he had climbed no stairs, he emerged a moment later in the mezzanine which only moments ago he'd looked upon from below.

He stood a moment, perfectly still in the heart of the Gallery of the First, Kether, the Godhead, the sphere from which all others emerged and to which all belonged. The scarlet stained-glass in the lancet windows dyed the failing afternoon light the color of fresh-spilled blood. Within that sanguine dark, the books along the shelves looked like nothing more than shadows, the midnight darkness between the most distant stars distilled to its essence and machined into paper, glue, leather and metal. They had, Cronan realized with a teeth-rattling jolt, all the substance of things caught between states of being—caught between worlds.

"Ah, the Fool himself," Pylorus' voice came again, ubiquitous yet now identifiably resonating from just ahead, a shadow among shadows in the crimson gloom. "You know the old wisdom, Douglas—no fool like an old fool."

Cronan opened his mouth, tongue ready with an answer—and found he had no breath in his lungs, no strength in his legs.

"I must apologize for the state of the Library," Pylorus went on, voice gleeful yet thick, his and yet not his, the imitation of a skilled mimic. "Old Jacopo Bon's Kabbalistic scheme wasn't too far off the mark, but neither he nor any of that breed ever properly understood the relationships between things—not even comparatively simple things like the Chambers and the Passages. We needed something a tad more … M. C. Escher."

"You've twisted the very fabric of reality," Cronan panted, bent over his cane's silver handle like a hunchback.

"Is that a hint of admiration I hear in your tone, Douglas?" Pylorus cooed. "It should be—the rites I've worked within these walls outstrip the greatest of Adepts to go before me. But even that was only a necessary step on path to the completion of our great work."

"That work must *never* be completed, Myles," Cronan said, forcing himself to stand upright even as the strength drained from his sinews. "I've come to put a stop to it."

"Douglas," Pylorus' voice chastised, its tone at once amused and deathly-earnest, "you're far too old to trifle with me ... and far too late. Come, come and see. . ."

Summoning whatever strength he had left, Cronan hobbled closer to the black shape beneath the rotunda dome. Nearer now, he made it out to be the Grand Librarian's desk, the tall elegant chair behind—and in the seat, a figure from beyond the fringes of nightmare, human yet not, a fluid darkness whose outline only suggested that of a man, because no form within the known universe could contain or describe this entity whose inside was its skin, whose back was its front, this thing without eyes or mouth or limbs yet capable of sight and speech and grasp. Cronan flinched away, eyes fluttering shut of their own volition—to look upon such an impossible being for more than an instant would surely inspire insanity, shatter a mind like fine crystal under a hammer's blow.

"I feared the final book might take years to understand," that semi-human voice muttered. "Feared the ancient madman's code might prove daunting. But no! No, Douglas my old old friend! The volume spoke to me here within the Library in a voice louder and clearer even than that with which it called to me in that peculiar shop in London. It desired my understanding, ached for my unique comprehension."

"I always worried that you were bound for madness," Cronan murmured, his eyes still averted from the undreamable thing behind the desk. "Clearly my fears were only too well founded." The effort of forming the words left him breathless, wheezing sickly.

"I have known the darkness, Douglas," Pylorus whispered, and even his complete inhumanity could not disguise the pride in his voice. "I have gazed into the abyss that underlies everything, and it has gazed into me.

"It isn't empty. There are things within the darkness—things that tear the mind and gnash the soul, borers in the axis, incarnations of chaos and entropy. They're always felt—oh yes!—but only a few of us ever see them." Cronan heard his diction slipping, his affected upper-crust accent growing thin, pretenses forgotten now. "But now—Douglas, but now! This Library is the lock, and I've got the key. When I turn it, the door will swing wide and everything that dwells in the abyss will slither and scurry out and no one anywhere will be able to look away. The Creator is nowhere to be found—but a single word from me can unleash the agents of the world's destruction!"

"Myles, you've lost your mind! You mustn't—"

"No feeble objections, Douglas, I beg of you," Pylorus said, raising that façade again, almost playfully. "You haven't come all this way to save the world—we both know that it's far beyond saving. You've come to join me in this moment of culmination, in this instant when all our years as stumbling foolish members of that childish fraternity finally come to meaning something. To be here when I speak the word and the doorway is flung wide at last."

Douglas Cronan opened his mouth to object—but the words withered on his tongue. Pylorus' argument had the weight of years behind it, all that time spent searching for the precise volumes, locating their exact places within the Library—nearly a century lived for that one purpose. At the mere thought of completing it here, now—of finishing what millennia of men had scarcely begun—his failing muscles grew strong, his cold flesh warm and vital again. He felt a smile rise on his parched lips.

"Ah," Pylorus whispered, "I knew. . . I knew that you would at last see the darkness with me ... Master Calchas." And despite his taunting, he sounded strangely pleased by this, perhaps even relieved.

Cronan said nothing, the tired machinery of his mind working, slow but potent.

In the gloom of the Library rotunda, he heard the sigh of a page being turned in a large book. He had no need to see the tome to know what book, or what page.

Despite himself, he opened his eyes then, and looked up.

The shape of Myles Molan Pylorus had cast off the last semblances of humanity and now revealed a thing altogether given over to the darkness at the heart of existence, to the chaos and insanity that swirled in the abyss underlying the paper-thin façade of prosaic reality.

"So ... you see me as I truly am," Pylorus guttered. "I am but the foreshadow of what is to come ...."

The sense of power drained from Douglas Cronan at once, all notions of strength and importance and meaning undone by that single glance, that black promise. He sank to his knees, propped up only by his cane, and some final lingering idea of duty.

"You can't," he said, voice tiny yet carrying within the strange dimensions of the Library. "I won't ...."

He slouched over his cane, forcing himself to breathe slow and deep—then summoned the very last of his strength and threw himself at the nearest wall sconce. As much falling as lunging, he plucked the candle from its holder and, investing its flame with the final ounce of his life's energy, tossed it at the ancient book spread open on the Grand Librarian's wide black desk.

The paper took the flames at once, feeding itself to them in large curling yellow leaves. The Pylorus-thing splashed or flailed away, screeching some incoherent string of frenzied syllables, and the fire leapt across the desk. In that split-second of lunatic clarity, Cronan saw that the blaze cast no light upon anything in that nighted rotunda—neither on the desk nor the chair nor the thing slouching away from it, neither on the abysmal books nor upon the shelves that held them. The fire's hot light fell over him alone—the last remaining entity within that chamber not yet given over entirely to the otherworld. He took all this in even as the flames jumped and spread, starting on the bookcases now, moving fast. Surely it would take no more than a few hours for the fire to reduce the entire contents of the Library to charcoal and ash.

The shadow which had been or seemed to be Pylorus only twenty-four hours ago spilled from its place and rolled and writhed, screeching—but not agony, Cronan realized with a stab of icy terror. The creature was, in its unthinkable way, *laughing*.

"You fool!" it cried, in a tongue alien yet grotesquely comprehensible, "you incredible fool! You're too late! The door is open! I've already spoken the word!"

Cronan slouched against a burning bookcase, choking, unable to see anything now but sable shadows and scarlet smoke.

"A lie," he muttered, perhaps only to himself. A deadly heat had replaced the cruel chill and he knew he would never have the strength to drag himself out through the collapsing maze of the Library, not now.

"No lie!" Pylorus wailed, mad with glee. "You heard me speak it!"

Cronan flopped to the floor, retching and shaking his head with all the fury he still possessed—but even as he did so, he recalled that hideous chord of sound Pylorus had uttered as the book went up in flames. Not a cry of rage or horror at all—it had been the word, the final turning of the well-hidden key in the long-forgotten lock.

As if feeling the despair in Cronan's mind, the Pylorus thing squealed in hateful delight.

"The door is open! The denizens of the abyss emerge! Chaos will swallow the world!"

Cronan managed a few staggering, directionless paces, then dropped to the cold marble floor. Some still-functioning part of his mind sensed things in the smoky darkness with him, hideous mewling chittering things with shapes not meant for the world beyond the Library doors. Denizens of the Abyss. . .

"Douglas! Do you see!" Pylorus cried from the core of the inferno. "You've done what I couldn't bring myself to do! You've smashed the lock and buried the key! You've ensured that the door can never be closed again!"

The being in the flames might have said more, but Douglas Cronan heard none of it. By then, another sort of darkness had already claimed him.

Originally appeared in the limited-edition anthology *Bound for Evil: Curious Tales of Books Gone Bad* from Dead Letter Press, edited by Tom English.